'Lyndsay Faye is a superstar-caliber writer . . . *The Gods of Gotham* is a gift to the genre that readers will surely relish'
Matthew Pearl, bestselling author of *The Dante Club*

Timothy Wilde hadn't wanted to be a copper star. On the night of August 21st, on his way home from the Tombs defeated and disgusted, he is plotting his resignation when a young girl who has escaped from a nearby brothel crashes into him; she wears only a nightdress and is covered from head to toe in blood.

Searching out the truth in the child's wild stories, Timothy soon finds himself on the trail of a brutal killer, seemingly hell bent on fanning the flames of anti-Irish immigrant sentiment and threatening chaos in a city already in the midst of social upheaval. But his fight for justice could cost him the woman he loves, his brother and ultimately his life . . .

'A historical romp of a read that's as sexy as it is adventurous'
Elle magazine

'Faye's novel is as fascinating a historical novel as it is a crime tale, especially as the serial killer is fanning political and sectarian flames in a bid to wrong-foot potential pursuers. Reminiscent of Dennis Lehane's *The Given Day* in its ambition and style' *Irish Times*

'Faye has clearly undertaken meticulous research and creates a convincing insight into a world of death and decay, riots and religious fervour, where Irish Catholics are deemed to be sub-human. The whodunnit element is very clever ___ he ending comes as a complete surprise' S___ ___land

Author photograph © Gabriel Lehner

LYNDSAY FAYE is the author of critically acclaimed *Dust and Shadow* and is featured in *Best American Mystery Stories 2010*. Faye, a true New Yorker in the sense that she was born elsewhere, lives in Manhattan with her husband, Gabriel.

Visit www.lyndsayfaye.com to find out more.

More praise for *The Gods of Gotham*:

'Slips into 1840s New York with ease . . . Faye strides the historical crime path with confidence' *We Love This Book* magazine

'Exquisite . . . A raucous underworld of criminals and chiselers, the infamous Five Points, where thieves speak their own argot . . . Faye's prose crackles with historical authenticity so cunningly rendered that readers will lose themselves from the very first turn of the page' Katherine Howe, bestselling author of *The Physick Book of Deliverance Dane*

'A fascinating backdrop, neatly observed historical detail, an intriguing protagonist, and beautifully written, with the added bonus that many of the characters speak "flash", aka the argot of New York's criminal underworld: it's a potent blend' Declan Burke, www.crimealwayspays.blogspot.com

'This is a new and exciting historical novel which has everything that will entrap a reader . . . an inferno of a book' www.crimesquad.com

'Faye's a fantastic, talented author; one with a fluid, distinctive writing style and great attention to historical detail. I look forward to reading more of her work. Highly recommended' www.civilian-reader.blogspot.com

'The sights, sounds and smells of the old city are there, they leap off the page at you and there is a lushness and febrile intensity to the writing which put me in mind of *The Crimson Petal and the White*, it has the same slight edge of decadence and something vaguely rotten in the air' www.randomjottings.typepad.com

THE
GODS OF
GOTHAM

LYNDSAY FAYE

headline
review

First published in Great Britain in 2012 by
HEADLINE PUBLISHING GROUP

First published in paperback in Great Britain in 2012 by
HEADLINE PUBLISHING GROUP

3   .

Cataloguing in Publication Data is available from the British Library

ISBN 978 0 7553 8676 5 (B format)
ISBN 978 0 7553 9442 5 (A format)

Typeset in Goudy Old Style by Avon DataSet Ltd,
Bidford-on-Avon, Warwickshire

Printed and bound in Great Britain by Clays Ltd, St Ives plc

Headline's policy is to use papers that are natural, renewable and
recyclable products and made from wood grown in sustainable forests.
The logging and manufacturing processes are expected to conform to the
environmental regulations of the country of origin.

HEADLINE PUBLISHING GROUP
An Hachette UK Company
338 Euston Road
London NW1 3BH

www.headline.co.uk
www.hachette.co.uk

For my family,
who taught me that when you are
knocked considerably sideways, you get up and keep going,
or you get up and go in a slightly different direction.

In the summer of 1845, following years of passionate political dispute, New York City at long last formed a Police Department.

The potato, a crop that can be trusted to yield reliable nutrition from barren, limited space, had long been the base staple of the Irish tenant farmer. In the spring of 1844, the Gardener's Chronicle and Agricultural Gazette *reported anxiously that an infestation 'belonging to the mould tribe' was laying waste to potato crops. There was, the* Chronicle *told its readers, no definite cause or cure.*

These twin events would change the city of New York forever.

The rogue fraternity have a language peculiarly their own which is understood and spoken by them no matter what their dialect, or the nation where they were reared. Many of their words and phrases, owing to their comprehensive meaning, have come into general use, so that a Vocabulum or Rogue's Lexicon, has become a necessity to the general reader, but more especially to those who read police intelligence.

George Washington Matsell, Special Justice,
Chief of Police, New York, 1859

SELECTED FLASH TERMINOLOGY*

AUTUM. A church.

BAT. A prostitute who walks the streets only at night.
BENE. Good; first-rate.
BLOKE. A man.
BURNERS. Rogues who cheat countrymen with false cards or dice.
BUSTLED. Confused; perplexed; puzzled.
BUTTERED. Whipped.

CAP. To join in. 'I will cap in with him.'
CHAFFEY. Boisterous; happy; jolly.
CHINK. Money.
CRANKY-HUTCH. An insane asylum.
CUPSHOT. Drunk.

---

* Excerpted from George Washington Matsell, *The Secret Language of Crime: Vocabulum, or, The Rogue's Lexicon* (G. W. Matsell & Co., 1859).

DEAD RABBIT. A very athletic, rowdy fellow.
DIARY. To remember.
DIMBER. Handsome; pretty.
DUSTY. Dangerous.

EASY. Killed.
EGROTAT. Sick.
ELFEN. To walk light; on tiptoe.
EYE. Nonsense; humbug.

FAM GRASP. To shake hands.
FIB. To beat.
FRENCH CREAM. Brandy.
FUNK. To frighten.

GINGERLY. Cautiously.

HASH. To vomit.
HEMP. To choke.
HEN. A woman.
HICKSAM. A countryman; a fool.
HOCUS. To stupefy.
HUSH. To murder.

INSIDER. One who knows.

JABBER. To talk in an unknown language.
JACK DANDY. A little impertinent fellow.

KEN. A house.
KINCHIN. A young child.
KITTLE. To tickle; to please.

LADYBIRD. A kept mistress.
LION. To be saucy; frighten; bluff.
LUSH. Drink.

MAB. A harlot.
MAZZARD. The face.
MOLLEY. A miss; an effeminate fellow; a sodomite.
MOUSE. To be quiet; to be still.

NATURAL. Not fastidious; a liberal, clever fellow.
NED. A ten-dollar gold piece.
NISH. To keep quiet; to be still.
NODDLE. An empty-pated fellow.
NOSE. A spy; one who informs.
ORGAN. Pipe.
OWLS. Women who walk the street only at night.

PALAVER. Talk.
PATE. The head.
PEERY. Suspicious.
PEPPERY. Warm; passionate.
PHYSOG. The face.
PLUMP. Rich; plenty of money.
POGY. Drunk.

QUARRON. A body.
QUASH. To kill; the end of; no more.
QUEER. To puzzle.

RABBIT. A rowdy.
RED RAG. The tongue.

SANS. Without; nothing.
SLAMKIN. A slovenly female.
SMACK. To swear on the Bible. 'The queer cuffin bid me smack the calfskin.'
SQUEAKER. A child.
STAIT. City of New York.
STARGAZERS. Prostitutes.
STOW YOUR WID. Be silent.

SWAG-RUM. Full of wealth.

TOGS. Clothes.
TONGUE-PAD. A scold.

UPPISH. Testy; quarrelsome.

YIDISHER. A Jew.

THE PILGRIM'S LEGACY

Those daring men, those gentle wives – say, wherefore do they
*   come?*
Why rend they all the tender ties of kindred and of home?
'Tis Heaven assigns their noble work, man's spirit to unbind; –
They come not for themselves alone – they come for all mankind:
And to the empire of the West this glorious boon they bring,
'A Church without a Bishop – a State without a King.'
Then, Prince and Prelate, hope no more to bend them to your sway,
Devotion's fire inflames their breasts, and freedom points their
*   way,*
And in their brave hearts' estimate, 'twere better not to be,
Than quail beneath a despot, where the soul cannot be free;
And therefore o'er the wintry wave, those exiles come to bring
'A Church without a Bishop – a State without a King.'

Hymn sung following a lecture at the Tabernacle,
New York City, 1843

PROLOGUE

When I set down the initial report, sitting at my desk at the Tombs, I wrote:

On the night of August 21, 1845, one of the children escaped.

Of all the sordid trials a New York City policeman faces every day, you wouldn't expect the one I loathe most to be paperwork. But it is. I get snakes down my spine just thinking about case files.

Police reports are meant to read 'X killed Y by means of Z'. But facts without motives, without the *story*, are just road signs with all the letters worn off. Meaningless as blank tombstones. And I can't bear reducing lives to the lowest of their statistics. Case notes give me the same parched-headed feeling I get after a night of badly made New England rum. There's no room in the dry march of data to tell *why* people did bestial things – love or loathing, defense or greed. Or God, in this particular case, though I don't suppose God was much pleased by it.

If He was watching. I was watching, and it didn't please me any too keenly.

For instance, look what happens when I try to write an

event from my childhood the way I'm required to write police reports:

In October 1826, in the hamlet of Greenwich Village, a fire broke out in a stable flush adjacent to the home of Timothy Wilde, his elder brother, Valentine Wilde, and his parents, Henry and Sarah; though the blaze started small, both of the adults were killed when the conflagration spread to the main house by means of a kerosene explosion.

I'm Timothy Wilde, and I'll say right off, that tells you *nothing*. Nix. I've drawn pictures with charcoal all my life to busy my fingers, loosen the feeling of taut cord wrapped round my chest. A single sheet of butcher paper showing a gutted cottage with its blackened bones sticking out would tell you more than that sentence does.

But I'm getting better used to documenting crimes now that I wear the badge of a star police. And there are so many casualties in our local wars over God. I grant there must have been a time long ago when to call yourself a Catholic meant your bootprint was stamped on Protestant necks, but the passage of hundreds of years and a wide, wide ocean ought to have drowned that grudge between us, if anything could. Instead here I sit, penning a bloodbath. All those children, and not only the children, but grown Irish and Americans and anyone ill starred enough to be caught in the middle, and I only hope that writing it might go a way toward being a fit memorial. When I've spent enough ink, the sharp scratch of the specifics in my head will dull a little, I'm hoping. I'd assumed that the dry wooden smell of October, the shrewd way the wind twines into my coat sleeves now, would have begun erasing the nightmare of August by this time.

I was wrong. But I've been wrong about worse.

Here's how it began, now that I know the girl in question better and can write as a man instead of a copper star:

On the night of August 21, 1845, one of the children escaped.

The little girl was aged ten, sixty-two pounds, dressed in a delicate white shift with a single row of lace along the wide, finely stitched collar. Her dark auburn curls were pulled into a loose knot at the top of her head. The breeze through the open casement felt hot where her nightdress slipped from one shoulder and her bare feet touched the hardwood. She suddenly wondered if there could be a spyhole in her bedroom wall. None of the boys or girls had ever yet found one, but it was the sort of thing *they* would do. And that night, every pocket of air seemed breath on flesh, slowing her movements to sluggish, watery starts.

She exited through the window of her room by tying three stolen ladies' stockings together and fixing the end to the lowest catch on the iron shutter. Standing up, she pulled her nightgown away from her body. It was wet through to her skin, and the clinging fabric made her flesh crawl. When she'd stepped blindly out the window clutching the hose, the August air bloated and pulsing, she slid down the makeshift rope before dropping to an empty beer barrel.

The child quit Greene Street by way of Prince before facing the wild river of Broadway, dressed for her bedroom and hugging the shadows like a lifeline. Everything blurs on Broadway at ten o'clock at night. She braved a flash torrent of watered silk. Glib-eyed men in double vests of black velvet stampeded into saloons cloaked from floor to ceiling in mirrors. Stevedores, politicians, merchants, a group of newsboys with unlit cigars tucked in their rosy lips. A thousand floating pairs of vigilant eyes. A thousand ways to be caught. And the sun had fallen, so the frail sisterhood haunted every corner: chalk-bosomed whores desperately pale beneath the rouge, their huddles of five and six determined by brothel kinships and by who wore diamonds and who could only afford cracked and yellowing paste copies.

The little girl could spot out even the richest and healthiest of the street bats for what they really were. She knew the mabs from the ladies instantly.

When she spied a gap in the buttery hacks and carriages, she darted like a moth out of the shadows. Willing herself invisible, winging across the huge thoroughfare eastward. Her naked feet met the slick, tarry waste that curdled up higher than the cobbles, and she nearly stumbled on a gnawed ear of corn.

Her heart leaped, a single jolt of panic. She'd fall – they'd see her and it would all be over.

Did they kill the other kinchin slow or quick?

But she didn't fall. The carriage lights veering off scores of plate-glass windows were behind her, and she was flying again. A few girlish gasps and one yell of alarm marked her trail.

Nobody chased her. But that was nobody's fault, really, not in a city of this size. It was only the callousness of four hundred thousand people, blending into a single blue-black pool of unconcern. That's what we copper stars are for, I think . . . to be the few who stop and look.

She said later that she was seeing in badly done paintings – everything crude and two-dimensional, the brick buildings dripping watercolor edges. I've suffered that state myself, the not-being-there. She recollects a rat gnawing at a piece of oxtail on the pavement, then nothing. Stars in a midsummer sky.

The light clatter of the New York and Harlem train whirring by on iron railway tracks, the coats of its two overheated horses wet and oily in the gaslight. A passenger in a stovepipe hat staring back blankly the way they'd come, trailing his watch over the window ledge with his fingertips. The door open on a sawdusty slaughter shop, as they're called, half-finished cabinetry and dismembered chairs pouring into the street, as scattered as her thoughts.

Then another length of clotted silence, seeing nothing. She reluctantly pulled the stiffening cloth away from her skin once more.

The girl veered onto Walker Street, passing a group of dandies with curled and gleaming soaplocks framing their monocles, fresh and vigorous after a session with the marble baths of Stoppani's. They thought little enough of her, though, because of course she was running hell for leather into the cesspit of the Sixth Ward, and so naturally she must have belonged there.

She *looked* Irish, after all. She *was* Irish. What sane man would worry over an Irish girl flying home?

Well, I would.

I lend considerably more of my brain to vagrant children. I'm much closer to the question. First, I've been one, or near enough to it. Second, star police are meant to capture the bony, grime-cheeked kinchin when we can. Corral them like cattle, then pack them in a locked wagon rumbling up Broadway to the House of Refuge. The urchins are lower in our society than the Jersey cows, though, and herding is easier on livestock than on stray humans. Children stare back with something too hot to be malice, something helpless yet fiery when police corner them . . . something I recognize. And so I will never, not under any circumstances, never will I do such a thing. Not if my job depended on it. Not if my *life* did. Not if my *brother's* life did.

I wasn't musing over stray kids the night of August twenty-first, though. I was crossing Elizabeth Street, posture about as stalwart as a bag of sand. Half an hour before, I'd taken my copper star off in disgust and thrown it against a wall. By that point, however, it was shoved in my pocket, digging painfully into my fingers along with my house key, and I was cursing my brother's name in a soothing inner prayer. Feeling angry is far and away easier for me than feeling lost.

God damn Valentine Wilde, I was repeating, *and God damn every bright idea in his goddamned head.*

Then the girl slammed into me unseeing, aimless as a torn piece of paper on the wind.

I caught her by the arms. Her dry, flitting eyes shone out pale grey even in the smoke-sullied moonlight, like shards of a gargoyle's wing knocked from a church tower. She had an unforgettable face, square as a picture frame, with somber swollen lips and a perfect snub nose. There was a splash of faint freckles across the tops of her shoulders, and she lacked height for a ten year old, though she carried herself so fluid that she can seem taller in memory than in person.

But the only thing I noticed clearly when she stumbled to a halt against my legs as I stood in front of my house that night was how very thoroughly she was covered in blood.

CHAPTER ONE

*To the first of June, seven thousand emigrants had
arrived . . . and the government agent there had
received notice that 55,000 had contracted for
passage during the season, and nearly all from
Ireland. The number expected to come to Canada
and the States is estimated by some as high as
100,000. The rest of Europe will probably send to the
States 75,000 more.*

New York Herald, summer 1845

Becoming a policeman of the Sixth Ward of the city of New
York was an unwelcome surprise to me.

It's not the work I imagined myself doing at twenty-seven,
but then again I'd bet all the other police would tell it the
same, since three months ago this job didn't exist. We're a
new-hatched operation. I suppose I'd better say first how I
came to need employment, three months back, in the summer
of 1845, though it's a pretty hard push to talk about that. The
memory fights for top billing as my ugliest. I'll do my best.

On July eighteenth, I was tending bar at Nick's Oyster Cellar, as I'd done since I was all of seventeen years old. The squared-off beam of light coming through the door at the top of the steps was searing the dirt into the planked floor. I like July, the way its particular blue had spread over the world when I'd worked on a ferryboat to Staten Island at age twelve, for instance, head back and mouth full of fresh salt breeze. But 1845 was a bad summer. The air was yeasty and wet as a bread oven by eleven in the morning, and you could taste the smell of it at the back of your throat. I was fighting not to notice the mix of fever sweat and the deceased cart horse half pushed into the alley round the corner, as the beast seemed by degrees to be getting deader. There are meant to be garbage collectors in New York, but they're a myth. My copy of the *Herald* lay open, already read back to front as is my morning habit, smugly announcing that the mercury was at ninety-six and several more laborers had unfortunately died of heatstroke. It was all steadily ruining my opinion of July. I couldn't afford to let my mood sour, though. Not on that day.

Mercy Underhill, I was sure of it, was about to visit my bar. She hadn't done so for four days, and in our unspoken pattern that was a record, and I needed to talk to her. Or at least try. I'd recently decided that adoring her was no longer going to stand in my way.

Nick's was laid out in the usual fashion for such places, and I loved its perfect typicalness: a very long stretch of bar, wide enough for the pewter oyster platters and the dozens of beer tumblers and the glasses of whiskey or gin. Dim as a cave, being half underground. But on mornings like that one the sun cut through wonderfully, so we didn't yet need the yellow-papered oil lamps that sent friendly smoke marks up the plaster. No furniture, just a series of booths with bare benches lining the walls, curtained if you wanted although no one ever closed them. Nick's wasn't a place for secrets. It was a forum for the frantic young bulls and bears to scream things across the room after a twelve-hour stint at the Exchange, while I listened.

I stood pouring off a gallon of whiskey for a ginger boy I didn't recognize. The East River's bank swarms with rickety foreign creatures trying to shake off their sea legs, and Nick's was on New Street, very close to the water. The lad waited with his head tilted and his little claws on the cedar bar plank. He stood like a sparrow. Too tall to be eight years old, too scared to be ten. Hollow boned, eyes glassily seeking free scraps.

'This for your parents?' I wiped my fingers on my apron, corking the earthenware jug.

'For Da.' He shrugged. 'Twenty-eight cents.'

His hand came out of his pocket with a ragtag assortment of currency.

'Two shillings makes two bits, so I'll take that pair and wish you welcome. I'm Timothy Wilde. I don't pour shallow, and I don't water the merchandise.'

'Thankee,' he said, reaching for the jug.

There were dark treacle stains at the underarms of his tattered shirt due to the last molasses barrel he'd gammed from being too high, I saw next. So my latest customer was a sugar thief. Interesting.

That's a typical saloon keeper's trick: I notice a great many things about people. A fine city barman I'd be if I couldn't spot the difference between a Sligo dock rat with a career in contraband molasses and the local alderman's son asking after the same jug of spirits. Barmen are considerably better paid when they're sharp, and I was saving all the coin I could lay hands on. For something too crucial to even be called *important*.

'I'd change professions, if I were you.'

The bright black sparrow's eyes turned to slits.

'Molasses sales,' I explained. 'When the product isn't yours, locals take exception.' One of his elbows shifted, growing more fluttery by the second. 'You've a ladle, I suppose, and sneak from the market casks when their owners are making change? All right, just quit the syrups and talk to the newsboys. They make a good wage too, and don't catch beatings when the molasses sellers have learned their sly little faces.'

The boy ran off with a nod like a spasm, clutching the sweating jug under his wing. He left me feeling pretty wise, and neighborly to boot.

'It's useless to counsel these creatures,' Hopstill intoned from the end of the bar, sipping his morning cup of gin. 'He'd have been better off drowned on the way over.'

Hopstill is a London man by birth, and not very republican. His face is equine and drooping, his cheeks vaguely yellow. That's due to the brimstone for the fireworks. He works as a lightning-maker, sealed away in a garret creating pretty explosions for theatricals at Niblo's Gardens. Doesn't care for children, Hopstill. I don't mind them a bit, admiring candor the way I do. Hopstill doesn't care for Irish folk either. That's common enough practice, though. It doesn't seem sporting to me, blaming the Irish for eagerly taking the lowest, filthiest work when the lowest, filthiest work is all they're ever offered, but then fairness isn't high on the list of our city's priorities. And the lowest, filthiest work is getting pretty hard to come by these days, as the main of it's already been snapped up by their kin.

'You read the *Herald*,' I said, fighting not to be annoyed. 'Forty thousands of emigrants since last January and you want them all to join the light-fingered gentry? Advising them is only common sense. I'd sooner work than steal, myself, but sooner steal than starve.'

'A fool's exercise,' Hopstill scoffed, pushing his palm through the sheaves of grey straw that pass for his hair. 'You read the *Herald*. That rank patch of mud is on the brink of civil war. And now I hear tell from London that their potatoes have started rotting. Did you hear about that? Just *rotting*, blighted as a plague of ancient Egypt. Not that anyone's surprised. You won't catch *me* associating with a race that's so thoroughly called down the wrath of God.'

I blinked. But then, I had often been shocked by the sage opinions bar guests had gifted me regarding the members of the Catholic church, the only breathing examples they'd ever seen being the Irish variety. Bar guests who were otherwise – for all appearances – perfectly sane. *First thing the priests do with the novice nuns is sodomize them, and the priests as do thoroughest work rise up the ranks, that's the system – they aren't even fully ordained until their first rape is done with. Why, Tim, I thought you savvied the pope lived off the flesh of aborted fetuses; it's common enough knowledge. I said no way in hell, is what, the very idea of letting an Irish take the extra room, what with the devils they summon for their rituals, would that be right with little Jem in the house?* Popery is widely considered to be a sick corruption of Christianity ruled by the Antichrist, the spread of which will quash the Second Coming like an ant. I don't bother responding to this brand of insanity for two reasons: idiots treasure their facts like newborns, and the entire topic makes my shoulders ache. Anyhow, I'm unlikely to turn the tide. Americans have been feeling this way about foreigners since the Alien and Sedition Acts of 1798.

Hopstill misread my silence as agreement. He nodded, sipping his spirits. 'These beggars shall steal whatever isn't nailed down once they arrive here. We may as well save our breath.'

It went without saying that they *would* arrive. I walk along the docks edging South Street only two blocks distant on my way home from Nick's pretty often, and they boast ships thick as the mice, carrying passengers plentiful as the fleas. They have done for years – even during the Panic, when I'd watched men starve. There's work to be had again now, railways to lay and warehouses to be built. But whether you pity the emigrants or rant about drowning them, on one subject every single citizen is in lockstep agreement: there's an unholy tremendous amount of them. A great many Irish, and all of those Catholics. And nearly everyone concurs with the sentiment that follows after: we haven't the means nor the desire to feed them all. If it gets any worse, the city fathers will have to pry open their wallets and start a greeting system – some way to keep foreigners from huddling in waterfront alleys, begging crusts from the pickpockets until they learn how to lift a purse. The week before, I'd passed a ship actively vomiting up seventy or eighty skeletal creatures from the Emerald Isle, the emigrants staring glassy eyed at the metropolis as if it were a physical impossibility.

'That's none too charitable, is it, Hops?' I observed.

'Charity has nothing to do with it.' He scowled, landing his cup on the counter with a dull *ping*. 'Or rather, this particular metropolis will have nothing to do with charity in cases where charity is a waste of time. I should sooner teach a pig morals than an Irishman. And I'll take a plate of oysters.'

I called out an order for a dozen with pepper to Julius, the young black fellow who scrubbed and cracked the shells. Hopstill is a menace to cheerful thought. It was hovering on the tip of my tongue to mention this to him. But just then, a dark gap cut into the spear of light arrowing down the stairs and Mercy Underhill walked into my place of employment.

'Good morning, Mr Hopstill,' she called in her tender little chant. 'And Mr Wilde.'

If Mercy Underhill were any more perfect, it would take a long day's work to fall in love with her. But she has exactly enough faults to make it ridiculously easy. A cleft like a split peach divides her chin, for instance, and her blue eyes are set pretty wide, giving her an uncomprehending look when she's taking in your conversation. There isn't an uncomprehending thought in her head, however, which is another feature some men would find a fault. Mercy is downright bookish, pale as a quill feather, raised entirely on texts and arguments by the Reverend Thomas Underhill, and the men who notice she's beautiful have the devil's own time of it coaxing her face out of whatever's latest from Harper Brothers Publishing.

We try our best, though.

'I require two pints . . . two? Yes, I think that ought to do it. Of New England rum, please, Mr Wilde,' she requested. 'What were you talking of?'

She hadn't any vessel, only her open wicker basket with flour and herbs and the usual hastily penned scraps of half-finished poetry keeking out, so I pulled a rippled glass jar from a shelf. 'Hopstill was proving that New York at large is about as charitable as a coffin vendor in a plague town.'

'Rum,' Hopstill announced sourly. 'I didn't take either you or the reverend for rum imbibers.'

Mercy smoothed back a lock of her sleek but continually escaping black hair as she absorbed this remark. Her bottom lip rests just behind her top lip, and she tucks the bottom one in slightly when she's ruminating. She did then.

'Did you know, Mr Wilde,' she inquired, 'that *elixir proprietatis* is the only medicine that can offer immediate relief when dysentery threatens? I pulverize saffron with myrrh and aloe and then suffer the concoction to stand a fortnight in the hot sun mixed with New England rum.'

Mercy passed me a quantity of dimes. It was still good to see so many disks of metal money clinking around again. Coins vanished completely during the Panic, replaced by receipts for restaurant meals and tickets for coffee. A man could hew granite for ten hours and get paid in milk and Jamaica Beach clams.

'That'll teach you to question an Underhill, Hops,' I advised over my shoulder.

'Did Mr Hopstill *ask* a question, Mr Wilde?' Mercy mused.

That's how she does it, and damned if it doesn't fasten my tongue to my teeth every single time. Two blinks, a gauzy lost lamb expression, a remark she pretends is unrelated, and you're hung up by your toes. Hopstill sniffed blackly, understanding he was good as banished from the continent. And by a girl who turned twenty-two this past June. I don't know where she learns such things.

'I'll carry this as far as your corner,' I offered, turning out from behind the bar with Mercy's spirits.

Thinking all the while, *Are you really going to do this?* I'd been fast friends with Mercy for well over a decade. *It could all stay the same. You lifting things for her and watching the curl at the back of her neck and working out what she's reading so you can read it too.*

'Why are you leaving your bar?' She smiled at me.

'I've been gripped by a spirit of adventure.'

New Street was aswarm, the sheen of polished sable beaver hats punishing my eyes above the sea of navy frock coats. It's only a two-block street terminating to the north at Wall, all giant stone storefronts with awnings shielding the pedestrians from the scorching blaze. Pure commerce. From every canopy hangs a sign, and plastered to every sign and glued to every wall is a poster: PARTI-COLORED NECKERCHIEFS, TEN FOR A DOLLAR. WHITTING'S HAND SOAP A GUARANTEE AGAINST RINGWORM. All the populous streets on the island are papered in shrieking broadsheets, no exceptions, the flaked headlines of yesteryear just visible under the freshly glued advertisements. I glimpsed my brother Val's smirk translated into woodcut and tacked to a door, then caught myself stifling a grimace: VALENTINE WILDE SUPPORTS THE FORMATION OF THE NEW YORK CITY POLICE FORCE.

Well and good. I'd probably oppose it, in that case. Crime is rampant, robbery expected, assault common, murder often unsolved. But supposing Val was in favor of the violently debated new police, I'd take my chances with anarchy. Up to the previous year, apart from a recently formed group of hapless men called Harper's Police, who wore blue coats to advertise themselves as fit for beatings by the spirited, there was no such thing as a Peeler in this town. There was a Watch in New York, certainly. They were ancient hangdogs parched for money who toiled all day and then slept all night in watchmen's booths, ardently watched by the brimming population of criminals. We'd in excess of four hundred thousand souls prowling the streets, counting the perpetual piebald mob of visitors from around the globe. And fewer than five hundred watchmen, snoring in vertical coffins as their dreams bounced around like tenpins inside their leather helmets. As for daylight keepers of the peace, don't even ask. There were nine of them.

But if my brother Valentine is in favor of something, that something isn't particularly likely to be a good idea.

'I thought you might want a bruiser to get you past the throng,' I remarked to Mercy. It was half a joke. I'm solid, and quick too, but a bantam. An inch taller than Mercy, if I'm lucky. But Napoleon didn't figure height stood between him and the Rhineland, and I lose fights about as often as he did.

'Oh? Oh, I see. Well, that was very kind, then.'

She wasn't actually surprised; the set of her robin's-egg-blue eyes told me that much, and I decided to watch my step. Mercy is very difficult to navigate. But I know my way around the city, and around Mercy Underhill. I was born in a cheerless cottage in Greenwich Village before New York even touched its borders, and I'd been learning Mercy's quirks since she was nine.

'I wonder something this morning.' She paused, her wide-set eyes sliding my way and then dropping off again. 'But it's silly, maybe. You'll laugh.'

'If you ask me not to, I won't.'

'I wonder why you never use my name, you see, Mr Wilde.'

New York's winds are never fresh in the summer. But as we turned onto Wall, bank after bank scrolling past us in line after line of Grecian columns, the air turned sweeter. Or maybe I just remembered it that way afterward, but suddenly it all seemed pure dust and hot stone. Clean, like parchment. That smell was worth a fortune. 'I don't know what you mean,' I said.

'There, yes. I'm sorry – I don't mean to be cryptic.' Mercy's bottom lip slid underneath her top one just a little, only a fraction of a warm wet inch, and I thought in that moment I could taste it too. 'You could have just said, "I don't know what you mean, *Miss Underhill*." And then we wouldn't be talking about it any longer.'

'What does that make you think?'

I spied a jagged hole in the pavement. Pivoting quickly, I guided Mercy out of its path with a swish of her pale green summer skirts. Maybe she'd caught sight of the little cave herself, though, for I didn't startle her. Her head didn't even turn. Escorting Mercy down a block, depending on her mood, you might not be there for all the attention she pays you. And I'm not exactly Sunday, so to speak. I've never been a special occasion. I'm all of the other days in the workweek, and there are plenty of us streaming by without notice. But I could fix that, or I thought I could.

'Do you mean to make me theorize that you like the topic of my name, Mr Wilde?' she asked me, looking as if she was trying not to laugh.

I'd caught her out, though. No one ever answers her questions with questions, just the way she never acknowledges answering questions at all. That's another fault of Mercy's I'm fixed on. She's a reverend's daughter, to be certain, but she talks clever as a jade if only you're keen enough to notice.

'Do you know what I'd like to do?' I questioned in return, thinking that was the trick of it. 'I've managed to put some money away, four hundred in cash. Not like all these maniacs who take their first extra dollar and play it against the price of China tea. I want to buy some land, out on Staten Island maybe, and have a river ferry. Steamships are dear, but I can take my time finding a good price.'

I remembered being two years orphaned, scrawny and pale skinned and twelve. Wheedling my way through sheer tenacity into the employment of a hulking but kindly Welsh boatman during one of the leaner periods Valentine and I had ever faced, having lived off of mealy apples for a week. Maybe I was hired on as a deckhand because the fellow suspected as much. I recalled standing at the prow of the ferry before the rails I'd just polished until my fingers were peeling, head thrown back as an ecstatic midsummer thunderstorm exploded in the still-blazing sunshine. For five minutes, spray and rain had danced in the dazzling light, and for five minutes, I'd not wondered whether my brother back on Manhattan Island had yet managed to kill himself. It felt wonderful. Like being erased.

Mercy quickened her grip slightly. 'What has your anecdote to do with my question?'

Be a man and take the plunge, I thought.

'Maybe I don't want to call you Miss Underhill, ever,' I answered her. 'Maybe I'd like to call you Mercy. What is it you'd like best to be called?'

I was a touchstone at Nick's Oyster Cellar that night, a lightning-bright lucky charm. All my pale glorified card sharps, all the faro-champagne-morphine-and-what-else-have-you addicts, the freaks who haunt the Exchange and make deals with damp handshakes in the back rooms of coffee houses – they all saw kismet on me and wanted a taste of it. A drink from Timothy Wilde was as good as a slap on the back from an Astor.

'Three more bottles of champagne!' shouted a weedy fellow called Inman. He could scarce breathe for being jostled by black-coated elbows. I wondered sometimes what made the financiers head for another sweltering cock-pit the moment they quit the chamber of the Board of Brokers.

'Take a glass for yourself on my account, Tim, cotton's higher than an opium fiend!'

People tell me things. Always have done. They hemorrhage information like a slit bag spills dried beans. It's only gotten worse as I've manned an oyster cellar. Incredibly useful, but it does get to be draining at times – as if I'm part barman and part midnight hole in the ground, just a quick-dug hollow to bury secrets in. If Mercy would only manage to fall into the same habit, that would be something miraculous.

A stream of honest working sweat trickled down my back by nine o'clock, when the sun went down. Men sweating for other reasons demanded drinks and oysters as if the world had spun off its axis. Apparently there was nothing for it but to annihilate the feast before we all slid off. I was moving fast enough for a dozen, juggling orders, calling back friendly insults, counting the shower of coins.

'What's the good news, Timothy?'

'We've got enough cold champagne to float an ark on,' I shouted back at Hopstill, who'd reappeared. Julius materialized behind me, hoisting a bucket of fresh-shaved ice. 'Next round's on the house.'

The way I figured it, Mercy Underhill hadn't said no to any of my remarks. Nor 'You seem to have the wrong idea,' nor 'Leave me be.' Instead, she'd said a good many completely unrelated things before I left her at the corner of Pine and William streets, a breeze picking up from the east, where the coffee houses churned rich burning smells into the heavy air.

She'd said, 'I can understand your not liking my family name, Mr Wilde. It makes me think of being buried,' for example. She'd said, 'Your own parents, God rest them, had the generosity to leave you the surname of a lord chancellor of England. I'd love to live in London. How cool London must be in the summer, and there the parks have real grass, and everything electric green from the rain. Or so my mother always told me, whenever a New York summer seemed too much to bear.' That was a regular catechism of Mercy's, whatever the season – a little prayer to her late mother, Olivia Underhill, a native of London who'd been odd and generous and imaginative and beautiful and wonderfully like her only child.

Mercy had added, 'I've finished the twentieth chapter of my novel. Don't you think that's a thrilling number? Had you ever expected me to get so far? Will you give me your honest opinion, once it's finished?'

If she aimed to discourage me, she was going to have to up her game.

And I might not be a scholar in title, or a churchman, but Reverend Thomas Underhill liked me fine. Barmen are pillars of the community and the hub of New York's wheel, and I had four hundred dollars in slick silver buried in the straw tick of my bed. Mercy Underhill, in my opinion, ought to be called Mercy Wilde – and then I'd never know where another conversation was headed for the rest of my life.

'Give me fifty dollars and I'll see you're a rich man by the end of the fortnight, Tim!' shrieked Inman from yards away in the roiling vat of bodies. 'Sam Morse's telegraph can make you a *king*!'

'Take your fairy money and go to hell,' I returned cheerfully, reaching for a slop rag. 'You ever play the market, Julius?'

'I'd likelier burn money than speculate it,' Julius answered without looking at me, deftly pulling the corks from a row of drenched champagne bottles with his wide fingers. He's a sensible fellow, quick and quiet, with fragrant tea leaves braided into his hair. 'Fire can heat a man's soup. You calculate they know the Panic was their doing? You think they remember?'

I wasn't listening to Julius any longer by that time. Instead, I was dwelling thick as laudanum on the last thing Mercy had said to me.

Don't think you've hurt my feelings. I'm not married to the name, after all.

It was the only sentence directly to the purpose I'd ever heard her say, I think. At least, it was the first since she was about fifteen, and even so, the remark had a sideways charm to it. So that was a heady, graceful moment. The moment when I discovered that Mercy saying something near-plain is every bit as beautiful as Mercy talking circles like a flame-red kite in the wind.

At four in the morning, I passed Julius an extra two dollars as he propped the mop handle in the corner. He nodded. Worn to a thinly buzzing alertness, we headed for the steps leading up to the awakening city.

'You ever wonder what it's like to sleep at nighttime?' I asked as I locked the cellar door behind us.

'You won't catch me in a bed after dark. Keep the devil guessing,' Julius answered, winking at his own joke.

We reached the street just as dawn flared with grasping red fingers over the horizon. Or so the corner of my eye thought, as I settled my hat on my head. Julius was quicker to catch on.

'*Fire!*' Julius bellowed in his low, smooth voice, cupping his hands around his sharply defined lips. '*Fire in New Street!*'

For a moment, I stood there, frozen in the dark with a streak of scarlet above me, already acting about as useless as a broken gas-lamp inspector. Feeling the same sickness in my belly the word *fire* always causes me.

CHAPTER TWO

The explosion was heard at Flushing and supposed to be the shock of an earthquake. Cinders fell on Staten Island, and for several miles over in New Jersey, the sun was obscured by smoke during the forenoon.

New York Herald, July 1845

The third floor of the storefront across the street from us looked as if it had imprisoned an amber sun. Fierce yellow tongues were eating away the outer windows, the fire already laying claim to what must have been a vast inner storeroom. Fires in these parts are about as common as riots, and every bit as fatal, but here one raged in plain sight without anyone having yet given the alarm. So whatever the cause, it had been horribly quick – a lamp left lit near a pile of cotton wool, a cigar end in a rubbish bin. Any small, stupid, deadly mistake would serve. It's a large warehouse that faces Nick's, taking up much of the small block, and my heart took a second dip in my chest when I recognized that a glow so very bright must have reached throughout the entire floor and now surely raged against the wall of the adjacent building.

Julius and I were racing toward the blaze an instant later. You run toward as-yet-undiscovered fires in New York, not away from them, offering your own help until the all-volunteer fire companies arrive on the scene. People have roasted for want of a hand out a window. I glanced behind us, longing for the clang of the fire bell even though I detested the sound.

'How can no one have seen it yet?' I gasped.

'It's not sensible.' Stopping, Julius sent up the cry of 'Fire!' again and then hurtled after me.

Neighbors trickled into the street under the charcoal sky, staring in awe and with a weird city-dweller's thrill-seeking pleasure at the wide ribbon of flame on the upper floor. Behind us, at last the nearest fire bell rent the air with its shocking peals – single clangs to summon help to Ward One. Moments later, the answering echo erupted from the cupola of City Hall, beyond the park.

'Wait,' I said, pulling sharply at Julius's shoulder.

The remaining windows of the storage facility began lighting up like a series of matchsticks – sparks had clearly invaded every story, fire devouring the interior as if the huge building were made of paper. Glass shattering in sudden pistol shots that I couldn't quite understand.

Then I did understand, and that was far worse.

'This is Max Hendrickson's store,' I whispered.

Julius's brown eyes went wide.

'Jesus have mercy,' he said. 'If the fire hits his stock of whale oil—'

Red flannel flashed past us as a volunteer fireman with his braces hanging off and his curious leather helmet drooping over his face careened around the corner of Exchange Place. *Hell-bent to claim the nearest fire plug for his own engine company,*

I thought with my familiar slight flare of disdain. *And thereby all the glory.*

Meanwhile, it occurred to me that my future was now less than certain.

'Go, fetch your valuables,' Julius ordered before I said anything. 'And pray you have a house an hour from now.'

I lived in Stone Street, two blocks below the southern terminus of New Street, down Broad, and I sprinted around the corner away from the doomed building with nothing but Mercy, my residence, and its four hundred dollars in silver on my mind. I would get that money if it killed me. Storefronts I'd passed a thousand times went by in an eyeblink, handcrafted chairs and leather-bound books and bolts of cloth just visible behind the darkened shop displays, my boots flying over eroding cobblestones, running as if hell were at my heels.

That was my first mistake. Hell turned out to be in front of me, over a block away from the New Street fire.

The instant my foot touched Broad, a detonation like a volcano erupting burst 38 Broad Street into a plume of rock, granite missiles the size of grown men sailing above me. The structure had hurled a quarry's worth of stone into the buildings opposite by the time I skidded to a halt.

At first I thought, *Holy Christ, someone's set a bomb in our midst.* But 38 Broad, I remembered in the back of my hellfire-dazzled mind as the mammoth warehouse rent itself in pieces before my eyes, was presently a saltpeter storage facility. It held shipments of gunpowder belonging to the well-liked merchant duo of Crocker and Warren. Which was a shame for New York, really. As thunder nearly shattered my eardrums, I thought, *Bad luck. A window must have been open,* for cinders from the oil fire in New Street had obviously been borne on the wind across the thoroughfare and into a room of powder kegs. Amid the fury, airy curlicues of ash hung perfectly still high above the cobbles. Maybe it was thick of me to even ponder the role of luck at the time, but exploding saltpeter warehouses seem to have a slowing effect on my wits.

Belatedly, I turned to run. I'd taken two steps when I saw a woman flying past me, her mouth open and her face fixed in surprise, her hair streaming backward in a lazy arc. One shoe was blown from her foot, and the foot itself had a smudge of blood on the instep. And that was when I started seeing things funny, just as I realized that I was flying too. Then I heard – no, *felt*, for the world was silent – the entire earth ripping in half as easily and raggedly as an old piece of cotton.

When I opened my eyes again, the planet had inverted itself. And it was still busily exploding.

My head rested against a door still within its frame, but doors aren't meant to be horizontal. I wondered why this one was. And why there seemed to be hulking pieces of stone surrounding me on all sides.

A tiny matchstick's worth of flame nuzzled at the woman's red calfskin shoe six inches from my hand. That single spark angered me terribly – its smug, devious approach. I wanted to save the shoe, return it to the flying woman, but I couldn't seem to move my arms. The index finger of my right hand twitched, the movement of a dull-brained little animal. I glimpsed the sky through a crevice and wondered how dawn had risen so quickly.

'*Tim!* Timothy!'

I knew that voice. I felt a flood of irritation, and also of plain, stupid fear under the shock. He wasn't too full of morphine to be standing, then. Of course not. That would be so *easy*. Instead, he was clearly striding into the very center of the bull's-eye, with shrapnel and brimstone raining freely down upon his person. How very like him.

'*Timothy*, call out where you are! For the love of God, Tim, answer me!'

My tongue stuck stubbornly to the back of my teeth. I didn't want that voice to see me sprawled in a Chinese dancing girl's pose, unable to so much as lift a singed shoe. I didn't want that voice anywhere near a warehouse acting like the world's biggest cannon, either. But all I could register was a cottony sense of *no*.

Something sticky and metallic was running down my cheek. *Light. Too much of it.*

A flickering yellow blaze like a god-sized fireplace struck my eyes when someone began tearing away the rocks. Only my upper body had been partly buried. My legs were in the open air and soon enough my face was too, when a cleanly shaven but bearish figure tossed aside a heavy iron shutter.

'Christ, Tim. Julius Carpenter just saved your hide, telling me which way you'd gone. There's nary yet breathing in this street.'

I blinked at my six-years'-elder brother, the soot-grimed mountain of a hook-and-ladder man with his ax swinging freely from his belt and his face obscured by the inferno behind him. The anger in my chest grew watery, mingled with sudden relief. When he pulled me up by the arms, I bit down on a yell and managed by some miracle to keep my feet once I was upright. He threw my arm over his coarse red shirt before setting off fast as I could keep pace with him, back the way I'd come, both of us stumbling through the rubble as if it were ankle-deep sand on a beach.

'There's a girl, Val,' I rasped. 'She landed very near me. We have to—'

'Gingerly, gingerly,' growled Valentine Wilde. I'd never

26

have heard him through the pervasive ringing if he'd not been two inches from my ear. 'You're more than half hocused, aren't you? Wait till we're out of this and I can see you better.'

'She—'

'I saw a piece of her, Timothy. She'll be put to bed with a shovel. Shut your head a moment.'

I don't remember much more until Valentine had reached a brick wall under a gaslight back on New Street and propped me up against it. What had been a half-deserted stone business thoroughfare was now an overturned hornet's nest. At least three volunteer engine companies had already arrived, and a viciously tight thread of visible tension ran between each and every man in a red shirt. Not a one was brawling, or bickering over fire plugs, or donning brass knuckles. Every time one firefighter met another's eye, his only expression was *And next? And next?* Half of them were looking at my brother, their eyes skimming toward him and then fixing. *Wilde. Wilde isn't afraid of anything. Wilde sees his way clear. Wilde runs into infernos as if they're rose gardens. All right, Wilde. And next?* I wanted to force them all quiet with my bare hands over their mouths, make them stop calling out to him.

What exactly do they expect him to do about the city exploding?

'You're well and truly buttered, my boy. Get to the nearest dispensary,' Valentine ordered. 'I'd cart you up to the hospital, but it's too far and the boys need me. The whole stait'll burn if we—'

'Get to it, then,' I coughed bitterly. Maybe if I went along with him for once, he'd see reason out of pure contrariness. Nothing makes me more furious than my brother's obsession with open flame. 'I have to stop home, and then I'll—'

'Don't rig with me,' my brother snapped. 'Get to a doctor. You're hurt worse than you think, Tim.'

'Wilde! Give us a hand, it's spreading!'

My brother was swallowed by a bedlam of red shirts screaming orders at one another and sending feathers of spray from their hoses to slice midair through the lazy pincurls of smoke. Looking away from Val purposefully with a hard jerk of my neck, I could see the bloated figure of Justice George Washington Matsell shepherding a clutch of whimpering females away from burning apartments toward the Custom House steps. Matsell is no mere politician; he's half legend to locals, a highly visible figure, not least because he weighs about as much as a bison. Following a trusted civic leader like Justice Matsell seemed a likely direction to head for safety.

But I, either because I was infuriated or because I'd been knocked in the head, staggered toward my home. The world as I knew it had gone mad. Small wonder I had as well.

I walked south through a snowstorm in which the flakes were the color of lead, feeling reckless and unmoored. Bowling Green has a fountain at the center – a glad, gushing fountain, rivers tumbling over its lip. The fountain burbled away, but a man couldn't hear it because the surrounding brick buildings had flames pouring like waterfalls out their windows. Red fire raged upward and glassy red water pounded downward and I staggered past the trees with my arms around my stomach, wondering why my face felt like I'd just stepped out of the salt water at Coney Island and turned in to a cold March wind.

Stone Street, when I reached it, proved a battlement of fire, my own house disintegrating into the earth even while it was being carried away on the updrafts. Just the sight of it pulled me to pieces a little. In my mind's eye, as the wasted runoff from the fire engines began to trickle past my feet, soon gushing with chicken bones and bits of trampled lettuce, I imagined my molten silver coursing along the cobble cracks. Ten years of savings looked like a mercury river, painting mirrors on the soles of my boots.

'Only chairs,' sobbed a woman. 'We had a table, and he might have grabbed the linens. Only chairs, only chairs, only chairs.'

I opened my eyes. I'd been walking, I knew, but they must have been shut. I was at the southmost tip of the island, in the middle of Battery Gardens. But not as I'd ever seen it.

The Battery is a promenade for those who have time for recreational walks. It's blanketed with cigar stubs and peanut shells, yes, but the wind from the ocean carries the care right out of my bones, and the sycamores don't stop my view of the New Jersey forests across the Hudson. It's a grand place, and locals and tourists alike lean on the iron rails in the afternoons, all staring off over the water alone together.

But the Battery was now a furniture warehouse. The woman rocking back and forth over her chairs had four of them – while to my left, a small hill of cotton bales had been rescued from the fire. Chests of tea were mounting like a dizzying Tower of Babel above a gigantic pile of broomsticks. The air that had been foul with summertime half an hour earlier reeked with the cindery dust of burning whale oil.

'Oh, my dear God,' said a woman carrying at least fifty pounds of sugar in a neatly stamped sack, peering at my face. 'You ought to see a doctor, sir.'

I barely heard her. I'd slumped to the grass with the rocking chairs and sacks of flour. Meanwhile thinking the only thought an ambitious fellow from New York would've indulged in as he lost consciousness while the city was erupting.

If I have to save for another ten years, she'll pick somebody else.

*

When I woke up a pauper, nauseated and disoriented, my brother had already picked a new profession for me. Unfortunately, that's the sort of fellow Valentine is.

'There you are. Bully,' my brother drawled from the chair he'd pulled up to my bedside and then sat in backside front, dangling his thick blond arm and half-chewed cigar over the sanded cedar. 'Some of New York is still standing, by the way. Not your ken or your workplace, though. I checked. Those look like the inside of my fireplace.'

We were both alive, then, which seemed pretty favorable. But where? The windowsill a few feet from me hosted a series of herb pots and a bowl of cheery upright asparagus, either decoration or future dinner. Then I spied a huge, glorious painting of an American eagle bearing arrows in its talons on the far wall and winced inwardly.

Val's place, on Spring Street. I'd not been there in months. It's the second floor of a fine cozy row house with hysterical political posters and the usual strapping patriotic pictures of George Washington and Thomas Jefferson blanketing the walls. Firemen are New York's heroes, and the heroes make an actual living by way of politics, as they aren't paid for running headlong into blazing infernos. So their days break down thus: for recreation, they douse fires, beat the good nature out of rivals from other engine companies in organized gang brawls, and drink and whore their way up and down the Bowery. And for work, they get their friends elected or appointed to city jobs, so that they all manage to elect or appoint each other. People would object louder to this system if they didn't worship the firemen. Who's against a flash-man when he's dressed in red cotton and you're handing your baby out a window?

I haven't the stomach for any of it. Politics or prolonged exposure to Val.

Valentine is a Democrat, in the identical way some men are doctors or stevedores or brewers, and his goal in professional life is to crush the hated Whigs to powder. The Democrats don't worry much over the few scattered Anti-Masonics, whose only aim is to convince America that the Freemasons intend to murder us all in our beds. Nor do they lose sleep over the Liberty Party, because as glad as New Yorkers are that slavery here was abolished entirely in 1827, joining an entire political engine dedicated to the welfare of blacks is extremely unfashionable. What chafes Val's hide are the machinations of the Whigs: they're merchants and doctors and lawyers generally, most of the well-to-do and everyone with pretensions in that direction, gentlemen with clean hands who make a tremendous racket about raising tariffs and modernizing banks. The accepted Democratic response to Whig arguments is to praise the natural virtue of the peasant, and then to throw the ballot boxes coming from Whig districts into the Hudson.

The main difference between them isn't political, though, to my mind. As I grasp the matter, the Democrats would like every last taxpaying Irishman to vote for them, and the Whigs would like every last taxpaying Irishman to be deported to Canada.

It all repulses me. I'll own that my brother lives pretty comfortably, though. And for a man who always neglects the top two buttons of his fireman's shirt and thinks of morphine the way most people think of tonic water, he's laughably clean in domestic habits. He sweeps the floor every morning and polishes his andirons with rum every other month.

'Thirsty? Water, rum, gin, or small beer?' My brother went to rummage in the kitchen and deposited two mugs on the table next to me when he returned. 'Here, have your pick of

31

the first pair. Would you believe that thirty-eight Broad Street, apart from the saltpeter, had its basement stuffed with French cream? Barrel after barrel of brandy, Tim. Worst streak of luck I've ever seen . . .'

As he continued, I squinted, focusing my vision. Val wore a halfhearted attempt at his typical Bowery Boy glory, sporting a fine white shirt and black trousers with a silk waistcoat covered in peonies only half done up. Clean and healthy, but clearly exhausted. My brother is the living spit of me on a thirty-percent-larger scale, with a boyish, dimpled face, dark blond hair with a deep peak at the brow, and pensive bags under his bright green eyes. They aren't much to do with deep thinking on either one of us, though. Particularly not Val. No, Val is more the type to stagger out of a bawdy house having just knifed someone, with an adoring moll under each gnarled arm, lush with gin and laughing like the bass clef of a pipe organ, the very living definition of an American dead rabbit. When my brother laughs, he flinches, as if he shouldn't be laughing. And he shouldn't. A darker-minded gentleman never stalked the festering city streets in brushed black tails.

'It was a sight, Tim,' Val concluded with a one-sided grin. 'And the light-fingered sort at work within seconds. Damned if I didn't spot a clever old toast of seventy years who'd hooked so many cigars he had to carry 'em in his togs. Tied the canvas of his trousers with two strings at the ankle and filled on up.'

That was when I realized what was wrong, apart from actual injuries: I was up to my eyebrows with laudanum. My brother had dosed me so high after the doctor (so I hoped) departed that the image of a man's trousers overflowing with cigars seemed pretty nightmarish. Valentine is careful about how much vinegar goes in his fish gravy, and careful about boiling the milk for his coffee, but a man with so many drugs in his veins is apt to miscalculate opiates. Meanwhile, a mysterious pain gnawed at the side of my head with burning reptile fangs. I wanted to feel it. Identify it, maybe.

'Never mind cigars. How did I get here?' I asked with a thick tongue.

'I found you on the Battery in a fortress of Holy Writ. One of the fire-boys had spied you keeping company with the Bible Society, flat on your back with all your lights out – I *told* you to find a sawbones, you incarnate tit – but of course, any Party man would know you for my brother, and they sent me word straightaway. These autum-bawlers were standing guard over your lifeless hide and their one thousand, two hundred and sixty-one Bibles salvaged from Nassau Street.'

Autum-bawlers. Churchmen, then. I had a vision of three fellows in drab clerical tweeds outlined against the murky starlight. Arguing over the safety of leaving one man behind with me and the stacks of Bibles, sending two to fetch parts of their press. Then one had suggested fetching a doctor instead, and the others told him not to be ridiculous. God would give me strength provided they saw that His presses remained unscathed. I hadn't been in a position to argue at the time.

'When I arrived, they handed you over,' Val continued casually, picking an errant piece of tobacco off his tongue. 'You have two nasty bruised ribs and . . . well, nothing else that'll keep you down long.'

'Sorry you missed any of the *fire*.'

'Anyway, I've set us both up easy,' Val announced, as if getting back to a topic we'd accidentally left behind. 'We've both a new occupation, my Tim. One you'll take to like a bird to air.'

I wasn't minding him.

I was fiddling with my fingertips at the oily cotton wool bandaging over the upper right-hand quadrant of my face. My eye was fine, I knew, for I could see clear as church glass, though the drugs glossed everything. And by Val's own account, it was miraculous that the worst of my injuries had been a couple of bruised ribs. So I couldn't have been brained too badly. Could I?

I kept hearing my brother's words, though, bitten out regretful but hasty as he'd turned away to pull people out of disintegrating row houses. He'd sounded dry as sandpaper. A voice I'd not heard in years. And so, picturing myself suddenly made my blood run slick and slippery as an eel.

You're hurt worse than you think, Tim.

'I don't want your setups. To run for state senate or work as a hydrant inspector,' I grated out, ignoring my own thoughts.

'It's plumper than oyster pie, I'm telling you.' Standing, Valentine began doing up buttons, leaving the wet cigar end at the side of his expressive mouth. 'Got us both appointments only this morning, through the Party. Course, mine is . . . a bit higher up. And in this district. You, I only managed to post in the Sixth Ward. You'll have to live there, find a new ken, since roundsmen are required to live in the same ward they patrol. But that's no matter. Your house is getting hosed off into the river by now.'

'Whatever it is, *no*.'

'Don't get so peppery, Timothy. There's to be a police force.'

'Everyone knows that. Anyhow, I saw your poster. It didn't endear them to me.'

Despite my misgivings or maybe because of them, the police saga had been the first political tale I'd closely followed in years. Harmless citizens were shrieking for a system of constables, and less harmless patriots were bellowing that the freemen of New York would never stomach a standing army. Legislation passed in June, a Democrat victory, and the harmless citizens had won out at long last thanks to tireless thugs like my brother – men who liked danger, power, and bribes in equal measure.

'You'll come round soon enough, now you're a policeman yourself.'

'Ha!' I barked bitterly, sending a twinge of suffering through my pate. 'I call that nice. You want me trussed up in a blue strait-waistcoat for the real men to throw rotten eggs at?'

Valentine snorted and somehow managed to make me feel even smaller than I normally do in his company. No easy trick. But he's an expert.

'You think a free republican like me would be caught walking around in blue livery? Dry up, Tim. We've a real police now, no uniforms, and with George Washington Matsell himself at the head. For good, they're claiming.'

I blinked blearily. Justice Matsell, the equally infamous and obese civic figure I'd seen in the thick of the fire, shooing gawkers toward the oasis of the courthouse. I'd also heard from diverse sources that he was a degraded lump of blubber, that he was the righteous hand of God come to bring order to the streets, that he was a power-hungry troll, that he was a benign philosopher who'd owned a bookstore selling the sordid works of Robert Dale Owen and Thomas Paine, and that he was a damned dirty Englishman. I'd nodded at all accounts as if their gospel verity was unassailable. Mainly because I didn't give a damn. What did I know about governance, after all?

As for joining the new police force, that was clearly a plot of Val's to make me look ridiculous.

'I don't need your help,' I declared.

'No,' Valentine sneered, snapping one of his braces.

With considerable calculation, I sat up in his bed. The room reeled around me as if I were a maypole, and a hot molten flash branded my temple.

Nothing is as bad as it seems, I thought with the last remnants of my dense optimism. It couldn't be. I'd already lost everything once, I'd been ten, and so had countless other people I knew, and they all picked up and kept going. Or they picked up and went in a slightly different direction.

'I'll go back to bartending,' I decided.

'You have any notion of how many people are out of work this morning?'

'At a hotel or another of the better oyster cellars.'

'How does your face feel, Tim?' Valentine snapped.

Sulfur drifted through the air now. A hot and grainy sort of rage tugged at my throat.

'Like it was slapped with a laundry iron,' I answered.

'And you're supposing it looks sprucer than it feels?' he mocked me more quietly. 'You're in difficulties, little Timothy. You took a dose of hot oil where it'll be noticed. You want to tend bar from behind a three-foot pine plank up the arse end of a vegetable grocery, I'll drink to your fortune. But you're likelier to be hired on at Barnum's American Museum as the Man Who Lost Part of His Physog than you are to tend bar at a hotel.'

I bit the end of my tongue hard, tasting gunmetal.

I wasn't thinking any longer about ways to earn money so I wouldn't have to eat Valentine's goddamned chicken fricassee. My brother can cook as well as he cleans. I wasn't even figuring the odds of my being able to stand up long enough to punch him in the jaw.

*No, I was ruminating, it seems that two days back you had a
pile of silver and a whole face.*

I wanted Mercy Underhill like I wanted to breathe air, and
then in the same heartbeat hoped she'd never see me again.
Mercy could have her pick. And I'd gone from being a man
with a great many things in his favor to another sort: a highly
disreputable fellow whose sole possessions were a scar I
couldn't imagine seeing for myself without my neck flushing
clammy, and an equally disgraceful brother who earned his
bread giving concussions to somber swallowtailed Whigs.

'I hate you,' I said with very careful clarity to Valentine.

That was comforting, like bad whiskey burning my throat.
Bitter and familiar.

'Then take the sodding job, so you don't have to sleep in
my ken,' he suggested.

Valentine dragged his fingers through his tawny hair,
ambling over to his desk to pour himself a measure of rum.
Completely, entirely unmoved, which so happens to be the
most infuriating thing about my infuriating older brother. If
he cares a rotten fig that I hate him, I wish to Christ he'd be
more visible about it.

'The Sixth Ward is hell's privy pit,' I pointed out.

'August first.' Valentine drained his spirits and then
adjusted his braces with a second snap of impatience. His
green eyes raked over me as he went for his beautifully shining
black coat. 'You have ten days to find a ken in the Sixth Ward.
If you were political, I could've done better, settle you here in
the Eighth, but you aren't, are you?'

He raised his brows while I attempted to look properly
defiant about my political shortcomings. But it hurt my head,
so I relaxed against the pillows again.

'It's five hundred dollars a year, plus whatever you can

make by way of rewards or letting the flusher rabbits you nab grease you. Or you can always foist off the brothels. I don't give a damn.'

'No,' I agreed.

'Like I said, I arranged it all with Matsell. You and I both start August first. I'm to be a captain,' he added with more than a touch of brag. 'A respected metropolitan figure, and making steady chink at it, too, and plenty of time left for fighting fires with the lads. What do you think of that?'

'I think I'll see you in hell.'

'Well, that's true enough,' Valentine shot back with a smile that would have looked cold on an undertaker. 'You'll be living there, after all.'

The next morning, when I was sober enough to see straight, I awoke to my brother snoring on a flat pallet before his fireplace, smelling vividly of absinthe, and a copy of the *Herald* set out for me on the side table next to the bed. Val could read a lawyer's own brief and then argue him into an early grave if he liked, but he's better used to making news than mulling over it in print. So I knew the paper was mine. And here is what I read, after gasping my way through a burn so fierce that I thought my face must surely have been newly afire:

EXTRA New York Herald, THREE O'CLOCK P.M: TERRIBLE CONFLAGRATION: The greatest, the most terrible fire that has occurred in this city since the great conflagration of December 1835 has spread destruction throughout the lower part of the city. Three hundred buildings, according to the best calculation, have been burned to the ground . . .

My eyes faltered, not wanting to follow any further.

It is a close estimate to set the loss at from five to six millions of dollars . . .

Now, there was a fact I already knew instinctively, couldn't fail to have grasped despite my sorry physical state. A great deal of money had gone up in smoke over the Hudson. That was apparent. It wasn't dollars or buildings that plagued my unconscious brother, though, tracing a line between his brows. He must still have been drunk as a lord. Val's single redeeming quality consists of his method for calculating fire losses. And the code is stamped deep in his ribs, somewhere gripping and permanent. Thus I felt a hurt greater than my own real wounds, a raw and sympathetic sensation, when I read:

It is supposed that many lives have been lost by the terrible explosion.

The number, thank Christ, was thirty when all was said and done – a low figure of fatalities when the unholy chaos was considered.

But it wasn't low enough for Valentine. Nor for me. Not by a long mile.

CHAPTER THREE

> [T]he popish countries of Europe are disgorging upon
> our shores, from year to year, their ignorant,
> superstitious, and degraded inhabitants, not only by
> tens, but by hundreds of thousands, who already
> claim the highest privileges of native citizens, and
> even the country itself.
>
> American Protestant in Defence of Civil and
> Religious Liberty Against Inroads of Papacy, 1843

The key to being poor in New York is to know how it's
done: you make shortcuts.

Valentine and I, when we were sixteen and ten, respectively,
and one day woke up the only Wildes, learned that life-or-
death trick fast. So three days after the fire, perfectly able to
walk about but flinching like a gutter cat every time a loud
noise set my ears humming, I knew my options were limited
to taking Val's offer of police work or else moving to the
interior and learning agriculture. So I decided that, as I'd
apparently woken up in a permanent nightmare, I'd start with

the police work. And quit the instant I found something better.

On the morning of July twenty-second, a strong wind from the ocean cutting through the summer stench, I headed down Spring Street, past the pineapple vendors and the barrel-organ man in Hudson Square, to find a dwelling place. One with shortcuts. I was going to need plenty of shortcuts on five hundred a year. Nick's had paid me still less, but that hadn't been a problem. Not when all the extra coin had been considered, the half-a-neds and coach wheels and deuces slipped into my palm by madmen in French shirtsleeves, the jacks that clinked in Julius's and my pockets as we parted ways at the end of a shift. Wages were different – stable and frightening. I was looking at a fraction of what I'd earned previously, supposing I wasn't inclined to extort madams for extra chink.

Neighborhoods in New York change quicker than its weather. Spring Street, where Val lives, is a mix of people in the usual everyday sense: blue-coated Americans with their collars over their lapels and their hats neatly brushed, laughing colored girls waking your eyes up with canary yellow and shocking orange dresses, complacent ministers in brown wool and thin stockings. There are churches in Spring Street, eating houses smelling of pork chops with browned onions. It isn't Broadway north of Bleecker, where the outrageously wealthy bon ton and their servants peer down their noses at one another, but it isn't Ward Six either.

Which is where I was headed.

When I entered the district via Mulberry Street with two dollars of Val's money poisoning my pocket, I knew first that there were no shortcuts to be taken advantage of in that row of godforsaken Catholic misery. Second, I thought, *God save New York City from the rumor of faraway blighted potatoes.*

As for the swarms of emigrants gushing ceaselessly onto the South Street docks, I'd found out their next stopping place: the entire block consisted of Irish and dogs and rats sharing the same fleas. Not that I hold any truck with Nativists, but I couldn't prevent a shiver of sympathetic disgust constricting my throat. There were so many of them, scores passing to and fro, that I focused on one individual just to stave off a rush of dizziness. I lit on a still-sleepy peasant youth of about thirteen in trousers worn through the knees, entirely shoeless but wearing blue stockings, who stumbled past me into a corner grocery store. He bypassed the pale putrid cabbages set for show outside the entrance and headed straight for the whiskey bar. His posture matched the building he was patronizing. The Sixth Ward was built over the top of a swamp called the Collect Pond, but if you didn't know that, you'd wonder why the buildings lean at lunatic angles, seemingly stitched onto the sky in crazy-quilt seams.

I stepped over the fresh corpse of a dog felled by traffic and carried on, edging through the crowd. All the men walked with a purpose into groceries that didn't sell edible vegetables, the women's hands blazed redder than their hair from hard labor, and the children . . . the children seemed by turns harrowed and merely hungry. I saw one respectable fellow as I passed. A priest with a perfectly round head, faintly blue eyes, and a tight white dog collar. But he was ministering to the most wretched of the occupants, or so I hoped.

No, there were no shortcuts for an American on Mulberry. And my face simmered in the heat, rendering fat into the already greasy bandaging. Or something else, possibly. Frankly, I didn't want to dwell on it.

My face hadn't been a Michelangelo exactly, but it hadn't ever served me wrong either. Oval tending toward youthful roundness, and near enough identical to my brother's. Broad and high brow, deeply arcing hairline, hair indifferently blond. Straight nose, small mouth, with a little upside-down crescent where lips turn to chin. Fair skin despite our merciless summers. I'd never spent overmuch time mulling over my mazzard previously, though, because when I'd wanted a friendly hour or two with an idle shopkeeper's daughter or a hotel maid with appetites, I'd always gotten it. So it was a good enough face – it didn't cost me money when I needed a tumble, and I've been told my smile is very reluctant, which apparently makes people want to tell you their life histories and then pass you two bits for your patience.

Now I had absolutely no notion of what I looked like. The physical pain was already bad enough to make me steal a little of my brother's laudanum without added aesthetic horror.

'You're spooney,' my brother had announced, shaking his head as he studiously roasted coffee beans. 'Don't come over all squeamish on me *now*, for God's sake. Have a keek at yourself and be done.'

'Sod off, Valentine.'

'Listen, Tim, I can understand perfectly why you'd keep shady at first, in light of when you were just a squeaker and all, but—'

'By tomorrow at the latest I'll be clear of this house,' I'd replied on my way out, effectively ending the conversation.

Cutting across Walker Street, I turned up Elizabeth and then all at once shoved my fists in my still-sooty pockets in shock.

The structure directly before me was a miracle. A carefully printed wish list of shortcuts.

Thresholds and shutters on this block weren't quite gleaming, but they'd been scrubbed with vinegar and glinted respectably. The laundry strung along the hemp lines between buildings, fickly fluttering in the sun, was mended instead of lagging in limp shreds, giving me a settled feeling. And neat and humble and right before my very eyes stood a two-story brick row house wearing a ROOMS TO LET BY DAY OR MONTH sign. On the first floor, attractively lettered on a small awning, MRS BOEHM'S FINE BAKED GOODS held court. Not ten feet away from the entrance stood a pump ready to gush out clean Croton water.

That was potentially four shortcuts, if you're counting.

First, the pump meant pure Westchester river water and not the filthy stew drawn from Manhattan's sunken wells. Having the Croton River piped in your home means your landlord paying up front for the service, which happens just as often as the Atlantic freezes so a man can walk to London. Better to live by a free public pump. Second, residing above a bakery meant cast-off day-old bread. A baker is a thousand times likelier to give neighbors the surplus rye loaf than a stranger. Third, bakeries stoke up their ovens twice a day, which come November meant a pallid fraction of most people's heating costs, since the ovens would be baking caraway rolls while heating my floor.

Finally, Mrs Boehm's meant a widow. Women can't start their own enterprises, but they manage to inherit them when very careful. And I could see where the sign's paint was fresher on the 'Mrs' than on her surname. Making shortcut number four. If you're short on rent and a widow needs a roof mended, you might not find yourself back on the streets.

I pushed open the door to the bakery.

Very small, but well loved and well cared for. A simple pine counter displayed stacked rye and plain brown farm loaves, the smaller treats arranged on a wide flower-patterned serving dish. I could see sultanas poking out of a thousand-year cake, and its smell of candied orange peel livened my senses.

'You would like some bread, sir?'

My eyes swept from the baked goods to the woman who'd made them, approaching me as she rubbed her hands against her apron. Mrs Boehm looked around my age, closer to thirty than twenty. Her jaw was firm and her faded blue eyes alert and inquisitive – which, combined with the newness of the 'Mrs' above her door, led me to believe her husband hadn't long been absent. She'd hair the color of the seeds dotting her sunflower rolls, a dull shineless blond that looked nearly grey, and her brow was too wide and too flat. But her mouth was wide too, a generous sweep that oddly reversed how thin she was. When just her lips were considered, I could picture Mrs Boehm scraping ample butter over a thick slice of her fresh farmer's loaves. I liked that at once, felt strangely grateful for it. She didn't seem *mean*.

'What's your best seller?' I was pleasant but not smiling. Smiling sent a burn like a brand through my skull. But it doesn't take much effort for a barman to sound friendly.

'*Dreikornbrot*.' She nodded at it. Her voice was low, pleasantly rough and Bohemian. 'Three seeds. A half hour ago I baked it. One loaf?'

'Please. I'll be having it for dinner.'

'Anything more?'

'I'll be needing a place to eat dinner.' I paused. 'My name is Timothy Wilde, and I'm pleased to meet you. Has the upstairs room been let yet? I'm in terrible need of lodgings, and this seems the perfect fit.'

That afternoon, I bought a fresh and nicely stuffed straw tick mattress with Val's money and hauled it back to Elizabeth

Street over my shoulder, ribs protesting with every step. My new home had two rooms: the main chamber measured twelve feet by twelve with a pair of stunted windows overlooking the chickens in the dull brown yard below. For the moment, I ignored the windowless sleeping closet in favor of bedding down in the living area.

Laying the rustling tick before my open windows, I stretched out just after the sun vanished in a lingering smear of red. At least in the main chamber I could get a breath of cool starlight. Which was much to the good, for I felt like the only silent point in a geography of alien noise. A dogfight howled somewhere in the distance, wild and exultant. German men hunched around tankards of beer in the crowded house adjacent sent a low thrumming through the thoroughfare. I missed my books, and my armchair, and the particular blue of my lampshade, and my life.

I'd live here, I thought, and I'd do police work though nobody knew how, least of all me. And it would get better in slivers. It had to. I'd been knocked considerably sideways, so the trick was to keep right on moving.

I dreamed that night that I read Mercy's novel. The gorgeous saga she'd always intended to write from the day she finished *The Hunchback of Notre-Dame*. Three hundred pages of cotton-soft parchment, bound up with a green ribbon. Her writing gushed in watery ripples over the pages, penmanship that called to mind the maddest intricate Belgian lace. Wrought on a pin's head but stretching for miles if unraveled. The sort that leaves its creators blind.

On August first at six in the morning, having visited a slop shop with more of Val's funds and purchased a good second-hand set of clothing including black trousers and hose, a

simple black frock coat over a blue waistcoat and white neckerchief, and a revolutionary-hued scarlet kerchief at my breast as
a temporary nod to politics, I presented myself at the Halls of
Justice in Centre Street. I also wore a round-brimmed hat,
wider than had been my habit. The moment I put it on, eye-
catching as it was, somehow I felt very pleasurably invisible.

The air surrounding the newly assigned police headquarters
was spun from a sandstorm that early morning, just pervasive
grit and sharply slanting heat until a man couldn't think
straight – which was at least appropriate to the architecture. It
had taken all of a fortnight, from what I understand, for the
combined prison and courthouse to be nicknamed the Tombs
when completed. The slabs of charcoal granite weigh on a man
the instant he sets eyes on them, pulling the breath from his
chest. All the blank windows stretch two stories high, but are
themselves imprisoned by iron frames, each big enough to
serve as a fire grate to a giant. Carved in morbid lead-colored
rock above each window is a globe wearing a pair of delirious
wings and a set of serpents trying to wrestle the planet back
into orbit.

If their goal was to make it look like a place to be buried
alive, they did a pretty spruce job on a quarter of a million
dollars.

A little knot of ten or twelve protesters came into focus as
I approached the entrance, all men whose cravats were
hideously colorful and carefully knotted, and whose noses
had been broken on at least one occasion. Several wore
mourning bands but no actual mourning attire, which I took
to be an act of symbolic protest, and one held a sign reading
DOWN WITH PIG TEERANNY/POLICE YOUR DAYS ARE NUMBERED.
That flint-eyed fellow spat just in front of my feet as I passed
them.

'What's the mourning for?' I asked, curious.

'Liberty, freedom, justice, and the spirit of the American patriot,' drawled a bruiser with half an ear.

'I'd go so far as a black neckerchief, then,' I suggested as I walked into the prison.

All that can be seen from the outside of the Tombs is a thick wall lined with the double-height windows clapped in irons. But I learned after walking up the eight steps leading under those unrelenting pillars that the interior is a quadrangle, and already I was intrigued in spite of myself. There are open spaces, and four-story cell blocks separated by gender, and a profusion of courtrooms for deciding the length of the prisoners' entombment. A pox-scarred brute with a dirty white cravat directed me to the largest of the court-rooms, where I gathered the police would be addressed regarding their duties.

As I walked through the open air where the gallows stood on hanging days, a queer creature fell into step beside me. I couldn't help but stare at him. He was dressed very shabbily, with a dribble of egg staining his threadbare black sack coat, and his gait was slightly bowlegged. Downright crablike. The mad walk impaired his height to the point that he was almost as short as I am. From his face, pinched and chinless with pale hazel eyes staring out, I was sure he'd crawled from the ocean that morning. I'd have guessed his age at sixty. But his boots were square and Dutch and of a style older still, and his wispy grey hair flew wildly about in a wind that didn't touch anything else.

We entered the courtroom in the same stride. He scurried off to find a seat and I did the same, taking in the scene as I settled onto a bench usually devoted to trial lawyers. Here the walls were neatly whitewashed, the judge's high altar standing empty before us. I raked my eyes across my new cohorts.

A fool's motley coat would have looked uniform next to the seated mob. There seemed about fifty of them, and again I felt like a patch of vacant silence in the middle of a tumult. Irish aplenty, their laborers' hands choked with veins and their chins jutting with red side whiskers, looking wary and combative in dingy blue coats with long tails and old brass buttons. Black Irish too, pale and thick shouldered, squinting cannily. Scattered Germans with patient, dogmatic expressions, arms folded over their chests as they spoke. Americans with their collars turned down, whistling Bowery music-hall tunes and elbowing their laughing friends.

Finally, me and the crablike old man in the Dutch boots, awaiting orders. He with considerably more visible enthusiasm than I.

'Welcome, gentlemen! I'm proud to be addressing the police of the Sixth Ward of the First District of the great City of New York.'

Scattered clapping. But I was too deeply struck by the man who'd just launched himself through the small judges' door to the left of the judicial bench to bother. I'd last seen him in the middle of an inferno, after all, so I spent a moment to look him over more carefully. If there was a single new policeman Justice George Washington Matsell didn't fascinate, I'll own I missed the fellow.

Matsell, I later learned, was only thirty-four when he was selected by a Democratic majority in the Common Council to serve as the first New York City chief of police. But the man before us, standing ponderous as a walrus and twice as weathered, seemed much older. His twin reputations for holiness and debauchery must have preceded him, but – apart from realizing that he was unforgettable in person – I don't think anyone even began to take his measure that day. I can say now for a fact that he's equally intelligent and bluntly forceful. He's also near enough to tipping three hundred pounds on the scale. His whole fleshy face is based on the shape of a capital A: small brows drawn tight toward his nose, deep folds from his nostrils to his thin, downward-pointing lips, fainter creases continuing from his mouth down his jowls.

'That pack of dead herrings known as Harper's Police, or the bluecoats, has been permanently disbanded, thank Christ. Congratulations on your new appointments, to be terminated at the end of one year,' Matsell called out in a flat baritone, pulling a piece of notepaper from his yards of grey sack coat and peering at it through round spectacles. 'After election results – should the balance of the Common Council and the assistant aldermen remain the same – naturally you're welcome to reapply.'

He'd just described why men like Valentine are so very busy: a big enough political upset means all your friends are out of work and living in broken-down abandoned train cars north of the porous borders of civilization around Twenty-eighth Street. Elections decide which horde of rats gets to gnaw at the bones. I felt a bit like a rat just knowing how I came to be there, for if there were any voters save Democrats present, they kept good and snug about it.

'Some of you,' the chief continued, 'look as if you're itchy to know what exactly you're going to be *doing*.' A few dark laughs and a shuffling of boots. 'Your shifts are sixteen hours. During those sixteen hours a day – or night, of course – you are charged with the prevention of crime. If you see a man breaking into someone's ken, arrest him. If you see a vagrant child, collect it. If you see a woman pick the pocket of a tourist, collar her.'

'How about if she's just a mab strolling the back drags for a gentleman friend?' called out a slouched rough. 'Do we arrest her? Ain't whoring a crime?'

About a dozen men laughed outright at this question. Two or three whistled. Silently, I agreed with them.

'Sure thing,' Matsell replied placidly. 'Second thought – she'd have to go with you nice and quiet and you'd need the men who bought her to testify in court, so why don't you start by building the world's biggest holding cell and let us know when you're finished.'

Another ripple of laughter, and for the second time I felt a barbed twinge of interest. This was obviously going to be a job that required some thought from day to day, not work that turns a man into a glorified donkey.

'Back to it, then: if you start dragging every owl you see into the station house on whoring charges, I'll send you to hell myself. No one has that kind of time. Fees from the city have been abolished, but whether you accept rewards from pleased citizens is your own business,' our chief announced, reading down his long nose from his scribbled notes. 'We've sacked the following inspection departments: streets, parks, public health, docks, hydrants, pawnbrokers, junk shops, hacks, stages, carts, roads, and lands-and-places. Those men are now you. The Sunday temperance wardens and the bell ringers are gone. Those men are also you. The fifty-four fire wardens are gone. Who are they now, Mr Piest?'

The crab-faced old scoundrel in the Dutch boots jumped to his feet with his wrinkled fist in the air crying, 'We are! We're the fire wardens, we're the shield of the people, and God bless the good old streets of Gotham!'

A round of applause and crude hoots that were exactly half sardonic and half approving went up.

'Mr Piest here is one of the old guard,' Chief Matsell coughed, pushing his spectacles up his nose. 'You want to know how to find stolen property, talk to him.'

I privately doubted whether Mr Piest, who'd discovered the egg on his vest and was scraping at it with his thumbnail, could find his own arse. But I kept dark about it.

'The majority of you lot will be appointed as roundsmen today, but there are a few special positions still open. I see a great many firemen here. Donnell, Brick, Walsh, and Doyle, you're fire liaisons and I'll be appointing more. Anyone here speak flash?'

I was almost startled by the reaction – dozens of hands shot into the air, primarily from the wickedest-seeming American dead rabbits, the Britishers with tattoo marks, and the most scarred-up Irishmen. The Germans, almost universally, held their peace. Meanwhile, the air had turned lightning-sweet and thunderstormish. Whatever these positions were, they obviously were the shortest route to direct dealing with New York's underbelly.

'Don't be modest, Mr Wilde,' Matsell added mildly.

I glanced in shock at our chief from under the brim of my hat. I'd felt downright transparent an instant before, but seemed like I'd been wrong.

Flash, or flash-patter, is the curious dialect spoken by foisters, panel thieves, bruisers, dice burners, confidence men, street rats, news hawkers, addicts, and Valentine. I've heard tell it's based on British thieves' cant, but damned if I've ever heard them compared. It's not a language, exactly – it's more like a *code*. The words are slang substitutes for everyday speech, employed when a bloke who already knows the patter would prefer the bespectacled accountant sitting next to him to mind his own bloody business. The word *flash* itself, for instance, means a thing is about as spruce as possible. Of course, most of the men and women who speak it are poor. So some of our street youth grow up jabbering nothing else. And every day more honest workaday folk accidentally use flash terms like 'my pal' and 'kick the bucket,' but those are pretty amateur corruptions of everyday language. Matsell meant a higher level of expertise.

And not only was every damn rogue and rabbit present now staring at me, I couldn't see how Matsell had worked out who I was when only my lower face was visible.

'I'm not a bit modest, sir,' I answered truthfully.

'You mean to tell me you can't understand your own brother speaking, or Captain Valentine Wilde of Ward Eight lied when he said you'd be our most apt new recruit?'

Captain Wilde. Of course. Same youthful features, same deep hairline, same muddy blond coloring, except for only half the size and three quarters of the face. I set my jaw so hard my raw skin began throbbing under its light layer of bandaging. Typical Val. Not enough to get me a position I wasn't suited for and didn't want. Everyone had to be watching when I, as it's said, kicked the bucket.

'Neither,' I replied with an effort. 'I'm no dab hand, but I can work on it.'

That was flash for 'I'm not proficient'. But I'd every intention of doing my best.

Mr Piest's arm shot up like a Fourth of July rocket. 'Will there be training for us and for the new recruits before we go on duty, Chief?'

I've never seen George Washington Matsell snort, but that was as close as he's yet come to it in my viewing.

'Mr Piest, it's as much as I can do to get us launched without our noble populace screaming out "standing army" and aborting us out of pure patriotism. I need hardly add that the loudest patriots are currently wholesale villains. There isn't a moment to lose – the captains will take you through your paces and hand out scheduling assignments according to my guidelines, flash speakers where they're most needed, and you start tomorrow. Good morning, and good luck.'

Chief Matsell moves with remarkable speed for his size, like a bull charging, and was gone in another eyeblink. A wave of murmurs rustled the crowd, the energy muttering in my breast. The pair of captains, who seemed to be the tall black-Irish man in the plug hat and the native Bowery type with the greased sidelocks and calcified eyes next to him, exchanged puzzled looks. *What did he mean by 'paces'?* I saw pass the American's lips. It's an easy skill, one I learned within two months of tending an oyster bar that sounded like a mob riot. Tough to pass a fellow a drink if you can't tell what he wants.

They ought to be knowin' how to march in case of riots, which would be a danger to the entire city, the Irishman replied, nodding sagely. *A well-formed marchin' police force, that would go a fair way to breakin' a mob.*

By Jove, if that isn't the very thing.

So we spent the next three sweat-drenched hours learning to march in formation in the Tombs courtyard. It didn't do much to help us learn policing. But it sure seemed to give the inmates being led from the court to the cell block a pleasurable time.

I was nearest the door leading back to the courthouse when we were through the ridiculous parade training and thus the first to be assigned. When I was seated on a pine stool before a wizened clerk and asked about my qualifications, I flinched inwardly but played the hand I'd been dealt. 'I speak flash a little,' I said.

God help me.

'In that case, we'll route you past where Centre crosses Anthony. Four in the morning to eight in the evening is your shift,' the clerk announced. He pulled a sketched map from one of several piles. 'Here is your course when you make rounds. No drinking, carousing, or other entertainment while working. Your number will be one-zero-seven. Report for duty here at the Tombs tomorrow at four.'

I stood up.

'Wait a moment.'

The clerk reached into a large leather satchel and pulled out a pin shaped like a copper star. He placed it in my hand with a muttered, 'When you're on duty, you're not meant to take it off, mind.'

I passed my fingers over the metal. It was a plain thing, a bit misshaped. Just a hammered star, with a dull polish the color of the dead leaves blanketing City Hall Park in the autumn. Nothing much to look at, but then, they'd made them in a hurry, I thought. I touched the crown of my hat to the clerk and was the first man out the wide granite doorway.

An officer of the New York City Police Department.

There are fifty-five of us in the Sixth Ward, and a wider range of pure and half-bred scoundrels you won't find. But there's a common vein to us nevertheless, and I put my finger on it as I walked home to Elizabeth Street and a growler of Bavarian lager.

We're damaged right down to the last man, I've discovered, we 1845 star policemen. Perforated. There's something the city hasn't given us quite yet, or has taken away, a lacking shaped a little different every time. We're all missing bits and pieces. For each of us, there's a gap no one can quite ignore.

I was still puzzling out the best way to both hide and ignore my own unsightly punctures when the blood-covered girl appeared, three weeks to the day later. Pulling at her hair like an Irish widow of half a century, the moonlight painting her dress a dull stiffening grey.

Her name is Aibhilin ó Dálaigh. *Little bird* is what it means – Bird Daly. And she was about to turn the city upside down. August twenty-first was also the date, as it happens, when we found that poor baby. But I am getting ahead of myself.

CHAPTER FOUR

*At No 50 Pike Street is a cellar about ten feet square,
and seven feet high, having only one very small
window, and the old-fashioned, inclined cellar door.
In this small place, were lately residing two families
consisting of ten persons, of all ages.*

*Sanitary Condition of the Laboring Population
of New York, January 1845*

Mrs Boehm's naturally early baker's hours had already proven a godsend, for my landlady willingly rapped at my door at three thirty, before the day broke. A sallow stain from her taper's light would be just visible, and I'd call out, 'Good morning!' before rolling to my side with a groan. Such was my new routine. The silent trickle of honey-colored light would drift back down the stairs as I changed the dressing on my face in the near-dawn gloom, relishing the half hour of cooled air before the sun contaminated it.

I will look at my face, I thought every morning, though in truth I hadn't a mirror of my own. Followed by *Why haven't you stolen a keek at your face in some shop window or other by this time?* in the afternoon. Next would clang *You're spooney* in my brother's voice, each and every night as I blew out my bedside candle, and then I'd plummet into exhausted slumber. Telling myself all the while that my face was really an unimportant factor in the grand scheme of things. My ribs had healed quick enough, after all, and wasn't it better to dwell on good news? I was strong as I'd ever been, though I'd not yet grown used to the fatigue dragging at my bones when I was awakened before the sun had yet caressed the lip of the world. *Good looks are trivial*, I'd think. Or *I'm not a vain person.*

And I already knew more than enough about it, didn't I? *You were lucky*, I heard the stooped, nasal-sounding doctor telling me the day before I'd quit Valentine's, *not to have lost your eye. As it is, the damage will probably not affect your range of facial movement in the* regio orbitalis *— the scarring will be extensive, but the muscles of the* frontalis *and* orbicularis oculi *will work normally.* So I knew the medical jargon, and I knew that all the skin from the level of my right eye upward, covering my temple and a third of my brow and even a bit into my hairline, felt perpetually aflame, and I knew the expression that flickered across my brother's face when he supposed I didn't savvy he was watching me. That was plenty of information, wasn't it?

Truthfully, my stoicism was all bluff – the thought of seeing myself turned my stomach. It was a coward's avoidance, not a resigned and phlegmatic survivor's. But no one I encountered knew me well enough to either notice or mention that niggling fact, and I was back to scrupulously avoiding Val, and so it was fine. *Everything was fine.*

On the morning of August twenty-first, for the first time my own body awoke with a gentle slip into consciousness at around three o'clock. It ought to have been a sign, but I didn't notice. And so I watched the veil of clouds from my window that would smother the city until the storm broke. An atmosphere like being drowned.

Downstairs I left a penny on the clean countertop and took a roll of bread from the basket of yesterday's leavings. Shortcuts. Placing my wide-brimmed hat on my head and the roll in my pocket, I set off for the Tombs, where my day's long shift commenced. My beat had for a fortnight been a pretty fascinating blur, though I was wary about admitting as much. But I may as well be frank: I was a roundsman on a very interesting circuit. As for what *roundsman* entails, the word is its own definition: I walked in a circle until someone wanted arresting. Simple as that, and yet how engaging it was, to pass steady and silent through scores of people, casually scrutinizing them, making certain none of them needed any help or meant any harm.

After I signed in at the Tombs, my route took me up Centre Street. The trains with their enormous horses lumbered past me, wheels churning thick cinders into pavement dust for the bootblacks to erase. When I reached the imposing gasworks building at the corner of Canal and Centre, I turned left. Canal seemed to me a wonderful pulsing fray of a street – greengrocers crushed up against haberdashers, windows stuffed with gleaming shoes, windows packed with bolts of turquoise and scarlet and violet silks. Above the profusions of clocks and of straw hats lived the clerks and laborers and their families, men's elbows resting on high sills as they sipped their morning coffee. On the north side as I reached Broadway stood a hackney stand, the tops of the four-wheeled coaches thrown open to the pinkening sky, drivers smoking ninepin cigars and gossiping while awaiting the first fares of the day.

Broadway was my cue to turn south. If there's a wider street on earth than Broadway, a street more roiling, a street with a more dizzying pendulum swing between starving opium fiends with the rags rotting off of them and ladies in walking gowns bedecked like small steamships, I can't imagine it nor do I want to. Colored footmen sitting atop phaetons and wearing summer straw hats and pale green linen coats whirred past me that morning, one nearly colliding with a Jewess selling ribbons from a wide hinged box hung around her neck. Ice delivery men from the Knickerbocker Company, shoulders knotted with painful-seeming muscles, strained with iron tongs to hoist frozen blocks onto carts and then wheeled their cargo into the opulent hotels before the guests awoke. And weaving in and out, mud crusted and randy and miraculously nimble, trotted the speckled pigs, rubbery snouts nuzzling the trampled beet leaves. Everything begrimed but the storefront windowpanes, everything for sale but the cobblestones, everyone pulsing with energy but never meeting your eye.

From Broadway I turned east onto Chambers Street. On my left rose the elegant brick-fronted offices of lawyers and the coolly shuttered consulting rooms of physicians. To my right, meanwhile, squatted City Hall Park, encompassing not merely City Hall but the Hall of Records. Everything in it either sordid or brown. When I'd reached the end of that grassless canker, I'd find myself at Centre Street and make straight for the Tombs once more.

It was where Centre Street crossed Anthony, just a block before the Tombs, that things got leery.

In the two weeks I'd been a policeman, I'd made seven arrests. Each within spitting distance of where Centre crossed Anthony. Two gang coves on the mace, which is what my brother and the rest of the swindlers call swindling, selling fake stock certificates to emigrants. Three men I'd collared for being drunk and disorderly, which had been a challenge only in the sense that I had been forced to explain to them, 'Yes, you are required by law to go with me; no, I don't care that it will break the heart of your sainted mother; no, I'm not the smallest bit frightened of you; and yes, I am willing to drag you to the Tombs by your ear, if required.' Finally, I'd a pair of minor assault cases to do with hard liquor, weary working-men, and the whores who'd been unlucky enough to get in the way. In Anthony Street itself, in either direction as your eyes cross the railway line, the houses are dark charcoal streaks from an unsteady hand dragged across the sky, and they come too cheap. They're hungry buildings. Man-eaters, ready to swallow the nearest emigrant down a broken stairwell or rotting floor. Stuffed near to rupturing with Irish, of course. And on that morning, by the time I'd made my eighth slow circuit and the sun had burned past rose into yellow, they were calling my name.

'Timothy Wilde! Mr Wilde, can that be you?'

I flinched slightly within the borders of the wide-brimmed hat. The expression sent a wave of hurt along the edge of my brow.

'Reverend Underhill,' I called back, walking toward him.

'It is you, then. Forgive me, but . . . I don't know quite what to say. Since the fire, everyone has misplaced one another.'

The Reverend Thomas Underhill reached for my hand, his keenly intelligent face oddly pale. Reverend Underhill has the same delicate-blue eyes as Mercy. But his hair is more brown than black, greying at the temples, and his face above the simple clerical suit is on a narrower scale. Mrs Olivia Underhill had been an English beauty, lost in one of our cholera epidemics tending to dying foreigners – she'd wide-set eyes like Mercy's, the same divide in her chin. The reverend doted on her. Switched all his warm feelings to the congregation of Pine Street Presbyterian and to Mercy after Olivia died, and I couldn't fault his choice. He's a deft, capable man, eyes radiating focus, hands expressive. But something had badly frightened him. He looked a fraction of his age and lost in an angry mob, tugging at his pale yellow waistcoat when it was already lying flat.

'I'm fine,' I announced, being hearty about it. I felt a performer who'd stumbled onto the wrong stage. 'And how is . . .'

Your daughter, I would have said before, as I wanted nothing better than to replace her surname permanently.

'Miss Underhill?' I asked.

How I managed it I'll never know. Something tight came untethered inside my rib cage, slithering thickly through my veins like cold lead.

'She's well. Mr Wilde, I was looking for help when I spied you. Will you please come with me and . . .' He paused, his eye catching the dull glint of my copper star. 'My God. That emblem on your breast – are you a policeman?'

'If not, I don't know who is.'

'Oh, thank heaven, what a providential chance. I was just calling on a poor man who made an appeal to us for charity and on my way out of the tenement, I heard a baby screaming from within another chamber. I knocked at the door repeatedly, but discovered it locked. Then I set my shoulder to it, hard, but—'

'Babies scream pretty often,' I observed.

But I'd never once seen him frightened since his wife's death, cold sweat beading at his temples, so I started running into Anthony Street. Then the reverend passed me, leading the way. In about ten seconds, we reached an old brick building. The reverend didn't pause at the entrance. Instead he plunged down the alley between the residence in question and the structure next to it.

The front tenement reached four stories, scores of laundry lines running over our heads with streamers of beige rags pinned to them. A little boy, his sun-browned face pinched and blank, guarded the washing. But we were making for the rear building. In their infinite desire to house would-be Americans, property owners had recently taken to erecting residences in the rear yards of existing brick town houses. Usually a patch of open ground is left behind a dwelling place, for air and light and other extravagances. But canny landlords were now constructing second buildings at the back of the first, reached by the street-side crack between the structures, their windows facing nothing but walls. I edged swiftly around the pieces of a broken carriage wheel and then a mossy cistern head. The ground grew danker by the inch as we progressed through the fissure. By the end, we were three inches deep in runoff from the overflowing trough between the outhouse cesspool and the shallow sewer.

The wet yard the corridor led to proved to be planked over. A speckled grey dog lay on its side by the wooden outhouse, snoring in the sunshine. Just beyond it rose the second building. This one was wood, three stories, and already crumbling. Destined to be a hell before they'd even finished building it. As we hurried across the wood-slatted yard, sludge from between the cracks pressed up to lap at our boots.

The reverend paused just inside the shadowed doorway. A staircase to our left played host to a pair of drunks, nothing more than faintly breathing piles of whiskey-scented laundry.

'It's just down this hall.' He nodded, pointing deeper into the ground floor.

The door in question was indeed sturdier than it looked. But the two of us together soon bested it, the slats flying open with a muffled bang. And here is what we saw.

It wasn't a room at all, but a closet with a pallet set along one side. My brother could probably have reached his arms out and touched either wall. Extraordinarily clean. A woman wearing a torn lace cap that might have been a cobweb sat in a chair, sewing a sleeve onto the torso of a cotton dress. Twenty or thirty more pieces of cheap nankeen lay folded at her feet. Her hair was the pale red hue of a pumpkin rind, her freckled face serene, though tight lipped. She didn't look up when her door burst open and two men tumbled nearly into her lap. And by that I knew something was very, very wrong.

'Where is your baby?' the reverend demanded to know, trying hard to rein his urgency. 'I heard it crying from within this room. It sounded . . . Where is it?'

The needle slowed but didn't stop moving as the woman's red eyelashes tilted up. She was around twenty-five, I calculated, not long in the country – little scratches had sprouted up all over her fingertips from the unfamiliar needlework, none of them healing proper. Her blood was likely still pretty thin from eating nothing save hardtack and spoiling meat on the voyage over. She looked as if she hadn't seen fresh fruit for six months or more, her entire body as tender as an open blister. Meanwhile, she sat silent, seeming not to understand us.

'What's your name, ma'am?' I tried.

'Eliza Rafferty,' she replied in heavily accented English.

'And you've a baby, I take it? Whereabouts?'

The hazel eyes lost their bearings, slid back to her needle.

'But I haven't any baby. 'Tis a mistake you're makin'.'

'No?' I countered, motioning to the reverend not to lose his patience. Something had gone queer about her focus. Unsettled and hovering, a bird with no place to land. I'd never seen the likes of it before, and I've seen a hundred different looks on a thousand different faces. 'Whose are the infant's clothing in the basket, then?' I asked, gesturing at the corner.

Her chin dipped, quivering, but her face was still a mask. And not a mask of her own making either. Not a word we were saying made sense to her.

'They must be piecework,' she whispered. 'I haven't any baby, I'm tellin' you. I've dress parts to finish. Three cents apiece. Mr Prendergast might ha' sent those by mistake.'

'Madam, it is a grave sin to lie about—'

'I don't think she's lying,' I murmured. It's only a knack formed by talking to people for a living. But lies have a flavor to them, something smooth and sugared, and this wasn't it. 'Mrs Rafferty, did you hear the reverend knocking? He was anxious over you.'

'I heard him. I knew his voice. I'll not call the pope a liar, not denounce him, I tell ye. Not even for good cream like he promised the last time, and I on my knees already begging for it.'

I glanced at Reverend Underhill and he winced, his eyes pained. 'My charitable resources are extremely limited. It shames me, and daily. But we haven't time for this. We must—'

'What would you have used the cream for, Mrs Rafferty?' I inquired.

'For Aidan.'

Her dappled eyes went a little wider when she'd heard herself. The reverend and I exchanged dark looks. So there was an infant, and no place in that cell to hide so much as a bent copper penny. I went down to one knee so Mrs Rafferty could see me better. Her gaze was pretty pinched already from doing piecework in bad light. At the rate she was sewing, she'd be stitch-blind in ten years or less.

'After the reverend knocked, but before we came inside, you took something out, didn't you?' I inquired gently. 'I wonder what it was?'

'Only a rat,' she whispered. 'They bite me something terrible at night. They get in through the floorboards. I put this one in the sink yonder at the end of the corridor.'

'Weren't you frightened,' I asked her, my stomach going hollow, 'to pick it up and carry it?'

'No,' she said, her lips trembling like the wings of a moth. 'It was already dead.'

I turned a desperate eye to the reverend. But his boots were already racing down the hall beyond.

She was frightened, I thought with dull insistence as I pushed to my feet and dove through the door, *and she forgot the baby when she disposed of the rat. Yes. Yes, the rat is in the sink and the baby is doubtless in a basket of some sort beside it and she went in a daze back to her room without . . . Aidan was the name. Aidan Rafferty is in a basket at the end of the hall.*

The reverend muffled a sound against his dark sleeve. Standing in silhouette at the end of the peeling hallway, outlined by the light of the single window above the filthy public sink. I watched my feet advancing past droppings from the free-roaming chickens that had gotten through the door. I was seeing things in fragments again, I realized. The sink had once been a cheap wooden basin and was now the mold-blighted home of several buzzing flies, disturbed by Reverend Underhill.

'We'll get a doctor,' I said stupidly, before even looking. I could fix this, I *had* to fix it. 'We'll get a doctor at once.'

'A doctor isn't any good,' the reverend replied, having regained a little control of himself. His face was pure white, though. White but burning, a white like the glory of God. 'She'll want a priest.'

I've asked myself a thousand times since that day what pierced my brain about that particular death. Death, as they say, is common. And death of children even more so. They're subject to so many cruelties that I'd not believe their survival remotely possible had I not once been a child myself. Suppose their parents love them? Still they're playthings at the whim of disease and of violent accident, a holy brightness in their family's lives shining as fickle as the stock market. Suppose their parents do not love them? Then they're released into the world far too soon, forced to sell steaming cobs of corn for pennies a customer on Broadway, or else lured into far worse vocations due to the insistence of ravenous survival. Or they vanish entirely. Dissolve like a scent on the wind.

Suppose their parents die while they're yet kinchin?

I knew how that played out. And it could have been far worse for me, I understand that, though in a grudging sense. Had Val not been there with me in the days of our orphaned youth, I'd have been considerably less persecuted, but very likely deposited in a shallow grave one winter or another. I've absorbed that gift, deep within me, and on days when I have already decided to depart for Mexico, where there is no Valentine Wilde, I remind myself of the fact. And I stay. In spite of everything.

No, it isn't that the notion of a kinchin dying shocks me. And unfortunately, the concept of children being murdered isn't a new one either. Imagine a terrible thing that couldn't possibly happen, and it's been performed on the New York stage with applause and encores more times than you would ever believe possible.

What mattered about that death, as I came to understand it, was that the week before, Mrs Rafferty had apparently been pleading with the reverend over cream for Aidan. Wanting, *needing*, her boy's hunger to lessen. Sharing his suffering with every shallow breath, every feeble beat of her son's heart. She'd fallen to her knees over his welfare, stopping only at the moment when she thought her very afterlife threatened, and supposed an eternity with her child superior to three days' worth of fresh dairy supplies.

And today – lacking the cream, and maybe the lemon juice to restore her mind, and possibly a sodding *window*, God only knows what she was most desperate for – she'd supposed that same boy a rat. Mrs Rafferty appeared behind us looking out from her closet door, the needle still in her hand. Her fingers had grown palsied.

' 'Tis dead,' she said. 'I'm frightened of them too, but 'tis dead already, and the pair of you grown men. Why are you both so frightened? It's shameful, I tell ye. 'Twas only a rat.'

'God have mercy on you,' the reverend whispered in a voice edged with fire.

And with that, I made my eighth arrest of my new career.

Twelve hours later, I sat at a scratched wooden desk in the Tombs in one of the office chambers, a quill topped with a hint of deathly black feather in my hand. Staring at the paper before me, mainly. Not writing. I wanted to be sick in the corner by that time. It would have at least marked a difference, proven my ability to move, maybe lessened the nausea after the fact, and I couldn't stop staring or start writing to save my life.

Instead I thought about the reverend, wondered if he was faring any better. The reverend, who'd left behind him at age eleven a cheerless cottage in the Massachusetts woods with an ominous hickory cudgel leaning in the corner to earn his bread on a ship at sea. He's a precise and traveled man, known all over the city as a fearless Protestant with a voraciously demanding mind. His congregants think of him as the shepherd who keeps their lives in godly order, and that's exactly what he is; he was an abolitionist in his young days as a preacher because the idea of slavery disgusted his sense of logic. When he talks about it, he says *justice*, but *logic* is what he actually means. I think sometimes he battles poverty simply because the imbalance of it offends his aesthetics. That sounds like a weak reason, but only if you've never seen him peeling an orange like he's cutting the facets of a raw diamond.

I thought about the last time I'd seen him so pale, shortly after Olivia Underhill's death. The reverend had adored his wife, and I know what adoration looks like. After lowering her into the ground the day of her passing, her body shriveled and scarcely recognizable, he hadn't quit his securely locked study in the space of three entire days. No amount of pleading, even by fourteen-year-old Mercy, would coax him to emerge. Finally, seconds before Val meant to christen his new lock picks, the door had opened, and Thomas Underhill had kissed his weeping daughter, held her close and stroked her hair, and then announced that the small outbuilding of the Pine Street Church had required reroofing for long enough, and he intended to see to it. He'd left the room without a backward glance, my brother and Mercy and I staring after him numbly. Mercy found nothing in the study to indicate what he'd been doing all that while until months later, when she discovered that every separate page of her mother's extensive book collection had been meticulously bordered by hand in black ink. Thousands and thousands of sable mourning bands silently edging the parchment.

No, the reverend couldn't possibly be faring any better than I was, not by a long lonely mile. Not when the question of cream was considered.

Footsteps approached. I looked up from under the brim of my hat. It was Mr Piest, taking his single shift break for coffee. I could smell it. But he'd a pair of tin cups in his hands, not a single one. His flyaway grey curls waved a manic greeting at me as he set one of the cups down.

'Patriot, I salute you,' he declared gravely.

On his way out, heavy Dutch boots thudding, he added, 'You'll grow more used to it, Mr Wilde.'

That's a load of shit, I replied in my head with a vengeance.

But when I'd taken a sip of the oily coffee – which was rich, far better than it should have been – I managed to set quill to paper.

Report made by Officer T. Wilde, Ward 6, District 1, Star 107. Entered No 12 Anthony Street eight a.m. on suspicions raised by the Reverend Thomas Underhill of No 3 Pine Street. Made for rear building, ground floor, and discovered resident Mrs Eliza Rafferty in state of grave confusion. Infant Aidan Rafferty missing from chamber. Mother, claiming to have been plagued by a rat, led us to sink of same rear tenement, where infant had been placed.

Arrested Mrs Rafferty, who continued to display incomprehension of events, though she had by this time grown most emotionally disturbed. Called at once for aid by

*way of Reverend Underhill, and first to arrive on scene were
Roundsmen York and Patterson, who summoned the
coroner. I escorted Mrs Rafferty to the women's wing of the
Tombs, where she was incarcerated under prisoner number
23398 and awaits questioning.*

Stopping, I marveled at my handwriting. Perfectly clear. What
an appalling thing that was. Unfeeling in a way that made my
gut twist, repulsed by the even letters. I supposed reasonably
that they'd need it legible, and next thought that any man who
was capable of writing it all this neatly was a disgrace.

*Official coroner's report on body of Aidan Rafferty, aged
approximately six months, pending; marks on the neck
clearly indicate strangulation as the most apparent cause of
death.*

My script stared back at me, a monument to steady-
handedness. Revolting. When I saw how crisp the sentence
looked, how distant minded, I took the cursed star badge
off and hurled it against the whitewashed wall as hard as
I could.

Walking home that night under blazing August stars with the
dead copper star in my pocket, I wondered how best to make
my brother pay for bringing about the day I'd had. I was
thinking pretty hard, thinking *God damn Valentine Wilde* over
and over again as I reached Elizabeth Street and Mrs Boehm's
bakery.

Then something soft and frantic drove itself right into my
knees.

My hands reached for the little girl's arms before my brain

registered that the collision had been with a little girl. It was a good thing, too, for she was pulling at her hair, touching a piece that had come loose from a top knot, and she would have crashed to the spattered cobbles. When I set her upright, she looked at me as if from on a ship's deck midriver. Not really there. Not really anywhere, yet. In-between.

Then I noticed that she was wearing a night shift, and it was soaked in either tar or blood. A lot of it.

'My God,' I murmured. 'Are you hurt?'

She didn't answer me, but her square face was working on something other than words. I believe she was trying not to cry.

Maybe a professional policeman, like the ones in London, would have marched right back to the Tombs and delivered her for questioning even though he was off shift. It's possible. Maybe a professional policeman would have rushed her to a doctor. I don't know. It ought to be clear by now that there wasn't much in the way of professional policemen in New York City. But even if there had been, I was through with them for good and all. Aidan Rafferty was being buried by that time, so was his mother at the Tombs in another sense; I was a man used to pouring gin in a glass for double the money, and the copper stars could go hang themselves.

'Come with me,' I said. 'You'll be all right now.'

Gently, I lifted her up. I couldn't get to my key with her in my arms. But by chance Mrs Boehm had seen me out the window by that time and stood with the door open. Her dressing gown was wrapped tight around her bony frame, her face a study in blank surprise.

'Dear God,' she breathed through her widely drawn lips.

Mrs Boehm ran for the fireplace next to the ovens and stoked it furiously as I entered with the limp little kinchin, reaching with her other hand for a pail to draw water at the pump.

'There are rags in the corner,' she said while flying at the door. 'Clean, for the loaves.'

I set the girl down on a flour-smeared footstool. Mrs Boehm had left the lamp sitting on the broad kneading table, for the moon was high and the pump just outside the house. In the better light, it was apparent the huge stain on the child's dress couldn't have been anything other than blood.

Her grey eyes shifted about so skittishly that I moved back a little when I'd settled her on the stool. I went for the clean slop rags in the corner and brought back several soft cotton ones.

'Can you tell me where you've been hurt?' I asked quietly.

No answer. A thought occurred to me.

'Can you speak English?'

That stirred her a little, her jaw angling quizzically. 'What else would I speak?'

Unaccented English. No, that was just to my ears, I corrected myself. New York English.

Her arms started shaking. Mrs Boehm returned making long strides and began to heat the water. Muttering to herself, she lit another two lamps, bathing the bakery in caramel light. As she did so, and I looked the girl over more carefully, I noticed something peculiar.

'Mrs Boehm,' I called.

Careful and slow as we could, we pulled the dress off the girl. She didn't object. Didn't move a muscle save to help us. When Mrs Boehm gripped a warm, wet rag in her hand and brushed it over the child's lightly freckled skin, my instincts were proven correct.

'She isn't hurt physically at all,' I said in wonderment. 'Look. It's all from her dress. Covered in blood and not a mark on her.'

'They'll tear him to pieces,' the little girl whispered, eyes brimming with tears. And then I caught her for the second time, arms tangling with Mrs Boehm's, for she slipped into a dead faint.

Chapter Five

When Potatoes are attacked with this disease, the
first thing that is observed is a drying-up or shriveling
of the tuber . . . [W]e have lately received
communication from our correspondents complaining
of their Potatoes, and in some instances we make little
doubt that they are suffering from the disease we have
just described.

Gardener's Chronicle and Agricultural Gazette,
March 16, 1844, London

Mrs Boehm helmed the task of getting all the blood off
the poor girl while I held her limbs steady. Then Mrs
Boehm found an old, soft blouse, dressed the child in it, did
up the plain shell buttons, took all the pins out of her dark
auburn hair, and deposited her in a trundle pulled out from
under her own bed. Queerly methodical about all of the chaos,
which made me grateful. When she quit her bedroom on the
second floor, closing the door behind her, she met me coming
up from the bakery carrying a small plate of sliced day-old

bread with two cuts of salted ham and some cheese I'd found in a little pot of brine.

'I'll pay for it, every cent,' I said, trying to sound gallant. I think I sounded ill. 'I thought you might join me.'

Mrs Boehm made a clucking sound. 'Wait,' she commanded, ducking back inside her bedroom. When she came out again, she held a bit of wax paper of the sort used to wrap chocolate.

We set plates at the table with a pair of lit tallow candles, turning down the lamps to save oil. Mrs Boehm disappeared and then returned carrying a stone jug of table beer, and she poured it into two mugs from the cupboard. I noticed her looking at me a bit keenly, even for her, and in another moment I swept my hat off obligingly. It was like taking off my underclothes. Obscene somehow.

'Fire downtown?' she asked softly. 'Or accident?'

'Fire downtown. It doesn't matter.'

She nodded, the corners of her broad mouth twitching. 'Tell me. The girl was outside, on the street, and to bring her in is what you decided?'

'You object?' I inquired, surprised.

'No. But you're police.'

The implication was clear. What were police for, if they didn't take blood-covered children to the station house and learn what had happened to them? I nodded, feeling about six inches to the left of myself ever since I'd taken off the hat. I hadn't noticed I'd been relying on it quite so heavily. Meanwhile, I could hardly admit to my own landlady that I was abandoning my only steady source of income.

'When the poor kinchin wakes up, we'll find out what's wrong – where she lives, where the blood came from. There's no point in policing with her asleep.'

Ravenously hungry, I reached for a slice of thick rye and tore a piece of the cheese curd away. Mrs Boehm just pulled a cigarette from a pocket of her dress and lit it with one of the candle flames. The dusty dull wheat color of her hair flickered for an instant, and then the taper was back on the table. I noticed a periodical lying open where she had been reading a short story, an installment of the hugely popular series *Light and Shade in the Streets of New York*, and smiled inwardly. It's a very keenly written collection – but equally lurid as lyrical, and the author hints ripely at sex whenever possible, which I suppose is why it's penned by 'Anonymous'. I liked my landlady better the more I knew of her. Meanwhile, when she caught me reading upside down, she blushed along the edge of her cheekbones and flipped the cover shut.

'Children like that are trouble,' she noted in a regretful voice.

'Irish children?' I wasn't surprised she thought so. Even if the girl talked American, her hair and her skin dappled like a plover's egg marked her as first generation. And living in the Sixth Ward, Mrs Boehm had certainly seen plenty of them, and sometimes they *were* trouble. Often enough taught that private property is a myth.

'Not Irish children.'

'Runaways?' The question puzzled me. Wouldn't Mrs Boehm run if someone covered *her* in blood?

Mrs Boehm shook her head with her bony arms crossed and her cigarette at her lips. 'Not runaways. You didn't notice.'

'Notice what?'

'She is a . . . what do they call it? Kinchin, you said. A kinchin-mab. The little girl is a kinchin-mab.'

The bread stuck in my craw. Taking a sip of Mrs Boehm's house brew, I set the sweating mug down and then leaned my elbows on the table, carefully running my fingers over my brow. How could I have been so blind? Being exhausted and hungry and three miles past horrified was no excuse for having the perception of a puppy.

'Her hair,' I muttered. 'Her hair, of course.'

Mrs Boehm's weirdly broad mouth curved into a dark smile. 'You look at people close. Yes, her hair.'

'It could be a mistake.' I leaned back, letting my fingers trail along the grainy wood. 'She could have been playing with an older sister earlier today.'

Mrs Boehm shrugged. The gesture had all the weight of a beautifully penned argument.

For who in their right mind would do up a little girl's hair like that of a woman of eighteen and then allow her to run, shoeless, out into the streets? Grown whores leave their hair down as a rule, trying to look as young as they can. Parade with their flimsy shirts open to their navels, their parched, brittle locks trailing behind them like brushwood twigs, hoping at least in appearance to shave off a few years' worth of being poked with knives and cudgels and every other tool known to man. The children, though. Kinchin-mabs are most often hidden away indoors. But when they do walk abroad, they're painted to look like tiny society women. Hair pinned up like the belles of a ghastly miniature ball.

'You think she escaped from a disorderly house,' I said. 'If she did, she's for a religious charity if she likes and back on the streets if she doesn't. Never the House of Refuge. Not if I have a say in it.'

The House of Refuge is an asylum for orphaned, half-orphaned, vagrant, and delinquent children, just north of the populated city at Twenty-fifth Street and Fifth Avenue. Its aim is to remove homeless kinchin from the streets, where they are visible, and set them on an enlightened path from behind closed gates, where they are not visible. The main sticking point being less about the enlightenment and more about whether the self-satisfaction of New York's upper classes is in any way threatened by the sight of starving six year olds huddled in sewage troughs. I happen to be unimpressed by the establishment's precepts.

Nodding in agreement, Mrs Boehm set her rib cage against the wood, unwrapping the wax paper and then breaking off a piece of the dark chocolate she'd revealed. She ate it pensively, pushing the small treasure toward me.

'What do you think she meant by saying "They'll tear him to pieces"?' I asked.

'Animal, perhaps. Into the backyard she goes, she has a favorite pig, the pig is killed, she runs. Blood from slaughter, I'm thinking. A cow, even, or a pony with broken leg sold for glue. Yes, her beloved pony. Of course they would tear him to pieces. We will find out tomorrow.'

Mrs Boehm stood up, lifted a candle.

'Tomorrow I've only a half-shift,' I lied to the friendly little knobs of bones running down her back under the dressing gown. 'You needn't bother waking me.'

'Very good. I am glad you are a police. We need police,' she said thoughtfully, collecting her magazine. Then, after a pause. 'It was only her pony, I am thinking.'

Mrs Boehm was a practical woman, I told myself. And she was right: the blood could have come from anywhere. Only a pony's, or even a dog's, run down by a carriage and then promptly swarming with rats. I relaxed a fraction.

But the thought of rats left me sick and shaken again, staring uselessly across the room at a hairline crack in the plaster. I wondered, when carrying the other candle up to my chambers, just what it would take after a day like that to get my usual self back.

Next morning, I awoke from a dead slumber to a pair of grey eyes examining me.

I stared, not comprehending. Still flat in bed and yet thrown off balance. Sunlight streamed through my window, which never was the state of things when my eyes opened. My straw tick was still up against the wall, for the thought of bedding down in the sleeping-closet depressed me beyond words, and I'd have been pretty shocked the day before to think I'd ever be entertaining any company. Yet here I was. Wearing only loose drawstring smallclothes that stopped well above my knees, with enormous ash-colored irises pinned to my frame.

The little girl wore the lengthy shirtwaist Mrs Boehm had given her the night before. It hung to mid-thigh, and under she boasted a small boy's set of nankeen trousers. Interesting, I thought. Her rosewood-colored hair was down now, tied back with a piece of kitchen twine.

'What are you doing in here?' I asked.

'I've been looking at your paintings. I like them.'

There weren't any paintings, but I could see what she was getting at. Ever since I was a young kinchin I've scrawled things on any spare paper I could find when my brain wants quieting. And every day before the start of police work I'd drawn something. Going out in the heat made my face burn, and I hadn't wanted people. I'd taken the Madison Line omnibus to the northeast frontier of the city, to Bull's Head Village at Third and Twenty-fourth, where all the pens, cattle yards, and butchers migrated when driven off Bowery. It reeked of recent death there, and the animals screamed a good deal. But they had thin brown paper to wrap meat in for next to nothing, and

I bought a pretty huge roll of it. Then I took a sack and filled it with spent coal from an abandoned brazier near the sheep yard.

Shortcuts. I know how they're done.

'You need to leave, so I can dress.'

'This one,' she said, walking up to a brown swath tacked to the wall depicting the Williamsburg Ferry leaving Peck Slip beneath a lowering July thunderstorm. Just precisely as I like to think of river travel, the way it still echoes in my mind – a boat cutting through a wide, placid river, seconds before a delirious collision of sunlight and rain. 'I like it particular. This one is flash. How'd you learn?'

'Hand me my shirt,' I commanded. 'There's one by the washbasin.'

She carried it over, smiling. A genuine smile, I thought, but double purposed: it was real charm coated on top of a measuring device. How was I going to respond to simple friendliness? Did I like that? I'd sized people up so myself, but I was better at it. Inwardly, I shook my head. This girl had been soaked in gore not eight hours previous, been subjected to God knows what beforehand, and I was worried about my apparel.

'I'm Timothy Wilde. What's your name?'

'Everyone calls me Little Bird,' she said with a tilt of one shoulder. 'Bird Daly. I can say the real one for you if you'd like me to, though.'

I said certainly, go on ahead, as I pulled on my shirt and wondered with an increasingly mortified feeling where my trousers had got to.

'Aibhilin ó Dálaigh. I didn't used to be able to say it proper, so I called myself Bird because Bird is easier. But they mean the same thing exactly, only different languages, so Bird is just as good as the other, is what I think. What do you think?'

Trousers, I thought. I now owned two pairs, and they'd

never seemed so very important. Finally, my bare foot hit black worsted and I pulled them on quick as I could.

Now Bird was staring at a large sketch of a cottage in the forest, obviously and violently on fire. The woods surrounding were a blackly burned-out no-man's-land, a dreamscape, and the whole thing smelled of incineration. I'd done it in spent fuel, after all. Whatever den she hailed from, she'd peered at paintings before. Her eyes were comparing new art to art she'd already seen. Not a Five-Pointer, then, from our blackest pit of all, and not from the saltwater East River dives either. Too well fed, expensively dressed, and critical of charcoal studies.

'We need to talk about yesterday,' I suggested gently. 'About what happened to you, and your nightdress, and where you belong.'

'Did you do this one when you were younger? It looks different.'

'No, they're all pretty new. We'll go and find Mrs Boehm, see about some tea while you tell me what upset you last night.'

Bird paused before another patch of paper-covered wall, frowning. It was a simple portrait of a pale woman with black locks and a scholarly air, her cleft chin in her hand, looking off with wide-set eyes. Just Mercy, caught in a brown study.

'You like her,' Bird announced darkly. 'You probably kiss her quite a lot, don't you?'

'I . . . as a matter of fact, I don't. Why—'

Pondering the sketch, I realized that the feelings of the artist toward his subject were, indeed, apparent to a ten year old. It didn't aid my flusterment much. Meanwhile, Bird's brooding face slipped into another – agreeable, pliant, erasing the trail of her mistake. 'Not everyone likes kissing. Maybe you don't? Anyhow, if you like her, I'll go on and like her too. Since you brought me inside and all.'

'You won't be seeing her. She's a very . . . admirable lady, though.'

'She's your mistress?'

'She is not. No. Listen, part of what we need to talk about is where you lived before. Because they'll be wanting you back, and if they don't deserve to have you back, well, we must find you a fresh start.'

Bird blinked. Then she smiled again, it having been safe the first time.

'I don't want to talk about it,' she admitted. 'But I'll try if you want me to, Mr Wilde. I think I'll cap in with you from now on, you see. So I'll try.'

'You will tell me,' Mrs Boehm said in a very kind voice, 'what last night happened to your nightdress.'

Bird, sitting at the wide bakery table with a cup of heated currant wine mixed with water and a lump of sugar held prettily in her small hands, looked down at a wisp of steam. Her face colored hotly, then faded again. I was reminded of being asked by my father long ago whether I'd finished polishing the tack in the stables with whale oil, being suddenly terrified because I hadn't, and then catching Val winking at me reassuringly from the corner of the room in a rare moment of rescue. It was the same quick flash of panic I'd just seen in Bird's eyes, the sort that steals your breath.

'It's a very pretty nightdress,' I mentioned from my seat on a chair in the corner.

The compliment rolled right over Bird, pulling her eyebrows up a fraction. I was grotesquely reminded that, while some children gobble encouraging remarks like gingerbread, Bird Daly had probably been subjected to *flattery*. And far worse obscenities.

'It did suit me, but it's probably ruined now. I like your hat,' Bird said shrewdly. 'It suits you too.'

When I perceived that she spoke like an adult because ninety per cent of her interactions had been with grown men spending coin on her company, I felt my face darken before I could prevent myself. I made the decision then and there that I wasn't going to be able to talk with Bird as if she were a kinchin and I a former star policeman of twenty-seven. Being outflanked because I'm not smart enough to drive the conversation is almost exhilarating. But being outflanked because I've read the opposition wrong is an outrageous embarrassment.

'I know you're frightened,' I said, 'because anyone could see that something terrible happened last night. But if you don't tell us what it was about, we can't help anyone.'

'Where do you live, Bird?' Mrs Boehm put in quietly.

Bird's generous lips twitched, reluctant. It occurred to me in a distant way, like looking at a rosebush, that she was beautiful. Then I had to fight my stomach back down from my gullet again, which was getting very tiresome.

'In a house west of Broadway with my family,' she said simply. 'But I'll never see it again.'

'Go on,' I said. 'We won't lay into you, so long as you tell us the truth.'

The somber budlike lips convulsed again, and then words began gushing out of them. Wetly, as if she was crying. Though she wasn't, not in a visible way.

'I can't. I can't. My father arrived, and he cut her with a shiv. He would have gotten me too, but I ran away, though I'd already dressed for bed.'

I exchanged a look with Mrs Boehm, or I tried to, but her faded blue eyes were fastened to Bird.

'Who did he cut?' I asked gravely.

'My mother,' Bird whispered. 'My mother was cut right across the face. She was carrying me up to bed, and there was blood everywhere. He's mad when he's been at the lush, but before he'd only used his hands. A walking cane he carried. Never a knife. My mother dropped me and she told me to run, told me not ever to come back because he blames me for costing extra money for food and togs.'

She stopped, rubbing at the rim of her cup with a trembling finger. Her eyes fixed onto a tiny chip in the china.

And I thought about it, pretty thoroughly.

It wasn't a pleasant picture, but it was such a *possible* one. Countless families are eviscerated every day by the price of whiskey. 'Mother of God,' a careful Sligo man with steady hands had said to me after calling for a drink in Nick's one late afternoon, 'I'll write to my cousin and tell him straight he shan't come here – back home the food may be scarce, but at least the whiskey is dear.' It was all so very possible.

Then I thought about her hair. I thought about what sort of Irish child might call her mum *mother*. And never *mother* as the subject of the sentence, never as a name. My mother dropped me. Not *Mum dropped me and she told me to run*.

'I think you should tell us what really happened,' I objected.

Bird looked shocked, her mouth in an O, and that was when I realized that she was actually a very good liar. Only good liars are surprised at being caught. And you probably had to be a good liar, in any case, if you wanted to live through her kind of work.

'I can't,' she replied shakily. 'You'd be angry. And Mrs Boehm says you're police.'

'Nonsense,' Mrs Boehm tutted. 'Go on with what really happened. Mr Wilde here is a good man.'

'I didn't mean to do it,' Bird muttered. Broken sounding,

pushing her thumbnail painfully into the table.

'Do what, dear?'

'*Anything,*' she whispered. 'But he – I think he was drunk, because he kept pulling at a little flask, asking if I wanted some of it. And I said no, and then he poured it on my pillow and said that would make me used to it, and I thought he was mad. He had a box of lucifers, and he kept lighting them. One by one. He said they were like my hair, and he put one close to my face, and I said to get away from me, he'd already . . . he'd already paid me. So. But he wouldn't, and he pushed me onto the wet pillow and came down with the lit match. He was going to set me on fire. I started screaming, and I pushed him back hard as I could. He . . . he fell on the floor. There was a knife in his belt . . . but I didn't *know* that, I swear to God I didn't. He cut his side, and when he picked me up, the blood stained my dress. They'd heard me screaming and rushed into the room, and that was when I managed to get away. He isn't dead, I swear to you, and I didn't mean it. He was trying to *burn me.*'

This time when Bird stopped, Mrs Boehm sent out a hand and brushed it lightly over her wrist. Because that story, I thought, could be nothing but true. Details so strange that it would never have occurred to a kinchin to invent them.

Pouring whiskey into a pillow and then setting a flame to a little girl's hair.

That had all happened. But it wasn't why she was here.

'Bird, I'm sorry to hear that,' I told her. 'But if a man was stabbed even by accident, he'd have made a terrible racket. You'd never have gotten out of the house yesterday. We need to know if anyone's truly been hurt. I have to take you down to the station house.'

The cup of cordial smashed into the wall, flung by an outraged fist. The next instant, Bird looked horrified, staring at her right hand as if it belonged to someone else. She touched it with her left, blinking rapidly.

'Please don't. Let me stay here, let me stay here,' she begged in a weird little chant. 'Everything's all right. You don't need to worry. No one is hurt.'

'But you said—'

'I was lying! Please, I was lying, but . . . but you don't think I'd want to talk about where I really live, do you? Let me stay here, I can't go back. They'd lay into me something terrible. I'll pay for the cup, I always pay when things break. Please—'

'Tell us again,' I interrupted, 'but the real story.'

Bird's lower lip trembled violently, but she pulled her chin up at the same moment.

'I couldn't live there anymore,' she said in a flat voice. 'I was tired, you see. I was so tired, and they never let me sleep. She says it's because everyone likes me, but . . . I couldn't, so. It's awful not being able to sleep. Last night I took a few dimes I'd hid downstairs with me. Just down back, where the chickens are. We were to have curry for dinner. I paid the boy who killed the chicken for some blood, said it was for a spell I wanted to try on someone. We put it in a pail in the hen yard and I had my night shift with me and I – I soaked it in the blood. That night when I slipped out, I thought they'd chase me, or maybe I'd be sent to the House of Refuge, but – but if I was bloody, I could say I was running from murderers by the docks. And anyone would believe me. They'd see the blood and let me stay with them.'

Bird stopped, looking back and forth at Mrs Boehm and me with eyes like a cornered fawn. Hope scratching at her insides with tender claws, pulling hard at her ribs.

'But you *will* let me stay with you. Won't you?'

*

Marching for the Tombs with my badge in hand and a ringing resignation on my lips, I mulled over the best way to go about telling a ten-year-old stargazer that she wouldn't be residing with us. I'd stayed quiet, before. And Mrs Boehm had confined her response to shaking her head with a sad clucking sound. But in any case, no matter what our separate sympathies, there wasn't an extra room.

However, when I reached the deathly dour building, I found my brother, Valentine, talking earnestly with the imposing figure of George Washington Matsell on the massive front steps. Even Val seemed deferential where Matsell was concerned. His hands weren't in his pockets, one of his broad thumbs merely tucked into the gap in a waistcoat that seemed to have lily of the valley sprouting all over it. It was telling.

'Captain Wilde,' I said. 'Afternoon, Chief Matsell.'

'Where in God's name have you been all this morning?' Matsell demanded when he saw me.

'Tending to a girl covered in blood. Never mind that, it came to nothing. How are you, sir?'

'Not well,' he answered.

Valentine rubbed at his lips distractedly.

'Why is that?' I asked, clasping my star badge in glad readiness to hurl it at my brother's eye.

'Because we've found a croaked kinchin on Mercer Street, in my ward,' Val replied. 'Sans clothing, all slashed apart, enough to make you hash your breakfast. He was a dimber little fellow, too. Handsome as they make them. We're trying to keep it snug, but that's easier said than – where in hell is your copper star, young Jack Dandy?'

To my own very great surprise, when I pulled it out of my pocket, I didn't throw it in his face at all. I put it on again.

CHAPTER SIX

*All the persecutions which the true church has
suffered from Pagans, Jews, and all the world beside,
are nothing compared with what it has endured from
the unrelenting cruelty of this most insatiable
murderer of men.*

Regarding the pope, from the Orange County
Protestant Reformation Society, 1843

I didn't head back to my rounds that morning. Matsell let
me go with Val to the tree-fronted new station house of the
Eighth Ward, on the corner of Prince and Wooster streets.
Granted, I insisted pretty ferociously. Word of my finding
Aidan Rafferty had spread, meanwhile, which might have had
plenty more to do with the allowance. I figured the chief to be
indulging a shaken-up new recruit, since finding a dead infant
is high on the list of bad ways to spend a morning, even in New
York. As Valentine, in his infinite tact, reminded me in the
swift-trotting hired hack we took northward.

'I heard about the stifled Irish chit. You were keen to clear out, weren't you?' he asked, his hands resting on the top of his cane, his legs spread casually as was possible in a small hansom. Val's youthful face was tight with vexation, the ever-present bags beneath his eyes grown taut. 'That would have made a nice time for me, Tim. I promised Matsell you were up to snuff.'

'I don't recall having asked you to do anything of the kind.'

'You're welcome nevertheless. Don't be a tongue-pad.'

My eyes idly passed over my brother's hand dangling across his weighted walking stick and caught sight of a tiny tremor in his fingertips. Glancing up, I checked his pupils.

'You're sober,' I mused. I'd supposed he'd be glazed over with morphine next I saw him, pining for his precious fires. 'Why is that, I wonder.'

'Because I'm a captain, a trusted figure, and we've a Democratic committee meeting this afternoon. Why do you want a go at another stiff kinchin, I wonder? Finding out you've a taste for undersized grinners?'

By grinners, of course, he meant skulls. 'Don't be disgusting. Tell me what happened.'

Valentine explained that a whore by the name of Jenny had been walking her usual mindless circles in search of a patron that dawn when she'd passed by a trash barrel outside an eating house. This keg was apparently a predictably rich source of food, and Jenny had spent the last of her coin on a morning mug of whiskey, so she pulled the top off the barrel thinking to find, as she often did, some crusts of oyster pie or a duck carcass. Perhaps, if she was very lucky, some half-eaten fried veal. What she'd discovered instead had set her screaming her head off, and eventually she found a roundsman who'd spirited the corpse to the station house. And what would have happened to it *before* we police existed, it suddenly occurred to me with a little flutter of surprise, was anyone's guess. I like to think a watchman would have looked it over thoroughly, maybe even called in his captain, before sending it to a potter's field, but who could say?

'Thank Christ he did jark it off to the station,' Val added as we pulled up to the curb and he flicked two bits up to the driver. 'It really won't fadge, the police only just formed and dead kids thrown out with the oyster shells. Right this way, he's in the cellar. I'm to meet with a doctor in a few minutes.'

The street was quiet and dotted with greenery, the building an ordinary brick one, with an official-looking desk at the front and a black-Irish policeman standing behind it wearing a frozen expression that made something slither along the back of my neck. A closed, wounded look. I was actually glad of my brother being there for a moment as we crossed the small room. And then told myself, in his words, not to be such a bloody milch cow.

Down the back stairs we went, not needing a lantern because the room below was lit. The chamber we emerged in was more a dry cave than a cellar. A sack of apples in the corner for hungry men on night duty, three large oil lamps turning shadows sharp and black as threats. It was cooler by ten degrees below than it was above. I caught a smell like trees and topsoil, a pleasant underground aroma from when I was very young fetching potatoes for our mum. But mixed in with that was another odor – filthy-sweet and raw. Something lay on a table in the middle of the room under an ashy tarp.

'Go on,' Val challenged. 'You wanted to see what a rum job it was. Be my guest, Timmy.'

If there's one word on earth that operates on me like a bald dare, it's the word *Timmy*. So I walked over and threw back the tarp.

And the thing is, at first I couldn't accept it. Val was right, I wasn't man enough for this, and the same twisting, falling feeling I'd had looking at Aidan Rafferty's tiny curled fist passed through me. But then, staring down at the body, a slight metallic *click* slotted in my brain like a window shutting. I needed to be able to ask Bird clearly about this later, ask her to better explain *They'll tear him to pieces.* I needed that deep down in me for some reason.

And in the meantime, something else didn't make sense.

'There isn't much blood, is there? For what's happened to him.'

'You're right,' is all he said. Surprised. Val folded his thick arms and walked over to join me.

The boy was around twelve years old. Clearly Irish. Fine fair skin and curls the color of rosy sand, his face drawn but his eyes peacefully closed, as if exhausted. He wasn't just dead, though. And he wasn't precisely slashed apart, as Val had said. The lad's torso had been sawed open with something like a hacksaw, in the exact shape of a cross. Bits of muscle dangling, organs staring back at us, ribs jutting out. It was a pair of enormous intersecting cuts. I didn't know what any of the pulled-apart strings of flesh and the shards of snapped bone were called. But I knew that a cross had been hewn into the poor kinchin's torso, and that there was a weird cleanliness to the gaping rib cage. Bird's blood-dyed nightdress flapped before my eyes like a flag from a war.

'Who is he?'

'How the deuce should *I* know?' Val answered irritably, green eyes flashing.

'Has he been reported missing? Has any child who looks like him?'

'If you don't think that's the first thing we checked, you're a noddle. Anyway, he's Irish as they make 'em. You have any notion how hard they're looked for when they go missing? Might as well tell the parents to keep a tenderer watch over their fleas.'

'When did this Jenny open the keg, then?'

'Quarter of seven.'

'The barrel itself is full of blood, though?'

'Come to think of it, it isn't. I did palaver for a spell with the restaurant owner, and the cook, and the oyster boy. There's two waiters employed, but they'd not arrived yet. We talked down here so as to have a little atmosphere,' he added, rubbing a hand over his knuckles in an unconscious power gesture that was completely wasted on me. 'It's their damn scrap hogshead, they ought to know what's in it. Who's in it. Well, they didn't, and they didn't know who the kid was, either. I made sure that they didn't. Never mind how.'

I was about to tell Val that I hadn't asked and in fact would prefer not to know how when we both heard tentative footsteps. Our heads swiveled identically. Frustratingly enough.

'Dr Palsgrave,' said Valentine as a very small man entered the room. 'Glad you came.'

'Oh, God have mercy,' the other fellow cried when he viewed the ghastly table.

And, as happens shockingly often in New York, in particular to barkeepers, I knew him by sight. Dr Peter Palsgrave is the last descendant of a prominent old family, the lucky sort who'd held on to their money and the town house on Broadway. He's known citywide as an expert in children's health. And that's what makes him so peculiar – no one specializes in children's health. A doctor is a doctor, after all, unless he's a surgeon or an asylum keeper. Dr Palsgrave has animated eyes of a golden amber color, a pair of neatly trimmed silver side whiskers, and a queerly erect posture from his old-fashioned habit of going corseted under his gleaming white shawl-collared waistcoat. His beaver hat was quite tall that day, his sapphire coat very fitted. In all, a riveting mixture of jumbled-up nerves and expensive polish.

'Not my cup of tea either, Doctor, though my brother Tim here can't stop keeking at it.'

This was, amazingly, not the worst introduction I'd ever received from my sibling.

Dr Palsgrave mopped his broad forehead with an expensive piece of hemmed green silk.

'I apologize, gentlemen, but my heart is forever impaired,' he confessed. He sure enough looked it, for my money. 'Rheumatic fever at a tender age, which has led to many compensatory measures on my part. If the Hôpital des Enfants Malades or anything like a children's facility existed in this country of ours, I might not be so vulnerable to startlement. As it is, my pulse is racing. Now. You are Captain Wilde, I take it?'

'The genuine article,' my brother affirmed.

'You're well aware that I am no coroner. Yes? And yet I received an emergency summons from this . . . this so-called police force. You'll tell me why, and at once.'

'Actually,' Valentine said with a razor-lipped smile and a sweep of his hand over his high tawny hairline, 'you'll now take a good look at that boy's mazzard and tell the captain of Ward Eight whether you've ever tended to him in a charitable way before, or I'll knap you off to the Tombs for a few days. Don't try to lion me. And I thank you for your help.'

Dr Palsgrave looked ready to suffer a second heart episode. Then he shifted his weight and tried to make himself . . . well, taller than me, because we were dead even, and nowhere near as tall as Val. It didn't work too well. Meanwhile, I felt a rare glint of family pride that I quashed like a cockroach in the pantry. The forcible bluntness of Val's approach couldn't be denied – but then, neither could its potential.

'It's *outrageous*. You wish me to attempt to identify a child I may never have seen, and out of thousands that I have?'

'That's just it,' Val agreed coolly, running a thumb over his vest buttons. 'Plus tell us whatever else you happen to notice, purely as a favor to the copper stars.'

I smelled imaginary money in the air, prettily metallic. It was the moment when – knowing my brother – Valentine could have offered a bribe. Unless he decided that the subject wasn't worth it and didn't bother. Val said nothing.

He was dead on.

Shrugging, Dr Palsgrave approached the corpse, linking his arms behind his back. When he reached the lifeless husk, his face softened quickly, as if the sight of death still grieved him despite his anatomical education.

'He is between eleven and thirteen,' he reported in a clipped tone. 'I can see no clear sign of what caused his demise, but it was not these . . . twin wounds. They took place postmortem. Perhaps a foreigner raised upon heathen spells intended to steal his organs and was interrupted. Perhaps he swallowed a valuable and someone sought to recover it. Perhaps someone was in desperate need of meat. Whatever it was, he was already dead.'

It was all more than a bit thick, the nod to cannibalism in particular. I found myself glancing at my brother for some sort of anchor to reality, and to my shock found him already looking at me. I snapped my eyes back to the doctor.

Dr Palsgrave's eyes were almost tender now, deeply regretful, and he brought one hand out from behind his back and passed it gently over the kinchin's stiff arm, 'Poor little soul. As for who he is, I have not the *slightest* notion. Doubtless he is a street arab who scavenges for his daily bread and met with a fatal misfortune.'

'He isn't,' I said, not really recognizing my own voice. 'His fingernails are clean. You ought to look closer.'

Val's entire gaudily clad chest fell back an inch as he laughed. Wincing as he always does when laughing, because the subject isn't ever a fit one for humor. Meanwhile, I heard in my head *We've a new occupation, my Tim . . . one you'll take to like a bird to air*, and beat back hot twin urges to be either irked or else to smile myself.

'Do you mean to tell me,' hissed Dr Palsgrave to my brother, 'that I am to be subjected to the . . . the *insolence* of this fellow?'

'Yes, but only so long as he's beating you at physicking. Go on, Tim. Where's he likeliest come from, this little one?'

'From either a respectable house or from a brothel,' I said, very carefully. 'But even if he'd washed his hands, his complexion is all wrong for summer in the open. He's very pale. Won't you tell us what you think he died from, Dr Palsgrave?'

Reluctantly, the angry flush seeping away, the doctor bent back over the corpse. We hadn't any tools for him, so he took his cuffs off and searched with his fingers, my brother standing over him wearing a very encouraging scowl. He pulled back the lad's eyelids, and he poked in his chest cavity, and, swooping down, he smelled the boy's lips. There was a palpable reverence to his movements, a respect for what had once been a boy. Finally, he turned to wash his hands in a stone basin near the table.

'Nearly faded marks on his body indicate that he was about

a year ago subject to varicella. That is chicken pox to the layman, and *highly* contagious. His health was not overall good. He is, as you say, a boy of attentive hygiene – however, he is quite thin, and his lungs give every indication of having suffered a serious case of pneumonia at the time of his death. I should identify it the cause of death outright, for there are no other signs of violence to his person other than these terrible postmortem wounds, but I cannot be completely certain.'

He cleared his throat. Hesitated.

'His spleen is . . . missing, which is undoubtedly peculiar. It could *very* easily have been absconded with by a rat, however – there are clear signs this carcass has been picked over by vermin within the open abdomen.'

Valentine, as a reward to us all for good behavior, went to pull the grey tarp back over the nameless kinchin. The poor lad left behind him the smell of lifeless tissue not yet gone to rot. Also a rapidly increasing dislike on my part for unanswered questions.

'You're dead to rights that you've never tended this pup before now – at a hospital, or inside private digs?' my brother persisted.

'I tend to thousands of children and have few colleagues willing to assist me. Why I, a doctor of medicine, should be expected to recall their *individual* faces I cannot say,' Dr Palsgrave huffed, drying his hands. 'You'd be much better off asking a charitable worker. I bid the pair of you good day.'

'What charity worker would be best?' Val drawled with a smile that meant unfinished business would be tolerated with bad grace.

'One who has a good eye for faces, is trustworthy, and who is willing to visit Catholics, of course,' Dr Palsgrave snapped, reattaching his cuffs to his sleeves. 'An anomaly amongst charitable types. You'll want Miss Mercy Underhill for that, I shouldn't wonder. I work intimately with the Reverend Thomas Underhill in poor Protestant wards. But there aren't many who venture where Miss Mercy does, not even her father. Now for the last time, *goodbye*.'

His quick, nervous footsteps thudded up the stairs. Something had gone wrong with my mouth. It was dry as bones. If I moved it, I thought, it might possibly splinter apart.

'Well, if that isn't a ream bit of luck for us.' Valentine slapped me on the back. 'You can find Mercy Underhill blind in the dark with your hands trussed, can't you now—'

'No,' I said clearly. 'No. I only wanted to help you, to help you with the body. That's all.'

'Why in hell would you want to help me? And once you'd wanted to, for whatever cracked reason, why would you stop?'

'I won't make Mercy look at that. Not for anyone.'

'Not for the dead kinchin himself?' When my mouth opened furiously, Val lifted a wide and admittedly authoritative hand. 'You saw a croaked Irish chit and it funked you, so you came with me to learn whether you had the nerve to do it twice. I savvy, Tim. But you were aces. Listen, I'm going to have his body cleaned up and put in a robe, so all she'll have to ruminate on is his name. I'll even send it to St Patrick's, it's only six blocks down Prince, and see whether they recognize him first. It's possible the priest will know where he hails from.'

'I'm not even posted to this—'

'Matsell was ready to sack you this morning, chit or no chit, so I'll tell him I need you to sort this out for the Eighth. It's perfect. I'll mention what you said about fingernails. That was sharp. Comes of tending bar, I suppose?'

'But I don't know how to—'

'And who does, Tim? All my men are questioning the neighbors as they make rounds, and I'll sling you the fresh news when you report back to me tonight. I'll be at the Liberty's Blood after ten. You can cock an organ with me.'

'Please tell me that means smoking a pipe.'

'What in buggering hell else would it mean?'

'I can't just go and interrupt Mercy's entire— '

'It's for a murder. She's a game sort, and plenty brainy, she'll be white about it. Farewell, Tim, and best of luck.'

'This is not just about murder!' I snapped, rubbing at my own high brow in despair.

Valentine was already halfway to the stairs. 'Oh,' he said, stopping.

I braced for ridicule. But he only flipped me a coin with a knowing smirk on his face. 'That's a shilling, I think. Get yourself a mask to match that flush hat of yours. Something patriot-red and bully and mysterious.'

Fisting my hand over the coin, I protested, 'A mask is never going to solve—'

'Give that tired red rag in your mouth a rest, Timothy. I didn't say it would. There's a whole world of things I can't solve, much as it may surprise you.'

His voice had been positively greased with sarcasm. Then quick as a wolf, Val grinned at me with an honest dazzle of teeth. 'But it'll help, eh? It'll help. Go to it. Then find Mercy Underhill and figure out who'd crack open an Irish lad like a lobster. I don't mind telling you, I'm keen to know as much myself.'

CHAPTER SEVEN

*The Annual Reports of the City Inspector show that
nearly one-half the deaths by consumption are of the
foreign part of the population, and that more than
one-third the whole number of deaths are of
foreigners. Such an immense disproportion can only
be accounted for on the supposition that some
extraordinary causes of death prevail among the
strangers who come to reside among us.*

*The Sanitary Condition of the Laboring
Population of New York,* January 1845

Red masks are for bandits in Bowery theatricals and
possibly Italian pantomime artists. My rogue of a brother,
of course, wouldn't know the difference. But the idea itself
was infuriatingly sound. So I bought a charcoal grey strip of
soft cotton, and I tied it angled around my head over the thin
oiled sheet, so my eye was exposed. Then I went to the Pine
Street Church.

I wondered as I hastened along Pine past the all too familiar three-story lawyers' practices, and the shop windows full of modern oil lanterns and hothouse flowers, why I wasn't racing toward Bird instead to ask her all about the boy with the cross dug in his chest. Two reasons emerged as I thought it over. First, Bird had said *They'll tear him to pieces*, and I felt poorly about telling her she'd been right. Supposing the bowl of chicken's blood another fabrication, of course. More important, I thought, no one outside my house needed to know about Bird quite yet. Did they? The sweet-faced young liar who'd been drenched in gore and could have seen far too much. *I'd* help Bird, and then *I'd* see her on her way.

I hadn't been south of City Hall Park since a massive slice of city had burned to the ground. The closer I came, the slower my feet went. Smoke assaulted my nostrils even though there wasn't any, embers pulsating within the rubbish heaps. Eager hammers rang out like the pounding of the city's pulse. Buildings – still intact, plastered with clothing and medical and political advertisements – grew ever more scorched. Occasional structures, formerly wooden, were missing entirely. And therein lay the source of the hammering: Irishmen, hundreds upon hundreds of Irishmen, were sweating through their shirts with nails in their teeth while a native or two looked on, drinking from a flask and calling out jeers.

'I've been sawing lumber all my life, learned it off my own father, and you call that *craftsmanship?*' a ruddy bearded man was screaming as I approached William Street. 'A *nigger* wouldn't work for so little, nor would a nigger *do so poor a job!*'

The Irish fellow gritted his teeth and very sensibly said nothing, preferring to keep his employment than to indulge in a street brawl. But he flushed scarlet as the man continued screaming epithets, the native having moved to the subject of the Irishman's mother, and, as I passed the emigrant, the dull, helpless look in his eyes was one I recognized very well. I've seen tattered Yidishers with threadbare head coverings wearing it, coloreds being literally thrashed out of shops wearing it, ridiculed Quaker farmers wearing it, Indian craftsmen with rain running down their black braids as they sit stoically before a table of beaded work and carved bone wearing it. It's always *someone* in these parts, being made small, being made to wear that look. I've worn it myself. And it isn't comfortable.

When I stepped onto Mercy's street, I saw the devastation. And then there was nothing else to look at. Not to a man bred here, who had known New York before fire took it away. I stared into a beautiful hive of swirling man-made invention. Dozens of half-formed thoughts had somehow erupted into buildings. Fresh-cut stones amid the rubble, coloreds running water to men about to perish of heat stroke, black tree roots with the branches burned away, under which sat flowering window boxes shipped from Brooklyn or Harlem.

And because New York is the only place in the world like it, just watching it happen made a part of it *mine*. I'd expected sight of the wreckage to set my face newly afire. Instead, I looked on and thought, *Yes. We keep going. Maybe in another direction, maybe even in the wrong one. But by whichever God you fancy, we keep going.*

The Pine Street Church is modestly blushing red brick, at the corner of Pine and Hanover, with the rectory adjacent. When I pushed open the thick chapel door, I spied vague movement at the back, heard hushed tones. My shoulder blades tingled at the thought it might be Mercy, but even without much light, I knew it wasn't. A pair of women stood near the pulpit, sorting through donated clothing spilling gaudily from a great canvas sack onto a plain oak table.

'This we can put in the usable pile, can we not, Martha?' asked the younger of the two as I approached. A widow, I took it when I was close enough to spy her ring, for married women who wear homespun have more important domestic tasks at four in the afternoon than sorting through slops. She'd coarse blonde hair and a squashed nose like a pressed flower, but her voice was gentle. 'It's quite good, I think.'

'Far too good,' the older woman sniffed after glancing at the plain rose-colored nankeen. 'Any destitute woman would look above her place in such a dress. The very idea, Amy. Put it in the pile to pawn instead. Can I assist you, sir?'

'I'm Timothy Wilde, member of the copper stars,' I explained, gesturing at the blasted thing.

An expression composed half of curiosity and half of severe distaste flashed over her features.

'I need to find Miss Underhill quick as possible,' I sighed, ignoring it.

'Oh! Dear Miss Underhill – has something happened?' the one called Amy squeaked.

'Not to Miss Underhill. Do you know where she is?'

Martha pulled all the edges of her sallow face into the shape of a moldy lemon. 'She is with her father, at the rectory. I would not interrupt them, were I you.'

'Why not?' I asked, already half turned.

Smothering a pleased look under a thick smear of prudishness, she reported, 'Voices were raised as they went indoors, and the argument is one she ought to listen to. Miss Underhill has been tending to low Irish families, against all sense. She'll end up in the earth next to her mother, consorting with drunken foreigners like this – where does she suppose cholera comes from? And then where will the reverend be, the poor noble man?'

'Safe in God's keeping,' I answered dryly, tipping my hat. 'Your God, of course, so you needn't worry.'

I left behind me a pair of open mouths.

Exiting the side door of the church and following the little path through the apple trees to the dark-leafed hedge that borders the rectory, I stopped short when I caught sight of Mercy and her father standing before the bay window in their parlor. And they were arguing, to be sure, Mercy's teeth worrying her thumbnail, her father's posture stern. On my life, I never meant to spy upon them, but something in Mercy's eyes made my feet stop just short of the hedgerow – and in any case, seeing her again had just done something very uncomfortable to my heart rate.

But they are not even Christians, Mercy, I watched him say, making a decisive movement with his hand.

Missionaries tend to the poor in Africa, and the tribes there have more gods than they can count. There isn't any difference, she said, gazing wide eyed at him.

The tribesmen are merely unlettered, innocent.

And the Irish merely poor. I can't—

The reverend stalked a few feet away, steps swift and angry, and I lost sight of his response. But whatever it was caused Mercy to flush like a sunrise, and wince her eyes shut as she stood with her face to the window. His speech lasted for perhaps ten seconds. When it had ended, Thomas Underhill stepped back into my line of sight with an anguished expression, pulling Mercy's dark head to his chest. She went readily, gripping his arm, and the last thing I saw before turning away from a scene far too intimate to view was the reverend speaking once more, his chin resting lightly on his girl's head.

It terrifies me, he was saying. *I'd not risk your health for a thousand lost souls.*

Guilt would have gnawed at me, witnessing a scene like that, had I not been well aware of what they were arguing over. Society charity types limit their usefulness to hosting themed teas with generous slices of tongue pie, lemonade soirees where they feelingly discuss ways to rid the earth of vice. Mercy isn't a society type, though. She frankly isn't any specific type at all that I can discern despite my constant scrutiny, and after all she comes of abolitionist stock. If any breed of charity worker is willing to dirty their hands, and at any hour of the day they're called on, it's an abolitionist. So I don't muse over the fact that Mercy's equally impassioned mother died by walking into a sickroom full of sufferers, the way her father does. I don't muscle Mercy back into the light and air when I see her do it. I wait it out, or she'd never speak to me again.

Such were my dark thoughts as I rounded the corner of the house. When I reached the front door, it swung open, and then Mercy turned to shut it once more.

I froze stiff for no reason at all. Mercy copied me when she reached the footpath, the swinging basket over her arm marking off seconds. As she recognized me, I watched her face shift from pale to bloodless. A tiny piece of hair had just caught at the edge of her lower lip, and most people would have wanted to brush it back for her. That would have ruined the expression, though, whatever it was.

'I'm headed for the Browns, though I haven't nearly enough flour for them,' Mercy said in a rush. Apropos of nothing, as usual. 'Mr Wilde, I've a very urgent visit to make. Are you here to see Papa?'

I shook my head, still tongueless.

'Then do please escort me to Mulberry Street, and after that . . . please talk with me. I fear I'm all out of sorts for conversation just now. Will you go?'

She may as well have asked whether I'd any interest in a holiday from a stint in hell. So I nodded. With my hand on her arm once more as we hastened down the road, after the usual rush of quiet joy, everything looked closer, focused. Seen through a gently curving lens. I almost forgot why I'd come for a moment. I wouldn't get to have her, so *Today*, I thought, *is better than all the days stretched in front of it will be, because today we're seeing the same view.*

Nearby, Mulberry Street was sweltering. Blackened produce melting through its crates into the pavement outside groggeries, buildings swooning against each other in the heat. Packed with people, and nary a man there by choice. Seventy-six was a wooden structure – built of matchsticks and twice as flammable, to my eye. We entered and without pause climbed to the second floor. Going to the end of the hallway, Mercy knocked at the door on the right. When a low murmur answered her, she pushed it open, nodding at me to wait in the passage.

I could see three-quarters of a bare room that smelled cloyingly of illness and had an oily human texture to the air. For about the dozenth time in my life I stopped myself from hauling Mercy bodily out of a strange sickroom. But I know precisely the sort of agony that churned through the mind of the reverend that morning. Because every time, it feels like being pulled in half.

Three children sat on the bare floorboards. The youngest maybe two years old, though he could have simply been underfed, naked, and sucking on four of his fingers. Two other girls in streaked cotton shifts, eight and ten by the looks of them, hemmed handkerchiefs. From the bed, a reedy voice sounded. American, for my money, though she could easily have had Dutch grandparents. Mercy set the little sack of flour in a teakettle, as there wasn't a table or cupboard in sight.

'The temperance tract women were here again. I'm to clean the floor and wash all the linens before they deliver the potatoes, but I haven't any vinegar. Nor ash, nor turpentine.'

The woman speaking, blond hair plastered to her brow and flushed with ague, didn't look game for standing, much less scrubbing floors. Mercy pulled a blue bottle and a little glass vial out of her basket.

'Here is turpentine, and I've an ounce of quicksilver for the bedbugs. If you share both, will Lacey Huey help you to clean?'

'She'll do it,' sighed the sick woman in relief. 'I did her washing last month when her gout was bad. Thank you, Miss Underhill.'

'If I'd any potatoes today myself, I'd leave them, worse luck.' Mercy made a wry face that tugged one side of her lips down. They spoke for a few moments more, of the woman's fever and her kinchin and what exactly the temperance tract ladies had demanded be done to the wretched chamber before its occupants deserved any food. Disease, the clergy and the scientists agree, is caused by weak living. Rich foods, bad air, rotten earth, lazy hygiene, liquor, drugs, vice, and sex. The sick, therefore, are generally supposed something lower than angelic and thus not to be directly associated with by virtuous charitable workers. Mercy and other radicals flout that system gleefully, and – despite the terrifying danger to her – I do see her point. I don't know what causes illness. No one does, really. But I'd been sickly more than once as a child, and Valentine, who can't be accused of owning many virtues, has the constitution of a draft horse. It doesn't quite wash.

'Thank you for coming,' Mercy said to me after warmly bidding the kinchin farewell and closing the door. 'We'll take this staircase back down; the other is rotten in three places.'

Sunlight dazzled my eyes as we regained the street. Recalling with a jolt just how foul my errand truly was, I prepared to warn her that I'd a terrible request to make. But Mercy spoke first, as I angled our feet toward St Patrick's Cathedral.

'My father had the most grotesque nightmare,' she said. 'I came down this morning and there he sat in the parlor, with a pen and paper and a book. Not reading or writing or notating, only sitting, before he attended to his duties. He could hardly speak to me. It made me quite worried for your own recovery. Are you well?'

It took me a second or two, but then I realized she wasn't speaking of the fire. She meant Aidan Rafferty.

'It was a hard day,' I admitted.

'I confess myself sorriest of all for my father,' she said with a painted-over look. 'I suppose the infant is in heaven, and maybe you do as well. Or in the cool earth, perhaps. Only my father imagines it in hell. Who do you pity most, Mr Wilde?'

The mother, I thought. *Sitting in the Tombs with a fogged mind, and only rats to talk it over with.*

'I don't know, Miss Underhill.'

Mercy isn't surprised very often – and so I watched this second instance like the collector I was. At the sound of her name, her lips fell open, and then she bit the lower one gently.

'Haven't you thought about it, then?'

'I try not to.'

'Why have you come to find me, Mr Wilde? Here I thought us old friends, and you disappeared without a word, following a great disaster. Do you imagine us heartless, not the sort to wonder where you'd gone?' she added, her eyes ricocheting to the side.

'If I caused you or your father any stray anxious thought, please forgive me.'

'Surely you see that it isn't like you?'

'I'm wearing a copper star and living in the Sixth Ward. Do I *look* like myself at the moment?'

Mercy's black brows drifted apart. Contemplating her equally, I lost my bearings for an instant. When we resumed walking, she'd inexplicably found something to smile about. It teased at the edges of her mouth, more audible in her breath than visible on her face.

'I'm sorry for your recent misfortunes,' she said softly. 'All of them. I learned of them only yesterday, from Papa, of course, and wish I'd known sooner.'

'Thank you,' I said, feeling ungrateful. 'How's the book coming?'

'Well enough.' She sounded almost amused. 'But I find it difficult to credit that you're here without reason, from the sound of you. Are you about to tell me what it is?'

'I am,' I replied reluctantly. 'Dr Peter Palsgrave thought that you could maybe help the police identify a deceased boy. If you don't wish—'

'Peter Palsgrave? My father's friend, the doctor working on an elixir of life?'

'Is he? I thought he only tended children.'

'He does, which is how Papa and I came to know him. And yes, he is. Dr Palsgrave has long been after the formula for a cordial capable of curing any illness. He vows it's science, but I find it all rather impractical. Ought one focus so very hard on a magical cure-all while so many are dying for want of perfectly simple cures like fresh meat? But why should he think of me— Oh, I see,' Mercy sighed, shifting her basket up her slender arm. 'Is the boy native?'

'If you mean were his parents born here or have they the accents and money to pass for it, I don't know. But he seems Irish.'

Mercy gave me a brief smile like a darting kiss on the cheek, one corner of her mouth sweeping toward me. 'In that case, I will certainly help you.'

'Why should his being Irish make you help us?'

'Because,' she answered, and the needle had crept back into the elegant weave again, 'if he's Irish, no one else in this city would dream of it.'

Viewing the body – by that time clean and shrouded, I assumed, and only yards distant at St Patrick's on Prince and Mulberry – was more difficult than we'd imagined it would be. There first was the problem of my reluctance to approach the rough stone wall of the five-windowed side entrance with Mercy on my arm, knowing I was about to show her a corpse. More important, though, there were the thugs.

'We'll burn Satan's palace to the ground!'

A giant of over six feet with thick black side whiskers, who couldn't possibly have yet reached twenty-five years in spite of those facts, stood before a small knot of workingmen wearing fierce faces. All their wrinkles etched deeper than they ought to have been. Men of honest work who'd just finished butchering swine or pounding nails and had donned their best coats to pelt a cane basket full of river rocks at the Irish. They resembled Val in their tight black swallowtails and careful breastpins. Val wanted Irish votes, though, and Nativists wanted Irish deaths. They were men with hard lives, showing as much in their cold eyeblinks and their readily clenched hands.

'I'll see to this,' I said to Mercy, nodding at the corner to tell her to wait.

'You inside-out niggers don't dare to face down a single freeborn American! Come out and play, you cowards. We'll drown you like a sack of pups!' the boy giant shouted, all teeth and carefully combed bear's fur.

'Not today,' I suggested.

Eyes swept in my direction like vermin to a carcass.

'And you are, my sweet little skip-kennel?' the huge young fellow questioned in a voice that could only have come from New York.

'Not a footman. A copper star,' I said, translating *skip-kennel*. I needed a gesture, so I flicked my thumbnail over the badge the way I'd all too often seen Val do with mere buttons. For the first time, I felt something about that star other than rage or annoyance. 'Find some pups who want drowning and leave the church as it is.'

'Oh, a *copper star*,' sneered the giant rough. 'I've been meaning to give a copper star a beating for weeks now. He talks big though, don't he? Seems to savvy flash.'

'That's all just smoke,' slurred a drunken sort whose face seemed to have been mistaken for bread dough and rearranged. 'There's but one of him. And he don't understand us.'

'Smack on the calfskin, I understand you. And I don't need more than one of me,' I replied. 'Get out of it or I'll see you to the Tombs.'

As I'd predicted, the lanky monument they all looked to stepped forward. With his hands curling into their natural shape.

'I go by the name of Bill Poole.' He breathed downward, the gust tangy and ripe. 'And I'm a free native-born republican who can't abide the sight of a standing army. You'll be flat as a sounder in a strammel when I'm through with you, copper star.'

111

Whether he was capable of beating me flat as a caged pig, I couldn't tell. But I could tell he was drunk and loose in the limbs. So when he swung down at me, as a taller man will do when overconfident, I stepped in close past his fist and felled him with an elbow snapped up into his eye socket. Bill Poole dropped like a sack slung from my shoulder.

'Practice makes all the difference,' I advised candidly as his followers scrambled to get him upright. I touched the star again, wildly pleased with it now. 'Get away from here before more of me arrive.'

Maybe there really is something to enduring hundreds of brawls with my older brother, I thought, *if it helps me fight low and filthy for good reason*. The roughs, meanwhile, dragged their leader and their rocks away. I adjusted the cloth over my face while hope pulled hard and insistent at my spine. Mercy was behind me, after all. Mercy was . . .

Not behind me. The door, prettily curved at its top, was open.

Hope, I've discovered, is a sad nuisance. Hope is a horse with a broken leg.

Inside the cathedral, twelve enormous pillars like the roots of mountains supported the distant roof, each ringed at the top with four globes of muted light. Dim despite the glow, and the air thick with incense and ritual. When I spied Mercy, she stood earnestly listening to the priest I recognized from my visit to Mulberry Street in search of lodgings only weeks before. He must have struck me at the time, for I remembered him though we'd never exchanged either words or money. His head wasn't bald, to start with; it was spherical and hairless, as if hair had never grown there. The features below that sphere were cut strong and bullish and intelligent, however. His eyes flicked to me, interested.

'Mr Wilde, I take it.' The prelate offered me the steady hand of the man who presides over the walls and the roof. 'They told me you'd be payin' me a call. Bishop Hughes is in Baltimore at the moment, in conference with the archbishop, and I'm servin' as administrator. I live just adjacent to the cathedral in any case, and oversee the grounds. Father Connor Sheehy, at your service.'

'Thank you. The Bowery types have left your doorstep, you might want to know.'

'Sure, and they leave every afternoon about this time, afore the Catholic day laborers are through with cartin' manure and want a dust-up.' He smiled. 'We pay them no mind, Miss Underhill and myself. I get the feelin' you humiliated them, though, which is all to the good o' the copper stars. No, I do charitable work in Five Points with Miss Underhill here, and . . . your brother Captain Wilde seems to have sent me somethin' grave. You'll be wantin' to see the lad. He's in one of the side chambers. Come this way.'

The room's trappings were so different from the police station's that I couldn't quite get my head around its being the same corpse. I could see the boy better in the free-flowing window light from high above, and here equally still pictures of saints surrounded him, keeping fit company. He wore a white gown now, facing the freestone ceiling, a cloth pulled up to his breast. You couldn't take him for sleeping, though, not when you've seen death before. Dead things look *heavy*. Earthbound in a way living things don't.

Mercy went right to him, setting her basket down. 'Yes, I've the feeling I've met him before, but I can't place him,' she said. 'I take it you don't know the boy, Father?'

'I do not. I wish I could say otherwise, seein' what was done to him.'

'What was done to him?' Mercy questioned quick as thinking.

I shot Father Sheehy a glare fit to melt the ice blocks daily shipped down the Hudson. 'Do you truly wish to know, Miss Underhill?' I asked. Willing the single word *no*.

'Are you reluctant to tell me, Mr Wilde?'

'A very deep cross was carved into the lad's torso,' Father Sheehy explained, adding a far too knowing glance of sympathetic apology in my direction. I ignored it.

'To what purpose would someone do such a terrible thing?'

My memory slid dizzily back to Dr Palsgrave and his un-speakable three-item list of *satanic spells, treasure hunting, food source.*

'We're working on it,' I said truthfully. 'Every suggestion thus far has been ridiculous, from religious mania on down.'

Showing us the back of her slim hand as she brushed her fingers along her neck, a more stricken Mercy murmured, 'He did not die of that, did he?'

'No, no,' I promised her. A half-formed thought was tapping at the back of my head. 'He died of either pneumonia or else something less traceable. Miss Underhill, last year, did you treat any poor families who'd taken ill with the chicken pox?' I asked in a rush, snapping my fingers.

Lowering my head, I crossed to the body and pulled the kinchin's gown down just an inch or two, at the shoulder. The nearly faded marks were scattered across the skin, less visible than his freckles but still clear.

Mercy frowned at one side of her mouth. 'Last season was remarkably quiet regarding varicella cases. He could have had it without ever seeing me, of course, but I did go about for some two weeks with brown paper, soaking it in molasses, then plastering the children to reduce inflammation of the skin. There was a row of houses stricken, on Eighth Street between the Harlem Railroad and the cemetery. Those were poor natives, though. A patch in Orange Street, all dreadfully ill, but they were Welsh. Oh,' she said with a little start, 'a few houses in Greene Street, where . . .'

Peering down at the body, Mercy's blood began a retreat from her beautiful face.

'He's from a bawdy house,' I said quietly, putting a hand on her elbow. I was reasonably sure in that instant I did it for her, not for me. I hope I did. 'He's a kinchin-mab, isn't he?'

'How could you know that?' Mercy questioned, her lips slack and startled. She took a step away from me, falling silent – as if I knew things I shouldn't, had patronized such places myself and learned their roster of fleshy distractions.

'No, God no, I've never visited a den like that,' I protested. 'There are particular clues. Where does he come from?'

After a pause, she continued. 'I met him in a vile brothel in Greene Street last year, one owned by a Madam Marsh. Silkie Marsh. How did you guess?'

'I didn't guess. I've an inside source, and I'll tell you all about it. What's the address? I need to question this Madam Marsh.'

Father Sheehy, his arms calmly folded over each other with an air of quiet fortitude, cleared his throat.

'You won't be findin' it easy to question Silkie Marsh, for I can tell you that St Patrick's has tried to set the fear of the most holy Trinity in that woman before now, and to no avail. Irish orphans wander into her den from time to time, you see, and they find it a great task gettin' out again. She has connections.'

'What sort of connections?'

'Political ones.' He raised his brows in my direction, polite but incredulous. 'Is there another kind?'

Mercy touched her fingertips to the child's hair. 'No wonder I didn't recognize him. I saw him a year ago,' she said to herself, her voice strained. 'He's . . . he's so much older now.'

'Be very careful about visitin' that brothel, won't you?' Father Sheehy advised, angling his perfectly smooth head meaningfully.

'Should I be frightened of a madam who follows politics?' I scoffed.

'Not a bit of it. I only mention it because I wonder if you are aware of how very put out your brother, Captain Valentine Wilde, would be to know you're harassin' a major Democratic contributor of his.'

'A contributor,' I repeated. It stuck on something fishhook-shaped that had sprung into my throat.

'Oh, and a mighty large one.' Father Sheehy nodded, smiling darkly. 'A benefactor. One might even say a very personal friend.'

And with that, the priest departed on other business. Leaving me with the finest girl ever born, a brutally deceased kinchin-mab, an angry flush that felt wasteful and stupid since I already knew my brother as well as I did, and a single notion in my head. It wasn't to go and talk to Madam Marsh any longer, not by a long haul.

Poor Bird Daly, I thought, was going to tell me the truth, or else have a pretty fair number of unforeseen consequences on her innocent hands.

CHAPTER EIGHT

. . . this sympathy with criminals has always been characteristic of the Irish peasant, and while it may be vain to account for such a morbid feeling, it is undeniable that its existence is the fruitful source of outrage and murder.

New York Herald, summer 1845

Mrs Boehm was standing in the middle of her kitchen beyond the neatly swept bread counter when I arrived home, her hand pressed hard over her pleasant crescent of a mouth. Not moving, precisely, and not standing either. Something 'twixt the two of them – rocking her scant weight back and forth, blinking.

'What on earth is the matter?' I asked her, ducking around the display of seeded loaves.

'I gave her slippery elm tea,' she answered tightly, not looking at me. 'Slippery elm tea is best when blood's humors are unbalanced. And a poultice, after. That works very well.'

'Has Bird fallen sick?' I exclaimed.

'I sent her out.' Mrs Boehm shifted her weight to her left foot, half turning again before swaying back. 'Just down the road, for a fresh fish for luncheon. Not far, but this terrible heat. I never meant to – I did not think it would tax her. She can hardly move,' she finished, tapping a loose fist against her lips with a disordered expression like a field freshly ploughed.

Imagining that Bird would be in Mrs Boehm's bed, I raced up the stairs. The door to the darkened room creaked slightly when I opened it. A hurt, pleading sound. It was a remarkably featureless chamber for a woman with her name on the building, I thought as my eyesight slowly sharpened in the dull brown shadows. A spindly chair, a single picture on the wall and that not even of a person. It was a lush pastureland scene, unrepentantly green and very much reminiscent of my childhood. The sufferer was clad in a thin linen shift and lying on her back. Her hair fell over the pillow in a jungle of dark woody tendrils. A warm poultice smelling strongly of roasted apple and tobacco sat on her chest, sending me a sharply unwelcome memory of being eleven years of age and suffering through Valentine's notions of how to cure a severe head cold. Her eyes fluttered open when she heard me. A pair of grey moths in the dim light.

'What's happened to you?' I questioned in a soft tone, walking to the bed.

'I came over all feverish,' she scraped past a dry throat.

'Coming back from the fish stall? Where are you troubled, Bird?'

'I've red marks, and it hurts to breathe.'

'Mrs Boehm seems very worried about you.'

'I know. I'm sorry to be any bother.'

I sat on the side of the bed, about to tell her the outrageous lie that she wasn't any bother at all. Debating with myself, and fair heartsick over the question, whether it was worse to tell a very ill little girl that her friend had in fact been torn to pieces, or allow said friend to go unavenged. The answers I needed would cut right down to this kinchin's bones in the telling of them, I thought. But before I could say anything, I spied something odd.

'What were you speaking of before you went out for the fish?' I asked conversationally.

Bird's eyes drifted to the window, pupils suddenly bottomless and inscrutable. 'I can't remember,' she whispered. 'Is there water?'

I held the glass up to her lips, watching how carefully her head moved, how very carefully, like a doll's and not a girl's, and then I set the water down again.

'What if I said that Mrs Boehm is very upset, and already told me what you talked about?' I not-quite-lied.

A tiny flinch. Barely a hairsbreadth, skin snagged on a bent pin.

'She wants to send me to a church orphanage,' Bird sighed. 'And I'll go, if she really does hate me so. I told her I'd pay for the cup, that I'm sorry when that happens, but she kept saying "better suited". I think *you* would let me stay here, if she didn't peck at you so. If she didn't force you to *mind* her. But I'll go, when I'm well again.'

'In that case, we'd best not let you run dry of beet juice. Or is it mulberry? I can't tell.'

The expression on Bird's face when I revealed her pretended illness isn't one I like to think back on. Kinchin look angry when you find them out in a charade. I know for a fact Val had been furious one morning long ago, having smeared himself with wild strawberries to absolutely no avail in an effort to avoid helping to cure the hide of a horse we'd lost to hydrophobia. Tanning is foul work, after all. But Bird's face flushed and collapsed the way an adult's does. A bloom of guilt, and then the falling flap of a dove shot from the air. I wanted to tell her to unlearn it somehow, to go back to being hot with anger at the snubs children suffer.

'The poultice is too hot, isn't it?' she asked in a normal voice, smiling a little. Charm following discovery. She looked down. Artfully done red blotches on her neck and chest were just barely beginning to pinken the sharp-smelling cloth sack. She sat upright and dropped it with a wet, disappointed sound on the side table. 'Generally beet juice won't run. I stole one from the pantry before I left and had a newsboy cut it with his pocketknife.'

'Clever.'

'You aren't angry, then?'

'I will be, if you can't manage to stop lying for ten seconds at a stretch.'

Her eyes contracted slightly, appraising. 'Pax, then. I'm through spinning yarns.' She scrambled out of the sheets and sat before me, Indian-style. 'Ask me something.'

I paused. But she was already riven in so many sinewy places under her skin, maybe all of us were, and waiting out of charity's sake was no charity at all. Hesitating only a moment longer, I removed my hat and set it on the red-and-blue patchwork coverlet. Bird's eyes widened again at the obvious signal that something grave was hurtling in her direction.

'Do you know a woman named Silkie Marsh?' I questioned.

She startled, a frightened hand gripping the sheets as she jumped to a kneeling position. 'No, no. I've never—' Stopping, wincing because she knew she'd already given herself away, Bird pulled a deep breath in through her mouth.

'I know for a fact you hail from there. So you needn't tell me, if it pains you,' I said gently.

'She's here, isn't she? She found me. I won't go back, I—'

'She isn't here, and I shouldn't have frightened you. I never would have, but I need answers more than you need rest at the moment. I'm sorry for it. Bird, when you said they were going to tear someone to pieces . . . We found a body. About your age, a little older, and from the same house.'

Bird said nothing at first. Shifting so that she sat with her legs to the side, she asked in a perfectly even voice, 'How did you know we were from the same ken?'

'I had some help identifying him, though I don't know his name. As for you, well . . . there was your dress. And what you said about . . . someone being hurt. And you all had the chicken pox last year. See for yourself.'

Bird ducked her chin to look at the two almost completely faded pox scars at the base of her slim neck and then lifted it with an unlikely and heartfelt grin. A tooth residing in her lower jaw was crooked, amiably jostling with its neighbor.

'You're mighty fly, Mr Wilde. Nothing gets past you. Is that because you're a copper star?'

'No,' I admitted, shocked I hadn't upset her more. 'It's because I used to tend bar.'

She nodded wisely. 'Well, you're a plumb sort of fellow, plumber than most. I could tell straight off, like I said. I'm sorry I tried to queer you earlier, but it's . . .' Bird cleared her throat, another weirdly adult gesture I wanted to rid her of. 'What do you want to know?'

'The truth.'

'You won't like it,' she said dully, fidgeting with the hem of her shift. 'I don't.'

'What was your friend's name?'

'Liam. He didn't have another. He was from the dockyards, lived by begging scraps from the sailors and stevedores. Came to us two years ago. He said he was sick of giving something free they ought by rights to pay for, and in any case the food at Marsh's is pretty fine.'

I sat frozen. Trying not to let my body say the things that my mouth would wrestle bleeding to the ground before allowing them to escape. *There shouldn't be such ways in the world.*

'And what happened to him last night?'

Bird shrugged, the most helpless and the least apathetic shrug I've ever seen. 'Last night the man in the black hood came.'

'And the man in the black hood is the one who hurt Liam?'

'Yes.'

'You don't know his name?'

'No one does, nor what he looks like. I think he's a savage of some sort. Maybe a Red Indian or a Turk. Why would he hide his face otherwise?'

I could think of several reasons, but failed to share them. 'And how did you come to be covered in blood?'

Bird's jaw closed, a ferociously shut door. 'I don't want to talk about that. It was Liam's. I went in, and I saw . . . I *don't* want to talk about that.'

I thought about pushing, then turned disgusted with myself. Enough questions existed without my harping on the worst of them. For now.

'Why did this man in the black hood hurt Liam?'

'There isn't a reason that I can tell. Like I said, he could be a savage. But I think maybe he likes it. They like funny things sometimes. His step is always so light and quick, as if he's about something wonderful and not . . . He's the one cuts them to pieces, all right.'

My heart stuttered badly, a matchstick held to a wet wick.
'*Them?*'

'Yes, them.'

'How many of them?'

'Dozens of us.' Her throat worked suddenly, thrashed like
a tied-down animal. '*Them.* I live here with you now.'

'And how in God's name am I supposed to help you if you
tell me one outrageous lie after another?' I demanded to know,
passing my fingers through my hair. 'First you expect me to
believe you ran from your father, or that you accidentally
shivved a man, or that you soaked your—'

'Or that my blood's out of humor, but not now! Truly, not
now,' she cried.

'Bird,' I attempted, my bones feeling fragile and crisp with
exhaustion, 'this is unfair. You've done nothing but lie to me,
and now you expect me to believe that *dozens* of children have
been cut to pieces by some sort of . . . of child-loathing
maniac?'

Bird nodded, her perfectly trained face wavering without
her permission. The whole look brought to mind a loose
carriage wheel navigating slick mud and malicious stones.

'Without anyone noticing? Without . . .'

I trailed off.

Who *would* have noticed, after all? The police were two
weeks formed, and not a soul considered it good taste to listen
to the Irish. Hell, *I* no longer considered it sound judgment to
listen to Bird, and of course she was exaggerating. Of course.
Two or three of her mates had gone missing, and she'd inflated
it to *dozens* and a Turk in a hood.

'How am I to trust you?' I pleaded.

Bird's entire ten-year-old body suppressed a shudder, a
quake of revulsion from the base of her spine.

'I could show you where they're buried,' she whispered. 'But only if you agree to let me stay here.'

'Two weeks,' Mrs Boehm had said, the edges of her mouth as anchored to the floor as her feet. Something about Bird's deception had shrunk her skin several inches too small for her. There would be punishment involved if it were her child, she'd said darkly, but she guessed Bird knew her own mind, didn't she? So two weeks before she must leave. It was like watching a jail sentencing in reverse.

'I'm sorry,' Bird had said, taking what she could get. 'See if I can make it up to you, though. I could—'

'Two weeks,' Mrs Boehm had said, and then pounded the piece of dough in her fists as if expunging the sins of many worlds.

And now Bird and I were walking to the Tombs, the heat sending sharp wafts of scorched horse urine and baked stone into our nostrils. Bird had changed back into the boy's pair of trousers and the long buttoned shirtwaist, but had added a scrap of burlap for a belt. She looked like a street sweeper working a corner for spare pence.

'How do you know where these dozens of kinchin are buried?' I asked. Trying to prevent *dozens* from sounding like a snide *millions*.

'I overheard them once. When the man in the black hood came before,' she answered, her attention continually darting from left to right at the doorways of the cobblers and liquor grocers. 'My friend Ella was gone and I glimpsed him arriving that night. Getting out of a carriage. He went to the room he uses, down in the cellar. I didn't find that for ages, you know, it's locked better than all the others and I had to pinch the key. When he left, I was at a window. They loaded a bundle into the back of the carriage with him and he said, "Ninth Avenue at Thirtieth".'

'There's nothing at Ninth Avenue and Thirtieth but woods and farmland and empty streets.'

'Then why else would they go there?'

Feeling I was about to be made a fool of, a sadly familiar sensation, I led Bird up to the enormous entrance to the Tombs. She'd been so cowed by the thought of going before that I wondered if she'd bolt at the sight of it. But she only stared upward in a sort of stilled awe.

'How'd they make the windows tall as two floors, straight through the wall?' she asked as we stepped into the cooler air within the solid rock.

It was just as well I didn't have to answer her, for I hadn't the slightest idea. And someone was shouting at me down the cavernous cathedral-like hallway from the direction of the offices, in a stirring baritone that straightened your posture.

'Wilde, get over here!'

George Washington Matsell had a sheaf of documents under his thick arm and a glare under his steely brows that turned my shoes heavy. We went up to my somber and elephantine Chief of Police. He didn't look at Bird, not directly. He absorbed her presence with a steely but encompassing gaze trained solely on me. It made him seem a regal monument erected in his own well-deserved honor.

'Your brother, Captain Valentine Wilde,' Matsell began, 'is a man who accomplishes things. When the Democratic Party would benefit by an action, he fulfills that action to the letter. When a fire is raging, he removes the living from its clutches, and then he puts that fire out. He'll bring the same decisiveness to the police, I think. And that is why I was forced this morning to replace a missing roundsman. Was it

inconvenient to me? Yes. Do I trust your brother? Yes. So tell
me, Mr Wilde, what the roundsman I replaced has been doing
this afternoon to prove his brother right.'

'The deceased child's name was Liam, and he lacked
another,' I answered. 'He hailed from a bawdy house owned
by one Silkie Marsh, with whom my brother is apparently
acquainted. This is another former resident of that den, one
Bird Daly, who states that other kinchin have been dispatched
in like manner, and claims to know where they were disposed
of. I propose to investigate her claim, and for that I need help.
And some shovels, I imagine. With your permission, sir.'

The smile that I'd seen hide behind Matsell's teeth flashed
into its full force. He quickly grew grave once more, though,
dark thoughts quivering behind his eyes.

'Silkie Marsh, you say,' he repeated quietly.

'I do.'

'Refrain from saying it again on Tombs grounds, if you
would. Other kinchin dispatched, you say.'

'Yes, but—'

'If they're there to be found, it's us who'll find them,' he
concluded, already striding away.

We decided that traveling by rail northward would have
placed us considerably too far east of Ninth Avenue to be
practical. And so, an hour later, I found myself in a large hired
carriage shared with a subdued Bird Daly, a sober Chief
Matsell, and Mr Piest, whose untamed silver hair flew about
his head like so many eager exclamation marks. Matsell
apparently trusted him, God only knew why. Three shovels
clattered beneath our feet, and whenever Bird's gaze fell on
them by accident, her eyes bounced quickly away again, out
the open top of the hack at the ever-dwindling buildings as we
left the mighty temples of brick and stone behind us. My own

nerves were vibrating like a violin string at the thought that Bird had fabricated a dozen corpses purely for the sake of distracting me. Odd, since I wasn't meant to care about police work.

'Beg pardon, but have you really the time to spare for this sort of investigating, sir?' I asked the instant it dawned on me that Chief Matsell actually meant to wield a shovel.

'If Silkie Marsh has aught to do with it, yes, not that it's any of your affair,' he answered placidly, taking up the space of two men on the padded leather seat. 'Now, how'd you come to know so much so quickly?'

Skipping Bird's various theatrics, I found the tale easily reported. Chief Matsell fell into a brown study at the end of it, ignoring us completely, while Mr Piest beamed at me with what could only be called ardor.

'First-class finding skills, Mr Wilde.' His ragged sleeves rested neatly in his lap, Dutch boots awkwardly clanging against the shovels. 'I've been a watchman all my life, and by day I also worked as a personal finder of lost property. Finding missing things, for a reward at least, is what I've always done. But finding a *name*,' he said, tapping a craggy finger to his chin – or rather, where his neck met his face and a chin ought to have been – 'that's hardest of all, sir. I salute you! Indeed yes. The chicken pox. By this hand, tonight I shall drink to your health.'

Bird and I exchanged a look that said clear as print *mad but harmless*. It sent a pretty little golden spark of kinship flaring between the two of us. And then she was staring at the brownstone houses, quite alone again. Biding her time until we reached the edge of the ever-growing metropolis.

So near the churning Hudson that happened at around Twenty-third Street. The grid continues as if branded into the earth, of course, though some roads shift eerily from stone to dirt while others are daily being recklessly paved. Broadway and Fifth Avenue are well populated even so far north and growing ever more so, for example. But Ninth Avenue is still downright pastoral. Had our mission been different, and a knot of worry failed to tighten just above my pelvis as we stepped down with our shovels, it would have been very homelike for me. We'd left behind the roaming street pigs along with the market stalls, and the air beyond the city was richly clear. No wood smoke, no upturned chamber pots, no rotting fish guts. Just the occasional fenced-in farm, corn husks shimmering bright as the numberless glittering rock formations thrusting up through the switchgrass, and the smell of the sugar maples that watched us as we marched to the vague intersection.

Idyllic, under different circumstances.

We stopped at the roughly delineated crossroads. Each of us subtly looking from left to right and back to front. Bird slipped a very small-boned hand into mine and looked up as if to say, *I only know so much. Not everything. If I knew everything, I wouldn't be alive.*

'Tell me,' George Washington Matsell suggested out of the side of his mouth, 'in what sort of light they would generally come here. Dawn, for example? Or by cover of darkness?'

'Dark,' Bird said in a very small voice. But I'd heard that sort of voice before, and it hadn't been used in the course of truth-telling.

'Then,' he sighed, 'if a gravesite exists – and I do hope for your sake, little girl, it exists, or I'll have you sent out West to live with a farmer who's lost his wife and needs a decent cook – then it exists at least a little away from Ninth Avenue. That's much traveled by night. Harlem dwellers use it to ride back from New York.'

'When was the last time you saw the man in the black hood before Liam disappeared?' I asked her.

Bird's throat seemed to clutch at her spine for a moment. 'A month before. I never saw him that time, but . . . but Lady was gone.'

I didn't ask her how old Lady had been, God help me, for I knew she hadn't yet grown to be a lady.

'Then if they're buried here, the vegetation will be very fresh,' I reasoned.

If it exists, my mind supplied me.

The grid location my tiny friend had overheard was so specific, we didn't bother to split up. We walked as far as the Hudson, where Tenth Avenue scrawled its way through the thimbleberries and cattails next to the sluggish slate river, and we walked back as far as where Eighth Avenue shot dusty and broad over stone-marred rills. There the sound of hammering reached our tender ears. Hacksaws barely audible in the stillness, rooftops barely visible over the crests of white walnut.

'There's nothing here,' Chief Matsell reported. And he was right.

The glance I shot at Bird was neither fair nor sensible. But it essentially requested that a ten-year-old girl not make a jackass of me. She glared back, a look that demanded to know how I could expect her ever to have been there herself.

'Mr Wilde,' Matsell said when none of us had formed a reply, 'my patience is dwindling.'

'But this has all been to the good,' exclaimed Mr Piest readily, passing a hand across his slack-jawed face. Far too alert for what I'd convinced myself was an ancient man. 'We've executed the preliminary search. Now, *where* in this terrain would make a safe hidden burial site?'

I hated Piest for an instant, though he didn't deserve it, when Bird made a coughing sound meant to cover a frightened shudder.

'You're right,' I said instead. 'We'll think it through.'

'The small forest over there,' Piest decided after a moment. 'That great mass of cottonwoods with the apple orchard beyond.'

'Wait,' I offered. 'If a man was shrouded in cottonwoods, he couldn't see another man's approach. If, on the other hand, he was behind one of the rock formations, he could look just around or just above to have a clear view of traffic.'

'Good, Mr Wilde. Yes. I see what you mean.'

I walked several paces into the sugary-smelling grass. The rest followed, eyes to the ground. And it wasn't long before we saw them: very faint signs of wheel tracks. Not where the flowers were absent, but where they were once crushed and hadn't recovered fully.

'Six feet wide,' I said.

'A carriage or a large cart,' Piest added from my left.

Matsell set off for the nearest mass of earth-piercing schist boulder and we followed. It was a great shimmering stone thousands of years old. We ought to have felt very isolated, but the farther into the woods and away from what passes for civilization you go in Manhattan, the more the island itself seems to be watching you. You either get used to being under thousands of eyes in New York, or you leave it altogether. But when you're at the outer reaches of the city, with the sky sprawled out lazy and clear above you, and the birds talking nonsense at each other, and the grasses whispering secrets underfoot . . . the feeling doesn't leave you. It's embedded in your skin by then. Something's *always* watching here, just as the shining grey stones and black ash trees watched us that afternoon. And it isn't always easy to assume that the presence is kindly.

Because it isn't. It can be pretty merciless, actually.

When we reached the back of the stone protrusion – the north side – we met with a horrifying sight. There lay a freshly turned meadow, all alight with wildflowers. Buttercups primarily, and clover intermixed with the tender grass. Innocent and very beautiful, so green and so yellow it hurt your eyes.

'God in heaven,' I muttered.

'Start digging,' said Matsell.

That field was so wide. It was wide, and it was shallow-dug, and nothing on earth could explain its being there. All I could think as I looked at the stretch of virgin growth was *far, far too long, and far too wide.*

I'll skip that part of the story. That part was only facts, and dark ones. No reasons and no meanings. And anyway, despite the heat and the sweat of the work, it took much too short a time. Whatever God was watching us, Protestant or Catholic, I can't imagine what His impressions were when we discovered at the same instant a thin white bone and a rotting arm, fixed with a crude snap between two shovel thrusts. Whose shovels, I can't recall exactly. Maybe Matsell and me, maybe Piest and me, but I remember my own instrument hitting not-dirt. I'll never forget it.

And only two feet down. The earth still soft above, the flesh still soft below, and the worms loving every loamy inch of it. It wasn't the arm that unsettled me, though. The fingernails were peeling away, yes, and skin melting greenly into sod. But next to it, the dead fingers curled around the object almost tenderly, was another bone. A part of a foot, considerably further decayed.

That bone told me instantly *many more than one*. And the flesh sent a secretive smell up as if to say, *Find us*.

Please find us.

We kept at work very hard that day, lifting heavy soil from what had once been children. But a single incident stands out in my mind. There are moments when you decide that you respect a man, and other moments when you decide you're on that man's side. The moment George Washington Matsell ordered Bird away from the view of her rotting companions marked when I felt something about the badge on my chest, and the man who trusted me to wear it, that I hadn't before.

'Get her away from here,' Chief Matsell said, still never looking in Bird's direction.

I dropped my shovel. Cursing myself for not having thought of it before, though we'd struck the first body only a bare three minutes previously. I ran for Bird, who stood frozen in a patch of clover with her lips clamped together to keep from screaming, and I soundlessly lifted her as I made for the nearest shimmering rock that would block that unholy sight.

'I won't go back,' she vowed once more, clutching my shirt in a death grip.

'No, you won't,' I agreed, though how I was to house a tiny stargazer I hadn't the slightest idea.

I hadn't been a copper star before. But I was then, I think, with Bird shivering so hard in my arms that she could scarcely breathe. And I am now.

For if not for us, who would ever have found them?

CHAPTER NINE

. . . There is a variety of ways in which POPERY, the idolatry of Christians, may be introduced into America, which at present I shall not so much as hint at . . . Yet, my dear countrymen, suffer me at this time to warn you all, as you value your precious civil liberty, and everything you call dear to you, to be on your guard against POPERY.

Samuel Adams, *Boston Gazette*, April 4, 1768

New York City inhabits the southern tip of Manhattan Island where the shipping industry booms, and when we run out of space to live and work, we naturally spread north. For instance, Greenwich Village, where I was born, is entirely encompassed by New York now, and the thought that high society actually inhabits the land north of Fourteenth Street constantly baffles me. While the urban city more or less ends just north of Chelsea, so many people share this tiny land mass that these few square miles are divided into twelve wards. And I was about to discover that when you've just unearthed an unholy burial site in the middle of the woods, it soon becomes a question of some urgency where you're meant to run for help.

Everything above Fourteenth Street, from Union Square Park to the squall of affluent construction on Fifth Avenue north of the House of Refuge, from river to river and farm to farm, was Ward Twelve. But the station house designated as Ward Twelve's was the Old Lock-Up, an unthinkable distance away from us through the woods in the stagnant and smiling green farming hamlet of Harlem, where fences crumbled pleasantly and Dutch wives waved to each other while having coffee on their whitewashed front porches, and it would have been nonsense to gallop up the Boston Post Road in search of help when help was much closer by.

So Mr Piest unhitched one of the horses from the hired carriage while I unhitched the other, which wasn't a bit to the hacksman's liking. But I can't recall our showing much concern over that, and we vowed to return the animals as fast as was possible. Piest rode hell for leather for the Union Market at Fourteenth Street, where Ward Eleven was centered, and I rode with Bird perched somehow both rigid and half fainting in front of me in the direction of Elizabeth Street to leave her with Mrs Boehm.

Matsell stood watching us go with one hand draped over his shovel. Jacket off, shoulders bullish, lips taut. Likely wishing his day had gone differently.

Mrs Boehm's anger vanished like steam when she saw Bird's posture – a concentrated movement that was at once balletic and unpracticed, as if she'd never learned to walk at all. I wanted to stay. But I burned also to see just what we'd found. So I tipped my hat to my landlady, who'd gathered the little girl into her skirts, and, as evening fell, I galloped back to the quicksilver, upward-feathering edge of New York.

Copper stars were everywhere. Two Germans dug deep at one end of what was now a wide, gritty ditch, an American rabbit and an ex-Britisher at the other, a knot of Irish between them putting matched bones into separate sacks. Piest bustled about, overseeing the lighting of torches. But they seemed only to make the twilight darker, and an evil-minded breeze was lifting the weight of human decay into our nostrils. There's nothing else that smells like that, and it haunts you for hours. Days. I walked up to Matsell.

'I can't credit it,' he said, not looking at me. 'That they're all from Silkie Marsh's house.'

'Why is that, sir? Surely, over the years, scores of children have passed through her brothel. That several are buried here isn't impossible.'

'No, Wilde,' he answered dryly, 'but you tell me if it's a shorter route to *impossible* when I tell you that so far we've unearthed *nineteen*.'

I made some sort of sound that wasn't a sound at all. Then I cleared my throat. My eyes cartwheeled over the scene. The bags, the white bones, the not-yet-white bones with frayed meat still lingering. Some tarps laid out, with pieces on them. Nothing made sense, least of all the conversation I was having.

'Could we have miscounted? Some of them . . . some of the pieces are very . . . They're fragmented, sir.'

'Heads, Wilde,' Chief Matsell said disgustedly. 'If you're as good at counting as you are at flash, I welcome you to try your hand counting heads. Piest!' he shouted.

Mr Piest scuttled over to us, more a spider than a crab in the torchlight and the expanding dark. Very kindly of him, I thought, that he ignored the fact I probably looked as if someone had just slapped me in the face. That was neighborly.

'Find me something,' Matsell said to Piest cordially.

'Yes, sir? What shall I find?'

'Anything. These are bodies. Only croaked bits of corpse. Less than useless, a waste of my time. Unidentifiable feed for the nearest potter's field. Find me a locket, a spade handle, a newspaper scrap, a rusty nail, a shirt button. A shirt button would be lovely. Find me *something*.'

Piest wheeled and disappeared.

'Wilde,' the chief said slowly, 'tell me how you're going to set about fixing this problem. Because as of now, you are fixing it for me.' Pausing to draw his fingers down his jowls, he met my eyes with all the fierce focus of an admiral planning a deadly offensive. I'd never been regarded so in my life, like a man being given a mission, and I held my breath a little as he continued. 'I haven't yet read you cover to cover. I think you'll surprise me. You can begin surprising me now.'

It felt like a dare. So of course, I plunged right in.

'Is the Democratic meeting over yet?' I inquired.

'An hour ago, perhaps.'

'Then I'll post up Captain Wilde, with your permission. Question Madam Marsh in his company. I need a better feel for the territory, and I don't want to walk into her brothel blind.'

'Wise precaution.' Matsell rubbed a hand up and down his craggy face, sending folds smashing into each other. 'Yes, by all means, go find your brother, and tell him that I want him in my office at six this morning. This is to be treated as the most jealously guarded secret in history, and also as a civic emergency. Why someone should slaughter children in this manner is beyond my ability to fathom, but we are going to find out, by God, and that person will hang in the Tombs yard at high noon. Go quickly. And do *not* visit Silkie Marsh without Captain Wilde accompanying you.'

'Why's that, sir?' A slick curl of doubt formed in my breast.

'Because,' the chief smiled as he turned to grip a torch being offered him, 'he's the only man alive to bed her and escape in possession of his faculties.'

Having a purpose grounds a man, steadies him. I felt better the instant I lit off southward in the long-suffering hacksman's carriage, now complete again and driven by its rightful owner. My brother was right where he'd said I would find him that summer night, its sky emptied of stars by the approaching thunderstorm. At the Liberty's Blood, Valentine held court in the back area as usual, beyond the crowded booths and the benches and the dozens of giddily filthy American flags, sprawled on a divan with his shirt half open and his gnarled chest visible, sipping something toxic with a stranger draped over his lap.

Typical picture. I'll confess to shock, however, at the gender of the stranger.

'Tim!' Val exclaimed. 'Jimmy, that's Tim. He's my brother. You wouldn't know it to look at him, but he's a right spit.'

The dark-haired, artistically slender fellow with arresting blue eyes glanced my way from the region of Val's lap and remarked with a cultured London accent, 'Of course he's your brother. Look, he's delightful. Hullo, Tim.'

The only thing I managed to come up with – and not adequate, I grant – was 'Something terrible has happened.'

Val was practically gleaming with the liquid shine of post-Party-gathering morphine. The passing seconds dripped off his eyes like blood from a wound. But then, all at once, he comprehended me. 'Up you go, fine young soldier,' he declared, and the unknown fellow called Jimmy was promptly evicted, leaving behind him an intoxicated and narcotic-impaired police captain and his grossly exhausted younger brother. Both of us missing key pieces of information.

'My God,' I said blankly, sinking into the rattan chair resting inches away from Val's. We reposed under a nicely stuffed American eagle draped in red and blue bunting, arrows glued in its flaking talons. 'I don't believe it. You've added sodomy to the list.'

'What list?'

Narcotics, alcohol, bribery, violence, whoring, gambling, theft, cheating, extortion, I ticked off in my head before giving up on a bad job.

Val cupped a hand to his mouth and shouted something merrily at a pal across the room before he registered what I'd said and turned to me with a genuinely surprised expression. 'Just a moment. What have I, young Tim, to do with sodomy?'

'That's what I'm wondering. In light of the chap who just left.'

Valentine scoffed at me, his entire face alive with flourishing dismissal, even as he poured us two gigantic clear drinks from a small stone jug. I smelled licorice and the bitter fire of diligently distilled spirits, and wanted a sip of it pretty badly. 'Brother Wilde, stow your wid. Gentle Jim is a pal of mine.'

'I could see that.'

'Jesus, Timothy, *listen* for a moment and I'll explain some basic principles to you. Regarding sodomy, since you're so keen on the subject.'

'I'd rather you didn't. But I see that you must.'

Having by now likely enough forgotten about my previous doomsday remark – and to be frank, in the shock of the moment, so had I – Val spread one hand wide, leaning over with the other to pass the drink firmly into my grip. I sipped and found it wonderful. It burned like sin's version of the Holy Ghost down my throat.

'Let's say,' my brother proposed, 'that you stay away from the ladies, all of them and all hours, and instead find your own sort and go up the back stairs to bed as a habit. You're a molley then. Am I right?'

I nodded, mute. The argument was unassailable.

'But then on the other hand, let's say you're *friends* with a molley – fine young Democrat, by the way, he lives here – and the molley likes you and very much wants to do you a French favor as a lark from time to time. You take my meaning, yes?'

I did. As well as another generous sip of spirits, while I recalled the long-ago night when I'd first seen that particular act, as a whore seated on a box crate in an alleyway earned her supper with her mouth.

'And then let's say you let him go to his knees every so often, and both parties are kittled as pie and no harm done. Where's the sodomy in that?'

I shook my head very hard, back and forth, thinking I could maybe fling some interesting but irrelevant thoughts about my kin out through my ears and instead focus on the relevant thoughts. The ones I was apparently now paid to mull over.

'There are nineteen dead kinchin, Val. Plus the one we already looked at.'

My brother's face darkened. 'What?'

'Don't make me say it again.'

In a very uncharacteristic display of understanding, Val leaned over to listen. I spilled. I spilled very nearly everything, including the tale of the ghostly gore-soaked apparition who'd collided with my knees, how she'd warned us of Liam's death, and explained that Bird Daly had led Matsell, Piest, and me to the terrible trove just below the ground. I left only one part out, which was that Bird yet lived with me. I simply didn't know how to explain that fact to my brother. Meanwhile, we were both eager enough to appear deaf to each other. Valentine didn't quite seem to grasp why Silkie's brothel was so important, for instance, not even after the sheer number of bodies was taken into account.

'There's a dozen brothels on every block, and identical, and anyone could have laid hands on the squeakers,' he said testily. The drugs were making him irritable, not to mention featherbrained as a whore with a guaranteed bed. 'Those dead kids couldn't possibly all have come from one place. Anyway, Silkie's are older. And why should she stifle her own source of coin? It's not sensible to think her involved.'

'Bird came from there,' I repeated. 'And Liam, the kinchin with the cross butchered into him. You recollect him, yes? The slaughtered kid you wanted me to identify today? So I identified him and found a score of others. Are you deflecting the point away from that monstrous woman because you bedded her, or because you're keen to have my fist in your jaw?'

'Because she's a Party asset. You don't even know her, so why call her monstrous?'

I pulled at my own hair. 'For employing kinchin as mabs?'

'What are you on about? They're none below fifteen, after all. How old were you when you first turned a moll's dress green in a meadow, Timmy? Or have you yet?'

'Sixteen. Bird Daly is *ten years old*. *Can* you tell the difference? Please say that you can.'

Val thought that one over. Pensive, he rubbed his nails against the arc in his plentiful hairline on the right-hand side. It didn't help, so he clasped his fingers together and arrested his knee with them.

'That's considerably too young,' he owned. 'You're sure she hails from Silkie's?'

'Are you stupid or just morphine-drunk?'

'Fooled,' he snapped. 'Silkie always savvies when I'm coming, after all.'

'No doubt. Do you want to know why I'm angry?'

'Not too keenly. You've been angry with me since eighteen twenty-eight—'

'I am angry with you,' I hissed, 'because we should be questioning this woman right now and instead I'm arguing with you over the principles of sodomy and whether ten is too early to turn stargazer.'

My brother stood up and drained his glass. I did the same, feeling the thickly sweet slide of the unholy concoction all the way to my gut. A malicious grin broke over Valentine's face. Somehow it turned a man with sandbags scored beneath his eyes into a boy in short pants.

'What a *copper star* you make, Timothy.' Rubbing salt into cuts as he always did. 'Such *enthusiasm*. I told you, didn't I? I did. Much better than my roundsmen; they haven't unearthed a thing all day. Let's to Silkie's. I'll even get you a tumble if you'd like one. On the house.'

It's a hard job to describe Silkie Marsh when you're looking right at her. The effect is all wrong. So instead I'll say how she looked in one of the massive Venetian mirrors in her front saloon. Surrounded by gilded walnut furniture lined in royal purple velvet, illuminated by a crystal chandelier that sparkled like glancing views of the inside of a diamond.

She wore a simple but perfect black satin gown the way the playhouse courtesans do, which led me to believe that she'd used to ply her trade in the third tier of the Bowery Theatre.

Plenty of rouge, artfully blended. The scent of violets hovered around her like a patch of spring. She stood with her white fingers draped over the treble end of a rosewood piano, a champagne glass in her other hand. Looking right at her, you'd think her beautiful. But looking at her reflection, you see that she isn't. Not the way Mercy is, with two or three flawless imperfections. Silkie Marsh had midsummer blond hair, piled loosely atop her head, and very delicate features. All of them even and feminine and fragile, soft in a way Mercy's aren't, with a mouth like a kiss blown through the air. But seen in the mirror, she looked like the theory of beauty and not beauty at all. Hazel eyes careless and blue in their centers, mouth smiling at nothing, making a perpetual wearied effort to look pleasing. Without giving any lasting pleasure.

And in the mirror, you can see that she's missing human empathy entirely. That little string tying people to strangers and acquaintances was cut clean through. I recalled Bird's face going white.

She's here, isn't she? She found me.

'I'm not certain that I should be flattered you're here unexpectedly, or very put out that you didn't give me enough warning to clear my entire night's schedule for you,' she said to my brother.

I'd just force-fed Val about two pints of lukewarm coffee with brandy in it, compelled him to dunk his head under the stream of a Croton pump, and fixed his copper star to his embroidered vest after he'd buttoned his shirt. He still looked like the edge of a serrated knife, fingers twitching like a smashed spider. But apart from that, and even apart from having the body of a fireman and the darkly merry, apple-cheeked face of a street urchin, something about him was compelling to look at in Silkie Marsh's front parlor. I wondered what it was.

'Or didn't you want me free to spend time with you?' she added coyly.

Valentine looked the same as he always did, I decided. I'd just never been in the same room with someone who was in love with him. Simple.

'It's business brings us, and not pleasure, my darling old shoe,' Val replied cheerfully as she handed us both champagne glasses. 'I've taken up police work alongside the firedogging, now there's policework to be taken up. So has Tim here.'

'I'm charmed to finally meet Val's brother,' she said with a calculated smile. 'He speaks so often of you.'

That was too frightening for comment.

'So I'm here to help,' Val continued. 'Go on. Palaver with me. What can we do for you?'

Silkie Marsh's angelic head tilted. 'Thank you, but I don't understand.'

'Your stargazers. One of them's been hushed. And I'm here to help.'

The pretty mouth parted, then wrenched in dismay. 'Do you mean to tell me that – no, it's too horrible. I'm not missing any of my sisters, but our page boy Liam has run away. Has he been found by someone?'

'Aye, and when we find whoever it was that found him first, we're going to have to string that fellow up by the neck, if you take my meaning.'

'Oh, God,' she gasped, hand clutching at Val's arm. It was a poor, cold excuse to touch my brother, I thought. 'We were so frightened for him, but we prayed he would come back.'

'This . . . page boy of yours,' I said. 'When did you miss him?'

'It must have been at least a week ago.'

And now I knew she was playing us. For it had been only twenty-four hours since I'd collided with Bird in Elizabeth Street, and that very morning I'd learned of Liam's body, identified him, and made the journey to the burial ground in the late afternoon. Therefore Liam was alive and still residing at Silkie Marsh's yesterday, for *They'll tear him to pieces* is a phrase undoubtedly couched in the future tense. Bird Daly, I thought, was nothing short of a godsend. Bird Daly was a liar pointing like a compass arrow at the truth. As I was thinking, I heard the unmistakable crack of a lash hitting flesh.

'Is someone being beaten in your establishment, Madam Marsh?' I questioned with steel in my tone.

'Yes,' she said, flushing slightly for my benefit. 'But I assure you that Mr Spriggs paid extra in advance for the service. With your permission, Mr Wilde, I'd like to cover the cost of Liam's funeral. Everyone will be so devastated to learn of his death.'

'That would be a nice gesture,' Val agreed, smiling. I stopped short of rolling my eyes only by the extremest effort of will.

'Are you certain that none of your other . . . sisters . . . have gone missing?' I questioned next.

'Why do you ask, Mr Wilde?'

'We're concerned for other innocents in the neighborhood,' I answered simply.

'People are in and out of here all day as if it were a firehouse,' she said with a resigned shrug of one shoulder, aimed square at Val. 'But I missed no one at supper tonight, if that reassures you.'

'In that case, might we take a look at your cellar, Madam Marsh?'

'My cellar? Will three dollars cover a simple ceremony, Valentine?' She drew her hand out of a red velvet purse and placed a few dollars in gold in my brother's palm. Fingertips lingering. 'Of course you can see my cellar. Whatever for?'

'A whim of mine,' I answered as Val pocketed the bribe.

We went down to the cellar with an oil lantern. And as I'd suspected, nothing was there. It was a pretty studied nothing, though. It was a square earthen-walled space, the air cool and well ventilated for being underground, with a few boxes piled helter-skelter and an eerie dressmaker's mannequin in the corner, stuck with pins that shivered in the light. Very clean. Too clean for a cellar – no cobwebs or roaches, and every cellar has roaches in the summer. If Liam had bled there and not in the barrel, as Bird's dress had already told me, no trace remained.

Then I snatched at the tail of an idea. A pretty spruce idea. A snakelike flit of excitement darted through me.

'It's good of you to pay for Liam's funeral,' I said easily, turning around. 'I wonder if all your sisters are as . . . generous as you. I'd sure like to meet one, if they are.'

'There's the spirit, Tim,' Val approved, pulling half a cigar from his pocket. 'Tip yourself a bit of velvet.'

'I'm happy to say that we're all fairly generous of spirit in this house,' Silkie Marsh replied with a knowing smile. 'Come, I'll take you back upstairs. One or two of my girls are very lonely this evening.'

I drained my champagne when we reached the parlor, and she poured the three of us more. Seating myself with my legs open in a masculine slouch, the way I'd seen my brother do thousands of times, I shot him a look from under my hat. He'd lit the cigar, and the smell of it crept like a spirit through the room.

'Rose is free tonight, and would be happy to know you better, Mr Wilde,' Silkie Marsh said, sitting perched on the arm of my brother's chair.

'I wonder . . .' I cleared my throat. 'You see, I'm a bit . . . particular. I don't like to be with . . . experienced girls. The ones who've had scores of others. I like to take my time, show a lass a thing or two, give her some fun. How old is Rose?'

Silkie Marsh blinked, running her fingers through my brother's sweep of hair. 'She is eighteen, Mr Wilde. But Lily is fifteen, you could wait half an hour for her.'

'That isn't quite what I meant,' I said slyly.

My brother flashed me a wink from behind Madam Marsh's back. 'My Tim over there is a bit of a devil,' he said. 'There's no harm in him, and he treats them square. Tender, even. But I'm afraid that it's unopened buds for my brother – once the rose has bloomed, you've lost his interest.'

It's a difficult job, forcing back a shudder. But I managed. I couldn't decide whether I wanted to slap my brother for saying something so foul, or wring his hand for catching on so quick.

'Oh,' Madam Marsh said softly. 'Well, I'm afraid we don't really cater to that sort of thing.'

'That's a shame,' Valentine sighed, 'because while Tim over there is kept busy . . . well, I'd need a way to pass my time, wouldn't I?'

Evil, evil, wicked man, I thought, standing up and applauding in my head.

Silkie Marsh's face softened. 'There *is* a girl here who helps me mend and sew, come to think of it.'

'Grand! You know what he really likes, though? When he's with a little miss, there's nothing Tim there loves better than to have a boy kinchin around as well. Show the squeaker the ropes, as it were, let him join in the game. Your Liam is out of the picture, and God rest him, but if you've . . . oh, I don't know . . . a stable lad or something, that would be rapture for Timothy Wilde yonder.' He passed her back the three gold coins.

I smiled seasickly at my horrible, depraved, ridiculously clever brother and held my tongue.

'And here I thought that there was no man in New York more wonderfully debauched than your sibling here,' Silkie Marsh said to me with a fond laugh, leaning back into his arm a little.

'You were absolutely right,' I assured her dryly. 'I just like to show the kinchin a good time.'

Assuring us that these requests would be no inconvenience, Silkie Marsh rose and rang a pair of bells. Their stable boy, meanwhile, had odd habits, she told me. Strange ways. But he was a good boy, and they loved him anyway. She knew I wouldn't mind his eccentricities.

Two children came down the stairs a few minutes later. One was a girl of eleven or twelve with her brown hair done up like Bird's had been, plump and sleepy faced, wearing a similarly rich nightdress, blessedly free of blood. The other was the identical bird-boned Irish boy I'd warned against stealing molasses before the fire destroyed Nick's Oyster Cellar, likewise wearing a nightdress, and lip rouge to boot. My jaw sank at the sight of him, and the air in my lungs went scorching of a sudden. Both were obviously under the quieting effects of a recent dose of laudanum.

'Wake up, darlings. Neill, Sophia, this gentleman would like to be kind to you.'

'That he would,' Valentine agreed, pushing to his feet. I rose as well. 'Is there anything upstairs that you'd like to take with you?'

Sophia, terrified, said nothing. Neill, in the unerring way sharp kinchin have, recognized me in spite of the grey strip of cloth and the brimmed hat. So he shook his head, his fingers flinching like the claws of tiny sparrows.

'Do you have shoes?' I added.

Another blank scared look, another negative.

'What on earth do you mean?' cried Madam Marsh. 'They live here!'

'Not anymore,' I said.

'Do you know, dear old hen,' remarked Val, 'that stargazing is illegal? I didn't either. I was just an unschooled fire rabbit hard after a tumble. But they told us it's against the law. Tough to credit, isn't it? So these two are leaving now.'

Silkie Marsh's rose-blossom features flew in several opposing directions, a flower savaged by a gale. Rage flickered past, then dull hurt as she gazed at my brother, then forced acceptance. I'm not a cruel man, generally, and I'm not proud of myself for gloating. But it was gut-deep satisfying.

'Is there anything else you'd like to take, then, Mr Wilde? Valentine?' She smoothed a hand down her black satin bodice. It was a brilliant piece of theater, for the fury had disappeared.

Val snapped his fingers. 'I'd near forgotten! We've a committee fund-raiser coming, Silkie, and I know you're a very scrapper for the Party. I'll have those three dollars back, with thanks for your pains. And a very good night to you, darling duck.'

Silkie Marsh passed him the money. Exit Valentine, her eyes charring his wide back. I wanted to linger, ask again if other of her kinchin-mabs were missing. Ask if she thought she could cross me when I'd pegged her as false. But the instant I did, she'd learn that I knew of Bird. And that gave me pause, thinking on Bird's trembling lips when she steadfastly refused to call Silkie Marsh by name.

So instead I tipped my broad hat coldly and quit that vile house with all speed. I found myself standing on the pavement with two shoeless kinchin almost identically dressed, wearing a madman's grim smile. My brother, his cigar hanging from the side of his mouth and his hands on his tapering hips, shook his head philosophically.

'That dirty slamkin,' Val mused. 'It almost disappoints me in the honesty of New York's population. I practically kept her for a ladybird a few years back, you savvy. And right in front of my face the whole time . . . I was drunk, though. Well, Timothy. I have one question for you.'

'Yes?'

'What, precisely,' Valentine desired to know, directing two stabbing finger points at each of the kinchin standing wide eyed on the street in the wetly thickening August air, 'are you going to do with *those*?'

CHAPTER TEN

Let every parent who wishes his children to be trained like human beings, improved in heart and enlarged in mind, beware how he ever allows a Jesuit to insinuate a single word into their ears.

American Protestant in Defence of Civil and
Religious Liberty Against Inroads of Papacy, 1843

The kinchin huddled together in the hack. Sophia's eyes snagged on things, uncomprehending, as if she hadn't been out of the house in a very long time. Maybe she'd never been out of it. But Neill's eyes were hooded. A brief, wild look of freedom had settled into dull silent shame. He'd wiped the lip rouge off with the sleeve of his garment, leaving a mark like a gash over his arm.

'When did you come to be in that place?' I asked. 'And how?'

He flushed along either side of his sharp little nose, through the freckles. 'Only these two weeks. Da was bricklaying, but he give it up altogether on account of the drink. She said her

house were like a theater, where people through wi' workin'
play games and eat fine things. I'd nary et in a week, save for
some apples I stole from a pig's trough. Then she wouldn't let
me out ag'in. Anyway, some of it were true,' he finished
defiantly, his reedy voice splintering. 'Some of it were true.
There was fish stew, and good fresh steak. I thought ye tended
bar,' he added. Suspicious, as he'd likely remain for the rest of
his life.

I explained it. All the while wondering if it was a proper
feeling for a copper star to want to wring Silkie Marsh by her
shapely neck.

'Neill, Sophia, I need to ask you something important.'

They said nothing. But Neill's ears perked, so to speak, and
Sophia looked watchful as she could through the mild
laudanum dose.

'I'm afraid that a friend of yours by the name of Liam isn't
with us any longer. Can you tell me what happened to him?'

'He were sick,' Sophia whispered.

'Yes?'

'In his lungs, like,' Neill explained. 'Bad off, he was. To see
him, though. Fightin' it.'

'I sent the maid out for strawberries for him wi' my extra
coin. He liked that. But he did na' get better,' Sophia told me
glassily.

'And did nothing strange happen then?' I questioned.

'Strange? Naught strange. He were just gone,' replied Neill.
Sophia nodded. 'Say, how do ye know of Liam?'

'I'm friends with Bird Daly.'

'Bird Daly.' Neill smiled, whistling through crooked white
teeth. 'Pretty chit. *What a liar* that girl is.'

'Bird is keener than you, and she mended my doll's dress
better than I could, Neill Corrigan,' Sophia snapped. 'She *is*

pretty, and her lies are pretty too. You've only lived there this fortnight, ye don't know. I'm *glad* her mother came back.'

'Her mother?' I repeated.

'Her mother come and took her. That's what Madam said.'

'Well, that isn't true. But she's out, and I'm glad of that. I'm glad of it for the three of you. Glad of nothing better.'

Sophia nodded, gazing tremulously out the window. Neill said nothing more for the rest of our journey. But he did unbend himself a little and sit as close to me as to Sophia, after two or three minutes more. It was a pretty generous gift on his part, I thought. Much better than I'd hoped for.

As for Bird – I liked her. Uncommonly. And despite her lies, the likelihood of a man in a black hood ever having existed would have been nil by that time, were it not for the evidence of twenty very real corpses.

We climbed down from the hack in front of St Patrick's. Getting inside after midnight, I imagined, would present a problem. But I didn't end up facing the great expressionless stones and forbidding entrance at all, because the cottage behind the cathedral had a studious light in the window. I knocked at the humble but well-made wooden slat door of Father Sheehy's rectory, flanked by grimy-footed kinchin. Sophia, as she heard footsteps approach, made a small frightened sound like the high chime of a warning bell.

Neill took her by the hand. 'Don't fret you,' he said, all authority in spite of the nightdress.

Father Sheehy opened the door still wearing his daytime clerical attire, his bald pate standing out sharp against the slick light from the oil lamp. Seeing who was with me and what they were wearing, he took a deep breath and widened the swing of the door.

'Come in at once.'

He seated the kinchin at his neat square table, going to his pantry for bread and a small cheese wheel. These he sliced as he spoke to us. I waited with my arms crossed and my back to the door, too full of rushing blood to be still. Father Sheehy very kindly asked them their names, and whether they had parents worth speaking of or no, and what had happened that night. Neill did most of the talking, and I was to glad see the priest wanted his trust before my information. Scant enough good he could do them if they were out the window the instant his back was turned.

'Eat this while I fetch you some things from the church storeroom, now,' he concluded. 'I'll take Mr Wilde here and be bringin' ye better clothes. Neill, see that she eats, yes?'

'I'll see to it, Father,' he replied. Neill, I thought, was a small man who liked tasks. Not a boy at all.

Outside in the dewy heat, air sparkling with almost-rain and smelling of the thunderclap that would surely soon engulf us, Father Sheehy peered at me, openly interested.

'I'd be grateful to know how ye stole property o' Silkie Marsh with her a devil and your brother the devil's best advocate.'

He waved me toward the nearest entrance to St Patrick's, iron keys in his fingers and a lantern in the other hand. I was willing enough to tell him, and I did, though there likely wasn't any art to it. I was too keen to go in a hundred directions at once, grow a thousand pairs of hands. Wanting to know Matsell's mind, if Piest had found a button and what the devil it would mean if he did, whether Bird's eyes had stopped looking like there were too many layers behind them. Father Sheehy's hands froze in the trunk of charity garb when I said the word *nineteen*, but otherwise he kept his marvels to himself.

'I want ye to know somethin',' he said slowly, folding a small dress and a set of blue trousers. 'When you need my help, you'll have it. And you will need my help, I fear. This is a keg o' gunpowder in a bonfire.'

My face twitched under the quarter-mask, burned slightly as if it agreed with him. 'Yes, but why do you say so?'

'Because at any moment, Mr Wilde, I fear your work on this case might be called off.'

Not only did I not fear any such thing, it had never occurred to me. A flush warmed the back of my shirt collar. I felt as if he'd insulted me, though he hadn't.

'The copper stars will leave the deaths of twenty kinchin a mystery? We're made of more iron than that, I hope. Though we're untested.'

Father Sheehy closed the trunk's lid with a decisive snap and leaned both hands on the table to look at me. 'Not twenty kinchin. Twenty *Catholic* kinchin who've nary been missed. For as long as this case appears *solvable*, and for as long as it marches in line with Democratic politics, ye'll be a man with a grave and awful mission. But neither George Washington Matsell nor Valentine Wilde will suffer the infant copper star force to be publicly humiliated, nor the Democrats to take a lacin' over a thankless task.'

'The day my brother and Chief Matsell take me off the case, I'll watch the pope shake hands with President Polk before a cheering crowd.' My voice was dark with indignation, harsh as penny pipe smoke in my throat.

'No offense meant, to be sure. As for His Holiness Gregory the Sixteenth, it would doubtless surprise most Gotham dwellers to learn that he's a bit too preoccupied with fightin' the slave trade, the modern rail system, and the terrorists in the Papal States to ruminate much over

America at all,' he added in a bone-dry voice.

'No offense taken,' I said tightly. 'What do you mean to do about Neill and Sophia?'

'I'll see that homes are found for them, better than their last if God grant us grace, and take them this very night to the Roman Catholic Orphan Asylum School. But I warn you: there's men as would have only one God in this city, and Him a Protestant. You'll learn it soon enough.'

'I know it already. But you'll soon learn that there are some men in this city more concerned with right than with God.'

'Separate things, are they, right and God?' he inquired slyly.

They are, in my opinion. But it would have been a fool's errand to argue so to a priest.

The storm began to break outside the leaded windows, fat droplets washing away the feeling of sweat hanging midair. The sort of rain that never lasted long and roared at the ground, welcome only in that you were no longer on tenterhooks waiting for it. The feeling a fellow gets after a beating or a fight. *At least now I know what the worst of it was.*

Father Sheehy gathered up the togs and his jangling keys. 'Ye needn't answer, though you'd never offend me anyhow. I like practical men. You'd quick see I am one m'self, forgetting the collar. And here you are, another practical sort – neither Catholic, nor Protestant, nor wicked, I think. Let us pray that you are not one of a kind, as in my experience your type tend to be o' tremendous use to God.'

I'd supposed the days following our dark discovery would be frantic and grueling. And I was right. But they didn't end up mattering very much, because the letter didn't arrive until

August twenty-sixth, and the letter was what caused all the trouble.

The morning after I delivered Neill and Sophia to St Patrick's, August twenty-third, we had a meeting of the copper stars of Ward Six, in the open judicial chamber in the Tombs, presided over by Matsell. As the rumor tearing through the police force like cholera had already informed most, nineteen children had been found beyond the city's settled spaces, he reported. Some of the bodies were as much as five years buried, some more recently interred. All seemed to be under thirteen, though that was a guessing game. Boys and girls alike. When the skeletons weren't too far disintegrated, they seemed all to have had crosses carved into their torsos. They were likely to be Irish, and certainly murdered. This was a secret, the blackest secret in a city where hidden confidences and midnight conspiracies were thick and prosperous as the rats. And it had better stay a secret, Matsell informed us, because the murder of an Irish chit called Liam in Ward Eight had been picked up by the newspapers and was now the full-throated cry of every bellowing newsboy. I knew this already, for I'd voraciously consumed the *Herald* that morning. The thought of the burial grounds likewise being dissected and shrieked about and speculated over sent a cold thrill down my spine.

'The mab who initially found the corpse has been going from paper to paper, trading story for coin,' Chief Matsell concluded. 'And if I find that any man of you has done the same regarding our other discovery, I'll make you *wish* you were a whore. You'll feel enough like one by the time I'm through with you.'

The room was a study by the time George Washington Matsell stormed out of it. Germans shocked but painting calm

156

looks on their faces. American rabbits lowly chattering. Irish, black and red alike, much more *Irish* suddenly, an undercurrent among them you could see in hard glances and mouths tense as fists before a brawl.

'Did you find any buttons?' I asked Mr Piest as the crowd dispersed. He sat in the corner like a shellfish in the crack of a rock.

'Mr Wilde, Mr Wilde,' he said, shaking my hand and sucking his withered cheeks in resignedly. 'I did not. Traces were as easily culled from that landscape as blood from a carrot. But I will find *something* for our chief, Mr Wilde, be it a thread or be it a sack of shovels. Mark me. I'll do it, or die trying.'

Mr Piest was laughable. But however laughably he was phrasing his subject, he spoke my exact mind. Maybe we were both mad, it occurred to me as I left the Tombs, going back home to look in on Bird. That wasn't exactly a practical destination, but it needed doing. I couldn't think straight otherwise. Since the gravesite, Bird had been much more convincingly unwell.

Mrs Boehm stood cutting pleasing scores into the tops of loaves, her ovens making her dark blue cotton dress cling to her tiny but vibrant hummingbird breasts. Her mouth was still turned down at its corners.

'Any change?' I asked her, setting a slender loaf of white sugar wrapped in the familiar purple paper on the table. A peace offering before there'd been any further war.

'*Danke*,' she said, looking surprised. 'No.'

We'd suffered an incident over a dough hook Bird had glimpsed Mrs Boehm using, just before I'd left for the Tombs that morning. I'd never heard anyone scream that way, ever. As if the sound could blot out everything else, make it all go white under a flood of noise. More pottery had been smashed, and again her hand had been blamed for it. Then she'd turned quiet, and that was worse.

'Speak with her, maybe.'

'I'll try.' I turned to head up the stairs.

'Good. And when you've tried, if she stays so quiet, I'll try again.'

'How's *Light and Shade in the Streets of New York* coming?' I added teasingly over my shoulder.

The rolling pin she'd just lifted froze midair.

'Don't worry, I read it myself,' I assured her. 'The one where the murderer hides the body within a display at Barnum's American Museum is my favorite. It's grand.'

Her lips parted, and then she hazarded a sly glance at me from under her barely visible lashes.

'Perhaps a scullery maid has been seduced by a visiting earl, perhaps not. If I read such things, I would know.'

'Bully,' I grinned, climbing up and out of sight.

I went into Mrs Boehm's bedchamber. But Bird, who'd been so still that you could see the currents roiling under the frozen-over lake, wasn't there. So I went into my own room, pretty scared she'd flown out the window as quick and soundless as she'd crashed into my knees.

She hadn't, though. Bird lay on her stomach in her long tunic-like shirtwaist and boy's trousers, a lump of coal in her hand. She'd taken one of my many wistful ferryboat sketches down from the wall and was adding to it. Snakelike forms threatening the ship from beneath the water, a hawk in a tree. Either the hawk had just caught itself supper, or another snake was forcing its way down the predator's gullet. When I came in, she glanced at me. Guilty over reinterpreting my art.

I picked up another piece of charcoal.

'I have to be along soon,' I said, shading the gently curled talons of the hawk.

Bird nodded, her hunched back beginning to look slightly less like a turtle's shell. We were quiet for a bit. I'd resolved to mention nothing of her friends' escape, not yet. Not wanting to say *Silkie Marsh*. She'd know of their adventure just as soon as the corpses left her eyes.

'What's your face look like, the whole of it?' she asked suddenly.

I turned glass for a moment. Brittle as a prism.

But then I took my hat from my head and thought, *It's better than Val tearing it from my pate when the liquor's turned him hateful and the morphine's wearing off.*

Better than doing it alone. Maybe.

'Find out for me, won't you,' I suggested. 'I frankly couldn't say. It's been a weight on me.'

Bird rolled up to her knees. Since I was also on the bare floor, she didn't have to reach far to pull the strip of mask off, tug the single piece of oiled gauze from my face. She let the fabric fall to the boards.

And then she tore out of the room.

A strange fearful sickness rushed through me, the drowning sort that can't be mastered even if a man supposes himself a man. But then Bird ran back in again with a hand mirror from Mrs Boehm's bedchamber, and she held it up.

'You look like a real flash dead rabbit, Mr Wilde. A regular brawler. Not such a one to scrape against.'

So I took a keek for myself.

The flesh surrounding my right eye as far up as my hairline was both new and ruined. A weird bright red with shallows rippling through it, the skin of a lizard and not a human. And she was right. It was so ugly as to be downright riveting. Previously, I'd been a scrapper in body and barely passable for handsome in feature. Youthfully healthy, anyhow. Now I was a wildman, a scoundrel who'd try anything, risk violent death over an acquaintance or a box of cigars.

It didn't suit a barman. But it looked pretty fine on a copper star.

'Should I tie the cover back on, so as not to frighten my enemies?' I joked.

'Yes,' she answered, smiling a little. 'But it would only frighten *enemies*, I think. Not anyone you aren't angry with.'

I was so grateful for her for a moment that I hadn't any words for it. I never did find them.

'I'd best be back to work.'

Bird reached for the flimsy cloth but winced in dismay at something. She held it up for me to see. There were charcoal marks from her fingers all over it, grey on grey smears of ashy dust.

'I'm sorry. I only wanted to see.'

'Never mind.' Hideous and unaware or hideous and well informed, I was still freakishly scarred, so I tied it back on, kicking the oiled cotton away in the corner as I rose. 'If you hadn't asked, I don't know when I'd have ever taken it off at all.'

I'd like to say that the ensuing afternoon was in any way satisfying. It was hateful, though. It involved me sitting at the Tombs with my teeth pressed together, writing:

Report made by Officer T. Wilde, Ward 6, District 1, Star 107. On suspicion of an unlawful burial reported by one Bird Daly, former resident of Madam Silkie Marsh's

brothel at 34 Greene Street, I accompanied Chief Matsell
and Mr Piest to 30th Street and Ninth Avenue.

I'd not hated a spill of ink so badly since Aidan Rafferty. And
two nights later, after a pair of miserable days spent speaking
with what seemed everyone in the city, I wrote this:

Report made by Officer T. Wilde, Ward 6, District 1, Star
107. Have interviewed various tradesmen (grocer, poulterer,
seamstress, coal merchant, liquor supplier, coachman,
maid, man of all work) connected with establishment of
Madam Marsh, to no effect. Apart from employment
practices, house above suspicion. Questions directed to
sparse residents near road where the burial site was
discovered report only unremarkable traffic.
  Positive identification of individual bodies deemed
impossible. No word of sinister stirrings has been unearthed
by questioning fellow Irish copper stars or their cohorts.
Growing most urgent and lacking other avenues, consulted
in detail with one Miss Mercy Underhill, charitable liaison
to the Catholics, after first obtaining permission from Chief
Matsell. Upon learning of the mass gravesite, Miss
Underhill knew of no one seeking out lost children, but
suggested the measure of conferring with her father, the
Reverend Thomas Underhill, as well as Father Connor
Sheehy, in strictest confidence, in hopes their own separate
but wide-ranging civic work may have suggested to them any
clue. By further permission of the chief, Miss Underhill
pursued this plan. However, no additional information was
garnered.
  Are we to imagine that these children were sacrificed
unmissed? Is it creditable? Is it possible?

It took every ounce of vinegar in me not to write next:

And what am I to do?

The following morning, August twenty-sixth, I came downstairs and sat at Mrs Boehm's empty table. She made delivery rounds pretty often, so I didn't miss her. Now I'd been assigned the specific task of investigating the mass grave, I rose at seven, being up rather late questioning folk who didn't want to be questioned. Bird, now that she was allowed to sleep, slept like a champion fighting for a title.

So the only thing to greet me that morning was the mail Mrs Boehm had left out next to my copy of the *Herald* and the sort of roll she'd come to learn I bought of a morning. Scouring the paper's headlines quickly, I found no word of the mass grave. Then I reached for an envelope marked *Mr Timothy Wilde, Copper Star, Elizabeth Street Bakery*, and I opened it.

Mr Wilde,
    There's sum citizens as says that the educating of Irish is throwing larning after pigs fer they might think themselves better than the white niggers they are once they do larn. Here's one Irish disagrees and see now I'm doing God's Work and am schooled enuf to write you this Letter.
    Romannists have suffered under Protestant boots for too long. But the weakness is ours and I know the sorce. Child Whores are an abommination against the Trinity and must be skurged. An Irish falt and an Irish sin and only An Irish can cleanse our own filth before God's eyes. Our most blessed Pope calls fer the swift hand of vengance upon Them only when clean can we be worthy clame what's ours and deliver New York into the hands of the holy Church of

Rome. Thus I marked the dead young ones hid north of the
City with the sign of the Cross they weren't fit fer other
treetment and know that I am apointed
                    The Hand of the God of Gotham

It's fair to say that I hadn't been so stunned in . . . well, three days by this point.

Because it was the most utterly *ridiculous* letter I'd ever seen.

Did the writer of the absurd thing truly expect me to swallow that the same man who'd write 'larning after pigs' would then coolly pen the words 'Romannists have suffered under Protestant boots for too long'? Barmen know how people naturally talk, and not even a madman would jabber so queer. Did the rank idiot suppose I'd believe that any Irishman would kill kinchin-mabs to gain a political upset? Did he suppose me the sort to credit that the pope breathed fire and yearly reinstated the Spanish Inquisition? Would any but a bouncing trumpeter of the arseward sort sign a letter 'The Hand of the God of Gotham' and expect me, an American born, to fear an Irish boot on my neck?

That left me with two questions, as I tapped the refolded paper against the table next to my swift-cooling coffee.

One: *How* in bloody hell had this whindling sheep learned of the cache of bodies? And two: *Why* in bloody hell had he sent the wretched letter to *me*? Any copper star could have sent it himself, I recalled within three more seconds. And if it had been a rare Nativist copper star, trying to stir up anti-Catholic feeling, I couldn't doubt that Matsell would have his hide one way or another. But it might not have been a policeman at all, so I moved on to the second puzzle. That one was simpler, of course. When I'd skimmed the contents again, it took me exactly four more seconds to figure the best man to blame for my address being on the envelope. I was meant to deliver a message to the Democratic Party.

'God damn you, Valentine Wilde,' I said out loud as I tucked the sick, twisted thing in my frock coat and ran out the door.

CHAPTER ELEVEN

Whatever point in this period of 150 years be taken
as the commencement of the power of Popery, it is
equally proved to be the Antichrist spoken of by
Daniel and John, inasmuch as its rise agrees with the
prophetic representation, and nothing else called
Antichrist does so agree.

American Protestant in Defence of Civil and
Religious Liberty Against Inroads of Papacy, 1843

I half expected him . . . I expected nothing good. But here's
how I found Val, when I burst into his rooms on Spring
Street. He was wearing naught but underclothes, this time in
the company of a stunning Irish lass with her ruddy hair
blotting up the white of his pillow (she being entirely naked, of
course, skin pale as dogs' teeth), and the following items
surrounding them: three pipes, each differently shaped. One
bag of what appeared to be dried mushrooms. A little brown
glass bottle labeled TINCTURE OF MORPHINE. Whiskey,
unopened. Half a hock of ham.

'Val,' I said, not caring about his wrath much, 'get rid of the hen.'

'I'll not. The very idea,' Valentine muttered halfheartedly.

The next ten minutes weren't entirely to the purpose. But soon enough, I had the stargazer out the door and my brother drinking coffee. Slowly. It was a challenge for him to hold the cup. I'd have pitied him, sitting in his linen drawers trying not to hash his guts out, were it not a tired and self-imposed picture.

'I've been sent a letter,' I said. Not kindly.

'And yes?'

'It isn't for me. It's for you.'

'Why say you?' He coughed messily. 'Did the culprit spell Timothy *V-A-L—*'

'It's a good job you can still spell your own name. Can you read just yet, or shall I tell it to you?'

'Best to call it out. And be quick over it, so it sooner comes time for you to leave.'

I read it to him. I caught his interest somewhere around the misspelled word *Romannists*. When I was through, he pressed his fingers into the postal sacks beneath his eyes and held out his right hand.

'Give it over, bright young copper star.'

I did. Valentine lifted the letter, holding it to the light of the window. Then, setting it down again, he pulled a box of lucifers from the pocket of his frock coat, which was draped over the back of his chair. Val lit one of the matches with his thumbnail and very deliberately held it to the paper.

'Stop that,' I gasped, snatching at it.

Val yanked his hand away and stood, to my endless surprise. I'd not have thought it in him an instant before, but now I was uselessly pawing for the letter high above his head as I watched it burn. Sometimes I can best him when he's glum enough from the night before. Sometimes. But he's not only taller, he's quicker. I felt six years old again, and he twelve with a harmless striped grass snake he planned to brain against a tree trunk. The snake didn't survive the adventure.

'Why?' Valentine questioned, watching the spreading feathers of flame. His fascination with fire makes me altogether ill. 'It's not any good for us, Tim.'

I tried a tack other than the physical as I watched the fibers being gnawed into slips of ash. 'But isn't it *evidence?*'

'Could be,' he admitted cheerily. 'But I think you mean wasn't it evidence. Now it's cinders.'

'You don't credit that it could have been written by the killer?'

'That heap of witless bosh? No. Do you?'

'Possibly not,' I growled, 'but how are we to find out who wrote it if it's *gone?*'

And it was gone, by that time. Val probably burned his thumb slightly, but he didn't show it. Just smoothed silken-thin bits of soot out of his hair.

'Who cares who wrote it?' Valentine asked.

'Whoever wrote it knew about the dead kinchin!'

'Ah,' he smiled. The rogue had completely recovered himself. It was such a powerful feat that I couldn't even despise him for it. 'I like that you think it could be anyone other than a rat Whig of a copper star – there must be six or seven of them – or else maybe a cracking mad copper star. Trying to stir up a mob against the Irish on account of every Irish mother's son being a Democratic-minded Party man. I like it almost as much as you supposing you can tell who wrote a letter just by keeking at it for long enough. That's rich. But a letter like that gets seen, and the party has a war on its hands.

Every half-starved Paddy off the boat turns loyal Democrat once he learns who his friends are, who'll give him a leg up, and a fine friend I'd be to the Irish if the Whigs saw this load of tripe – we'd be branded un-American, drowned in scandal. Voted out so fast our heads would spin.'

'And God forbid that the *Party* should suffer,' I said, sneering.

'Bless your lips, it's a fact.' He grinned. 'Thank you for bringing that scrap of blasphemy, Tim, you're right as an almanac it was for me, and thank you for the coffee. It was real white of you. If you would be so kind as to bugger off now, I'd be much endeared to your person.'

Breathing a bit too hard outside of Val's house, standing next to a post for tethering horses in Spring Street with no notion of where to go or what to do, I reviewed my options.

I could invade Madam Marsh's brothel and loudly demand to know what in hell went on there, on pain of imprisonment or worse treatment. She would either surrender or put me off. And if the second, the man in the black hood would be warned. Disappearing unpunished, should there be such a person. I could go stare like an idiot at the bones we'd stashed in a locked room at the Tombs, wondering who they were. I could badger an abused little girl with grey eyes into telling me things she claimed not to know. I could get drunk. Or find something stronger, if I wanted to resemble my brother even more than I already did.

In the end, I was weak. In a sorry state of willpower and growing sorrier with disgust, I went to the Underhills' house. Maybe I was a fool who only wanted to see something wonderful for a moment before admitting I couldn't avenge a score of dead children. But I thought to myself, on my honor, that I meant to get an earful of sound advice.

Val and I met the Underhills on the first occasion he took such a profound combination of toxins that I thought he wasn't breathing any longer. We were living in Cedar Street, in a windowless room resembling a breadbox with a single cooking burner and two pallets, and I arrived home one evening at age fourteen to find my twenty-year-old brother greatly resembling his own marble effigy. After trying to rouse him, I'd raced out of the house, witless with fright, and the first sign of help I could find was the lit window of the rectory adjacent to the church on the corner of Pine. When I pounded at the door, it opened to reveal a quizzical, sober man in his shirtsleeves, a pale woman deftly stitching by the fire, and an unforgettable black-haired little girl reading a book, lying on her belly on the braided rug with her ankles crossed.

There's some churchmen who aren't good for much beyond stirring speeches, but Thomas Underhill knows how to make use of hot water, smelling salts, brandy, ammonia, and common sense, and that night he employed all of them. The look he gave me as he quit our room was the kindest possible, as there wasn't a trace of pity in it. The next morning, apprised of the tale, Val had marched over to the Underhill residence and spoken with the reverend. It must have been the single most eloquent speech of all time, for we were invited to tea that afternoon, and I found myself sitting across from Mercy Underhill, watching in rapt fascination as she breathed cooling air over her Darjeeling. Val had then produced a bouquet of wild daisies for Mrs Underhill, vowing how sorry he was to have caused any trouble.

As for me, he stole a beefsteak from somewhere, since God knows we couldn't afford to pay for it, and cooked it shockingly well on our pitiful stove that evening. Saying not a

169

single word further regarding the night before, apologetic or grateful or otherwise. I was less than moved.

So by near-tragic accident I came to watch Mercy grow up. She wrote poetry and tall tales and one-acts every spare second, and Val and I and the reverend painted the rectory flowerboxes yellow each spring, and Olivia Underhill while she was living made the best election cake I've ever had. I could recall us sitting at their table after a fireman's ball countless times, Val flushing under the collar with gin and I flushing for entirely different reasons.

Being in a foul mood, I walked the distance, confident at least of bitter-chocolate-tasting distraction, rich and dark and irresistible.

The Underhills' lone servant girl, a pale waif of poor British extraction by the name of Anna, smiled when she opened the door. Then she frowned, doubtless curious to know why a quarter of my face had been deemed unworthy of daylight. But she told me right off that Mercy was seeing to a shockingly bad scurvy case along the East River, the entire family living off of day-old fish and week-old bread, and that the reverend was in the parlor.

It was like coming home, a little. There were all the countless bookshelves – I'd read most of their contents, waiting at different times for Mercy to show her face – and there was the clock with its sinister moon face, the window with the plush seat looking out at greenery and tomatoes tied to little scaffolds. But I wasn't expecting the reverend's expression when I stepped in from the foyer, my hat in my hand. The reverend himself is generally such an alert sort of person. Treating things like surprises when they don't actually surprise him, just to brighten the mood, that narrow face of his darting in your direction. But this was a look like a statue done poorly.

The parts fit together wrong, sad blue eyes clashing against the usual optimistic set of his lips. And none of it really seeing anything as he sat there with scattered papers before him.

'Mr Wilde,' the reverend said pleasantly. But something tense as razor wire crossed his face. And I knew what it was, too.

If he'd never seen me again, he'd still have kept seeing Aidan Rafferty, granted. In his sleep, in blank moments when adding fresh cream to white teacups, between the lines of tedious books. No matter what else he'd witnessed in his dark life, that vicious red welt along the white neck, the purpling of tiny fingertips – it would have left a gouge. But sharing the same sight, in two heads, without talking about it, just from looking at a person, is a different brand of indignity. I felt it as painfully as he did. I wondered if I shouldn't have come.

'I can't stay. You're busy, and—'

'I'm not.' He smiled fondly, pushing papers away from him. 'And I hope you would assume that even if I was busy, I'd want to know how you're faring.'

I sat when he gestured at the chair opposite. He was already on his way to the sideboard to pour us two very modest glasses of sherry. Unlike many Protestants, the reverend isn't a teetotaler. He believes humans should be able to control themselves, all humans, believes it like it's written down somewhere. Maybe it is. I think he keeps liquor in his house just to prove he doesn't need more than one drink. A stray drop from the lip of the bottle fell to the sideboard and he pulled out his kerchief, passed it three times over the spot, refolded the cloth, and returned it to his pocket. Ruthlessly efficient.

'Watching the pair of you growing up, living so near to us and doing so well by yourselves . . . you ought to assume my perpetual interest sealed,' the reverend continued, passing me the drink.

'And Val a captain now,' I said dryly.

I regretted it the second it came out of my mouth. I can rag Valentine all I like in my head, but I'm not meant to subtract from him publicly.

'Well, your brother has always danced a fine line between success and despair, but we do know why.'

I left that alone. Certainly our house had burned down, and our parents inside it, and yes, I'd seen their bones, and yes, that lived inside my own skeleton. Still. *I* didn't see the necessity of committing every social outrage alphabetically afterward, and then repeating the project, so why should my brother?

Of course, Valentine was already running with downright cross-cove rabbits by that time. He'd been halfway to rowdyism, 'borrowing' horses from livery stables and galloping them to Harlem and back, or convincing me that my ice cream wouldn't pain my head so if I warmed it first by the stove and then laughing when it melted into a puddle. Calling butter cow's-grease and sixpence a tanner. Taking a hiding for pelting rotten eggs at the retreating backs of churchgoers one day and the next teaching me how to smoke cigars. But when our parents were lost, so was he. Oh, he found us an apartment and learned to cook. Granted. After that, though, he either came home every night bloody and gin-sotted from a gang dustup, or else wild and ashy from a fire. Reeking of smoke that caused gaps in my heartbeats. And I hated him for it. He'd take himself away from me, I knew he would. He was doing it on purpose. And after that I'd have nothing at all.

How do you forgive a man for treating the only family you have left like a public dump? I wondered.

'Mr Wilde, forgive me if I presume too much,' Reverend Underhill requested gently. 'But these despicable killings Mercy mentioned to me last evening . . . have you learned anything?'

He gets to call her Mercy, I thought idly, picking at the wound. But I was still grateful. I needed a sounding board of sorts, and one I trusted.

'Could you ever give any credit to its having been a mad Irish doing the work of the pope?' I sighed.

The reverend steepled his fingers. 'Why do you ask?'

'It was suggested to me. I found it pretty hard to credit. I need a . . . professional opinion.'

Reverend Underhill settled back with his head at a thoughtful angle. Where Mercy answers questions with more questions, the reverend answers them with stories. Parables, I suppose, consequence of the job. So that's what he did, leaning the elbow holding the sherry on the arm of his chair.

'When Olivia was alive,' he said slowly, 'she did her best to convince me that popery was no indication of low intellect or morals. You recall when the Panic had well and truly taken hold, and people had begun literally starving in the streets, and we would find them in stables or frozen to death beside their own apple carts? Many of them Irish?'

I nodded. I'd been keeping bar, and Val had been snug with his fire and political appointments, but it was a cruel time nevertheless. An unforgettable one. And it wasn't just Irish. Former bankers were raining out of windows as a handy alternative to dying of exposure. They weren't brave or cowardly to my mind. Not after I'd seen enough cholera. I just considered them highly efficient.

'Well, Olivia claimed that those poor Irish were the biblical definition of "the least of these". And so she tended to and fed them as her own, be they lawful or criminal, and if the latter, be their chosen gangs the Kerryonians, Forty Thieves, Plug Uglies, or Shirt Tails. When the cholera she contracted in one of those dens took her, I asked myself before God why I'd never been convinced by her argument, as merciful and kind spirited as it was. Why I had insisted that charity must go alongside repentance and reform. After many months, God gave me my answer, made me understand how Olivia had been wrong.'

He leaned forward, setting his glass on the table. 'We do not countenance the sin of murder in this country. Or the sin of falsehood, or of theft. But we allow heresy – the greatest sin of all – to flourish. The Pope of Rome is worshipped as a very god in their religion, the sins of mankind atoned for not through repentance but through ritual, and what rank abuses flourish? What private atrocities cower behind closed doors when an organization is beholden to a man and not to God? You've seen the Irish here, Mr Wilde, their wills utterly depleted by the belief they must go through a mortal man to reach their salvation. They are drunk, they are diseased, they are loose, and why? Only because their very religion has robbed them of God. I no longer tend to those who will not renounce the Church of Rome, fearing for my own soul in fostering blasphemy. Olivia, may God rest her, was too generous of spirit to see her own error before their accursed contagion had infected her as well,' he finished in a grieved yet resigned tone. 'But I pray for the Irish, Mr Wilde, for God's forgiveness and for their own enlightenment. I pray for their souls every day.'

I thought of Eliza Rafferty, meanwhile, and the rats doubtless sharing her bunk, and her initial crime of wanting cream for her infant without denouncing the pope, and felt very tired of a sudden. If the reverend's prayers touched her, I couldn't see how.

'But you can't credit that a Catholic lunatic, leaving carved crosses in his wake, might be behind this?' I asked softly.

'Someone who has been raised by priests, perhaps, by the sort of men who hide sexual depravity beneath holy robes? Mr Wilde, the solution suggested to you does not seem impossible to me. It doesn't even surprise me.'

The moon-faced clock ticked morbidly in my head, a martial beat to a point of no return. It might seem stupid in such a giant metropolis to feel as if something bad is going to happen, because, well, of course it is. But the light seemed to me to have gone askew where it fell on the oak desk and the pretty braided carpet. Maybe it was the thunderstorm's retreat leaving us all alone, to deal with each other how best we liked. Which seemed pretty savage most of the time.

'Miss Underhill visits Catholics,' I pointed out vaguely.

'Against my will, she does indeed, though I can hardly categorically forbid her from emulating her late mother. But only in a charitable, never in a medical, capacity.'

My breath caught ever so slightly as I absorbed what he'd just said. Then I nodded, grateful for any facility I've been granted at hiding my thoughts.

He didn't know.

The reverend never accompanied Mercy on her missions, and she must have conveyed the impression that she was distributing good thread and cooking oil. And since he ministered only to Protestants, he had never so much as caught rumor of it. My mind flashed to Mercy changing the yellowed sheets of a typhus case on one of the occasions I'd escorted her to the east docks, and I swallowed a surge of disquiet. The day I had seen them arguing, it had been over entering Catholic households, not tending their sick at all.

'I'd sooner she minister in an actual slave pit of South Carolina than such slave pits of the human mind as she will insist on going to.' He made a queer little gesture with his usually nimble hands. 'It has changed her, in ways that I'm not sure I understand.'

My brain followed easily to the end of his sentence, but found the rest of his page blank. Granted, Mercy's spirit was an unlikely combination of her parents' – an oil-and-water mix of determination and whimsy that made her fascinating even when inscrutable. She had always been the most individual creature I knew, therefore, and so she couldn't change, could she? Mercy was already thousands of things I couldn't grasp. She could only become more herself.

'I'm only growing old, and mawkish,' the reverend added lightly when I said nothing. 'May God protect her in such places.'

There was a sentiment I could get behind. As I stood up to take my leave, something occurred to me.

'Reverend, if you don't mind my asking – feeling about blasphemy as you do, why should you be so tolerable about my brother?'

A quick smile flashed into life on his face. 'See those shelves?' he asked, pointing at all the books. 'My daughter's playground? You've read a number of them yourself, yes?'

'Yes,' I said, confused. 'A great many.'

'Well, when you weren't looking, so did your brother. If independence of mind is to be admired in the human race, then your brother is a most laudable man.' He stood, shuffling his papers into a neat stack. 'All the best to you, Mr Wilde, and please – I should like to be kept aware of your progress, insomuch as you can safely tell me.'

Walking out the door with a puzzled, anxious look dividing my brows, I realized that I was back to my Sahara-dry list of options. And getting stone drunk was edging further up the ranks by the second. When I'd shut the door behind me, however, I spied Mercy.

She was running. I hadn't seen her run in months, and she sprinted down the street with her black hair rioting against the tiny lace cap on her head, her swinging shoulders bare above the wide collar of her butter-yellow day dress, dozens of tucked pleats straining against her waist. Seeing me, Mercy came to a gasping halt with a smile forming on her face. I couldn't for the life of me fathom why.

'Are you all right?' I asked, only wanting a quick answer to the question.

Of course, I didn't get one.

'Mr Wilde,' she said. Breathlessly, on a laugh. 'I was looking for you, at the Tombs. But you weren't there, and now I see why.'

I tried again, harder.

'I'm grateful you found me, then. But what do you mean?'

'If I told you I badly needed your help, and that the matter is tied to your own stake in this evil business, you'd go with me immediately, yes?'

'*What's* happened?' I demanded bluntly.

'Mr Wilde,' said Mercy, her bosom still heaving, 'I think I'm right in supposing that you speak flash?'

Chapter Twelve

Ireland is in a deplorable condition – almost on the eve of a civil war. The police have seized a rioter at Ballinghassig, the people attempted a rescue, and were fired upon. Seven men and one woman were killed instantly. The police are said to have acted illegally and without reading the riot act before firing upon the men.

New York Herald, summer 1845

Ninepin *could* whiddle you both the whole scrap, if I *please* to. None trustier, and none belonging more heart and soul to Miss Underhill here,' said the lad before me, his pocketknife worrying at something foreign stuck to the sole of his boot. 'Tip us a wetting, copper, and I'll cackle like a right old tabby. Mr Wilde, that is to say,' he amended, glancing an unspoken apology at my companion.

I sat next to Mercy in a cellar coffee-and-cake saloon on Pearl Street, sharing one side of a grimy booth, staring down my nose at an uncommonly fine example of New York's news hawkers. This one had reached the ripe age of twelve, I thought, for the cigar in his grinning mouth was pretty well practiced, and his blue vest and knee-length purple trousers fit him well. He was experienced enough selling papers to afford to keep his clothing apace with his body, and anyway kinchin below twelve don't much like coffee. Rum, yes. But not coffee. The lad who'd introduced himself as Ninepin liked coffee considerably. We'd barely arrived, and he was through his second cup. Now he was asking me, not unexpectedly, for something stronger.

'Suppose you cackle *first*,' I suggested.

Ninepin scowled. He had fiercely blond hair, like a canary, his muscles of necessity and pugilism better developed than they should have been, and he'd scavenged a pair of gold ladies' reading spectacles. He kept taking them off, polishing the glass with a scarlet kerchief when making a particularly juicy point.

'Ain't as if I can't get it myself, is it? Free country and all that. Toady!' he called to the saloon keeper. 'A pair of French creams, if you please!'

The barkeep walked over readily enough with two brandies. Ninepin then paid for them in a style that was, I have to admit, pretty fine. He passed one to Mercy.

'Why'd you run off that way?' he coaxed suggestively. 'It don't fadge, my pretty bloss, and here you're back with a bobbie like enough to rub me to wit.'

'I've no intention of arresting you,' I simultaneously translated and replied.

He ignored me. 'We're flusher alone, Miss Underhill.'

'Do you think so?' she asked him with a skewed smile, passing her cup over to me and ignoring the child's, which he was already sipping.

'Dead to rights.'

'What if I told you that, while ever grateful for your company, I can't always quite grasp the sense of it?'

Ninepin blushed. Clearly unused to flirting, and newly sad of the fact. It was so raw that it was hard to look at. Like seeing a wet colt falling over. He pulled the cigar from his mouth, dipped the end in his coffee, and put it back.

'Don't patter naught other jargon, do I? Did I ever have kin what set me up with a brother of the quill? I ain't educated. Just in love,' he added slyly.

It was a good job I was staring ruefully down at the brandy a twelve year old seemed to have just purchased for me, because I know two looks flashed by under the brim of my hat. One was hearty amusement, which he wouldn't cotton to a bit. And the other was too embarrassing to admit to myself. So I let both pass.

'That were the reason you missed last rehearsal,' Ninepin said sadly. 'We ain't rhino fat blokes.'

'Wealthy sophisticates,' I said under my breath.

'Could it be possible, Ninepin, that I missed last rehearsal because I'd already given you the bolts of cloth you required, and I was needed elsewhere?' Mercy inquired mildly. 'Perhaps you'd permit me to attend the next one, after telling us both what you said this morning at City Hall Park?'

I'd been puzzled, but I saw the picture better then. Mercy had been spending her mornings wandering through City Hall Park for years, with plenty of bread crusts in her basket and plenty of bandages for those who awakened there and found themselves new-painted with blood. City Hall Park is ten acres of open grounds with about two acres of humiliated grass smeared thinly over it, the Hall of Records and City Hall presiding in the center. Three sorts of city dwellers populate it by night, and they keep pretty separate. The molleys like Val's friend Gentle Jim meet at the south end by a great basined fountain that doesn't work, wearing sensitive looks and pale scarves while waiting to do each other French kindnesses. The homeless girl kinchin who sell hot corn tend to shelter under the trees. As for the news hawkers, they lay claim to the steps of City Hall and the House of Records, where rival gangs of them sleep every night through our bafflingly long summers.

'A tale's what you want, a tale's what I'll weave.' The scamp grinned, showing a missing front tooth. 'This morning, Mr Wilde, we was up with the larks, and nigh keen to go buy our stiffs, when Miss Underhill here arrived with a jug of fresh cow's juice and we napped our regulars.'

I nodded. 'So you were about to buy your morning stock of papers when Miss Underhill brought milk, and you shared it. Then what happened?'

Mercy's blessed blue-eyed attention passed sidelong to me for a moment and then drifted off again as she tucked a little black strand of hair behind her ear.

'Well, then Miss Underhill asked us to blow whether we'd heard of any kinchin were put to anodyne, maybe flicked afore their ground sweat.'

I turned to her in surprise. 'You . . . you asked if they knew of kids killed and cut up before burial?'

The most perfect lower lip in the world tucked itself under Mercy's top lip for a moment, and it went straight to my gut. She'd not have wanted to ask such a thing of a band of boys, I thought, but how clever it was. After all, the news hawkers were as good as their own army. They had to be – they were the city's youngest independent entrepreneurs in a town where the word *cutthroat* applied to businessmen in both the literal and figurative senses. When the papers had produced a fresh edition, newsboys swarmed the offices, individually buying as many copies as they believed they could sell to the public based on the day's headlines and their own skill. No one bossed them, no one counted them, and I'd bet a double eagle that the employees selling them wholesale news didn't even know their names. They set fair prices for their wares among the various gangs, fought like pack rats for their own. The greenest of them was better equipped to answer Mercy's question than a society spinster of forty years.

'You did the right thing,' I told her fervently.

Ninepin coughed. 'So I said to her, she'd best look leery. Miss Underhill here is a kate, to be sure, a real iron insider, but—'

'Yes, she's wonderful. Now, sing it out,' I suggested. Mercy cast me a grateful look at last before returning her eyes to her folded hands.

'It just don't settle easy with Ninepin.' He pulled off his girlish spectacles and started cleaning the glass like a born scholar. 'A fine dimber mort like Miss Underhill palavering over stifled squeakers like that. Not with the cull in the black hood on the vag.'

My jaw dropped pretty far. Mercy, too refined or else too nakedly pleased to shoot me a look of triumph, cast it at the table instead, where it ricocheted back to me in spite of herself.

'You've heard rumor of a man in a black hood roaming the streets?' I repeated in shock.

Ninepin nodded grimly. 'I'm real sorry you thought you couldn't savvy me, Miss Underhill.' Brightening with an effort, he sipped the brandy as if he'd been practicing for this very occasion. Which he had, doubtless. 'Anything as I pattered strike you shady, Mr Wilde?'

'I understand you perfectly,' I answered, surprised. Val

had been speaking flash since before I'd known what it was, but I'd spent so much time avoiding his fellow rabbits, I never noticed my own expertise. 'Ninepin, it's very important that you tell us about this man in the hood.'

'On account of that hushed boy stargazer?'

'However did you learn about that?'

'Mr Wilde, I ain't educated, but I ain't a bottle-head.' He flashed a dazzling smile at Mercy. 'You think I sell stiffs without a mate reading me their headlines? You suppose I stand on street corners screaming out, "By your leave, nothing much happening today! Hot streets and crooked politics! More Irish arrive! Only two cents!"'

I was smiling before he'd even finished the joke. Mercy laughed, meanwhile, in such a way that I didn't suppose Ninepin would ever look twice at another woman in his life. Poor kinchin.

'Yes, we do want to know what happened to that stargazer,' she admitted. 'Will you trust us?'

'I'll parell it all to rights. But I can't go the proper way about it sans my lads. They savvy as much as I do, maybe more, and they'll leak once I own I've got the pig down fine.'

'Thank you for vouching for my character to your comrades,' I said with all the seriousness I could muster.

Ninepin winked at me, and then seemed to form an exciting new thought. 'Wait a tick. None of us like to give *you* any humbug, Miss Underhill – and I'll blow the gab, cross my heart. I'll deliver a proper rounding, and we'll not sing small, if . . . if you'll only trot along to the gaff on my arm.'

Mercy cast me a blank look.

'The gentleman would like to escort you to the theater in exchange for delivering information,' I explained, though I didn't understand it a jot either.

'There's another rehearsal,' he said a little shyly. 'Before the afternoon stiffs come off the press. If Matchbox stags you on my arm, he'll lose no time tipping it to Dead-Eye. And then Dead-Eye's cousin Zeke the Rat from the East River gang will have to button his lip, won't he, when I say as I know you personal?'

Mercy stood up. She reached for my untouched drink and took a sip of it, then rested her right hand on the pleats at her waist, offering her left for Ninepin's elbow. If God had granted a stockbroker second sight and a perpetually replenishing pharmacy, a human face couldn't look more joyful. It was futile, trying not to smile at it.

'Ninepin, the only project quite so important to me right now as learning about the man in the black hood is to put Zeke the Rat in his place,' she announced.

'Lord love a camel,' the youth replied in worshipful awe.

And I followed them up the stairs and out the door. Grateful as I very often am that Mercy doesn't spend overmuch time looking straight at me.

The theater, when we reached it following a six-minute walk, was a surprise to only one of us. But I'm pretty sure I made up for my two escorts.

We'd already been so close to the black heart of Ward Six where the world turns upside down, which is justly famous and called the Five Points, that I'd supposed we were actually going to that broken intersection. But we stopped on Orange Street, turning to a blank door. Permanent hooks were nailed into the wood for a sign to be hung, but the sign itself was on holiday. Ninepin knocked, a peculiar rhythm that reminded me keenly of when Julius hadn't any oysters to open and would drum curlicued tattoos on the bar top with his palms, and for a moment I wondered what the devil sort of other person I'd turned into so quickly.

Inside the door, though . . . we stood in a short hallway, where a wooden box big enough for a tall boy to occupy loomed next to the opposite door. The booth was poor secondhand lumber. Amateur carpentry, endlessly loving design. It had a window, with a piece of glass stuck in it that had once been in the Hudson, for a barnacle or seven clung to the green pane. No one was inside.

'Ticket booth,' explained Ninepin, looking back at me with the sort of glee that could fly a train over the Atlantic. 'Right this way. Step up, step right up.'

To my wonderment, seconds later I was standing at the top of a functioning playhouse. The deepening levels, the chairs (none matched and many burned), the light fixtures (two of them, rigged to either wall and black with smoke), the footlights (piles of wax with new candles perched atop their fallen brothers), the emerald curtains and the painted backdrop of a battlefield. Then there were the boys. About twenty lined up in a soldier's formation onstage. Or rather, what a child would think of as one.

'What do you reckon?' Ninepin demanded, but to me. Mercy had already seen his little bit of comfort, of course.

As it happened, *Valentine could have been a newsboy*, I thought. *Not a fireman. A newsboy. Just look at them. God knows none of these will first try morphine when they're sixteen.*

'It's flash,' I said, for I couldn't think of anything finer. 'It's dead flash.'

'Oy, it's a *rehearsal*, for Christ's sake, not a bloody morris dance,' snapped a taller kinchin from near the footlights. 'Don't be oafish, Dead-Eye!'

'Getting 'em into prime twig, eh, Fang?' jeered the newly important Ninepin.

Fang was a pock-faced boy of fourteen or so with his arms folded. The sort of strapping lad who came after you with a club and only remembered to apologize for the ordeal later, when all your pals were clear of the scene and it was cozy and the two of you could be human in secret. He started sneering before he even looked up, and then caught sight of Ninepin with Mercy.

We didn't have all that much trouble with anyone after that.

A few looked at my copper star and formed tiny scowls, but I was already well used to that. Fang strode forward with a little wooden stick he'd been using as a sort of director's baton, tapping it against his shoulder with his skinny arms yet crossed.

'What's it about?' he yelled. 'Might you kindly get that copper out of our theater?'

'How are you liking your proscenium curtains, Fang?' Mercy called down in response. 'To me the color looks very fine. Who hung them?'

'It were me, Miss Underhill!' shouted a tiny fellow with coal-black hair, waving from the assembled group with a wooden rifle. He was much older than his size, though – I could see it in the shape of his hands, his slouch, how deep-set his brown eyes were. Fourteen or even fifteen, and cursed with the bones of an eight year old.

'Was it, Matchbox? How did you manage?'

'Scrambled up with a rope, and Dead-Eye using the ladder and all.'

It didn't take long to spot Dead-Eye, who was blushing furiously and making use of a large cat's-eye marble in one empty socket.

'They'll do *The Thrilling, Gruesome, and Bloody Spectacle of the Battle of Agincourt* proper, Miss Underhill,' announced

Fang, knowing when he was outflanked. 'Supposing our Henry ever shows his mazzard at rehearsal.' He slung a dark look at Ninepin. 'We're none of us much for bobbies, though, since they've started marching up and down. What's this one after?'

'Are you questioning my closest childhood friend, Fang?' Mercy asked, stepping down toward the proscenium. 'I'd have thought you'd be happy to meet a copper star who thinks children are worth something other than packing off to the House of Refuge.'

Fang swaggered to the edge of the stage, where the first seats were placed. I headed down to meet him with Mercy. Ninepin, glowing like a lightning bug, took a seat in the house and began polishing his spectacles. When we were face-to-face, I saw that Fang had a scar running from his nose into his upper lip like the tooth of a snake. It seemed ever-ready to twitch up and deliver some venom.

'We like Miss Underhill plenty,' he said coldly. 'We don't like copper stars. Don't have much reason.'

'I'm Timothy Wilde. And I don't like the House of Refuge. Ever fam grasp a copper star, Fang?' I inquired, holding out my hand for shaking as sincerely as I could. A flutter of interest rippled through the boys, like a squirrel through dead brush.

'Are you waiting for a signal from God, Fang?' Mercy asked, amused.

'Here I am, come down to Gotham for a word with Fang,' Ninepin droned in a loud, genteel voice from the seats above us. 'Fam grasp the copper star, he's a bene cove. And buy Ninepin new cigarettes. You lost fair and square last night, you're shite at craps.'

A knowing clatter of laughter behind me. Ninepin was clearly the resident mimic. Fang lifted the white-gashed side of his lip good humoredly and shook my hand as hard as any man could.

'You're pretty natural about your friends, Mr Wilde, not minding shaking hands with a news hawker,' he said slowly.

'I've never yet been double-crossed by a news hawker.'

'Will you all tell us as much as you know about a very important matter, boys?' Mercy called to the stage at large.

A chair appeared magically behind her, carried by the gallant Ninepin. 'Miss Underhill and her pal need us to squeak about the cull in the black hood, mates,' he declared.

That altered the tone somewhat.

After protests, and a few sharp *no*'s, and one or two of the smaller faces going pale, I stood behind Mercy's chair with my fingers slung on its back while the tough-faced older youths gathered around and told us their story. And what a story. I'd set it in the original language, but it was recounted by over a dozen newsboys, with plenty of shouted profanity and disagreement leading to careful revision. It took the whole of my concentration to grasp it all. And the other half to believe any of it. So here is what they said.

Once there was a news hawker of the Five Points who went by the name of Jack Be Nimble. Or Jackie, when he was carousing with his cronies. From the time he was five, he could sell out of any paper, no matter what actual events the day before had held. Newsboys wait for disaster to strike the way merchants gaze out over the ocean for their ships to come home to port, but not Jack. He'd buy more than anyone and sell them all, even if the headline was that an opera house had been proposed, or a foreign aristocrat died in his sleep. He was loved. He was rich by his thirteenth birthday, or thereabouts, Jack not being able to remember when precisely his thirteenth birthday was. And one day soon afterward, heading to his favorite coffee-and-cake saloon for a dinner of custard pie and a glass or two of rum, he noticed something peculiar.

'Jack weren't no hicksam,' Fang put in emphatically. 'Jackie were always sharp as a shiv.'

Jack Be Nimble noticed that a carriage parked in front of a bawdy house was staffed better than the usual. There was a driver, naturally, for one. But also two others. The two other men were as big as houses, but very light and quick on their feet; and they'd wickedly cunning eyes, though their faces were hidden; and Jackie figured they were probably Turks, though granted it was dark; and the stealthy brutes could certainly kill a man without his ever noticing he was dead, though they did look dangerous from afar. Jack was a boxing enthusiast, which among the newsboys is akin to saying he breathed air, and so he decided that these rowdies were awaiting their boss: Abel 'Hammer' Cohen, the Chatham Street Jew. The only boxer rich enough to employ three thugs for one carriage, and the man who'd won a major prizefight a few hours earlier.

'Ever seen the Hammer?' Ninepin lay flat on his back and yet propped up on his elbows, moving the cigar from one end of his mouth to the other. 'He has the fastest cross-buttock throw I've ever clapped eyes on, and when he delivers you the floorer, half the time it's a nut-cracker. Sorry, Miss Underhill,' he added.

Jack and the boys who were with him – 'I were there!' shouted a grand and beautifully impossible chorus – hid behind a cluster of kegs at the mouth of an alley to wait for the celebrated man's exit. But when a chap did come out, it was only a servant from the household carrying a wrapped bundle in his arms. He deposited his burden on the floor of the carriage and returned inside.

Obviously, this bundle contained prize money. For that very evening, the Jew boxer had defeated Razor Daniel O'Kirkney, and after *only fifty-two rounds*. A badge of courage, a hero's wages. The clear thing to do was to pinch it.

Fang looked at me apologetically.

'We only meant to nap a bit of it. Like a good Christian tax,' he added helpfully. Aware already that, to avoid blame, God ought to be square in his corner.

Jack – and probably Fang and Matchbox, for their accounts had the workaday, cracked-bell tone of truthfulness about them – crept up to the parked carriage after having stealthily run round the block, approaching from the street side. The bigger boys hung back, fearing to be seen. A youth barely six years of age, which was ambitious even for a newsboy, who was called Fancy due to his insistence upon buying new socks when his old ones grew holes, was chosen to spy out the situation. He walked elfen as you please up to the street-side door of the carriage and looked in the bag.

'Came back all over egrotat.' Matchbox shook his head, a resigned false bravery in his weirdly adult eyes.

'Did he tell you why he felt ill?' I inquired.

He did not; the suddenly sickly Fancy refused to report what he'd seen in the bag. This wasn't exactly a mark of courage, and it went poor for him in a whispering and pinching fashion before Jack Be Nimble volunteered to see for himself. It was probably too much coin to fathom, or else something valuable to sell, and anyway Jack was determined to know the contents. He crept up to the carriage door quiet as a waft of cigar smoke. Hand poised over the cloth.

At the same moment, the man in the black hood exited from the brothel and took a keek in at the other side, about to step into his carriage.

The man in the black hood stood erect under a streetlamp, looking at Jack. Spine straight, eyes fathomless. An impersonal monster, the blankness of a nightmare you can't remember mingled with the sweaty solidity of a human threat. Every single child in the room, claiming to have been present on that fateful night or not, swore to have seen him again sometime or other afterward. In shadows, alleys, and saloons, mostly. In dreams. In their fathers, two of them pretty insistent that their fathers would stop at nothing to perform cruelties in the heaviness of New York nights.

'He's maybe a Red Indian, but then I didn't see his face,' trilled a child of possibly eight.

'He were never the Hammer, though. Abel Cohen had cigars with toffs at a chophouse uptown that night, everyone knew it by morning.'

'But he's a rum-togged swell, for certain,' Matchbox put in. 'Flush as you like, with a black cape.'

'You never saw him,' Fang jeered. 'Brave lad like you. You were back in the alley having a toss, or you'd ha' *stopped* him, eh?'

'I did see, you ugly sod,' Matchbox snapped, genuinely hurt. Fang had gone too far in front of a stranger. 'But he were peery by then, weren't he now, staring right at Jack Be, and anyway 'twas snitch! What could I ha' done better?'

Everyone was silent for a moment.

'We all turned tail,' Fang admitted. His eyes skated viciously over the room for a braggart claiming heroics, but came up empty. 'All of us. No one fights Old Nick in the dark.'

'What happened to Jack Be Nimble?' asked Mercy, her voice scraping against something rusted over.

The man in the black hood had greeted Jack, and Jack had stood straight and tall like a true-born American soldier.

Beckoning the lad over, the man in the black hood had pointed to the open door of the brothel, his posture kindly. He'd handed Jack a coin. They'd all seen it glint in the lamplight. Jack had thought it over.

And then he'd done a jaunty wave behind his back to his pals, leaving them behind. Walking into a door yellowed at the edges with welcome light. When he'd vanished, the carriage drove away. Jack had wanted to see inside pretty badly, they told me. From the street, it looked like a palace. But none of them had ever seen him again. Strategies had been plotted, and feats of daring I could never fathom had been attempted. The house had been long watched, whenever they were free of work, and regiments of men walked in and out again. But never Jack.

'We'd all thought he'd be back by dawn,' Ninepin sighed. 'I were only seven, then, but we wasn't . . . we thought he might a' paid for a tumble, see? We didn't *leave* him,' he added fiercely. I nodded. 'But we has to hawk our stiffs of a morning, don't we, so we must have missed when the man in the black hood came back and took Jack Be Nimble off.'

'What was in the bag?' I asked.

Fang shrugged. Matchbox blew air out through his lips dismissively. Several younger faces sought my attention like tendrils curling toward light.

'A dead girl,' one of them reported. As if in a classroom, repeating a lesson. 'Cut in half. At the front, like, in a cross. That's what the man in the black hood *does*.'

'Where is Fancy now, and may I speak with him?' I asked next.

'The bloody flux took him, something quick,' said Dead-Eye. *Dysentery*, my mind supplied against my will. 'He and John and Sixes, too. Last year.'

'And where were you rabbits when you saw the carriage before the bawdy house? Do you know the address?'

'I don't suppose I know any *addresses*,' Matchbox realized, laughing.

'It were Silkie Marsh's house,' said Fang. 'But Jackie never turned stargazer. *Never*. Don't think it.'

Mercy's skin faded and hardened at once, turning porcelain.

'Of course it was Silkie Marsh's house,' I said. 'When are you at work, selling papers?'

Dead-Eye glanced my way, interested. 'It don't take past nine in the morning to hawk the first set. Then we eat some flapjacks and chops, carry luggage down by the ferry docks for coin. Wait for the afternoon edition.'

'And after that's sold out?'

'Naught. We smoke, see the sights—'

'Could you recognize this carriage again, if you saw it?' I wanted to know.

The sudden pulse among them like a shout passing through silence told me they could.

'No.' Fang's pocky face was flushing around his neck and temples. 'We don't want a bit of that. Working for a copper star?'

'We're flush with lowre,' Ninepin added, assuring me of their riches.

Fang continued seething. 'Just look at this place, the new curtains, and anyway, *your* coin would ruin our reputation.'

'Fang,' Ninepin considered more slowly, 'Jack would—'

'Shut your bleeding head, Ninepin. Jack would want us to stay snug. We're out, Mr Wilde.'

And well he should be frightened, I thought. I'd have been frightened cross-eyed. But I'd already grasped by then that no one else in the entire city could tie that *particular* phantom to an *actual* carriage. My sole witnesses were half-criminal thugs-in-training. And richer than me, judging by their cigars. Meanwhile, they disliked me nearly to a man, and I'd only one thing I could possibly offer them since money didn't touch their spirits.

'You know what would spruce up a production like *The Thrilling, Gruesome, and Bloody Spectacle of the Battle of Agincourt?*' I wondered. 'But the setup here is swag-rum already. Very flash. You've probably thought of everything.'

'What were you fancying?' Matchbox asked, touchingly curious.

'It was a stupid notion.' I shrugged. 'One of you must already know how to make lightning. I've a lightning-maker pal, you understand.'

This was a brilliantly stark silence. The most tentative, *growing* silence. The little white rasp on the tail of the gun-powder stick creeping ever closer, joyful and greedy, biding its perfect time, and when it reached the firecracker at last, at last, green and orange and golden sparks would erupt into—

'We don't have a lightning-maker, Fang, we don't!' a sudden chorus exploded.

'I'll learn it, I've only one eye to lose!' Dead-Eye proposed with gravity and passion.

I glanced over at the boss of this less than democratic band. A growing hatred for me was curdling the fascination in Fang's hooded eyes, and his shoulders were getting steadily pugilistic. That needed solving.

'I think Fang should likely learn, and teach the rest of you,' I proposed.

Fang thought about that for a spell, chewing on it. 'That would maybe be a good arrangement. Supposing I can find the time.' Then, impossibly, a genuine smile broke over his face.

'Lightning! Just thinking on it – what Zeke the Rat will say when we have *lightning*.'

A door banged. The air around us exploded when a kinchin tore like an addict's blood through a side corridor. The wings, I think they call them in a theater. It was a stampede in the body of a single boy, his lungs clawing for air.

'You're missing it!' he gasped.

'What, a fight?' demanded Ninepin, sitting up farther and grinning.

'A hanging! Or better! The Irish have hold of a Negro, and they're to give him trouble. Quick, or you'll miss it!' shrieked the youth, streaming back down the corridor.

I didn't bother to let Mercy keep pace with me as I followed him, running for all I was worth. With any luck, I'd have solved the problem before she got there. With any luck, he'd been exaggerating. With any luck, it would have blown over by now.

But when did I ever have any luck?

CHAPTER THIRTEEN

*It is a singular anomaly in the Irish character, that
while the people are generous to a fault, and will
share with a stranger or pauper their last crust or
potato, they are deadly in their hatred against all
whose conduct has a tendency to restrict them of a
crumb, or deprive them of a beanstalk. Strange
inconsistency!*

New York Herald, summer 1845

We sprinted south, away from Five Points, where the
blacks and Irish are too poor to care a bent penny
about living together, flying toward the edge of the vast burned
area. The air rang weirdly quiet in my ears. The few people I
did see hunched sober faced over their little cobblers' stalls
and their poison-green apple carts, desperately minding their
own business. There ought to have been Irish quarreling hotly
with the peddlers, Yidishers hawking aprons, an Indian selling
pelts, someone other than the permanent fixtures of the
slumbering pigs. Even my boots pounded much too loud,

196

having outpaced the boys by half a block. I passed half a building plastered in oily soot on Nassau Street, and another, and another, and a tension like a finger on a pistol's trigger caught at my breath, and I knew I was almost there.

I could have said what the brawl was about without ever seeing it, because they're all the same. These mob mushrooms our city sprouts so readily. *It's about God. It's about money. It's about work. It's about helplessness. And whatever it's supposed to be about, it's about nothing at all.* But I'll be the first to admit that I turned ashen when I did reach my destination, for I'd been ill informed.

They weren't about to hang a black at all.

'You see this, the *price* ye pay for your *avarice?*' a grotesquely drunk Irishman screamed at a cowed little white native wearing a swallowtail coat and yellow breeches. 'The life of a nigger isn't much, I'll grant, but if ye sit up and take *notice*, by Jesus, he'll have served a grander purpose than his hide would ha' predicted!'

The speaker was a giant – black haired, his face heavily scored with lines and burned dark by our merciless August. His loose shirt hung ragged and filthy from his bullish shoulders and he'd no waistcoat, only drab nankeen trousers that had more than once been all night out of doors. I knew several things about him just by looking: he'd only enough money for the whiskey he'd drunk that morning. Not a cent more. There's a particular set to the eyes when that happens, whites hardening into bone. The turn of his mouth told me that something both terrible and wretchedly unfair had befallen him. His massive hands were a wreck, and that combined with his skin told me either construction work or hauling stones to the burned district had bought his last drink.

One of those hands was holding a torch in blazing midsummer daylight.

He'd two friends hovering nearby, likewise sloppy drunk and dividing their attention between sweating and standing. A non-threat for the moment. And just behind them, bound to a lonely support beam at the street edge of the unfinished building, was my colored friend Julius Carpenter, employee of Nick's Oyster Cellar when it was yet standing. A heap of pine faggots had been scattered around his feet. I stopped dead, gasping, right in front of the bastard who'd arranged the scene. I didn't grudge Julius's not greeting me, for they'd shoved a dirty turnip in his mouth, with a hole drilled through it for the rope to keep it in place. Julius was tied down too well for his limbs to be doing him any good. So his eyes were channeling all his useless strength away from his hands and his stretched-to-cracking lips, just a pair of pupils gnawing into my chest.

I doubt I'd have forgiven the stake and the torch in any event. I'm not a very forgiving sort, after all. I never have been. But Julius can taste the difference between twenty sorts of oysters set in front of him, even without their particular shells, and the manure-covered turnip had a hole in it for a rope. Planned. Specific. It was a *particular* evil, and it crippled my mercy with a leaded cudgel.

'What in *hell* do you think you're doing?' I thundered.

Volume was crucial. If the mob lost the thread of the conversation, I could easily pay for it. But this wasn't a proper mob at all, only an audience of miserable Irish and hardened natives staring at an arresting bloodsport. The same sort who watch lone terriers fighting hordes of rabid city rats. Not a black in sight, of course, I didn't even have to look for them. They were hiding their children in cupboards and burying their coin beneath the privy pit. The usual precautions.

'Settlin' a bit of an *argument*,' the blackguard sneered. 'With that *coward* over there!'

He waved at the yellow-trousered businessman with the mutton chops and the silver beard on his neck below his smooth chin, who stood wringing his hands fecklessly at a safe twenty-yard distance. I can't abide feckless men. Maybe it's another effect of growing up with my brother, and a better one than most, but that brand of weakling makes me feel a bit vicious. As if our all too pragmatic city wants me to run them off into the trees.

'You're already under arrest for disorderly conduct and assault and battery,' I reported to my real opponent, 'and you're already serving a stretch at the Tombs, but if you untie that man this *instant*, I suppose I *won't* make it assault with intent to kill.'

I'd memorized the list of things that were actually criminal versus theoretically criminal the day I started, thinking it might come in handy. It had, four times.

'And who's going to *arrest me*?'

'I am, you ignorant cow.' I flapped the left lapel of my frock coat with the copper star pinned to it.

'Oh. A *copper star*,' he spat. 'I've heard of you lot. About as frightening as a sow's teat. Ye can't bully me, you villain.'

'I'm not bullying you, I'm incarcerating you.'

The brute didn't react much to that. Seemed to be thinking, or whatever passed for thinking when he was in that black of a pit.

'Is that *really* a copper star?' a nervous male bystander behind me wondered. 'By Jove, I'd not yet seen one.'

'When I pictured them, I'd imagined them bigger,' another man remarked.

It wouldn't have been much to the purpose to respond to these comments, so I ignored them.

'They'd not told me that the copper stars were t' be nigger-lovers,' the soused Irish wretch leered. 'That'll make thrashing them all the better sport, though.'

Civilized conversation seemed to have reached a definite wall. But when I stepped forward to untie Julius, already in a hot rage and now practically seeing cinders, I had a waving torch in my face for my trouble.

I ducked. I ducked again.

Throwing myself a bit backward, I avoided a swipe that would have set my torso aflame.

Gasps breezed through the air all around me, a hushed cry from a weeping moll. *Steady yourself, you bloody milksop*, I was thinking as my heart tried to escape the cage of my ribs. *The only way he'll know you hate fire is if you tell him.*

I stopped ducking, therefore, and stopped dodging, and took two steps forward. Calling over my shoulder to the sniveling native gentleman with the infuriating yellow trousers.

'Just what is this mongrel's argument with you?'

'I . . .' The wringing hands pressed very tight together for a moment. 'I sacked my construction staff. I've every right! I own the building. The building to be built, rather, I own the *lot*, you see, and I couldn't conscience it any longer, I—'

'Ye couldn't conscience the *pennies* that you paid us above what you paid the *slave crew* you went a hirin' after!' the Irishman bellowed. 'And my wife in a *family* way!'

'You're paid the *same*, I tell you, that wasn't the— I can't be expected—'

'I'm going to make this very clear,' I announced loudly. 'I take it that you three, and your other mates with more sense than to be here, were all sacked and a black crew took your place. I'm sorry to hear it. But for every *second* that you don't untie that man, I'll add another charge to your accounting before the judge.'

'Ye can't even get *near* me, you gabby little weasel, and you expect—'

'Assault with intent to kill,' I interrupted. The crowd grew hushed.

'I'll set ye afire, you runty—'

'Fighting in the street,' I added.

'Fuck off,' he scoffed. 'Take my torch, lads, light the—'

'Insanity,' I snapped. 'Murder. Insulting females in the street, for I'm dead certain none of them want to be looking at this spectacle. Threatening life. Intoxication with disorderly conduct. Keep it up, why don't you.'

'Stop this,' a choked voice commanded from behind me.

I knew who it was, would have known that voice from the bottom of the Hudson. But I'd one eye on the torch and another on the crowd and the trio of thugs, and so before I could do anything, the voice was at my elbow. Maybe I'm less useful than I like to imagine myself.

'Miss Underhill, get away from here,' I said.

She didn't. Mercy walked right past me.

The trio of rowdies were too dazed with liquor and the strain of treading the desperate edge of their world to even object. Shocked into simply watching. Everyone fell silent as churchyards when a woman, and not a very formidable-looking woman either, but a woman with blue eyes set far apart and a grace like a cool wind off the ocean, marched up and started untying my former coworker.

It was suddenly a very, very bad situation.

'Get that uppish whore out o' this,' snarled the villain who'd started it all.

One of his two pals was just the right sort of drunk to think that wrenching a slightly built woman off a pile of timber and a black laborer was about his style. He tore Mercy away from Julius. When he did, I dove forward, and almost got a mouthful of fire as a consequence.

I didn't care, though, not by that time. Finally I managed to dart around the much bigger man, *finally* I was in the thick of it, and finally I was within two feet of the cur who was bruising Mercy's upper arms as she struggled wildly, and I determined to make the wretches bleed before they bested us. That being the way it's done around here. The one touching Mercy would get a fist in the throat, and then when they killed me I'd at least have died properly.

I planted my feet. Then, in the oldest trick known to street fighting, I screamed at the top of my lungs.

It startled the thug holding Mercy enough for him to loosen his grip on one of her arms, just before my fist landed where his neck met his collarbone.

He collapsed, windpipe half crushed, and I caught Mercy around the waist before she went down with him. The others listed drunkenly away from me, likely supposing me cracked. That was fine. It meant a wider berth while they took a better measure, the ringleader shoving his torch out in front of him as if I might attack at any moment. Shivering, whiskey stupid, but not a likely candidate for my pity. When Mercy had her feet back, she rushed for the makeshift funeral pyre. My pocket knife was out an instant later.

'Here, I have it,' I hissed, kneeling. 'Back away.'

'I won't,' she replied, tearing at the hemp ropes tying Julius down.

'Then for God's sake, get that thing out of his mouth.'

Not knowing how long he'd been trapped, I gripped my

friend's shirt at his lower back as I freed him from the ropes. But he was steady enough, though his hands trembled slightly below his bloody wrists. Julius broke away, half stumbling on the piled-up faggots. Bending over, he finally tore the repulsive object Mercy had been loosening from his mouth. He gagged once or twice, shaking. Meanwhile, I kept one eye on Mercy and one on the slowly recovering drunks, who stood whispering together in a poisonous knot.

'Are you all right?' I asked, glancing over my shoulder.

Julius coughed, his hands on his trouser knees. 'It's nice to see you again,' he managed. 'Thought you'd left town.'

'I moved to Ward Six.'

'Well, if that isn't the most damn fool thing I ever heard. What was wrong with Ward One?'

'Copper star,' came an evil singsong. One I was steadily tiring of.

The torch-brandishing Irishman had found not only his courage but a fresh stock of allies. Three new men, laborers from the crowd, I thought, now stood with the original set of criminals. Two had knives, and I caught the flash of brass knuckles from the third. Apparently New York was about to watch one of their new copper stars being cut to death. Fine entertainment.

'*Cease!*' thundered a deeply strange voice.

I could have laughed at that sound. But it's Val's job, after all, to laugh at things that aren't funny. And anyway, as I turned my head, I felt a rawboned idiot for having forgotten that there was more than one of me in this city.

Mr Piest stood in all his weird crustacean glory at the head of a band of copper stars – about twenty-five of us, fully half of Ward Six – everyone armed with cudgels and tapping them menacingly against boot tops. The native rabbits seemed pretty pleased about the situation. Or better pleased than the Irish police, who were pointedly not looking at one another. They stood just as iron faced, though, stalwart and neatly aligned, a picture of professional determination. Red hair and black hair and blond and brown packed all together, with already-tarnishing little stars pinned to their coats.

The Irishman screamed something in his own language. It sent an angry red hue over the faces of policemen I knew from the Tombs. Mr Connell's broad, intelligent face froze instantly, and the phrase slid a trapdoor over Mr Kildare's. I wondered why, knowing them both to be steady policemen of good character – people I'd swapped stories with of aching legs after a sixteen-hour shift, of being hissed at in the streets.

And then the drunken thugs flew straight at the copper stars in a fury. Like a family of ravens headed into a glass windowpane.

Breaking their cluster apart, several of the police shouted. I heard warnings, gleeful yells, one violently delighted 'Have at you, you dirty sons of bitches', but the outcome was never much in question. Flying cudgels, twisting bodies like an acrobat's routine at the Gardens, a shriek from one of the drunks as a particularly efficient copper star shattered his leg underneath him.

And then there was only the ringleader left standing, waving his torch at his enemies like a sword.

Mr Connell, a scarlet-haired Irishman I heartily liked and had twice shared my spent newspaper with at the Tombs, stepped behind him neatly and felled him with a graceful loose-elbowed cudgel swing to the back of the head. Once he was down, a few American boots headed for his ribs. More shouts went up, a midnight laugh that reminded me of Val's. I wondered whether we ought to be doing things like that, kicking felled culprits, but Mr Connell stepped in with a sober-faced snarl and solved the problem, shoving a pair of overly enthusiastic rabbits away from his captive.

I worked at getting my wind back. Everything slowly stilled. The news hawkers were gathering around me, suspicion wiped clean from their hardscrabble faces. It had been replaced by soft-lipped awe.

'That,' breathed Ninepin, his spectacles in one hand and his polishing cloth dangling in the other, 'were poetry. That were watching the devil at lying. "Insanity. Murder. Insulting females in—"'

'Where has Miss Underhill gone?' I questioned urgently.

'Run off, said she needed some quiet,' said Fang. 'And *Miss Underhill*! Lord, what a pelt she was in! She ought to be a queen, I tell you. Queen of Gotham.'

'Listen, will you stay here just for a moment?' I asked Julius. 'I need your statement, after a word with the other police. You're all right?'

He nodded, though he looked as if he'd prefer to be a great deal less visible. I ran over to the group of copper stars, who were triumphantly fitting clumsy iron bracelets on their several stunned captives. The brute who'd started it all slept the sleep of the wicked. And appeared considerably more misshapen than previous.

'That was timely,' I said.

'On your part doubly so, Mr Wilde, I take it!' Mr Piest exclaimed, shaking my hand. 'Now, I myself am a bit more cautious. It comes of long years on the watch. When a mob is forming next time, be in a mob yourself, sir! That is the New York way of doing things.'

'I suppose it is, yes. Mr Kildare!' I called to the roundsman whose beat had bordered my own.

'Mr Wilde,' he returned gruffly in his brogue thick as peat moss.

'What did that rough say to you? Before he rushed the copper stars?'

'That en't a bit important, are it now?'

'It seemed to be to you.'

Mr Connell brushed past me, dragging the smaller of the sottish henchmen toward a cart. He's a calm, square fellow who thinks hard before answering anything. 'In league wi' the landlords, Mr Wilde. We Irish copper stars, he meant. *Hirelings* o' the *landlords*. It don't have an exact translation. Serf, maybe,' he added over his shoulder, 'though slave comes closer for an American.'

Then I recalled the other scoundrel to blame for all this. Turning about, I finally spied the lot owner with the silver neck beard and the miserably sunny breeches as he woefully watched his former employees being carted off, looking caved in, dust settling around him.

'You've plenty to answer for, though none of it'll be charged to your account,' I growled. 'What the devil did you *think* would happen, sacking an all-Irish crew to gain a black one?'

'It isn't as if *Americans* will work for the wage I'm able to afford and thus spare me all this trouble, is it?' he whined. 'And I couldn't conscience an Irish crew any longer, not as I'm a Christian man, sir, nor yet a citizen of Manhattan!'

'But *why* would you say that, having already hired—'

My question died when Mr Piest plucked at my elbow, leading me a few feet away from the inept property owner and the self-satisfied copper stars. He scuttled behind a lamppost that didn't shield us in the smallest part and pulled a folded-up newspaper scrap from his fraying inner coat pocket.

'You were doubtless hot on the trail today from early morning without a second to spare for politics, but things have . . . changed,' he informed me gravely, his worried brows twitching like lobster claws. 'Matsell wants you in his office at the Tombs.'

He flitted away, and I opened the *Herald* clipping. I didn't need long to look at it to see what had happened, and my fist met my brow as I cursed myself for checking only the headlines that morning. It was a letter to the editor: 'Thus I marked the dead young ones hid north of the City with the sign of the Cross they weren't fit fer other treetment and know that I am apointed . . .'

'God *damn it*,' I swore under my breath, crushing the thing into a ball.

Somebody had more than one correspondent.

The yellow-trousered twit shivered as the police cart trundled past with its baggage of bruised rogues. 'I am not the only God-fearing businessman who has been affected by this, sir. Three of my colleagues who own properties west of here also replaced their crews, and my sister in the Village lost no time in sending me word that she had sacked their upstairs maid. Quite right of her, too.'

'I fail to follow you,' I said icily.

'Who knows what sort of wickedness lurked in that girl? We ought to round these papists up somehow, send them back where they belong. If God wishes them to starve there, then who are we to stand in the way of divine justice? Granted, it may require twice the effort on a white man's part to get an honest day's work out of a Negro, but at least they fear the devil – there is nothing these Irish won't sink to, as that letter proves. It shocks me, sir. The cruelty in what passes for fellow humans.'

'There at least we're agreed,' I growled as he turned away from me.

Julius came up from my left, the smell of the tea leaves braided into his wiry hair preceding him slightly. A strange bulge distorted his right-hand pocket. He looked at me for a few seconds and then rubbed at his nose with his nimble fingers.

'I owe you considerably.'

'You don't either. They pay me almost ten dollars a week.'

'So you're a copper star now.'

'Shockingly,' I admitted with more than a touch of pepper.

He shook his head. 'It isn't, by my way of thinking.'

'And you're a carpenter. You likely always have been a carpenter, and I didn't think of it. Is that where your father got the name from? Or your grandfather?'

'Father.' Julius smiled. 'Cassius Carpenter. See what I mean? You can't go ten minutes without figuring something down to the ground.' He cleared his throat. 'I'll help you any way you like, and anytime too, only I can't give a statement. It wouldn't do right by me. Nor anyone I know. Name something else, for your trouble. Please.'

I swallowed a pincushion and nodded. Julius could bring charges all he liked, even win his case, but I already had the bastard on several counts of violence against police. And to my friend, a statement wasn't worth wondering of a summer's evening how long he'd live before his ken was torched.

'Just let me get it right in my head,' I said slowly. 'A letter written by a mad Irish bent on taking over the city, supposedly killing kinchin as a means, came out in the early editions. Say, five this morning.'

Julius nodded, tapping his chin.

'That stunted worm over there read it and fired his crew,

208

and with the way things have been booming in the burned district, he'd replaced it with blacks a few hours later, losing only a bit of the workday. Some of the former workmen got soused off their pates and hatched the notion of a public demonstration. And you're the one they caught when your crew took to their heels. How close am I?'

'Shaving the bone.'

'Julius, there is one thing you can do for me. Do you savvy where most of the folk from the old neighborhood have got to?'

'Seen quite a few of them, one time or another. Always stopped for a word. Who are you after?'

'Hopstill. I need a lightning-maker.'

'Don't we all,' said Julius, with a philosophic little smile.

He gave me Hopstill's new address, in a wretched part of Ward Six not far from my own house. I thanked him, which was sensible, because he'd helped me. He thanked me again, which wasn't as sensible, since everything I'd done had been my job. Julius had shaken my hand and was already walking away when I idly asked him what was straining the seams of his right pocket.

'The turnip,' he called back.

'Why?' I asked, aghast.

'Because I'm still here,' he answered. 'I got a brick, a leather strap, and a rock from a slingshot too, all on a shelf. But look at me. I'm right here.'

I bit the inside of my lip hard as he walked off. Thinking about useless men, and men who are good for something. But I was wanted elsewhere. Before I saw Matsell, I knew I had to find Mercy, and I knew just where she went when she needed quiet. So I pulled the brim of my hat down and left the dwindling scene as the property owner scurried to clear the pile of pine faggots away from his precious lot. Proving conclusively, in my mind at least, the limits of what precisely that particular man was good for.

Entering Washington Square from the eastern side, having told the hackney driver to wait and there'd be a fare back to the Tombs for him plus extra, the silence of the place struck me like a shaft of sunlight through a window. Carriages trotted slowly past, to be sure. Parched leaves cracked underfoot. But so many other sounds were absent. People don't talk much in Washington Square. Either they live in the stately tree-fronted homes surrounding it, or they're leaving the jewel-toned Dutch Reformed Church, or – ever since it was founded fourteen years ago, anyway – they're students at New York University, reading as if their lives depended on it. Something about the triangle of the church and the school and the trees makes for quiet in that square, even in the amber-lit midafternoon. And soon enough I caught sight of Mercy, sitting on a bench with her hands in her lap.

Seeing her when she hasn't seen me yet is a drunk feeling, but not in any sense of giddiness. I mean in that half-cupshot way a tipsy fellow has of looking at tiny things far too close, all attention netted by the absolutely trivial, gaping at a single straw in a huge haystack with no desire whatever to drag his focus off again. I can talk about the intricacies of ferry travel for hours when I'm soused, remembering the cool, thick feel of river water on my face, and when Mercy doesn't know I'm looking, I can spend ten minutes on her nearer ear. But I didn't have time to squander. So I gave myself about five seconds of the single black tendril on the left side of the back of her neck that never, under any circumstances, allows itself to be pinned up with the rest of her hair. It would do in a pinch.

'Might I join you?'

She swung her eyes up, and they were packed full of troubles. Mercy wasn't surprised to see me, though. I was beginning to notice she scarce ever was. Nodding, she returned her attention to the littered leaves and joined her fingers together.

'There's nothing helpful to say about what just went on,' I told her. 'And I know you've seen as bad as I have in this city. Maybe worse. But that was a brave thing to do, for all I'd not have tailored it for you myself.'

It wasn't what she'd expected me to say at all. The cleft in her chin dipped toward the ground slightly.

'I wanted to see that you were well,' I explained. 'That's all. I'm not going to scold you, it would be offensive. And Julius would thank you, if he were here.'

Then we didn't say anything. A student passed by us, oblivious to the cruel events just south of him. His hat very baggy and his step very hasty and his hose very tight. There was someplace urgent he needed to be, and he wasn't going to make it there on time. It was a gorgeous calamity in scale, I thought. A lovely misfortune. Immediate and irreversible and very soon forgotten. We needed more troubles like that. Ones like burning supper or coming down with a head cold at an awkward time. I desperately wanted to pass through countless small, endurable problems with the girl sitting next to me. I didn't need much else. After all, had I funds enough to feed her whatever she wanted, and dress her as she pleased, I myself could live on small beer and artfully deflected remarks.

But I didn't have a thing to my name save a star badge with a bent point. And I had to go to the Tombs. I hadn't even the time to wait for her to speak to me.

'That's what I'm thinking,' I said at length. 'I wonder, before I go, what are you thinking?'

'Do you mean before you arrived?' she wondered softly. 'Or now?'

'Whichever you like.'

The smile was vaguely shaky, a porcelain cup with the tiniest hint of a crack. 'Do you ever think about London, Mr Wilde?'

At the word *London*, I knew she was missing her mother. The same way her mother missed London itself, I figure it. Thomas Underhill met his future wife on an abolitionist mission to England. Terrible things happened to them there, I think. Enough to drive them away forever. And they must have felt like failures emigrating back to the States. At least Olivia Underhill lived to see Empire-wide British emancipation from this side of the ocean, when I was fifteen and every newspaper was howling it on the front page. New York is a free state, of course, but Christ knows if we'll ever see American emancipation at all.

'You mean London specifically, or do I think of . . . someplace away from here?'

Mercy chuckled, but without any sound. 'I think about London, you see. I think about writing my book in a garret study with a window of stained glass, not in the corner of my room whenever I can spare half an hour. And I think about filling page after page, and how afterward all the things I've ever felt will be clear to me. Just the way the feelings of . . . oh, Don Quixote, perhaps, are clear to me. Imagine being Don Quixote, dreaming dreams so boundless as that, without having a book by Cervantes in front of you to make you clear to yourself. You'd drown in such feelings. They're bearable only because they are written down. And so I'd like to go to

London, as soon as I can. Because at times, this afternoon for example, I'd like to have a better . . . a better map for how I feel, to know its borders.'

'That would be a grand thing,' I agreed. 'I thought you had twenty chapters finished.'

'Twenty-two now, though it's very difficult to write here, without much in the way of privacy. But did you understand what I meant? Are books cartography, Mr Wilde?'

'Reading them, or writing them?'

'Does it matter?'

'I don't know.'

'Do you think me a bit mad?'

'No, I've always known you felt that way. I just didn't know the studying maps was to be in London.'

Mercy's eyes closed. I'd never seen her look so before, tired and brave and unstrung, and it annexed another piece of me. Where, I haven't the faintest idea, because I'd assumed them all conquered.

'I was speaking to your father,' I said slowly. 'About your visiting Catholics.'

Her eyes flew open again as a tiny gasp gripped her throat.

'No, no, I didn't tell him. And I didn't mean to startle you, but is it right he doesn't know that you tend the sick? Is it fair?'

Touching her knuckles to her lips, Mercy shook her head in frustration. 'It isn't fair in the slightest. Not to anyone – to me, to Papa, to the Irish who need help. I can't see people so . . . categorically as he does. But if he knew where I went, he would be very unhappy, and with every good reason. He's quite frightened for me. I'm grateful you didn't tell him. You won't say anything?'

'No. For the record, I think you've got the right end of it,' I answered. 'I hate to see you in those places, but I can't fault the Irish for living in tiny hells. And I don't think God sent them there.'

Mercy looked at me very hard for a moment, blue eyes glowing oddly, as if trying to read the back of my head. Then she stood up.

'I must be getting back to the parsonage. That was a brave thing you did too, you know, a wonderful thing. But you're a curious man, Mr Wilde.'

That one floored me. 'I'd thought you pretty well used to me by now.'

'Oh, of course. But the things you *fail* to do are so absolutely unexpected, you must realize.' She bit her underlip as she thought about it. 'Here you haven't taken me to task. And you haven't told me to run along home. Nor to stop spending time with news hawkers, or to cease visiting sickrooms,' she added with a flickering smile that looked like a flinch. 'You fail to do so very many things.'

'Is that all of them?' I asked, still a bit stunned.

'Well, you haven't yet called me Miss Underhill either, as you've suddenly been doing ever since the fire. But you're about to, perhaps?'

Washington Square was very big suddenly. It was an ocean of grass and trees without any borders to make it stop, to show a man where he was. One side of Mercy's wide collar had tugged down, so more of her shoulder was exposed there than the other. But it didn't need fixing, it needed to stay just as it was, that intoxicating lack of balance she has. The way her hair never stays where she wants it to, bits drifting like kite strings.

'Be careful getting home,' I said. 'I'm for the Tombs, but will see you shortly. I've a lightning-maker to deliver to Fang.'

Mercy waited another moment. But I didn't add anything. Only the faint birdsong marked the seconds passing. So she nodded politely and walked away south, trailing pale living yellow skirts through the dead yellow leaves.

People tell me things. They tell me all sorts of things. About their finances, their hopes like torches in the dark, their tiny rages, their sins when the sins feel too much like shells and they want to break out of them. But never in my life had the new facts made me feel I weighed less instead of more, caught me up on a breeze. Maybe I would never understand Mercy, grasp why she spoke so glancingly or guess what she was thinking. Still. I only wished for decades to keep trying.

I think about London, you see.

So could I, I found. And so I would do.

CHAPTER FOURTEEN

*In thus tolerating all sects, we have admitted to equal
protection not only those sects whose religious faith
and practice support the principle on which the free
toleration of all is founded, but also that unique, that
solitary sect, the Catholic, which builds and supports
its system on the destruction of all toleration. Yes, the
Catholic is permitted to work in the light of Protestant
toleration, to mature his plans, and to execute his
designs to extinguish that light, and destroy the hands
that hold it.*

Samuel F. B. Morse, 1834

When I turned up in Chief Matsell's office in the Tombs,
he was busy writing. I sat down when he motioned me
into a chair, looking with interest at the space the strangely
impressive man before me had molded to suit himself.

On the eastern wall hung a map of New York, of course, a
giant and lovingly rendered one, with our wards clearly
marked. One of those endlessly high Tombs windows loomed

behind the desk, with a shocking amount of inert beige light drifting in. The desk itself was noticeably not covered in paperwork. One project at a time, it seemed, however unlikely. Maybe that accounted for his casual but drill-bore focus. Several titles on his high bookshelf I recognized, confirming rumor. He did read radical civics and female reproductive texts, then. The south wall was devoted to politics: flag, Founding Fathers portrait (he'd gone with Washington, his namesake), freewheeling taxidermied eagle, seal of the Democrats. I was so absorbed that when he did speak, he almost startled me out of my chair.

'The copper stars' investigation into the nineteen bodies is over, Mr Wilde.'

I choked back something toxic, rising to my feet. 'What?'

'The article of this morning has made our position impossible. There were no dead kinchin. There are no dead kinchin. You're a roundsman of the Sixth, Mr Wilde, and please be on time henceforth.'

Disbelief vibrated through my head like a church bell next to my ear. *No,* I thought, and then, *I defended him, I said this wouldn't happen, so no.* And then there was nothing. I was so shocked it was ugly, it must have looked ugly, me standing there gaping – me with my three-quarters of a face and all my efforts and the things he knew nothing about. The news hawkers, the countless people I'd spoken with, Bird living at Mrs Boehm's. He went on writing. I felt like a street mongrel who'd been given a piece of fresh meat and then lashed out of the butcher's shop.

'Here,' I said, taking off the copper star. I put it on his desk and headed for the door.

'Wait.'

'I told New Yorkers we were better than this. You've just made me a liar, so—'

'Mr Wilde, *sit down.*'

His voice was quiet enough, but the force of it bulleted through my brain. Then Matsell looked up at me, lifting one brow. I don't know why, but I sat. That great dignified piggish man with the facial lines cutting like a railroad through his jowls was about to tell me something, I supposed. Depending on what it was, I might say a few choice words in return.

'I've come to a realization, Mr Wilde.' George Washington Matsell placed his pen very deliberately next to his sheet of foolscap. 'The content of it will surprise you, I think. Do you know what I am writing?'

'How could I?'

Again that suggestion that a smile might be forming, and then all of it blown away downwind toward the Battery. 'I am writing a lexicon. Do you know what that is?'

'A dictionary,' I snapped. 'I just helped to save a man from being burned at the stake, all because a mad letter was published exploiting twenty dead kinchin who'll now never be avenged. And you want me to know that you're writing a *dictionary.*'

Chief Matsell did smile then, tapping his quill feather against his lip once. Only once.

'All sorts of people comprise a metropolitan city. Unfortunately, the ones with the least respect for law and order are also the ones who've developed their own singular language, its origins lost in the fog of British history. What you see before you is the beginnings of a flash lexicon. A rogue's lexicon, if you will.'

'You won't need my help for that, knowing the ways of rogues so thoroughly yourself.'

He laughed. I looked at his writing, firm and a little arrogant and upside down. It was an inspired idea to record crime's language, I thought reluctantly. But what good was knowing flash if the actual solving of a crime didn't line up with the Democratic agenda?

'I don't need your help with the lexicon, Mr Wilde. I'd like you to spend your time in another way entirely, as a matter of fact. Now that I understand just how strongly you feel about this matter. I did wonder, you know. How you felt.'

'Only the way I figure a man ought to feel about dead kinchin,' I replied coldly.

'I understand you. What I would like you to understand is the fragility of this particular organization. Are the copper stars universally well liked, would you say, from your experience on your beat?'

I shook my head grudgingly. For every man grateful for our watchfulness, there was another ranting about free streets and the spirit of the Revolution.

'Harper's Police were useless,' Matsell continued, 'and that is why they failed. Not because this city does not understand deep within that we require law enforcement, but because New Yorkers eat incompetents for breakfast and because our criminal population couches their arguments in the language of patriotism. I am not incompetent, Mr Wilde, but I have been placed in an impossible position: it is extremely difficult to solve crimes of any significant age. Nigh impossible. A day passes, a week, and all trace of evidence the culprit may have left behind is gone. Here we have a series of crimes the nature of which would rock the city, perhaps threaten the voting base of the entire Democratic Party. And if we publicly fail to solve these murders, if we prove to be as inept as those blue-coated slackmouths we replaced, a future Whig victory and the dissolution of the copper stars would not surprise me in the slightest. They like their money funneled toward banks and industry.'

'The goddamned Party is all you people think about,' I hissed.

'It gave you this position, didn't it?'

'That's not exactly an honor. Any scoundrel who can swing a leaded stick is good enough for you.'

George Washington Matsell tapped his fingertips together with a frown. 'We both know that isn't quite the way of it. There are different kinds of police officers, same as with any set of men. Some wanting to guard the streets, and some wanting to gain an advantage on those same streets by wearing the copper star. I'll be the first to admit there are scoundrels in my employ, but for the sake of the Party it can't be helped. I argue that tolerating a few useful rogues is better than lacking a police department entirely. So there are dead rabbits, and decent men, all of them walking the rounds. Then there's you.'

'And what am I?' I didn't try to hide the scowl on my face. It felt permanently stamped.

'The rest of them are preventing crime, you see. The roundsmen, and the captains as well. But *preventing* crime is another matter from *unraveling* it once it's been committed. I suspect that's where you come in, Mr Wilde. The solving after the fact. Not everyone can attempt such a thing, you see. So by God, that's what you'll do. Solve the riddle, and report back to me and me alone.'

'Solve *which* riddle?'

He spread his hands out amiably, leaving them lightly touching his desk. 'Is there another on your mind?'

I glanced at Matsell's map, thoughts glinting hard and in

every direction like a knife fight. Staring at the point where the city ground to a halt, where the kinchin had been hidden beneath the wordless trees. I wanted to know how they came to be there like very little else I've ever wanted, and I'd never felt so about a *puzzle* before. It was Bird, partly, along with all the others, but it was simpler than that. Tending bar is a line in the dust drawn repeatedly, the same transaction over and over again, with daydreams of your own ferryboat and a piece of land on Staten Island so you can stomach it. Mind games built on common sense are also required to keep you interested enough to make any money, but no matter what you guessed right about a patron, you'd forget it an hour after locking up, the next day's tracks erasing the ones that came before. But this was a single goal, a mountain to climb and see the top with your own eyes, and *I needed to know.*

And here it seemed the chief burned to know too. Despite the Democrats.

'There's one on my mind, all right,' I said quietly.

'You'd better keep this, then,' he suggested, handing me back the copper star and managing somehow not to look smug.

'You turned me back into a roundsman just to see what I'd do?'

'It was much more clarifying than even I had expected.'

Thumbing the pin out, I shoved the star back into my lapel. It felt much better to have it there. 'I need a little money,' I admitted. 'I'll use it honest, on my word. I need to bribe the news hawkers.'

'Very clever of you, too. Get funds from your brother, if you would. He'll have a Party donations cash box at the committee meeting tomorrow morning that won't have been recorded in the ledgers as of yet. Say nothing of this to anyone save for Captain Wilde, and Mr Piest if you should need another ally. The man who wrote to the newspapers is a lunatic. There are no dead kinchin, there never were. Do you understand me? And if it was a copper star behind that disgraceful piece of trash, I'll have him by the bollocks. Before you leave, write out a report regarding that powder keg you stopped going off this afternoon.'

'Good luck with your lexicon,' I said apologetically from the door, touching my hat brim. 'It's really a very useful idea.'

'It's the most useful idea I'd ever had before the idea of assigning a specific copper star to detect a particular criminal,' he returned placidly. 'Get out of my office, Mr Wilde. And say not a word.'

I wrote out the report. Very intently penning 'assault with intent to kill', 'threatening life', 'public drunkenness with disorderly conduct', among other things. That went a fair way toward making up for spelling the word *turnip*. Then, not having the funds yet to bribe the newsboys, and wanting pretty badly to speak with Bird, I walked home to Elizabeth Street, the brim of my hat blocking the heavy spears of late-afternoon August light. Within twenty yards of my steps, I met a keen surprise.

A very fine carriage, such as would never stop in front of Mrs Boehm's bakery, waited outside my front door. Silt from the road dulled its perfect black paint.

I stopped, sizing up the object. The seated black driver hadn't caught sight of me, for his sweat-drenched back was to the west. Standing on my toes with my neck craning, I peered inside the vehicle. Expecting a doctor's bag, maybe – Peter Palsgrave come by magic to help us. Or the owner of a newspaper, there to drag a story out of me, leaving his notes for the morrow's edition in a case on the seat.

Instead I saw nothing. But mixed with smells of the street

and the hot leather upholstery, a hint of violets drifted sluggishly in my direction. Turning cold, I wheeled around, diving into the bakery.

No sign of Mrs Boehm. Nor of Bird, for that matter, and my muscles by then had a death grip on my bones. There Silkie Marsh sat, however, angelic and smiling with her soul a perfect blank, sipping a cup of cooling tea at the bread-making table. Smelling of violets and wearing the most ingratiating shade of green imaginable.

'I apologize for calling unexpectedly, Mr Wilde,' she said with a look of practiced shyness. 'I hope you don't think it too rude, but I was . . . I was very much disturbed in my mind. Your landlady was called away on a delivery, but was kind enough to make me some tea first. Shall I pour you a cup?'

I needn't look friendly, remember, I thought, *and it's natural to look surprised. Treat it as an opportunity, play close to the vest, and pray God that Bird has been upstairs all this while.*

'I haven't much time, Madam Marsh. And I confess myself a bit abroad. I'd have thought my brother would be the man you'd want, if you were . . . unsettled.'

Silkie Marsh poured me a cup of tea, molding her rosy lips into a regretful curve. To my horror, I registered what was folded neatly and sitting on a chair near the flour sacks behind her, scrubbed into cleanliness again by Mrs Boehm: Bird's nightdress. It ought to have been either saved as evidence or burned, but had instead fallen victim to good housekeeping habits within a tub of lye and stone lime. I'd no means of learning whether Silkie Marsh had glimpsed it, no way to ask without giving myself away.

'Valentine *would* have been the first man I'd dream of running to under such circumstances, long ago. But you must have noticed that . . . it's a painful subject.' She flinched, a real one this time. Artificial only in that she purposefully failed to mask it from me. 'Val is a lover of novelty, Mr Wilde. I can't help but fear that my devotion to him now goes unnoticed.'

'Most people's devotion to him goes unnoticed.'

Her patient look of suffering quirked into a knowing smile. A gift. A secret between us. 'You know him better than I, of course. As devastated as the loss of his attentions makes me, you're quite right – he is deservedly accustomed to being revered.'

'I don't know about deservedly. Tell me, what vexes you?'

'I read the newspaper this morning,' she confessed in a far more hushed whisper. 'It quite . . . I was very upset, Mr Wilde. Afraid.'

If children were being carted off regularly from her bawdy house by a man in a black hood who liked cutting them open, I couldn't rightfully blame her. Particularly not if she had something to do with it.

'What were you afraid of personally, Madam Marsh?'

She pursed her lips in pretended disappointment, blinking feathery lashes at me. 'On behalf of our city, Mr Wilde? Riots, perhaps. Chaos in the streets. On behalf of the Irish, and the future of the Democratic Party, to which I absolutely subscribe? Failure in the next election, of course. Or do you rather suppose that my interests are much more *personal*, since I am paying you a visit that must be awkward for us both?'

Confession, even partial confession, was a bold stroke. But people do tend to tell me things. I took a sip of the tea she'd poured, measuring the weight of the silence. The entire conversation had me balanced on the tip of a fishhook, but at least Silkie Marsh had learned somewhere that her voice was more persuasive when bright and forceful. Bird could hear us, surely, from upstairs. I hoped to God Bird could hear us.

'You employ kinchin as mabs, I turned up with Val and a dose of bitter news over Liam, and then carted off two of your youngest stargazers,' I summarized for her. 'And you want to know just how that came about.'

She shook her blond head decisively. 'I don't give a damn about what's past. I want to know if my sisters, my employees, everyone who lives at my residence, need be frightened for our very *lives*.'

'I'd say that the kinchin ill starred enough to live under your roof are frightened enough for their lives already. Such lives as they have.'

Her eyes sparked within the blue ring closest to her pupils. A glint that wasn't calculated – just bitter and tired. The sort of calcified resentment too ingrained to hide.

'You're not alone in failing to hold a high opinion of me, Mr Wilde. But I live well, and so do the residents of my household. I am a rich and independent woman. I'll not remark on the benefits of sewing piecework until one either starves or freezes, nor the joys of factory labor where favors are taken forcefully rather than paid for. But I own my establishment. I also own my time, which is far more valuable. It's not too much to suppose that some of my charges, when they grow up, will prosper also. Here I sit before you, though I was also a fragile thing at age nine.'

I blinked, to be sure. Because if it was true, if she'd suffered the same, if she knew all about what made Bird smash ceramics first-hand . . . then there was nothing I could say to the purpose. Some sorts of scars I can't see the depth of, not having the same variety myself. And if she was lying, well, then she wasn't worth speaking to.

Sending our conversation off the rails appeared to vex her. Silkie Marsh straightened, passing her spoon once around her teacup as if to dissolve a stubborn lump of sugar, though she'd clearly – from the lack of steam – been awaiting me for at least a quarter of an hour. When she met my eyes, her mouth was buoyant again, her cheeks blushing petal pink.

'Please, what really happened to Liam?' she asked quietly. 'Come to that, however did you learn who he was, where he resided?'

'A charity worker identified him in the end.'

'Ah. That would be Miss Mercy Underhill, I suppose.'

A startled jolt like burned coffee grounds hit my blood. I must have looked well bustled, for Silkie Marsh was suddenly very pleased. She tilted her chin at the same angle as my head.

'It wasn't very likely to be anyone else, Mr Wilde. I see her infrequently, but she is, after all, quite devoted to children. I cannot suppose anyone else would have recognized Liam after a brief acquaintance.'

A weird polish to her voice perplexed me still further. But once I'd got well past the fact of them knowing each other in the first place – and of course they did; Mercy couldn't possibly have tended to kinchin-mabs without meeting their mistress – I couldn't find much to wonder at in Silkie Marsh taking a profound dislike to the reverend's beautiful, educated daughter. It certainly accounted for the dark tone bleeding through the faint smile.

'Can you tell me nothing else?' she coaxed. 'I do wish to help, you see.'

'Because of my brother?'

'Whatever else you think of me, and you do give yourself free rein, I cannot let you suppose I care nothing for my own frail brothers and sisters.' There was deliberate heat in that statement, and I was meant to feel it in crackling, bitten-off consonants. 'I didn't build New York City, Mr Wilde, so don't ask me to remake it to your better liking. *Can* I be of any service?'

'No. But thank you. You're here to work me like a hand pump for information, so it's white of you to offer a trade.'

I'd thought to startle her, somehow knock the outraged smile from her ivory face. But the smile only widened.

'Valentine could have told you I'm very fair minded. But I don't take it that you listen to your brother nearly enough, nor quite know what to do with him.'

'And you've a better way of handling him, as I saw.'

That one accomplished what a direct insult couldn't. Of course it did. Whatever heart she retained, she'd clearly lent it to the wrong person. So I regretted it when her eyes stopped seeing me and saw Val instead, saw whatever the first callous thing he'd done to her happened to be. Her lips reeled for an instant and then were forced back under control as she smiled as if her life depended on it. It likely had. More than once.

Gracefully, rustling green watered silk, she floated to her tiny feet. She glanced about for her gloves, which lay on the bread display counter.

And in doing so caught sight of the nightdress. Silkie Marsh's head whipped back a fraction to peer at me.

'I couldn't very well deliver Neill and Sophia to a church in that rigging, could I?' I said disgustedly.

'Of course not, Mr Wilde,' she replied, all sugar and poison stirred together at boiling point. 'But nevertheless I do hope that you paid them their due for having . . . stopped the night here. Having so obviously been a source of valuable entertainment. I do always guarantee in my own establishment that they are properly *reimbursed* for their *time*.'

'And if I find you've employed another kinchin, by Christ, stargazing – any sort of stargazing, if done in your house – will seem of a sudden ungodly illegal.'

I'd known before meeting her that women were capable of writing *murder* across their eyelids and then sweetly blinking at a fellow. But I'd not seen it. It's pretty daunting, when it's done proper.

'It must be difficult, passing through life as Valentine Wilde's runt brother. I don't wonder that you seem a bitter man,' she said pleasantly on her way over the threshold.

'I'll give Val your best greetings, then?'

The door slammed shut.

I felt pretty raw myself by then. Relieved and angry and hectic and wrung with quick, clever fists. The instant Mrs Boehm returned home, I determined, I was going to inform her very courteously why that particular woman was under no circumstances ever to be allowed back in her house. Now that Silkie Marsh had been sitting at it, the floury table – which had been beginning to feel downright homelike – seemed angled wrong. The air was displaced, and I didn't know how to put it back where it belonged. So I took my hat off, walked to the cupboard where I kept my few domestic items, and poured a flash ribbon of brandy in my tea.

A footstep sounded behind me – a bare one, only a ghost of a tread.

'I was never *hiding*,' Bird announced.

I turned around. She was tying the makeshift burlap belt around her waist, her hair all down and dwarfing the rest of her, grey eyes terrified and New York accent steady as the Hudson.

'Of course not,' I scoffed. 'God, no. What I'd imagined you were doing – hoping, really – was spying. Away out of sight, like a regular paid nose.'

It was about time I took a fair turn at lying, the way I figured the landscape. My small friend's hands were shaking.

Nodding exhaustedly, Bird padded over to the table.

'Yes, that's it. I was nosing. Did you ever show her a backhander or two.'

'Did I?'

'I knew you were a match for her, and now I savvy whyso. I didn't rightly diary it in my mind, why I figured you for a round fellow from the start. But I recognized you, she brought it back to me. I remember now.'

Sinking into a chair with the laced cup, I leaned my elbows on my knees in her direction. 'But you'd never seen me before.'

'Not *you*,' she corrected. 'Whenever there was an out-and-out spree, I'd dress as a serving maid, carrying drinks to the rabbits. Mr V. He gave me an orange that was in his pocket. I'd have cottoned to it faster, if you were the same size.'

I sighed, and blackly too.

'He was a good sort?'

'Top marks. And you're the spit of him. Brothers, yes? That explains everything.'

'No, it doesn't. But it's a start.'

We listened for a while to the Germans next door. They seemed to be either fighting or dancing. I gave it fifty-fifty odds, from the steady pounding, uncontrolled shrieks, the occasional banshee laugh. But I hadn't the first idea which end was up by that time, so I sipped my drink and watched Bird drawing her name – the Irish one – into the white grit that never left the tabletop.

'If you *could* explain everything to me,' I asked her softly, 'you would, wouldn't you?'

Bird nodded gravely. But she didn't answer. Just traced line after line through her name on the table, being viciously thorough about the project. Until it was a clean streak of wood again and she had never been there at all.

CHAPTER FIFTEEN

Besides, it is easy to form a just estimate of popish
teachers and instructors, from the practical efforts of
education and instruction. Scarcely one in twenty, it
might probably be said one in fifty, can read or write.

American Protestant in Defence of Civil and
Religious Liberty Against Inroads of Papacy, 1843

I awoke with the dawn next morning, an invisible but jagged
bread knife sawing ineffectively at the back of my neck.
Drunk, then, I thought – drunk the night previous. *At last.* I'd
earned it. There was a fuzzy whiskey carpeting coating my
throat.

And what had I been about?

Ah, yes, I recalled once downstairs and out of doors in the
morning sunlight, emptying the basin I'd dunked my head
into over the slats of the front entryway to keep down the
dust. Losing at cards. To a kinchin whose skill at calling the
turn paid her out four to one no fewer than six times. I'd
broken even with Bird, though, with our wood chips from the

back area for money, each calling the other's outrageous bluffs.

Stretching, I went back inside.

Suddenly all I could see by dawn's soiled light was Silkie Marsh standing before the same table, frozen in my mind's eye, catching sight of the nightdress. Her head then turning back to mine as if pulled on a chain.

Fifteen minutes later, I stood fully dressed in Mrs Boehm's doorway, after quickly scouring the *Herald* for news. Matsell seemed to have been pulling strings, for an article therein announced that the letter regarding Irish kinchin-mabs was 'fiction of the most hellish, shameful, and risible variety'. Still, I hadn't any time to waste.

'Bird,' I called softly.

Bird blinked at me with watery eyes from the trundle as I heard the bakery doors unlocking below.

'You ought to come with me,' I told her. 'Get out of this ken.'

She hesitated. Having seen Silkie Marsh the day before, I couldn't fault the caution.

'I don't suppose,' I said, yawning, 'you want to know how a lightning-maker builds stage firecrackers.'

First, though, we needed a proper bribe for Hopstill, due to Hopstill's being the proper bribe for the newsboys.

After Bird and I had finished our rolls and hot tea, we headed south and west for about ten minutes on foot until we'd reached Chambers Street, opposite the resolute fungus on the face of New York known as City Hall Park. August had done a regular artisan's work of killing the trees along its border, and we caught a whiff off the band of rogue chickens setting up a bleak gravelly campsite under their branches. On

231

the north side of Chambers, however, looking picked up and transplanted, stood a neatly trimmed brownstone house banked by two brilliantly velvet-leafed green ash trees.

Lounging on three of the steps, of course, was a copper star. Dressed like a fireman, as many of us were, with the badge thrust into red flannel – unlit cigar, the entire rabbit uniform done proper. Blond, even fairer than my brother and me. He'd a moustache, though, above his fleshy lip, which was out of the common. His name was Moses Dainty, a Democrat on the level of Paul the Apostle being a Christian. The sort who thought carrying my brother's laundry an honor.

'You're another copper star, then, Wilde?' he exclaimed lazily when he spied me. 'Or is that you under there? Val said you'd taken a bad whipe from the July blaze. Hullo, young miss,' he added, spitting politely. 'They're hard at the politicking in there, so stay mouse, will you? For the Party's sake, little loll?'

'I'll keep nish all right,' Bird answered, vowing to stay quiet.

A Knickerbocker Company truck rumbled up, its horses looking half parboiled. Two men jumped down and threw open the dripping back door, hoisting a huge block of ice with their iron pincers.

'Just around back, boys, and I'll pay you when it's in the kitchen,' Moses called.

'Quite a bang-up affair, a Party meeting,' I noted.

'This one calls for a better spread. Ice for the cracked lobster and the rum punch, two roast pigs as well – it's one of our bulliest meetings all season. Stay for the luncheon, why don't you. Voters always welcome.'

Inside, the tall-ceilinged chamber was thoroughly packed with men. Men in tight black coattails and lightning-hued cravats standing on the small platform dais at the back of the room, men in flannel red as their hair leaning their backs against the wall under Washington's sacred picture, men sitting at tables before a wretchedly done mural of the Declaration of Independence, writ with ghastly foot-high signatures. Finally, a large group of men – and here's where I turned puzzled, Bird's brow making a neat vertical track of confusion at the same moment – standing in an orderly row, like a cashier's queue.

At first, I couldn't tack down what was wrong about them. There were maybe forty, all told, in a line. I looked closer. They seemed to be clutching ballots in their fists – but the next election was a considerable way off. Then I caught the sour-pine scent of digested gin and their equally pinelike sway, as if a forest breeze permeated the meetinghouse, and knew they were drunk as lords. Next, they were Irish to a man, black and red alike, but all wore thick beards, which wasn't an Irish fashion in the smallest.

Finally, none of them matched their togs. Not one. Every rough in the queue wore the garb of a professional. A man with construction-calloused hands the size of a grizzly's blinked at the wall wearing a too-short nondenominational parson's suit. Another, whose complexion of gently peeling lead told me he lived in a particularly vile cellar bunk for three pence a night, wore a satin neck-stock and a dented gold monocle. A pugilist with ears like flowering broccoli who'd succumbed to the gin and was dozing in the corner had an ivory-headed cane with a carved physician's symbol tucked dreamily under one arm.

'All right, boys,' Valentine bellowed from the front of the dais, green eyes dancing and his hands on his hips. Sober, as was apparently his habit at Party functions. 'If I don't see some improvement from that last spectacle, all you bloody mounters will be going without the rag-water next training session. I won't have the Party fleeced at the polls due to our own generous natures. Make it smart, now! Canavan, set to!'

The lush in the parson's togs held his scrap of paper in the air like a holy standard, then marched single minded for a green box resting where my brother was draped against the sturdy wood table. Just as he was about to stuff the sham ballot into the slot, Val caught his arm.

'Come off it, you're having a smirk at me,' Val mocked, painfully squeezing the flesh in his fingers. 'You're voting *Democrat?*'

'Aye!' squealed the emigrant.

'I'll give you a beating such as you've never had if you do. I'll break your bones, break them individual. I'll fib your quarron so bloody that dogs'll think it fair breakfast.'

'Y'shan't!' his victim screamed, blindly tearing free and shoving the ballot hard and final into the sacred green box.

At the end of this performance, a light round of applause fell from the higher-ups along the wall, a gently approving spring rainstorm. And I knew what they were doing by then. It was an elections rehearsal, of course, although I'd made it a specific point never to witness one and there wouldn't be an election hereabouts for months to come. A precaution against able-bodied male voters in Democratic districts being frightened away from the polls by Whig bruisers. Not that the Democrats wouldn't have their own slab-jawed roughs in place at Whig-dominated voting locations, naturally. There was nothing considered to be better worth bashing a few heads over than the vote of an eligible rent-paying freeman. Of course, the voters would be marginally less soused off of liquid Democratic bribery come an actual election day. Marginally.

'Good.' Val approved as the supposed parson reeled back to the chairs. 'A flash bluff, that was. Finerty! Put your best leg forward, then!'

The cellar rat wearing the creamy neck-stock that would have paid for a fortnight's rent in a decent ken approached. Tentative, though. Bird's eyes, I saw when I glanced down, were riveted to the floor show. And I admit, it was arresting to watch grown men running their liquor-bribed voters through the proper paces to ensure that the Party came out ahead by a furlong. Arresting, and also more than faintly disturbing.

'This one won't make it,' Bird whispered, tugging at my coat sleeve. 'He can't think out a play.'

I agreed with her wholeheartedly.

'A dollar says he wins through,' I suggested instead.

'That's no better than stealing.' She smiled, eyes sparking. 'But I'll take it. Why've they all beards?'

'I haven't the slightest.'

Wiping ginny sweat from his brow, the cellar mole suddenly spread his arms wide in welcome. 'My dear old friend! Is that my old schoolfellow, back Kilcolgan way? Thanks be to—'

The effort to deposit the ballot with his left hand while wringing Val's fingers with his right went unrewarded when Val twirled his arm like a waltzer, spinning Finerty entirely around and then giving him a hard shove. Finerty was laid flat against the boards. Hoots erupted. My brother seemed, if anything, disappointed. He waved at another favorite crony from his fire company, a hulking, swarthy engine man who had a broken nose and went by the name of Scales. Predictably enough, Scales wore a copper star. I was beginning to think I was already acquainted with half the force of Ward Eight.

'Scales, drag this thing out back and fill it with coffee until it's a man again,' my brother ordered. 'Go on, get Moses to help if it won't take its—'

Val caught sight of me standing perfectly still with my arms crossed, inspecting him from under my hat brim. It's a job that goes against the natural order, startling Valentine into quiet. But I guess seeing me at a Democratic meeting was enough to do it. There was something more, though, when he fell silent, a twist in the set of his mouth as if he suddenly held a new word on the tip of his tongue. He wanted to tell me something.

'We'll adjourn for ten minutes while we teach an Irishman how to handle his spirits,' he boomed in wearied annoyance. 'That should never be our job, gentlemen and voters all. That goes against all traditional sense. There's bread in the next room if you need it before the hot and cold luncheon. Ten minutes, and we'll stuff this ballot box like a bawd!'

A crashing wave of applause swelled, of course, as Val stepped down from the dais, lighting the cigar stub he'd found in his waistcoat pocket. He didn't bother to look at me as he passed, only waved me onward. I fell into step behind him, Bird at my heels like a shadow.

'That's a dollar,' she said happily.

'Wait a moment, I'll be getting it from him,' I answered, pointing at Val's back.

My brother stalked into a side room that clearly served as an office, crammed with posters on every shelf. They were red and yellow and blue and shocking violet, plastered with such purely admirable notions as being FREEMEN AGAINST DESPOTISM and THE SWORD OF CHANGE FOR THE PEOPLE OF NEW YORK. When Val turned to lean against the desk, one of the sandbags beneath his eyes twitched at the sight of Bird.

'You've another stray cat, Tim,' he said darkly.

'This is Bird Daly. I told you about her – she's been staying at my ken.'

Val's mouth dropped open, barely retaining the cigar and only out of long practice. He took a closer look, tucking his thumbs in his trousers.

'Silkie's miniature downstairs maid,' he muttered. 'I'll be damned.'

'Real pleasure to see you again, Mr V,' said Bird. And by God, it sounded true.

He shook her hand, glaring butcher's hooks at me. 'This is her. The kinchin covered head to toe in fresh ruby from that Liam chit, who led Matsell to— Jesus Christ, Tim, where's your head?'

'Have a care about it, will you,' I growled.

Bird seemed not the least bit put off. 'Why have they all beards, Mr V?'

Valentine's face softened abruptly as he glanced down at Bird. 'Ah. Well, those fine upstanding voters you saw were all three men, with three changes of togs. You savvy? We've barbers on duty across the city, and they need practice before the next election. Those individual coves were actually a man with a beard, a man with a moustache, and a man clean shaved. All of them loyal Democrats.'

A bitter look crossed my face, but Bird only laughed, thinking politics a good joke. She was onto something, maybe.

'Listen to me, little cat.' Val brushed his fingers into his hair distractedly. 'Go right out that door, turn left, and head up the stairs. You're going to find an unlocked room. The room is full of trunks. The trunks are full of togs. The togs are for poor voters and friends of the Party, but never mind that at the moment. The togs are where you come in. If you come back here before you've found a dress that suits you, I'll hang you out the window by your ears until they fall off your head. Yes?'

Bird ran off with a grin on her lightly freckled face, closing the door behind her.

'Timothy Wilde, you are out of your mind,' Val snapped. 'What has she told you?'

I explained that Bird's accounts of the situation were less than reliable, that she didn't know why any of the children had been killed or been disfigured, and that a man in a black hood seemed to be behind it, according to both her and the news hawkers.

'Tim, you grasp that the investigation is over, yes?'

'I did hear that.'

'Well, then mark after me for once in your life.'

In Val's opinion, I should be grateful to be back on roundsman duty. Dead grateful, for it wasn't near as likely to get a man's head staved in as going after a kinchin-killing lunatic. Meanwhile, all was well enough with the world, to his mind. There was a guard over the burial site, so nothing more could be dumped there without our collaring the bastard or bastards. As for Bird, I could drop her at a Catholic orphanage that very afternoon and wash my hands of it all. But I had a stubborn cast to my mazzard, he told me. Why fret over quitting such a sordid business?

'It's what copper stars are meant to do,' I said coldly.

'There won't *be* any copper stars, you oafish sack of fertilizer!' Val groaned, shaking his head despairingly. 'The public finds out, and we don't solve this – and we *won't* – presto! The end of the New York City Police! You want to make a mint, bet against the coppers after word gets out we can't find a kinchin killer with a taste for bared ribs.'

'The chief mentioned that. But I'm to keep at it, Matsell's orders. Sorry to disappoint you.'

'Sod Matsell,' he snarled. 'You take orders from *me*.'

'I'm not in the Eighth Ward.'

'Not as a policeman, as—'

'And I'm not *gutless* either. Like some.'

That one landed a bit better than most of mine do. Val blinked. His lip snagged so angrily, like a burned curl of bark twisting, I was ready for a fist to come at my eye. Then he blinked again and a sneer slid like a crooked carnival mask over the fury.

'There's something else,' I added slowly. 'Or you'd not be like this. What happened?'

Too disgusted for words, Val pulled a folded-up piece of paper from his inner coat pocket and threw it flat on the ground. Feeling vaguely as if I'd broken an unspoken rule, I walked over readily enough and picked it up. And it didn't take me long peering at it to know exactly why my brother had called the entire meeting to a halt purely in order to show me something. A smallish but cool trickle of guilt ran down my back. And guilt, no matter how scant the quantity, is damnably impossible to ignore.

The letter read:

> *Beware Protestant tyrants fer I am become the skurge of wickedness, vice has been punnished and fornication despised but more must be sakrificed before our knives spill American blood. Whore bodies shall be marked with the sacred Cross once more and the vermin feast upon their guts, they've earned such fer the weight of their sin and when the little devils are made quiet the end of your time is coming.*

God will raise us up and the Irish will danse on your graves.
Trust me for I am

The Hand of the God of Gotham

'Humbug or not and no matter who's writing them, these worry you,' I owned apologetically. 'I can certainly see why.'

Val didn't say anything. I'd caught him in the breadbasket, apparently. He pushed himself up, strolled over to one of the desk drawers, and took a whiskey bottle out. This he took three healthy swigs from before delicately wiping the mouth with his shirt cuff, replacing it, and shutting the drawer with a dismissive bang.

'This implies that more murders are planned,' I realized. 'God, Val. Do you credit it? That he's going back to work? That an emigrant with a broken mind is to blame for these deaths? Is that what's troubling you?'

'Whoever wrote that is cracked as an egg. Whoever thinks ripping guts out of kinchin is high sport is brainsick as well. The police are allied with the Democrats and the Democrats are allied with the Irish. You figure out what troubles me, Timothy, you've eyes in your head.'

'All the more reason for me to solve this, then, and quick as possible. Isn't it?'

'How do you manage to get up in the morning, lifting that bloody thick skull of yours? Right. Suppose these letters are real. Suppose you collar the twisted sod. Suppose you *do* lay hands on an Irishman who's been busying himself hushing kids – just how do you think this city would react to *that* bit of gossip?'

Much as it irked me to admit it, my brother was right. I was beginning to suspect that I'd disbelieved the first letter was from an Irish madman not because it wasn't credible, but because it would be very, very bad news.

'It would be chaos,' I agreed. 'This particular letter, though – need we concern ourselves over the newspapers?'

'Where do you think I got it from? We've paid off the newspapers, flush enough to hold them for a month or more. Any more letters, they turn them over to us. A clerk at the *Herald* found this somewhere in their mail pile this morning. Bastard must have been so chaffey at seeing his name in print, he fired off another.'

My brother held a hand out. I knew what he was after and hesitated. But it was beginning to seem that burning evidence might be a grand policy. Val flicked a lucifer against the desktop and watched, intent as ever, as the paper wove itself into cinder. I watched him in my turn, planning out a move. Any move better than the ones I'd played so far. But Val, as so often happens, prevented me.

'Continue this investigation,' my brother said in a voice as frozen and clear as the ice block beyond, 'and I will be selecting the flowers for your funeral.'

'Is that a threat?' I choked out.

'Think of it that way, if it helps. You know best. Or think of it like a prediction, Timmy. It's all aces to me.'

'That's flash, then. I'll remember. Now, give me the money that Matsell sent me here after, or I'll tell him that firedogs don't care to take orders from the chief of police, *Captain* Wilde.'

'Bully,' he said cheerily. 'If you're keen on getting yourself croaked, may as well go out in style. It's the new Democratic funds you're after, the ones yet unmarked? How much?'

'Ten dollars ought to do it. No, eleven. I nearly forgot.'

'You nearly forgot a single coachwheel?'

'The coachwheel is Bird's, rightfully. She bet that Finerty wouldn't stuff the box.'

'She's sharper than you, then.'

I let that pass. Val went to a blank, useless-looking box sitting atop a leaden safe and pulled out three ten-dollar gold pieces and a dollar coachwheel, thumbing them singly in an arc to me behind his back.

'This is too much,' I argued, catching them.

'Oh, but we're at high tide, my Tim. Buy your own coffin with the extra and save me the trouble.'

I thought about saying I hated him, but it was probably pretty clear from my face. If he'd been looking at me, that is.

'Silkie Marsh paid me a call. I gave her your compliments.'

Val's head swiveled back to me in real surprise. His teeth came together tightly for a moment.

'You stole three live valuables from her, and then she came to see you? You're dying quicker than I thought.'

'How nice for you. Do you mind telling me why a visit from Madam Marsh is such a bad omen?'

'Not at all, young Timothy, I simply recognize the circumstances,' he hissed through a steady pressure around his square jaw. 'She's tried to make me easy too, you know. Oh, yes. I didn't mention she'd once been keen to hush me? Never told you she nearly managed it, too?'

Bird threw open the door without knocking. She'd found a little satchel, claimed it, and stuffed her old togs inside. My friend now wore an ivory cotton summer dress with a scooped neck and a high falling waist, covered in orange poppies at the seams, sleeves just capping her speckled arms. A much better dress than I'd expected, though probably not a finer one than she was used to for going out. This one was hers, though, and she was saturated with joy over the fact. Fairly dripping with happiness over not wearing a nightdress in the afternoon.

I was so glad over it myself that I almost missed my brother's reaction. He was grinning boyishly from one side of his face while the other stayed partly eroded, about as pleased as he ever is. It beggared me of language for a second.

'If that isn't dimber, I'm no judge,' he said to the question in Bird's eyes.

'About as pretty a dress as I've seen,' I agreed.

'Tim, you'll do as I said,' Val added abruptly, turning to a stack of childishly bright posters and lifting them. 'I think I've told you what's like enough to happen otherwise. Farewell. I've mounters to train. Why a native ought to be expected to teach Irish to hold their liquor is past all sense. They might as well have set me up with hoops and brained dogs.'

Valentine stormed out, breezes whirling weightless and confused in his path. Bird turned to look up at me. She truly was a different person – not a kinchin-mab, not a hot-corn wench in pilfered nankeen trousers, but simply a little girl, furrowing her brow in a way I was growing used to.

'What's happened? Mr V doesn't really mean that. He likes the Irish.'

She was right. And I would have answered her, too, if I'd known what had just happened. And if Dr Peter Palsgrave had not at that very moment slammed through the door, corseted and gasping, mopping his brow with flimsy electric-blue silk, causing us both to dart back defensively.

'I require Timothy Wilde,' he breathed. 'I've had a letter.'

'How did *you* come to be here?' Bird Daly exclaimed.

Dr Palsgrave blinked, heart visibly fluttering in his rib cage. He sank faintly into the room's only chair. 'I— How did *you* come to be here?'

I stood there, looking from the one to the other of them.

Bird smiling broadly, her hands clasped before her, apparently delighted to see two old acquaintances in a single quarter hour. Dr Palsgrave tremulous and startled, but seeming no less gratified to have encountered Bird. And I feeling more than a little upside down, watching as each of them cast about for a reasonable explanation of the other's presence at a Democratic Party rehearsal luncheon.

CHAPTER SIXTEEN

*It is ascertained that in civilized communities,
one-fourth part of all the human race who are born,
die before attaining their first year; more than
one-third before arriving at five years of age, and
before the age of twenty, one half the human race, it
is supposed, cease to exist.*

*The Sanitary Condition of the Laboring Population
of New York, January 1845*

The conversation seemed to have hit a rut, and I didn't want Bird doing much storytelling, that being a risky venture. So I took the reins myself.

'You know Bird?' I asked Dr Palsgrave directly. 'She's from—'

'Madam Marsh's house,' she interrupted with her chin jutting boldly. 'The . . . the downstairs maid.' Amazing what a change of togs can do for a person. As for Dr Palsgrave, he blinked his alert amber eyes twice and then huffed out a breath, standing up again. His spine was now straight and his chest swelled out, a man molded into the shape of a bantam rooster with a shawl-collared waistcoat. He leaned stiffly over to stare down his nose at the openly smiling girl with the dark red hair. A visible fondness came into his eyes and then flickered away again.

'Was it Marsh's?' he questioned, righting himself. 'I suppose you would know better than I.'

'But you recognized her only a moment ago,' I said, puzzling.

Palsgrave waved his hand in the air, pacing queer little circles in the cramped room. 'I treated her for something once. I can't be expected to remember names; I see far too many faces, and they all grow so quickly when they manage to grow at all. It must have been a bad case, whatever it was, for me to know her.'

'Chicken pox,' Bird said happily. 'You gave us lard and stewed onion poultices. I hardly itched.'

'Ah! Good, good,' he exclaimed, equally pleased. 'That's wonderful. So you—'

'Asked how you came to be here,' I interrupted.

'I received a letter,' he explained, white side whiskers flaring like a hissing tomcat's. 'A *most* disturbing correspondence, regarding the recent . . . the rumored child deaths. Is the *Herald* to be believed, are they merely a hoax? You and your *insolent* brother were the first to introduce me to this sordid affair, and so I at once sought you out at the Tombs, having now been *personally* engaged. I wish to help you. Chief Matsell directed me here.'

'About this letter,' I said slowly.

'I have it, if you—'

'Let's look at it somewhere else,' I said emphatically.

Dr Palsgrave tugged at his waistcoat, running his palm over his tightly constricted torso. 'Follow me, then. My practice is only two blocks from here.'

Quitting the stone meetinghouse unnoticed, as Moses Dainty seemed to be occupied plying voters with coffee, we walked west along Chambers. It didn't much surprise me that Dr Palsgrave kept his office on the most prestigious street in the city for a medical professional and, as we approached the end of City Hall Park at Broadway, I was struck with an odd sense of time going the wrong direction. It was the route I'd traveled as a roundsman, only done backward. Then we passed the teeming, sweltering, pedestrian-packed intersection and were greeted by more stone houses, these with their flowerboxes nicely watered and their windowpanes slashing sunlight at our eyes.

At his own heavy oaken door, marked at the side with DR PETER PALSGRAVE, PHYSICIAN TO YOUTH on a brass plate, Dr Palsgrave pulled out his keys. Catching a glimpse of Bird as he did so, he frowned.

'Why, may I ask, is she—'

'I'd prefer if you didn't,' I answered.

If Peter Palsgrave hadn't thought much of copper stars before, I wasn't making us any headway, for he glowered. Something about his swift shifts between innocent delight and bristling ill humor satisfied Bird extremely. Every time his lips pursed like a shutting clam, Bird's tilted up at the edges. As the doctor stormed his way into his richly carpeted front hall, hanging his slick beaver hat on a peg, I nudged her arm.

'Friend of yours?'

She nodded as we trailed after the mincing little physician. 'He always shams not to remember anyone. Always. It's sweet, I think.'

'Why is that?'

'He likes to *save* kinchin, doesn't he? He's a flash doctor, you know, and if he diaries our names and later sees us . . . well, then we're sick again, aren't we? He failed. He'd rather forget, and never know us once we're grown, than remember and lose out to whooping cough.'

I'd meant to answer her, since the insight was pretty handily reasoned for a ten year old. But the chamber we were led into, part study and part laboratory, froze my tongue a bit. For I'd never seen anything like it in my life.

The large room was divided in halves, in a sense. The side flooded with light from two garden-facing windows was a fully outfitted laboratory. Sparkling blue glass jars sealed with wax, copper kettles buffed to a rich coral finish, all manner of clever glass tubing. There was a hulking iron stove, a huge table on which rested vials and measuring instruments and open notebooks filled with crabbed doctorly handwriting. On these walls hung gaudily illuminated pages in careful frames, flowing Italian script marking out the properties and principles behind skulls and trees and wellsprings and hearts.

Meanwhile, the windowless side featured massive bookshelves – far richer than the Underhills' library, and it struck me that it was for excellent reason that the very learned doctor and the very learned reverend worked so closely together aiding the Protestant poor. But these weren't literature, nor holy scripts. These were medical tomes, gigantic and sober in their garb of cracked leather, gilt-edged chemistry textbooks, dozens of foreign language titles with gold leaf painted onto their spines, thick with strange symbols. Alchemy volumes. They had to be, for I'd just remembered what Mercy had told me Peter Palsgrave's *other* project was, apart from healing sick kinchin.

'How goes the elixir of life?' I asked in a friendly way.

He whirled like a top, with his neat little boots and his thin-stockinged legs and his puffed-out chest in its rich blue coat. Bird's smile cracked wider.

'How could you . . . oh, of course. Yes,' he sighed. 'I sent you to Mercy Underhill. She must have mentioned my magnum opus. It isn't the elixir of life, really, but a healing cordial. It is tremendously abstruse experimentation, not the sort of thing I can explain to a layman.'

'Try me,' I said, nettled.

Peter Palsgrave looked pretty set upon, but he told me all about it. And he was fascinated enough by his subject that even Bird was swept along for the ride, cocking her head and twirling a bit of reddish hair around one finger.

Alchemy, he told me, was the science of creating processes that could turn one element into another. And alchemists, having sought long and hard after the wisdom required to achieve impossible things, had done just that. They'd distilled liquids so pure that they were merely *one* thing and not many – alcohol, for instance. They'd created glass so transparent that it was entirely invisible. But purification and refinement, he told us, were a means to an end. Intended by some villainous types to lead to such wicked achievements as turning lead into gold, which would destroy any healthy economy, he added in a weary voice.

The elixir of life, which had long been the Holy Grail of alchemy, was an impossible goal, he told us, with a light in his eye that couldn't be dimmed by the lowliness of his audience. Man was created to return to dust one day. But a cordial capable of curing any illness in the living – that was an achievable dream. Children, he explained passionately, were so fragile. So vulnerable to contagion. But if one could only discover the perfect remedy by combining the latest advancements of medicine with the most ancient truths of alchemy and the noblest techniques of chemistry – *there* was a prize to be won not for the sake of wealth or of fame, but of humanity, the queer little man standing dapper and impassioned with his golden eyes and his corseted figure told us. The young and the helpless would no longer be subject to the evil whim of miasma. What form precisely it would take he did not know, though he'd long been following the threads of suspicions. Subtle but distinct clues.

It was mesmerizing.

Dr Palsgrave was practically throwing off golden sparks, words clattering headlong down an iron railway, braking madly to keep himself in some sort of check. And what a goal it was. Of course it was utterly cracked, and yes it was wildly romantic and seemingly impossible. But what a goal. To take a desperately ill child and restore it to health, to die of old age one distant day. Improbably, I loved the idea. Without supposing with any hope it could be accomplished, but who knew? With all the magical discoveries already unearthed, what else in the world silently waited to be fully understood?

'I occasionally wish that my own condition were not so . . . precarious,' he concluded, waving his hand toward his rheumatic fever-impaired heart. 'But perhaps, were I a sound man, I should not have been inspired to my calling with such fervor. And for the children, every discomfort is but a small price. Now, Mr Wilde. Tell me.' He paused, smoothing his palm down his silk-covered rib cage in his queer self-calming gesture. 'Have the police truly found, north of the city . . . have they—'

'They have,' I affirmed. 'Nineteen of them.'

The fact seemed to offend him physically, a sentiment I

heartily respected. Dr Palsgrave waved a vial of smelling salts under his nose. 'Despicable. Monstrous. I must see the bodies at *once*, I may be able to help you. Don't touch that, you foolish girl, it's poisonous!' he snapped at Bird, who swiftly set down a small crystal decanter.

Once the potion was safely out of her delicate hand, he instantly relaxed. He gave Bird a warm smile of apology, his anger evaporating as if it had never bubbled up at all, and in that moment I could see why she liked him so well. The gruffness was wholly an act, the welfare of youth a genuine obsession. I liked him too.

'By all means,' I agreed. 'Under condition of utmost secrecy, even from the rest of the copper stars. I'm the only one pursuing this. About your letter.'

'It nearly finished me,' he muttered, the electric-blue kerchief reappearing. 'Take it, I never want to see it again.'

I glanced at Bird, still investigating the chemistry kit, but with her hands dutifully behind her back now. Then I sat down and read about the oddest thing I've ever come across:

I can see only it.

Once there was a man who did the work of his God and when that man saw what his work must be, he felt ashamed, though he knew it was his burden, and he hid himself, and he wept at becoming the Angel of Death.

I can see it and nothing else see it ever and ever amen only the body so small and so broken. Ravaged like that. And nothing else.

So small it's an abomination no I've chased it away now for a moment but now there again, back at once, God help me, God save us, I'd tear out my eyes if I could but I would still see the body painted into the holes. And you, when you

see the little ones with their eyes gone white and still as bone
what can you do, how do you manage it? I can see only
them. With their dead eyes like nothing. Like cold stars.
Fish scales frosted over.

I am a broken jawbone.

Finish your work and stop this they have no sight any
longer and they need you to finish it as do I finish at once.
Mend the broken things. I must break another, and I will for
it all to stop. No nearer, let me go no nearer.

'It's unsigned,' I said, clearing my throat.

It was a shabby attempt at a clever observation. But my eyes didn't quite fit in my head any longer. Palsgrave scoffed at me, rightly, but it ended on a shudder. Robbed him of his point scored a bit.

Staring at the thing, I tried to make a better go of it. I'd read the letter in Val's company that morning much too quickly, the first one at my digs in Elizabeth Street slower. Had I still possessed them, I could try to match up papers, handwriting maybe, ink color, because the sentiments within were largely the same. As it was, I'd a rum job in the physical sense to compare the first documents to this new, differently painted piece of dementia. I could find the first in the *Herald* if I liked, but in type. Not much use when it came to studying appearances. But I did my best to mull it over from memory.

I cast my mind back. Both original letters had been poorly spelled, of a purpose maybe. This was mad but highly articulate. The others had been done in large, clear, blockish writing such as a beginner might scrawl, writ entirely in capitals, revealing nothing of personality or character – perhaps because the author was capable of naught better. But perhaps he meant his script to be masked. This had been done with an educated but badly palsied hand, in parts barely readable. As if the writer was terrified of his own words. Under the influence of liquor or a drug, maybe, shying back from phrases full of a sad venom that hurt his eyes. Finally, the others had been suspiciously gleeful, melodrama ripe enough for me to suspect them sensationalist nonsense. To *hope* they were nonsense, as I now admitted to myself. For the city's sake, for the Irish, for the copper stars, maybe even for Val's bloody Democratic Party. There was dread here, though, not gloating, and the dread sounded genuine.

'I don't suppose you know this hand?' I ventured.

'It's nearly *illegible*, you imbecile, and why should I?'

'This person obviously knows of your work.'

'Everyone knows of my work!' the strange little man cried. 'That is why this – this – *malignancy* was addressed to me! I am a physician who works exclusively with *children*, I am the *only* one, I— *Put that down!*' he thundered, the skin around his silver whiskers flushing with lively pink rage.

Bird dropped a sinister knife blade with some sort of herbal residue yet clinging to it. Clasping her hands again, in front this time, penitent.

'I won't hurt myself, I promise.'

'Oh, God. Thank you,' he breathed gratefully. 'I would consider it a tremendous boon.'

'Will you go to the Tombs and examine the bodies?' I questioned. 'Matsell, when you've found him, will show you personally. You must speak to no one else.'

'I'll go at once.'

'May I keep this?'

'Mr Wilde,' he hissed, 'if I never see that piece of depravity again in all my days, I will be a man who ends on a note of satisfaction. Get it out of my home. Come along now, you –

you *child*. Quick march. Mr Wilde, you imply that you do not intend to accompany me.'

'I've another line of investigation,' I explained as we quit the building. 'If you're game, I'll stop by here tonight. See what you've learned.'

'If you must, and I suppose you must, mustn't you,' he sighed. 'Farewell, then.'

'Goodbye, Dr Palsgrave,' Bird said.

'What *does* she want? Ah,' Palsgrave huffed fondly, pulling a wrapped caramel from his pocket and tossing it to Bird. 'Kinchin. Such alarming creatures, really. Good day to you.'

'That man is mad,' I noted as the ramrod-spined gentleman waved for a hackney with his bizarre blue kerchief.

'Fit for a cranky-hutch,' Bird agreed as she unwrapped the candy. 'He's grand, isn't he, Mr Wilde?' Her face darkened as she looked up at me. 'Is that letter you have from . . . from the man in the black hood?'

'I don't know,' I answered, turning back from the road to help Bird up into the hack I'd just flagged down. 'But I will find that out if it is the last thing that I do.'

Mott Street near to the Five Points just south of Bayard gives a man the impression an infection is running rampant through the road's sewers. And in August the fever worsens, paint peeling and wood cracking like skin in a hospital ward, the hot, wet air shivering before your eyes. The pale glassy cast of the windows making the houses look stupefied. The smell of it. Every open casement vomiting chicken guts and trimmed vegetable leaves that are already spoiling, thrown down from kitchen bowls three stories above. I don't know that Bird had ever walked through such a hellhole, for she stuck close, eyes wide and careful. She passed the time glancing at blacks sitting in doorways, straw hats in their hands and jugs on their knees, wasted with loss of sweat; Irish leaning their elbows out of windows, smoking mindlessly, starved for honest work. The bone-deep ache in that road rises up from the very cobbles, seeping into your own tired feet.

Hopstill resided in an attic at number 24 Mott Street, or so Julius had told me. So when we reached the cancerous wooden structure, I walked right up to the door to make for the stairs. A boot caught my ankle as I stepped over the threshold, and I swiftly looked down. Following the stocking to the grime-saturated skirts, I discovered a woman, everything about her gone grey as dust, peeling potatoes with her fingernails.

'What do you want, then?'

'Edward Hopstill,' I answered the strange gatekeeper. 'He's in the attic, I take it?'

'He's nary,' she sniffed, letting a shard of potato skin fall to the floor. 'Moved to the cellar, didn't he. A month back.'

Thanking her, I stepped over the bowl, Bird keeping close. Hopstill had lived hand to mouth even before the fire ruined our homes, I knew as much. And yet . . . a cellar. I'd never even been overly fond of the scoundrel, and still my feet dragged, afraid to see anyone I knew personally lowered until they were under the very ground.

The stairs I found didn't have a door at the top, but I could see one at the bottom, blank and sinister. We tramped down. I knocked. The door opened. Hopstill's face appeared, its fleshy curtains badly shaved, his hair dank and possibly moldy, his sallow skin going ashy already. The acrid stench of gunpowder, burning lamp oil, and whatever stews underneath New York's houses met our nostrils.

'What on earth do you want?' Hopstill growled in his annoyed English cadence.

Boom.

The explosion wasn't a big one. But it was enough for me to throw a protective arm over Bird, for her to start like a cat whose tail had been stepped on, and for Hopstill's scowl to burrow a bit deeper into his face.

'Perfect. Thank you, Wilde. How am I to test whether a new sort of bombshell is properly colored when I don't even *see it go off?*'

Tentative, we followed him in. It was another laboratory, but the sooty workplace of a craftsman rather than the bright playground of a scientist. The lamps brooded a sulfur yellow, revealing an unmade bed, a single grated air shaft with flies buzzing around it, two large tables, and a small cookstove. Mortars and pestles, stacks of fire-crackers, sparking sticks, and corked bottles of lightning powder were everywhere. The walls were planked and exhaling some sort of foul earthy moisture, forming an ooze where the wood met the packed dirt floor. Either the chamber pot was full, or the rear tenement (I never doubted there was a rear tenement) used a school sink for sewage. It was altogether the most unlivable chamber I'd ever keeked into. Except for the striking fact that only one person lived in it and not ten.

'It's because of the fireworks, isn't it?' I asked.

'What?'

'You have to live alone. Because of the lightning. You have to rent an entire ken, and this is what you can afford.'

'What the devil business is it of yours, what is that young person doing following you, why are you wearing a copper star, and what are you doing in my home?'

I told him as much as he needed to know, which was

practically nothing. A thirty-second tale of how I'd come to work on the force. We were in a hurry, and Hopstill benefits from being dealt with abruptly.

The lightning-maker stood hunched angrily over his work. And I knew the man: sick at being caught out in a cellar. Since he figures God sends poverty to the unworthy, I didn't blame him a bit for being ashamed. He hovered above an iron retort, checking its hot contents, darting back to the mortar and pouring powdered red dye into it, siphoning off gunpowder, generally loathing our presence. And now, of all things, I wanted him to teach *children* how to make lightning. I claimed that, in return, they would work in a vague way as my spies. From his perspective, I was a pretty comprehensive arse.

'If you can convince me to do such a mad thing, I'll nominate you for governor,' he snapped. 'Get the hell out of my workshop, I haven't the time to grant favors.'

I was about to make him an offer, but Bird squealed in delight all of a sudden. The happy sound tugged at a piece of me, something lightly tethered to the back of my neck.

'This has a little handle,' she said. 'I've seen fireworks, over the river, but never held one. Is that what it's for? To hold it while it fires? What's the color?'

Hopstill's deep-seated loathing of kinchin seemed to retreat a fraction. 'It's silver.'

'However do you make it silver?'

'Powdered metal. I use the cheapest I can find.'

There was a small silence. One that could have dragged a bit had I wanted to make a point. But I didn't.

'For teaching the newsboys how to make lightning for their stage effects, I'll pay you enough to get out of this cellar,' I offered.

'Ridiculous. How much do you suppose that is, then?'

'Twenty dollars.'

His eyes sparked like crackers and then dimmed just as quick. Hiding the smoldering brimstone look of total desperation. I set the two golden neds on his table, twenty dollars in coin.

Hopstill blinked at it ravenously, mouth melting into a lost shape. 'I had never really thought to associate with anyone from the old neighborhood again, and now here you're getting me out of this tar pit. Pardon my skepticism earlier. But I've been sorely tried, and no familiar faces to speak of it with.'

'Julius seemed glad enough to have seen a former neighbor himself, and I'm grateful to him for telling me where you'd got to.'

Hopstill looked up from a bag of shining blue dust. 'Julius? Oh, yes, the colored fellow from Nick's. I did see him.'

'Who did you think I meant?'

'Miss Underhill, of course.'

I shuffled bits of my thoughts to and fro, tried out new patterns. None of them sensible. 'Why?'

'Well, she's everywhere, isn't she?' he muttered. 'In the dead of night, when all Christian folk are abed. In any event, I'll teach these lads to make a sheet of fire fit to terrify the popular theatergoer.'

'I'm grateful.'

Hopstill's head dropped into his palm in rank exhaustion. 'God, and I thought I'd likely enough die here come winter, when I'd need extra money for fuel,' he said to no one in particular. I wondered when last he'd eaten. There was no food on the shelves such as I could see. 'I was planning out a grand finale of all my stock over Battery Park. Better than pawning it for a few more miserable weeks, to watch all those sublime explosions. But I can forget that now. Sometimes things turn out all right after all.'

'Sometimes,' agreed Bird gravely.

When all Christian folk are abed, I thought, the phrase like an itch in my skull.

'Sometimes,' I said out loud. Just then, for instance, a great deal was going right. I'd money to spare from the elections fund, and my time was my own, and Hopstill would gain me the aid of the news hawkers.

Of course Mercy went abroad at night; sickness and want abide by no schedule.

What a splendid day.

I gave Hopstill the address of the Orange Street newsboys' theater, and he gave me his promise to pay them a call that evening. *The trick is to keep pushing,* I thought as Bird and I surfaced into the sunlight once more. *If you push hard enough, it won't matter that you haven't the smallest inkling of what you're doing.*

After leaving Bird with Mrs Boehm (who'd assured me that if she so much as glimpsed Silkie Marsh, she would lock every entrance and scream in her native tongue for the Germans next door), I went to the makeshift morgue in the Tombs, hoping to find Palsgrave still poring tirelessly over medical evidence. He wasn't there. But George Washington Matsell was, standing rotund and dignified in the wide cellar. Viewing what I was now viewing, lined up on hastily built tables. Not saying anything about it.

There wasn't much to say.

'Dr Palsgrave tells me that the letter he gave you is a nice stroke of madness,' he commented. 'It might make a difference to us.'

'I don't know how, but I hope it does.'

'Study it, then. Dr Palsgrave put this report in my hands, said if you needed him to explain any of it to you, to call around at his practice. But it isn't *medical* reading. More like something from that Poe lunatic.'

I took the papers, eager for the elusive fact that would make it all sane. I stopped, though. Took a breath. Because nineteen corpses, or the remnants of corpses, were laid out in front of me on wood tables. It was such a far sight from the beautiful imagined vision of health Dr Palsgrave had laid before me earlier that I could scarce bear to look. There were too many of them – God, how very many – and they were much too small. And no one's body should ever be bared like that – ripped open and displayed for all the world to see. I thought of my own inner organs, heart and spleen and kidneys, invaluable to no one save myself. And I wanted nothing greater than to lower our sole hard evidence of wrongdoing back under the ground, where what had once been tender and vulnerable could rest quiet.

'Surprise me, Wilde,' Chief Matsell said as he left the room. 'I'm waiting.'

How scattered they look, I thought. *A white flap of skin, a clump of red hair, the sheen of exposed bone.*

I opened the report. It had been hard to write, I supposed. Once I'd read its contents, I certainly hoped so, anyhow.

These nineteen bodies range from five years dead to very recent, but causes of individual death are impossible to confirm. All nineteen evidence severe violence enacted postmortem – specifically, breastbones are no longer intact, and the rib cage has been pulled asunder in every case. I can only suppose that the miscreant had intended to reach the organs. Aside from natural decay: in two cases, the heart is missing entirely; in three, the liver; four, the spleen; twelve, the brain stem; two, the spine. Whether animals did this before decomposition set in, or the murderer desired them, is open to debate, but I find it impossible to credit any circumstance apart from the latter.

When these deliberately carved crosses are taken into account, I cannot but wonder whether the letter published by the Herald *days ago was perhaps genuine after all. The theory of a religion-mad Irish would surely fit the violence done to these nineteen dead.*

Dr Peter Palsgrave

'*Finish your work and stop this,*' I quoted in a jagged whisper. '*Mend the broken things.* Dear God, whichever of you invisible lot might be listening at the moment, just what in buggering *hell* am I supposed to do now?'

CHAPTER SEVENTEEN

The social condition of Ireland is at present moment distressing – painful – most deplorable. The physical destitution of the people impels them to crime. The disputes about land give rise to assassination.

New York Herald, summer 1845

The only option left was to get back to work. In fact, I decided that hard, frantic work was the only route.

I turned out to be right, too. It just didn't happen to have been *my* work.

For three days, I waited on news from the boys who made a career of selling it. I suspected that they were being very successful at learning how to make lightning and coming up dry when it came to sinister carriages. I pored over the only letter that hadn't been burned. I avoided the morgue, and then the day before the bodies were to be secretly reburied, I went to the cellar with Mr Piest and searched through every bone and hair follicle, gaining nothing but a lingering queasiness and an oily feeling that wouldn't wash off my fingertips until

I used lye. I visited the police guards at the north end of the city, who were bored thin skinned at being stuck in the woods for sixteen hours a go. I earned some fairly ripe insults for my trouble.

By the end of the three days, on the morning of August thirtieth, I was so desperate I sat Bird down and told her to draw the man in the black hood for me.

'There you are, Mr Wilde,' she said when she was charcoal fingered and quite finished.

It was a picture of a man wearing a cape-backed cloak and a black hood which covered his head. I thanked her anyway.

Meanwhile, my brother's paranoia – as it was perfectly logical – had infected me. I devoured the *Herald* every morning as usual, but now the mere act of reaching for the familiar periodical sent a tipsy feeling through my rib cage. *Say nothing of kinchin*, I would beg silently. *Give me time.*

And so I would read of the frantic labor downtown, of shipping schedules and the roar of unrest in distant Texas, dreading to move my eyes lest I set them upon my own name: *It has been discovered that Timothy Wilde, copper star badge number 107, has been investigating the slaughter of Irish kinchin, and has failed in every way possible.*

I couldn't help but think that it was bound to happen. That it was only a matter of time.

Then on Saturday evening, feeling both wrecked and useless, and not knowing what else to do with myself, I returned to the Tombs. I encountered Mr Connell in the open yard, leading a slender and richly dressed man wearing a green velvet coat, with his wrists tied behind him. There was a grim air to my colleague. I nodded, and he angled his head in return.

'I say, sir,' the prisoner called out to me, 'please help – I am being detained against my will.'

'Sure, and that's pretty much the point of it,' Connell returned.

'What's the trouble?' I asked.

'I was accosted in the street by this – this *individual*,' the captive sniffed. 'A fine pass we have come to in this town when a gentleman suddenly finds himself being manhandled by some sort of bleached savage. Violence has been done to my person. I appeal to you, sir, to right this *at once*.'

'What's the charge?' I asked evenly.

'Passin' forged stock certificates,' Connell replied.

'Put him at the end of the eastern cell block,' I suggested. 'I hear there's a fresh litter of rats down there. They ought to get along fine.'

'Get your filthy paws off me!' the counterfeiter shrieked as Mr Connell pulled him away. Then to me, 'Don't you read the newspapers? Aren't you aware of what sorts of perversions these Irish are capable of? Their murderous debaucheries? You would leave me in *his* hands?'

'I don't know quite what ye've been doing these several days, Mr Wilde,' my fellow copper star said as we parted, 'but I wonder if you could be going about it a wee bit faster?'

It was such a fair question that I didn't even have the heart to answer it.

I went to the clerical common room for the copper stars within the depths of the Tombs. Once there, I began reading an argument for the complete expulsion of papists from America alongside an Irish manifesto of Catholic rights. Research born of total desperation. Scraping splinters off the bottom of an empty barrel. Then Mr Piest strode in, making an impressive racket in his five-pound boots. Manic eyed and wagging his chinless jaw up and down, he pointed at me gallantly.

'I have done it, Mr Wilde! I have found it. It has been discovered. At last,' he declared, 'I have found *something*.'

He dropped the *something* on the table. It was a male sexual shield. A good one, the sort long used by housewives who'd tired of miscarriage, or by whores who didn't fancy the notion of their noses eroding from Cupid's disease. Made of very neatly stitched-up sheep or goat intestine, forming a long reusable hood. Not fresh. Worn until a crack had formed, for one thing, though it certainly wasn't clean either. I stared at it dubiously.

'Where?'

'In light of your recent exhortation of hard, steady work, I expanded my range, Mr Wilde. You *greatly* affected me. I had been looking only thirty yards' radius from the site of the mass grave, but I found my answer fifty yards away, in a secluded little valley.'

'Good Lord. I thought you were still on roundsman duty.'

'I am,' the noble old lunatic confessed blearily. 'Matsell's orders. I take two hours every morning, to have the best daylight.'

Registering that Mr Piest's silvery hair was practically standing on end, and that his aged hands were vaguely tremulous, I started to say something appreciative and sympathetic. But then I trailed off.

'You don't mean to tell me,' I said, fighting whatever was crawling up the back of my throat, 'that before they've been killed, or even *after*, he—'

'No!' Mr Piest held up a single finger. 'Were that the case, I'd have found many more, going back five years. Would I not? As it is, I only found four, discarded when cracked, and none look more than a year old to me.'

He pulled the rest of them out from his stuffed coat pocket

and they joined their flaccid brother on the tabletop. I wanted very badly to jump up and wring the spooney old bastard by the hand. And then again, I didn't.

'You're a wonder at finding things, Mr Piest,' I said warmly instead. Then a tight little coiled-up thrill shot through me and I sat forward. 'You think that whoever used these goes there often. Very often. You think they might have heard something, seen something. There are scattered homesteads up there, small farms beyond the settled grid—'

'And these are all clearly home sewn, not bought, who would buy—'

'Shields from a druggist and risk exposure when you're copulating—'

'In the woods, so as to keep your sin a secret? These came from the wife of a cuckolded farmer, or a country maiden with an appetite and a keen sense of caution. Within walking distance, as will be obvious to you, Mr Wilde.'

I sat back in my chair, a feebleminded grin on my face. Sweeping my hat off, I made him a seated bow. Mr Piest bowed back, ridiculously low.

Leaning down, he grasped the pile of intestinal balloons and returned them to his pocket. 'I shall find the owner, Mr Wilde. I shall make inquiries. My questions will be the soul of discretion, and we will gain our answer. I must speak with the chief!'

He scuttled out again, whistling an old Dutch tune. The single oddest man I'd ever encountered. And worth his weight in fresh-minted guilders.

I went home that night much less heavy than I'd been, good luck floating under my boots. Merrier than I'd felt in days, ready for a pint or two of small beer, and then a glass or two of whiskey, and then bed, with hope loosening the knots in my shoulders. At Elizabeth Street, the front shop light was blazing as I went in.

Mrs Boehm stood at the counter, staring at the pair of nankeen trousers Bird had been using. She looked smeared somehow. All her edges gone slack, as if she'd been touched before the paint was dry. Her wide mouth adrift, and the set of her hands with their piece of kinchin's clothing resting uselessly on the wood.

'That was wrong of you,' she said in a dry cornsilk voice, weightless and empty.

'What? What's happened?'

'You should not have sent her away to the house. Not *that* house, ever. And not so soon. I was angry before, but my mind was changing, Mr Wilde. You ought to have told me.'

Gravity shifted its pull several times and simultaneously at that, a dizzy, panicked feeling.

She didn't just say 'house'. She said 'House'. House of Refuge.

'Where's Bird?' I demanded. 'I never sent her away. Where is she?'

Frightened dull blue eyes flew up to meet mine. 'There was a carriage. Two men, one very dark and tall. One lighter and smaller, with hair on his lip. They took her. I'd have stopped them, but they had papers, signed by you, Mr Wilde, and—'

'Was there a first name?'

'No. Only Wilde. They left five minutes ago.'

I ran out the door.

Every face on Elizabeth Street seemed to have a sneer on it, every indolent pig hoping I realized just how badly I could bungle a job I knew *nothing* about. Two men: one very dark and tall, and one lighter and smaller, with hair on his lip.

Scales, whose first name probably didn't exist any longer, and Moses Dainty – Val's men.

My feet struck the ground viciously, heading like a bullet shot for the nearest horse. It was tethered in front of a grocery and it wasn't mine, no argument in the world could have claimed it mine, but I tore the leather straps off the post and I swung myself in the saddle and I dug my heels in, ignoring its very reasonable startlement.

You live across the street. You can solve the crime of the stolen horse tomorrow.

I thought about cursing my goddamned interfering wicked-minded brother's name as I almost killed a pair of Bohemian pedestrians heading home from a beer hall. But by that time, cursing seemed superfluous.

The House of Refuge is located where Fifth Avenue, Twenty-fourth Street, and Broadway collide, its charity hidden well away from respectable people's eyes. In the countryside, east of where the bodies had been found – although recently men had begun building improbable mansions nearby. And I didn't waste an instant mulling over whether their stated destination might be a ruse. It was a reckless roll of the dice, and yes it made my breath stutter in my chest, and yes it made me bully the unfortunate stranger's chestnut gelding, and yes it was a guess based neither on evidence nor trust.

But I had nothing else to go on. I could fly toward the House of Refuge or else gallop toward India or the Republic of Texas. Gripping the reins, I swerved from Elizabeth Street into the mad lights of Bleecker, only a block from Broadway now and capturing the eyes of sable-hatted gentlemen and roughnecked Scots laborers alike as I thundered past.

My thoughts were pretty black as I traveled my route, earning squeals from stargazers and tourists and dignitaries, a weird and wild quarter-masked figure on a sultry summer night. They went in this fashion, most of them:

Valentine is warning you he means business. Valentine is despicable. Valentine seemed to like her, though. Valentine is a powder keg with his fuse running directly into the fingers of the Democratic Party, and Bird Daly is a witness to a scandal and therefore a liability.

The rest went like so:

Bird thinks you did this. She supposes evicting her your idea.

All the while I galloped, my eyes searched for a closed carriage. And I knew what it should look like, too. Something official enough to fool Mrs Boehm, who was no kind of fool. And neither was my brother, God rest his soul after I'd killed him for this. The coach, therefore, needed curtains and it needed good paint, preferably with a charitable-looking seal on its door.

But I saw no such thing. And so I rode like a scream on the wind up Broadway, skirting the omnibuses and the drays and the hackneys and the handcarts. Without much trouble, as it happened, because I was one man on one horse, and I hadn't the time to be afraid of a collision. Flying past the turnoff for Washington Square, I'd a perfectly still memory for an instant of Mercy sitting in a park speaking of London, having just walked open eyed into a smallish mob to free a black man. It whirled away from me all too quickly, replaced by ghastly things. The sort of things that happen to kinchin who go to the House of Refuge.

Bird will sew piecework until she goes stitch-blind at twenty-five. Bird will be shipped to a bleak prairie fit only for slitting your own throat to be the wife of a failing frontier farmer. Bird will die of pneumonia in the Tombs for stealing a rich man's purse once she figures out she can probably manage it without being caught.

Bird will return to her former profession.

I rode the poor beast still harder, my lungs chugging fast as its hooves, my entire body turned into some sort of ode to velocity.

As I hurtled along arrogant Broadway, hearing yells of satin-cloaked disdain in my wake, bypassing mansions with distantly glimpsed chandeliers as if they were so much washed-up tidal muck, I felt a ruthless thrill at my speed warring with a growing despair at my helplessness. I hadn't seen them yet. And I *would* have seen them, I knew I would. If they'd been present to notice.

Where had they taken her?

I was honestly considering turning back, spurring the innocent horse madly in another direction. Any direction. The right direction.

But then I stopped to think.

I was almost at the House of Refuge now. I'd passed Union Place's border at Seventeenth Street, its grass parched in the moonlight but its new-minted landscape irritatingly hopeful. Only a little farther to go. And if they'd been clever, and thought I might arrive home any second, ruining their scheme, what would they have done?

They'd have gone all the way around Washington Square and then cut back to Fifth Avenue, taking the wrong route a bit but still getting there directly. Because if they did need to flee my pursuit, I would surely come after them along Broadway.

Or so I was thinking as I rode up to the gates of the formidable House of Refuge. I reined in the gelding, waiting. Listening as my harsh breath broke the moonlit silence.

Hoping violently that I'd simply beaten them there.

It's an abandoned federal arsenal. The House of Refuge, I mean. Black as pitch in the steadily disappearing farmland surrounding it, blacker than the trees, blacker than an actual arsenal would be. As I mentioned, copper stars are meant to send vagrant kinchin there. But I'd never followed that particular order. And I never would do. They could penalize me however they liked. They could send me to the Tombs myself for insubordination, threaten any punishment, force me into hard labor, equip me with a leg iron, deliver me some licks with the cat while I was tied over a barrel, lock me up alone in a chamber the size of a closet without light for days. Because I was full grown, and likely enough to survive such treatment.

Some of the kinchin at the House of Refuge didn't.

The horse shivered, sweat pouring dark as blood along its neck as I waited. I rubbed at its mane, sensing its uneasiness under me, thankful it hadn't already decided I was more trouble than worth carrying. Crickets hissed at me from the void, and the sly whispered wings of dimmed fireflies hummed in my ears. The wall in whose shadow I sheltered was two feet thick. A stone fortress, more than high enough to foil most would-be escapees.

Not Valentine, though. Not by a long stretch.

The irony was that when he'd been incarcerated there, our parents had been enthusiastically alive. But it was an institution built to keep idle youth off the streets, then reform them by way of a pungent dose of 'moral and corporal discipline'. Well approved by the city elders, and by every parent whose kinchin were disinclined to steal liquor from groceries and drink it on the Battery.

Not Henry and Sarah Wilde, therefore.

It took my parents four days to find out where Val had been dragged off to. Eight more to secure an audience with a judge. As I was a runty six years old, I can only recall how silent our house was. How suddenly stamped with empty spaces. My brother's truancy at age twelve was passionate, but hardly regular. And whenever he vanished, I'd always assumed he'd come back. His coming back was the natural order. But everything was different that time: the way my mother couldn't sew a straight line, the way my bull of a father couldn't bring himself to finish his supper. When they did finally speak with the magistrate, the official observed that Val had been caught breaking windows. Asked for better documentation of his birth. Dismissed them.

Val arrived home two days later, when my parents were nearly beside themselves and hadn't stopped whispering for forty or so hours. His tawny hair was viciously shorn off, and he wore a threadbare uniform. He asked with a cocky grin on his face for a cut of meat and some small beer. My dad was nearer to him and the first to pull him into his arms, so my dad was the first to notice that Val's shirt had dried completely into the bloodied cuts crisscrossing his back.

Whether Val was boldly exaggerating about making brass nails, or about the infernal bells summoning them from place to place in soulless silence, or about the mortifying forced washings or the spoiled food, I never cared. I saw my brother's shirt for myself. Henry Wilde wasn't an easy man, but when my mum was soaking the fabric off Val's skin, I heard him clear as anything pounding his fists into the barn wall. Even six as I was, I'd a similar urge myself that I couldn't express with words, and so kicked apart a rotting box.

The thought of Valentine sending Bird to the same place was half horror and half awe. So wrong that it was a scrap of nightmare. I'd gained the same feeling once by dreaming of a monster with teeth at the ends of its digits and its mouth full of fingernails.

Hoofbeats approached me.

At a clean, swift clip, too. Not drawing attention. Neither losing an instant of time.

There was a breeze at my back, and it shivered along the prison wall, echoed by the muted snuffling of the stolen horse. I was buried in the high stone's shadow, and the driver the only man who could possibly see me. But my own vision of the clopping vehicle as it drew closer was very clear. It was a four-wheeled carriage pulled by a matched pair, with curtains over the windows, and I caught a glimpse of a seal of sorts painted on the door. And by then I had a plan.

Digging my heels into the ribs of the animal, I burst into the road again.

'Halt!' I shouted, waving my arms.

The set of black horses obeyed me an eyeblink before their driver did, as I was directly in their path. There ought to have been lights on that carriage by night. I could see the shadows of its lanterns hanging cold and unlit from its four corners, very tellingly.

'Who goes there?' called down the driver.

'Police.' I shook my lapel at him. 'I must speak with your passengers.'

I didn't give him time to answer. I clucked at the gelding and trotted to the side of the vehicle. Whether the horse trusted me because it was obedient by nature or because it preferred me to its usual master, I'll never know. I reached over and jerked the door open, my feet on a level with the metal steps.

Moses Dainty on the left-hand side, moustache twitching with vexed confusion. Scales on the right, breathing through his mouth because that's what he does when plans wobble or tilt. Sitting rigid and furious and tearful and perfectly healthy next to Scales was Bird Daly. She scowled at the sight of me, and then the scowl faded.

Bird can spot a lie, and who's been telling it.

'Hand her over,' I said gruffly. 'Whatever you were told, Madam Marsh wants her back.'

The pair of thugs glowered at me and then glanced at each other. Meanwhile, outrage flashed across the little girl's face before settling into a fixed shipwreck victim's expression. The blank look of a half-drowned person clutching a raft, waiting directionlessly for something to happen.

'You know better than to try to fun a Party man, Tim,' Moses argued, 'seeing as—'

'Whatever my brother told you, I'm here to say he's off his chart. Madam Marsh sent me here personally. You'd not want her coming down on the Party over a clear mistake, and when I was here to warn you? This one's spoken for. Pass me the chit and we'll say nothing else.'

'Madam Marsh? But wait,' Scales began stupidly, 'did she—'

'Yes. In person. Only an hour ago. I've galloped here, can't you see that? Fine. If you want Silkie Marsh thinking you a pair of jilters heaving her goods, I'll leave you to it. I'd not much like to see what happens when she goes back on you. Doubtless the Party will pay for the funerals.'

'This was all to be pretty straightforward,' Moses put in. 'I don't think we ought to—'

'Hand her over,' I interrupted, 'or I'll have my brother thrown off the copper stars. Watch me do it. I've my own neck to think of, should you finish this blunder the way you're so set on doing. Didn't you see me guarding her at the Party meeting?'

It took maybe ten seconds but it was the right combination

of words. Scales, who'd longer arms, half stepped onto the footrest, hauled Bird up by her armpits, and deposited her in front of me, sidesaddle so her dress wouldn't hamper my riding.

I didn't wait to say thank you. I was already thundering back into town, in the dark of night on a stolen horse, the instant I had a grip on her torso. When we were south of Union Square Park and obviously free of the baffled hirelings, I nudged her a little, slowing.

'Are you all right?'

'Where are we going?' came a tiny voice.

'Home. To see Mrs Boehm. Then off to find a better hiding place.'

Bird nestled in tighter, before I set us to flying again and the wind carried the edges of her words off.

'I never truly thought it was you sent me away, Mr Wilde,' she lied. 'I never did.'

I'd heard Bird tell a score of lies for her own sake already. For precaution, for defense, for misdirection, for sympathy. It was easy enough to stomach those lies, because Bird Daly needed lies the way some creatures need shells. And so I'd sat back and watched them tumble out like beads off a broken string. There wasn't any choice about it. I wasn't about to stomach that last invention of hers, though. Not for a minute. As I said, I'm full grown.

'Bird, don't lie for my sake,' I said as I nudged the horse back into life. 'Ever again.'

'All right,' she whispered after giving that some consideration. 'Then I'm glad it wasn't you.'

The lights in the bakery windows on Elizabeth Street were fair quivering with watchfulness. When I reined in the long-suffering horse and dismounted, reaching up to hoist Bird down, she was stolen from me again within six seconds. This time by Mrs Boehm, who flew through the door with her broad mouth cracked in a grin that didn't match the wet in her eyes.

'Are you all right?' Mrs Boehm snapped, sounding considerably put out that Bird had allowed herself to be kidnapped.

'I think so,' Bird managed. 'Are there any poppy seed cakes not sold today?'

I led the horse across the street to the grocery. Peered around me. All peaceful calm at the streaky sulfur-smelling cabbage display, all slurring good cheer at the plank bar within. Tethering the horse, I gave it a bucket filled at the Croton pump on the corner. I brushed it down a bit with a rag from our side yard and plenty more fresh water. It shivered happily. The entire grim adventure had taken less than an hour. Chalking up another point for the copper stars, I went back inside.

'Where is she?' I asked Mrs Boehm, sweeping my hat off and sitting backward in a chair pulled up to the table.

'Upstairs, with a cake and some milk.' Mrs Boehm had been wiping down her ovens, but she turned to look at me, her plain, friendly face wrenching sideways. 'I let her go. It was my fault, I—'

'It was nothing like your fault. We'll just make sure not to let it happen twice.'

She nodded. Sinking on a long, low exhale, she sat across from me.

'Mrs Boehm, I'm sorry about your husband and son.'

I didn't want to sorrow her, but it needed saying. Maybe it was selfish of me. Still. The name on the bakery redone to claim her ownership, matched against the steady stream of regulars far older than the paint. The way she talked with Bird, lacking the shadows of more adult concerns flickering along her face as the child spoke. She was actually *listening*. Practiced poultices, reserves of silent patience, and a pair of nankeen trousers kept locked away in a trunk.

'Thank you,' she said softly. Then, 'That was a question, I think?'

'Not if it vexes you. Just a fact.'

'There was a cattle drive on Broadway two years ago. Very sudden, the way they grew frightened. Lost control.' She hesitated, rubbing at a glassy streak of butter on the wood with her thumb. 'Sometimes I wonder if maybe I would sooner have heard the danger. The stampede, the hooves. But it was too fast for Franz, and Audie was on his shoulders.'

'I'm sorry,' I said again.

Mrs Boehm shrugged in a way that meant I shared no part in it, not that she no longer bled at the memory. 'I have a shop, and a home. A neighbor when it happened said I was lucky to keep so much and that it was the will of God. What a stupid woman,' she concluded. 'For God to make something young and perfect and then crush him. Why go to the trouble? Stupid people imagine God thinks like they do. Maybe God is not there, but I cannot believe God is stupid.'

A knock sounded from behind us. A quiet little *rat-tat-tat*.

Cautiously, I opened the door. There had been something odd about the noise even apart from its softness, and I saw what it was when I looked down. The knuckles were pretty undersized, and the striking point on the boards three feet below where it should have been.

'Neill,' I said. 'What's wrong?'

Neill was gasping with effort, his bony little shoulders rhythmically flapping. He wore a good quality set of charity togs – cotton shirt and frayed tweed vest and corduroy breeches that didn't quite cover his shiny half-shell knees.

'Father Sheehy is needin' you at St Patrick's. Not able to come himself. Sent me. Guardin' it, he is, best as he can, but needs ye, come on, I'm to bring you quick as possible. Please.'

'Has someone been hurt?' I demanded after snatching my hat and advising Mrs Boehm to open the door for no one save myself.

'Can't rightfully say,' Neill panted as we broke into a run. 'But someone's been killed, and killed all wrong, sure as there's a mad Irish devil prowling these streets.'

CHAPTER EIGHTEEN

They surely must have been demons in human shape,
permitted for a time to have their full sway on earth,
in order to strengthen the cause of a purer and holier
faith.

American Protestant in Defence of Civil and
Religious Liberty Against Inroads of Papacy, 1843

*T*here isn't, though, I thought stubbornly as we sprinted.
Please. There can't be. If there is, we'll pay too dear for it,
much too dear, each and every one of us. If a mad Irish devil is
prowling these streets, every reasonable thought is about to be driven
clean out of the public mind.

The scant few blocks north toward the dizzy twin pinnacles
of St Patrick's Cathedral passed unreal, falsely familiar. Paper
cutouts for a newsboy's stage. The air came hot so near the
ground, gritty and thick as we flew by a cloyingly stuffed
sinkhole, and as I yearned for more speed, I wished I hadn't
yet solved the crime of the horse I had just stolen from the
Elizabeth Street grocery.

We wheeled left at Prince Street, and there was St Patrick's, the pale moonlit monument to the Catholic God before us. It was the only time of night in New York when the streets even approach quiet: the sheltered alleyway of lost time lying between three-thirty and four in the morning. Not anywhere near two a.m., drenched in gin and smelling of late-night chops and after-opera coffee and back-alley sex. Not yet approaching five a.m., horses streaming back into the streets and roosters crowing maniacally. Between play and work, when a mab just heading for bed following an all-night debauch might bump into a still sleep-blinded stonemason trudging to his work three miles from home. I turned to Neill, slowing.

'There isn't a mad Irishman after Catholic kinchin,' I said, desperate to believe myself. 'It's only a sick rumor based on a worthless letter the *Herald* printed. They've already retracted it, Neill.'

Neill shook his head sadly at my ignorance, quivering blue veins visible against his white neck.

A small crowd milled before the triple doors of the cathedral. Mainly Irish. Some American. Most of them buzzing with something I'd seen before: the same sort of eager, frightened, childish looks the bystanders had worn watching half of downtown burn to the ground.

'I've said nay already,' Father Sheehy was stating, very deliberate. He held a pistol. Cocked and clearly loaded and obviously an old friend, pointed at the pavement, for the time being. 'I'll say it as many times as ye'd care to hear, for as long as you're lackin' for better employment!'

'And haven't we a right to see what the devil's work looks like?' a glowering old crone demanded. 'When 'tis visited on our own kin, no less?'

'He's no kin o' yours, Mrs MacKenna. Pray for his soul,

and pray for our people, and pray for God's wisdom, and go back to yer home.'

'And what *about* our homes?' demanded a black-bearded fellow with keen blue eyes. Obviously a man with his thoughts on a future Democratic election, and just as obviously a father – I read rational fright in his face, and not for his own sake either. 'What about our children? Our livelihoods, when this news comes to be spreadin' like wildfire? Can we not look the enemy square i' the face?'

Sheehy's lips were set tight as the stonework at his back. 'That lad were never the enemy, Mr Healy, though I take yer meaning proper. You've your family's best t' look out for, and I know how rightly to do it, son. Walk away.'

'Back away from the door,' I called out, brushing my fingers over the copper star.

The by-now familiar first twitches of sneers sprung onto the faces of the bystanders at the sight of a copper star. On several, they grew into angrily bared teeth. But on others, the expression froze and then retreated. I didn't follow why, though I was grateful enough it didn't look as if a fight was on my hands. Father Sheehy's eyes snapped in my direction and then back to his parishioners. He wasn't strung any less taut, but I'd taken a bit of the weight.

'Ye heard Mr Wilde, and none o' you are fixed to fall foul of a copper star. Go back to your work and to your beds. Pray for the lad's soul. Pray for the city.'

As I met Father Sheehy at the left-hand door, several strangers pointed at me discreetly and shook their heads. Opening the tall portal a fraction, the priest stood before it with a hollowed-out expression. I bent down to Neill.

'I'll pay you to run quick as you can to the Tombs and find an officer,' I said. 'He's about to check in and then leave for the north edge of the city. His name is Mr Piest. Jakob Piest. Can you find him?'

'Sure enough,' the lad answered, winging away again.

'How do they know me?' I murmured to Father Sheehy as he edged me inside.

'I don't suppose ye know anything about a policeman battled three mad Irish forty rounds on behalf of a black carpenter,' he sighed. 'That's mere Irish legend, I suppose. Come, quickly.'

I turned to the priest, a bit shocked at minor civic fame. We stood just within the entrance for a moment, my eyes blinking as they focused, and I thought myself ready to be enraged by a gruesome picture I'd viewed too many times. But ready as well – truly, I was flush with newfound competence – to do some work.

Then a slinking animal fear drew a cold line down the center of my back.

I still didn't see anything as yet. But there was a smell. A smell echoing the frozen copper penny sensation trickling from my neck to the ground. Something like an ironmonger's workshop and something like a cut of flank steak and something like a school sink. It tasted of knives and of wet earth. Already horrified, I whirled the rest of the way around.

There was a little shadow nailed hands and feet to the central cathedral door with something dark pooled beneath it.

I choked out words likely never before said in a place of worship. It was profane, whatever it was. Staggering backward, my hand clutching at my mouth. It wasn't my best showing for steady nerves. I'm glad of it. I'm glad even now. Father Sheehy winced, a shattered and wholly human expression, his eyes sliding from what I'd just seen back to me again as we quickly distanced ourselves from the unhallowed entrance.

'They'd a right to be askin' after the lad. The neighbors, I mean, though they'd not desire to set eyes on this if they knew it fer what it is. But the word is out this half an hour now. I was too late. Whoever did that unholy work, may we find the creature with God's own speed, left that door swung wide upon the street.'

I could only shake my head, my fingers over my lips so my heart wouldn't fly out.

What I was looking at simply couldn't be, but there it was, and two sane men staring into the gaping red jaws of lunacy. Neill hadn't seen it for himself, I knew without asking. He'd been ivory toned and papery, but steady. This death would've done far worse by him than mere news of a fresh murder.

'Then who discovered it first?'

'I couldn't say that, the door bein' open to the road, but I learned it from a beggar who sweeps the streets for coin on this block. She's not fit t' be seen, bless her. Lord knows who else has heard tell of it, for when I found her, she was screamin' fit to raise the dead. I've closeted her in the music room with food and drink and a plentiful dose of laudanum. God help me.'

Find Piest, I begged in Neill's general direction as my eyes flinched shut and then forced open again. *I need one thing just now, and that is a better pair of eyes.*

The yawning carved cross was really the least of my troubles. He was a slender young boy. Maybe eleven years old, by the looks of his face and the size of his very visible rib cage. Irish, obviously, the ruddy hair and speckled skin told me as much. Not a laborer when I forced myself to look at his hands. He'd been a kinchin-mab, I'd have staked my life on it, and there were traces of kohl at the edges of his eyes where either he or the murderer had failed to wipe it away completely.

But the rest of it . . . there was so much blood. So much blood, and the body so small. Soaking his torn clothes, pooling on the floor, dripping down the thick oak boards to which he was nailed hands and feet. Surrounding the body like a border were pale markings streaked messily onto the wood.

'What are the symbols painted with?' I asked hoarsely. 'These, these – all these crosses. I count seven of them. Why? It's different, that's never happened before. And what was used? It looks like ordinary whitewash to me. Is it whitewash? It looks so.'

'To me as well.'

'It's not dry, but it's close enough. That might be helpful.'

'What d' you mean?'

'How long does it take whitewash to dry?'

'Oh, I see. Yes, yes, of course, I should say not above ninety minutes, perhaps, when done tha' thickly?'

I forced myself a step closer, my upper body curved like a question mark. I took a breath. The air was stifling, greasy as lamp oil. Incense mingled with the tang of sacrificial blood.

'Do you know him, Father?'

'Nay, never by sight. I tried. I can't say who he is.'

We stared a while longer. Stupid with helplessness.

'This isn't right,' I whispered, though what I meant by that escaped me.

A banging from the other side of the abominable door sent me haring out of my skin. Father Sheehy hissed something between his teeth in his own language and passed his fingertips over the glossy baldness of his pate, lurching toward the undefiled entrance at the left like a badly mastered puppet.

'I must see Mr Timothy Wilde on a matter of civic emergency!' shrilled the voice of a lobster half-dipped into the bubbling pot.

My shoulders straightened. I'd never fought in anything resembling an army. Not a brigade, not even a gang of dead rabbits squalling over territory. But maybe that's what it feels like when reinforcements arrive, I thought. Like you're a man again. Simply because you aren't the only one. Alone, I was a bent-over ex-barman glaring terrified at death. Two copper stars turned me back into one policeman.

'Neill,' I said over Father Sheehy's shoulder into the blank, hushed air, 'thank you. Now I need Dr Peter Palsgrave. Quick as you can.'

When I'd delivered Neill the address and sent him away again, and Mr Piest had slipped through the opening with his lantern half dimmed, I stepped aside with Sheehy. My fellow copper star turned to have a look. Stood there, heart visibly stalling. Not paling, though. He turned bright as a fireman's shirt, his lips curling back over his jagged teeth, and that was when I realized that he was as enraged by this whole bloody business as I was.

'First,' Mr Piest said. 'First. What to do now. What is *first*?'

'Shall we take him down?' the priest asked, voice purposely roughened so as not to sound cowed. ' 'Tis an offense to the Holy Church. To God Himself.'

'No. Wait for the doctor,' I replied. The words fought like hell to lodge in my craw.

'And Chief Matsell,' agreed Mr Piest. 'I sent him word at once.'

I nodded, turning back to Sheehy. 'The front door in question was open, you said? But the cathedral surely was locked?'

'Yes, yes. I keep my keys in the rectory, ye've seen for yourself.'

'Has anything been broken? Windows, locks?'

'I can hardly say. It's all been so quick, and I had to be guardin' the entrance. Here are my keys, and they were right where I left them. Someone must have forced the door.'

'Have you not yet searched this entire sanctuary, then, Father?' Mr Piest inquired, stepping back from a more careful look over the body.

'I – nay, apart from makin' certain the fiend had gone. And shall I now, then?'

'Father Sheehy, take Mr Piest through the building and keep a sharp eye open for anything out of place,' I suggested. 'I'll borrow your keys. I'm going to see if I can find out how our man got in.'

'Very good. The chief will waste no time in arriving,' my colleague added, his hand hovering near the priest's elbow protectively. 'Let us find something to show him when he does.'

I took the small lamp Sheehy had been using, and Mr Piest drew back the shutters of his smoking bull's-eye. We separated, moving fast but careful. I could hear Mr Piest questioning Father Sheehy in a practiced monotone. Little questions designed as much to produce comfort as facts. What sort of night had he passed? A busy one, presiding at the cathedral over a joint Catholic and Protestant meeting debating proposals for a Catholic school. A dozen leading figures had been present. And dead set against him.

'You're wantin' the minutes of my meeting, when each and every one o' them slandered me?' he demanded. 'Shall I give ye the names? The men who don't supposed a Catholic kinchin ought to be raised *Catholic*?'

What time had he retired? At midnight. Had St Patrick's ever been threatened before? Yes, scores of times, never amounting to more than flung stones and brickbats. I slipped along the wall with the scene out of hell itself at my back, trying not to imagine that the wretched boy could see me. Trying not to imagine what might have happened to this one *before* he had died. That set me to flushing, which I'd noticed recently sent sharp needling pinpricks through my scarred face beneath its thin layer of cloth. I lost the sense of Mr Piest's gentle questioning when the pair disappeared into the organ loft on the eastern side. And the moment their voices had faded, I heard it again in my head.

This isn't right.

Then, *Of course it isn't,* I thought furiously.

The side walls of St Patrick's are intercut with narrow strips of stained glass. At the rear, where the pinnacles rise, and small rooms house vestments and sacramental objects I can't name, are three more doors. There was a cobalt suggestion that dawn would rise soon when I unlocked the right-hand door and stepped outside. A fever gleam to the sky's edge, quickening the breath.

Kneeling, I peered at each of the locks in turn, not certain what I was looking for. All of them were smooth, cool iron, and all of them pretty typical – ornate, a bit sour smelling. A tidy sheen to the surface. That gleaming polish wasn't scratched in the least. Picking a lock, I knew because Valentine had once considered it his duty to teach me how to pick locks, often leaves traces. I pulled the sharp edge of one of Father Sheehy's keys over the surface and sure enough it left a mark. But that didn't tell me much, after all. If a cold-blooded rabbit was skilled enough, and his pick small, it could be done without obvious signs.

I walked around to the front, where the hewn grey blocks ended and the dull red freestone greeted the passersby. People had started to mill about again, talking in whispers. Eyeing me. I paid them no mind, kneeling.

To no avail. The same untouched gloss held true for the front entrance locks, all clean and plain and defying me to learn anything from them as I shone the light into their keyholes. I paused for a second or two longer at the center entrance, seeing the reverse image through the door clear as second sight. Feeling the weight of the body there, hanging so much heavier in my chest than in the truth of its gravity.

Using the leftmost door, I came back inside. Mr Piest and Father Sheehy stood before the altar beyond, sharing the light and volatile kerosene-soaked expressions.

'Are there other sets of keys?' I asked, returning them.

'Naught,' Father Sheehy replied.

'Then the killer is simply very good with locks, which narrows our search to six or seven thousand dead rabbits in this town. I see you've done better by us.'

They'd laid several items out on a cloth spread over the frontmost pew. A bag of large iron nails, their shape now sickeningly familiar to my eye. A hammer. A hacksaw, wrapped in a piece of tarp but bloody nonetheless. A paintbrush gleaming ivory in the yellowish light, and a small pot of whitewash. A sack, emptied of its contents and draped beside them: in all, a neat little kit for the violation of all that's right.

'Where were these?' I asked.

'In my sacristy, hangin' with my vestments,' Father Sheehy answered. The words grated along, forced from his lips. I'd not known a man could hold so much outrage within using only his jaw.

'And the outer doors not forced,' Mr Piest added slowly, 'and you the only one with the key, and these tools hidden in your own private vestry.'

'Are ye supposin' that I, being a Catholic and a dutiful

servant to His Holiness and the Church of Rome, would think to end vice by committing a ruthlessness so profane it redefines the very idea of sin?' the priest snarled. 'This – this – *savagery*, this *barbarous wrong*, 'tis a lit match set to the dwellings of the New York Irish. I did not emigrate that I might *ruin my flock*.'

'No, no, sir, it is a point in your favor,' Mr Piest explained. 'Most decidedly.'

'And grateful I should be if ye were to tell me *how*.'

'Because no one behaves like that,' I replied, understanding my fellow copper star perfectly. 'Hushes a kinchin and then shows off where he hid his tools. Had we discovered these without your company, it might have looked different. As it is, the news is still pretty gammy.'

'How so?'

'Someone just butchered another kinchin, but this time he wants us to calculate it was *you*.'

'Do you suppose that's why the crosses are painted around him?' Mr Piest exclaimed, snapping his fingers. 'To point to the father here?'

'I can't say, though I like it better than the other explanation.'

'And yes?'

'That he's lost what little was left of his mind.'

Bang bang bang.

The sound thudded from the rear side of the cathedral this time. Mr Piest scurried off, snatching up the keys. I stayed with Father Sheehy, hoping he wasn't about to turn greenish or fall into a black study. I needn't have worried, though. He looked keen to restain a rainbow-hued church window by putting some sick bastard's head clean through it.

Chief Matsell came in, with Dr Peter Palsgrave at his heels. Mr Piest followed, having sent Neill away once more.

'Post me up,' said the chief. 'How bad is it?'

'If it can get any worse, it's beyond my imagining,' I answered, gesturing.

We all walked purposefully toward the front end of the church. I was about to explain further, Mr Piest and Father Sheehy striding deferentially behind us, when Dr Palsgrave started to scream.

It was an unearthly, horrible sound – something ripped from his throat that should have stayed there. A private noise. Anguished and terrified, like a pit had opened beneath him. All at once, he stopped, sinking into the nearest pew.

'Surely you've seen blood before, Doctor,' Chief Matsell pointed out, incredulous.

'It's – it's nothing,' Dr Palsgrave panted, clawing at his chest. 'Just my heart. Oh, my *heart*. Heaven have mercy, what has happened?'

'The same thing that's happened twenty other times,' I said, an edge to my voice.

'But this. This, this. Look at it,' Palsgrave cried, hauling himself to his feet using the back of the next pew. 'And done to a helpless little *child*. Who could stomach such an act? I can't bear to – it's completely *insane*.'

This isn't right, my head announced relentlessly.

'Our man's mental condition is deteriorating,' Chief Matsell agreed decisively. 'We've ignored his warnings, and he has been pushed into a state of violent lunacy. Now, tell me what else you've found, Wilde, while Dr Palsgrave here makes a preliminary study. Dr Palsgrave, master yourself.'

The semi-hysterical expert looked sick with fear, but he wrenched himself forward as if determined to ignore the violence taking place within his chest. I felt a little tender toward Dr Palsgrave, hearing Bird in my head. I could buy that he loved children. And could smell the blood myself from ten yards off. This was graphic waste, the antithesis of doctoring. *If he diaries our names and later sees us . . . well, then we're sick again, aren't we? He failed.* But the chief was right, and the doctor knew it, so he blinked very hard a few times and mechanically drew nearer to the center door.

It was only five minutes later that Dr Palsgrave wanted the body on the ground, nothing more being gained by viewing the dark glory of a madman's staging. So the chief nodded, and Father Sheehy fetched a crowbar, and between the pair of those iron-spined men, three minutes later it was done. We had the boy laid out on a stretch of canvas sacking, looking so much smaller than he had moments before.

After a few more fluttery minutes, Dr Palsgrave delivered us his final verdict.

'To my knowledge, I have never seen this child previously. He was healthy in life, approximately eleven years old, his organs are entirely intact, and he is dead of a laudanum overdose,' Dr Palsgrave announced.

We stared.

'There are traces of spittle upon his lips that suggest the onset of nausea. That in itself would not be very conclusive, but in addition, he shows every sign of asphyxiating – his fingernails are quite blue, as are his lips.'

'So he was strangled to death,' said the chief.

'By no means – there are no marks on the child's neck.'

'So he was poisoned? But—'

'Smell the stain on the boy's shirt collar for yourself and then tell me it isn't an anise-flavored opium paregoric!' the old man cried. 'Laced with morphine, I shouldn't wonder, for it appears to have done its work before the nausea had a chance to set in.'

'It's a bit far-fetched, don't you see, Doctor?' Mr Piest

attempted. 'The method, it's quite . . . humane. Is that likely?'

'We are dealing with a homicidal religious maniac, and you grouse to me about *likelihood*?'

'You mean to tell me,' Chief Matsell growled, 'that some sick-minded brute broke in here with a captive, poisoned him, and then after sending him tenderly off to sleep, nailed him up and sawed him open? For effect, like?'

'Oh, merciful God,' whispered another voice, very small.

No matter how snappish we were fighting, no matter how occupied we were with the boy on the ground, I still to this day can't credit *myself*, Timothy Wilde, not noticing the whisper of Mercy's steps until she was nearly upon us. Without her own lantern, her hair down, her face bloodless as the moon. Her eyes fixed on murder's latest sacrament. I did catch her as she fell, though, and as she fainted, she said something that might possibly have been 'Timothy'.

CHAPTER NINETEEN

And we ask again, Can Romanism be the religion for
America? As a religious system, it is an old fossil of
the Dark Ages, formed to awe a rude and
superstitious people, and in all its great peculiarities
in direct antagonism with the religion of the Bible,
which is the religion of these United States.

Letter written to Bishop Hughes of St Patrick's
Cathedral, New York City

Here is what happened that day, Sunday, August thirty-first, in the nineteen hours before New York City fell apart. From five in the morning, when Mercy arrived in the cathedral, when dawn's scarlet glow started burning across the East River's cool grey skin, until around midnight, when the match hit the fuse.

I missed the arrival of discreet copper stars charged with removing the body to the Tombs. Father Sheehy had lent me his keys again, and I was installing Mercy in his bed. The bedchamber was plain, dignified. Religious art on the walls, so it was no monk's room, kept blank for God's glory. So far as I was coming to understand Father Sheehy, it matched him: reverent, cultured, and honest. The bed was against a wall, covered with a plain quilt. I drew it back and settled my temporary charge on a pillow.

Her eyes opened. Slivers of pale blue showing through a cloudy sky.

'Marcas.' Her voice strained badly, though she herself was barely conscious. 'What happened?'

'It's all right. You're at Father Sheehy's. But—'

'What happened to Marcas, Mr Wilde?' There was a sheen to her eyes now, one that tore at me.

'That's his name, then,' I breathed. 'You know him. Whyever did you come here?'

'Was that – was that done to him first?' Mercy asked, biting her lower lip so hard I wanted to reach for it, gently pull it out again, and give her my knuckle for a substitute.

'It was laudanum. He didn't feel a bit of it. Please, just tell me what happened to you.'

'Do you know who did it?'

'Not yet. Mercy, *please*.'

Her dark head fell toward the pillow. She was working so hard to keep from crying that my speaking her name was enough to cut her strings and send her limp. It had done just about the same to me, once I'd heard myself say it, but one of us had to stay collected. And I could do it, too, if it was for her.

'I heard shouting in the streets,' she whispered. 'All Irish voices. Calling out to each other, cutting right through the dark. That there was a devil loose and he'd defiled St Patrick's.'

My skin went cold. The newspapers didn't matter any longer, then. Nothing we'd done to hide this foul investigation mattered anymore – we were exposed as that poor boy had been, hung up for all the world to see.

'I threw on my dress and my cloak without a light,' Mercy continued. 'I – I thought I might know whoever it was, thought I could help, perhaps. I thought you might be here. That maybe we could set it right.'

Something purely selfish decided to inhabit my arm. I reached out and slipped my hand into hers. I didn't calculate it, but it was only for me and not meant to comfort. Her fingers were cold, and she pushed them farther into my palm.

'His name is Marcas, but only because they call him that. And he's nothing to do with Silkie Marsh. His house is nearly in the East River, the southwest corner where Corlears Street meets Grand. It's all boys there. I once treated him for whooping cough. When I saw him, I – I'm sorry.'

Half a second later she was weeping on my shoulder, trying the whole time not to make any noise. My arms around her back and her mouth open on my coat. It's not charitable to say that it was the happiest moment of my life. But in the midst of the nightmare landscape I'd wandered into, I think it was.

She quieted quickly, blushed when she pulled back. I let her go and passed her my handkerchief.

'I need to present you with an argument,' I requested quietly. 'You're the only one I can trust to hear me out.'

Mercy sighed darkly.

'Shall I get out of this bed before delivering my expert opinion?'

We repaired to the kitchen. My head felt more or less packed with unlit fireworks. It didn't take me long to find Father Sheehy's whiskey, an endearing third of a bottle with six months of dust on it, and I poured us two generous glasses.

'Do you think,' I asked her, 'that murder has to have a reason?'

'In the mind of the murderer, yes,' she said slowly. 'Otherwise, why would it happen?'

'So,' I expounded, grateful just to hear her recovered enough to return questions with more questions, 'what is the reason in this case?'

Mercy squinted at me. Drew her head back and took a sip of spirits.

'Religion,' she reported, dead as dust.

'Not politics?'

'In New York, aren't they the same?'

'They aren't,' I objected. 'Look here: a man deciding to kill kinchin and defile their corpses in secret might be doing it for religion, or an insane corruption of it. But not for politics. Politics isn't about secrecy. It's about *press*.'

'Yes,' she agreed, 'but things have obviously changed since that – that – *cruelty* in the church, have they not?'

'Exactly. Which is why I think something's happened to our man. Maybe he's nervous, because we're getting to him. Maybe he's growing more ill. There's another letter, one sent to Dr Palsgrave, that suggests he might be. Maybe he wanted Father Sheehy implicated for some unholy reason. All I know is that this is beyond what we've seen before, and I don't believe that the other murders were done for politics no matter what's being written to the *Herald*. This was cruel of a *purpose*. The whitewashed crosses drawn all around the child, the staging. It was cruel to draw attention.'

Mercy's jaw was working again. 'I assume the cathedral was locked. How did he get in?'

'I don't know yet. But I'll learn it, on my honor.'

She stood up, gracefully finishing the whiskey. 'I pray you

do, Mr Wilde. And now, I left the house very abruptly. I must go.'

I'd not have expected anything more, knowing her as I did. But she stopped with her hand on the knob, casting me an angled eyebrow.

'Promise me you'll be careful?'

'I promise,' I answered.

Mercy Underhill left for home.

I grinned stupidly at my whiskey for a few moments. Thinking over my job, which was harrowing. My task, which was nigh impossible. My face, which was mangled. My savings, which no longer existed.

Draining the glass, I imbibed a silent toast to each and every one of those misfortunes before locking Father Sheehy's door behind me.

When I checked back in at the cathedral proper, much of the blood was cleaned away, Chief Matsell and Dr Palsgrave were gone, and Mr Piest was dropping the evidence we'd found into a sack. A few bleary-eyed clerics stood speaking in whispers, wielding mops with religious zeal. Father Sheehy had vanished.

'At the Tombs,' Mr Piest explained. 'He was taken in for questioning.'

'That's pure flam,' I snapped, forgetting myself. 'Don't tell me he was arrested?'

'No, but on the evidence – think of how Chief Matsell sees it. If we're right about Sheehy, he'll be free in two hours. But if we're wrong, and it comes out we were wrong and could have questioned him, it's the end of the copper stars.'

I nodded, a brushfire headache growing behind my right eye. The eye hadn't been hurt in the tragedy downtown, of course, but now I suspect I tense it when vexed. And I was about as vexed as was possible. Having already lost my temper once, I regained it so as to lose it again.

'Dr Palsgrave went with them?'

'He went home. Complained of severe heart palpitations.'

I opened my mouth, furious.

'He's a private citizen who can have nothing to do with this crime,' Mr Piest interrupted reasonably. 'I'll tell you what I mean to do, Mr Wilde. I mean to write out a report after looking long and hard at these tools. I mean to eat a few oysters and some bread and butter, quick as humanly possible. Then I mean to go north, and find the owner of those used shields. And you?'

Forgiving the old Dutch madman for every problem that wasn't his fault, I nodded. 'Miss Underhill identified the kinchin. Name of Marcas, from a bawdy house by the dockyards. I mean to learn how he was missed and who last saw him.'

'Wonderful,' he exclaimed. 'Best of luck to the both of us, then.'

'I'm grateful for your eyes, and you should know it, Mr Piest. I don't have much else to be grateful for in this investigation.'

'Seeing is an honest craft.' He smiled, an ugly and a wonderful expression. 'And a learned one. I do my best.'

'How did you come to be doing it?' I couldn't help but ask.

'My parents were Dutch fur traders.' He leaned forward with his palms on the back of the nearest pew. 'They lost their fortunes before losing their lives, and so I lost my inheritance. But one day a fine old friend of my father's complained that he had lost three hundred yards of very costly silk from his warehouse, which could only have been taken by someone who knew that the back window locked improperly, an employee or close friend, and it outraged him so badly that he offered to pay a ten-dollar reward to whoever could find it. The look on his face, Mr Wilde. The hurt at the feeling he'd been robbed by one of his own. I never forgot it and I never will. It haunted me, you see, because my own father's partner had embezzled heavily, which is how I came to be dismantling my bed for firewood. There is hardly a worse feeling than having something stolen away from you.'

I nodded, knowing it true. 'You found the silk and gained the reward, I take it, and discovered you'd a hidden talent?'

'Talent had very little to do with my original success, as I'd stolen it in the first place.' He laughed readily at my upraised eyebrows. 'My father's old friend offered me a position instead of the reward. But I took neither. The next day, I signed up for the night watch and also placed an advertisement in the paper. Lost valuables found at the rate of ten per cent of cash value. I've never been hungry since, and I'll never be rich. But I'm in the right work. Be careful as you go, Mr Wilde.'

I was halfway to the rear entrance before his voice stopped me.

'How did the young lady . . . Miss Underhill, you said? How did she come to be here?' he asked politely.

'Disquiet in the street before her window,' I called back. 'We must be doubly cautious now.'

'Ah,' he said. 'No doubt.'

But small mobs are as common in New York as the pigs. And not a thing – far from it, in fact – to leave the house over. As I quit the cathedral, I mulled over whether the rumor of one would ever have sent me from my bed unarmed before turning copper star. Still dreaming over the question and vaguely ashamed of myself for it when I reached Prince Street and Valentine Wilde.

My brother walked with his head drifting attentively from side to side, making sure of his surroundings. Scales and Moses Dainty flanked him, on the left and right, respectively. Val was watchful. When he spied me, his step hitched, though it was ever so small.

Here's the advantage to being someone's brother, whatever brand of man that brother happens to be: you can read him. Easier than strangers. Easier than yourself, truth be told. You know after watching two blinks of his green eyes how much morphine he's had (plenty, but at least four hours ago). You also know what sort of mood he's in (cautious, hedging his bets, but ready for a tussle if one finds him). You know why he's there (the Irish are near enough his entire voting population, and he's keen to hocus them into thinking he cares about croaked kinchin-mabs).

Knowing him doesn't mean you need to spare him, though.

'Tim!' Val boomed down the lightening street. 'What's happened? Good, you can post me. I had to—'

'Knowing you,' I hissed as I drew close, 'and for my whole life, I should have figured you'd order Bird off to the House of Refuge the second you knew where she lived.'

'Tim—'

'After everything else you've done in your days, I shouldn't be flummoxed that you'd send a battered little kinchin off to the same place as flogged you and then packed you into solitary confinement.'

He got quiet. It wasn't his angry quiet, and it wasn't his dark quiet either. His face hung still, prey only to gravity. It seemed a picture of Val as he actually *was*: tired, depraved, sick of it, and ever looking for another dose of distraction. And that disturbed me.

'Fine, Timothy,' he said through his remarkably good

teeth. 'What do I have to do to make you quit? How do I make you notice you're purblind muddy in the brains, and get out of it?'

'If your answer to this problem, to any problem at all, is to send kids to the House of Refuge, then I want nothing more to do with you,' I announced.

I meant it, too.

'It isn't,' he said carefully. 'But you have to stop—'

'Get out of my way,' I interrupted.

I didn't care that he was huge and I wasn't, didn't care that he was *better* in more ways than I'd ever dared to count and still dead set against me. Val let me go, the dumbstruck Democratic lackeys exchanging spine-sapped glances from behind him. I turned my face toward the salt air, and toward the docks.

Fighting with Val generally feels a bit like shaving, or buying a cup of coffee. But that one left me with my skin shrugged on wrong and my fingers twitching into fists. The man had punched me in the jaw for considerably less insult, and by the time I'd reached the masts standing thick as weeds along Corlears Hook, walking under a striped canopy of ship prows, I was itching for a brawl. Since I seemed to have just been robbed of one.

The Corlears Hook area down by the ferry stations is Ward Seven, and I don't envy whoever's beat takes him there. The ferry docks rippled with all sorts by the time I arrived, the lusty summer morning drying salt crust into the flapping sails. And so, mingling with the Brooklyn dwellers who come daily into the city for work, the East River's particular brand of whore was already making a frontal assault. Mabs in short pinned skirts and mabs with skirts slit. Mabs winking, sitting on pilings fanning themselves with old newspaper, and mabs in their own doorways, not having bothered to cover their breasts just yet. Mabs smelling of saltwater and gin and other people's sweat. They were covered in tinsel and likewise covered in nautical pox scars, and they make me feel equally as if I ought to be bundling them off to a charity hospital, or marching them indoors to improve the scenery. Irish, it goes without saying, teemed thick as the stench of the docks. I didn't know what shipping line had recently put in, but there were a hundred or so of them huddled in a crowd by one of the piers, bones showing through skin like the stays of a corset, looking at each other and at their alien surroundings with expressions of blank fear. All I could think as I passed them was that they'd picked one hell of an inauspicious morning to arrive.

Reaching the dwelling Mercy had indicated, I looked up. Typical of the neighborhood, it had once been a rich merchant's house. Built to impress with fine stone trim, then later converted to squalid housing and disreputable occupations. Edges crumbling, probably since the Panic, or maybe the fellow had struck still richer and decamped to Broadway, but either way, his house was left a corpse.

I went through the front door without knocking. I was in that sort of mood.

Outside had been better than inside. A piano caked with dust disintegrated next to a shelf filled with liquor jugs and a very badly done picture of the Greek notion of a pleasant afternoon in the woods with your men friends. The mistress seemed to be the person lying on a vermin-infested fainting couch and lazily pulling at an opium pipe. What air there was to speak of was near solid with the smell of it, half rotting sweet corn and half tar.

'You'll have to give me a minute, love. There's not one of them awake at this hour, it's not Christian.'

'I'm a policeman,' I said, showing the star. 'Timothy Wilde.'

'Does that matter, dear?' she wondered blearily.

'You'll find that it does. Who was Marcas's last client?'

'Bless me if I can remember. Must have been hours ago. Done something, has he?'

'When did you first come to miss Marcas?'

The hag's rhinoceros eyes drooped, puzzled. 'Haven't missed him a bit, have I? He's upstairs. Third on the left. Go on then, if he's your fancy, I needn't bother lining up the others.'

Turning in disgust, I ran upstairs. The third door on the left was open. In the room, I found a bed, a lamp, a chamber pot, a makeup table, and cheap theatrical paint in the first drawer. Not much else. So I quit that barren chamber and knocked at the next.

A small face of thirteen or fourteen keeked out at me. Not curious. In fact, so very deadly incurious about who I was and what I wanted that I could have sent my fist through his wall. His clothing was male but ridiculous – all cheap satin and lace cuffs and brass jewelry. He hadn't been sleeping, for his brown eyes were clear.

'I wonder if you could tell me when Marcas left this house. I'm a policeman, and it's important,' I said.

'We have policemen?' he asked, genuinely surprised.

'We do,' I returned wearily.

'As for Marcas, I wouldn't know. Might have been anytime, come to think, what with Missus riding the pipe these two days. Marcas was pogy as a sailor yesterday afternoon, could hardly stand up. One of the guests must've shared some of his rag-water. He left, you said?'

'Yes. Is anything missing from his room?'

The boy padded around his door and into the adjacent chamber. Looking about, he shook his head.

'Naught. Oh. His journal is generally there, on the vanity. He leaves it out for us. We'll visit when we've a free moment, write notes to each other. Jokes. I don't see it.'

After a quick search, the diary remained missing. I didn't see how that could possibly help me, though, and so soldiered on.

'Did Marcas have any particular friends?'

'You mean our sort, or the clientele?'

'Both.'

'Nah, Marcas has a stammer, doesn't he. An awful one. That's what the journal is for. We'll say hullo, he'll write back an hour later, we'll read it. Those as can't write draw pictures. It's a game we play.'

The lad's face clouded. There were already worry tracks for the lines to settle in, too. Thicker than they should have been, and deeper than Bird's. By three or four years, of course.

'You said *did* Marcas have particular friends,' he whispered.

'I've got just one more question, and then I'll explain,' I vowed.

'And what's that, then?'

'How long would it take you to quietly gather everyone below sixteen who works here, and find them all some shoes?'

There's some would argue that the precious minutes needed to march six boys – led by my enthusiastic new assistant, John, who turned out to be the eldest – downstairs and away from that pit might have been better spent. I'd not agree with them. And it might have taken a good deal longer, but the harpy with the opium pipe had fully surrendered to it by the time the seven of us left, piss stains yellowing her dress as she snored like a thunderstorm. Supposing I felt like throwing her headfirst in the Tombs, I'd be back. But just then I couldn't be bothered.

So, all told, it was only two hours later when I arrived back at St Patrick's, hoping Father Sheehy had been released by that time. He was in his small rectory garden with Neill and Sophia, sunlight reflecting off his bald head, everyone pruning the tomato leaves and sending their dark, peppery smell seeping into the humid air.

'And what's this, now?' he questioned when he saw me approach.

'Peter, Ryan, Eamann, Magpie, Jem, Tabby, and John,' I answered.

'God be praised.' The priest grinned. 'And here I was certain that nothing on His earth could make me smile today.'

I went home.

Mrs Boehm was baking, shoving her palms into the dough, leaning forward with her bony hips. She blew a piece of dull hair away from her mouth as I went over to her.

'Is there a place you can go that's safe?' I questioned. 'For a day or two, with Bird? If I keep the shop locked up and pay you daily what you'd earn? The Democrats would cover it, and I don't like the cast things are taking. Please say yes.'

She stopped kneading. Sent her watery blue eyes up and down me, calculating.

'My cousin Marthe, she lives in Harlem. Not a long journey. I always mean to visit her. Now would be a good day.'

'Thank you,' I said, hugely grateful. 'I need to talk with her first.'

'Thank you,' she returned as I climbed the stairs, 'for stealing that horse. Oh, Mr Wilde?'

'Yes?'

'It was a very good installment of *Light and Shade in the Streets of New York*. Plenty of . . . interest.' Her lips cracked into a shy smile. 'I left it outside your door.'

'Mrs Boehm, you're a treasure,' I told her, smiling in return.

Bird wasn't in Mrs Boehm's room. She was in mine, studying the amateur sketches and using my blank butcher paper with a pencil in her fingers. Her square face melted into a tiny smile when she looked up.

'Hope it doesn't vex you, Mr Wilde.'

'Of course not. But I'm not lucky enough to have a pencil. How'd you manage to lay hands on one?'

'Mrs Boehm gave it over. She doesn't seem as hot at me any longer.'

I sat down with my back to the wall a couple of feet from Bird, dreading what I was about to do. Altogether sour in the stomach over it.

I took my hat off first. Then the strip of cheap cloth. Setting them next to me, I slung my arms over my knees. Just me, and Bird, and my whole face, because she deserved that much, and the memory of a church door stained with blood. The image lending me some much-needed courage.

'I need to know everything,' I told her. 'It pains me, but I do.'

Bird's eyes turned panicked. Wide and split like thunderstorms. Then she closed them. Soon enough, gave a small shrug. Crawled the few feet over and likewise sat with her spine to the wall next to me, clutching her knees after she'd neatly arranged her embroidered dress, otherwise quiet.

If you want to know what courage looks like, I can't think of a better picture.

'True, this time,' she whispered.

'True,' I agreed.

We sat there for a little. Then Bird abruptly dropped into the story, and I tumbled along after her, fighting the sensation of falling every inch of the way down.

CHAPTER TWENTY

Keep always GOD before your eyes
With all your whole intent;
Commit no Sin in any wise,
Keep his Commandment.
Abhor the arrant Whore of Rome
And all her Blasphemies;
And drink not of her cursed cup
Obey not her decrees.

The New England Primer, 1690

'Liam wouldn't stop coughing,' Bird began. Her eyes were fixed very hard on her hands, hands fixed very hard to her knees. 'Not for days, and so they sent for Dr Palsgrave. He was so worried. He snapped at everyone no matter what they'd done, and then begged their pardon after and shared his caramels until he hadn't any left, and so we knew how it troubled him. Stayed with Liam overnight once, and he hasn't the time for that, there being so many children he tends to. Thousands and thousands, I guess. That made us all think that Liam might die.'

'From the pneumonia.'

'Yes. That was before, though, two weeks maybe. Liam began to get well, gain his color back. Because of Dr Palsgrave, though I'm sure he forgot about Liam the minute he could. But then Liam went outside one day, and the cough came back. It sounded terrible. Next morning, his door was locked and the mistress told us he felt better, but that he needed his rest and we mustn't plague him.'

Bird stopped. I didn't nudge her, exactly. Just shifted an inch so my elbow was in contact with her upper arm. She closed her eyes.

'That night,' she said.

'August twenty-first.'

'Yes.'

I waited.

'I came down the stairs, wanting some milk. Mistress never minded if we wanted things of that sort. Extra food. She's flush enough that the milk is always good, too, she doesn't mix it with water and chalk to cover the spoiled taste like some of the others said happened in their last houses. I poured some and drank it. I didn't have – there weren't any callers, save for one with Sophia, I think. So I went to the front room to see out the window, look at the ladies' dresses.

'The carriage was there. The one the man in the black hood uses. I knew it by sight, and I went cold all over.'

'Can you tell me what it looks like?'

'Big and dark. Four wheels pulled by a pair. There's a little painting on the side, but I could never make it out exactly.'

'What did you do?'

'Ducked away from the window. Thinking maybe I ought to hide in my bedroom, having seen what happens when— I'd never said anything about it to anyone. That I'd caught glimpses of us being carried away. Wrapped in black cloth, but I could tell what was underneath. I'd only broken things and not said anything. Teacups, a lamp once. She never whipped me for it, but her eyes got cold, and I had to be awake for longer for a few days.'

'How long had you lived there, all told?'

'I don't remember. Ages, polishing the silver. She says I was born there. I don't know if that's true or not. I went to work when I was eight, though. I remember that.'

My fingers flexed, but I held my tongue.

'I was already frightened when I saw the carriage. I didn't want him to come for me, too. But then I was worried for another reason, because . . . because Liam's door had been locked, you see, and what if that was because the man in the black hood had come for Liam? I thought maybe this time that I could let him out instead. I liked Liam, he knew bird calls. He said because of my name, I should know them too. We hadn't gotten to the hard ones yet, he was to teach me more that week.'

Bird had started to cry a little, but it didn't change her voice so much as a tremor. Tears just silently wetted her cheeks.

'The locks to the rooms aren't hard to pick. Robert taught me, when I was seven. Anyway, I fetched a thick hairpin from my bedroom and made certain no one was in the hallway. I picked the door open, keeping quiet as I could. Thinking I'd let Liam out the back. There were other bawdy houses he could go to, maybe, or— I didn't know. Maybe he could get well and go to sea. That's what I thought. But I was so stupid. *Stupid*. I didn't look under the door.'

'Why should you have?'

'Because it was completely dark in there,' Bird choked. 'If

310

he was there, and awake, his lamp would've been lit. And when I did get the door open, and I snuck inside, I was only few feet in, by the edge of his bed, when I tripped over a great bowl.'

I didn't need to ask what was in the bowl. Not the way her eyelashes were shuddering. Two terrified moth wings fighting the pull of a tallow candle.

'Did you light a lamp?' I asked instead.

'No. I could see Liam in the starlight on his bed. He wasn't breathing. There wasn't any blood in him. It was in the bowl. Just in the bowl. And all over the floor then, all over my dress.'

I passed an arm around her shoulders, very lightly. She didn't object, so I let it stay there.

'I ran back to my bedroom, where the lamps were lit. Needing the light. I wanted to scream, I think I was about to, so I put a pillow over my mouth until I knew I could be quiet. Then I tied some pairs of stockings together and knotted them to the window catch. I was frightened someone was watching me, so frightened my hands shook. Some places have . . . holes in the walls. I'd not heard of anyone ever finding one at Madam Marsh's, but maybe she was too clever for us. She's too clever for most. But no one stopped me. And then I ran. I couldn't live there anymore. I never saw the man in the black hood that night. Just his carriage. But I knew what he was about, all along. I knew he would tear Liam to pieces.'

It's not something I'd have figured I'm any good at. Sitting on the floor with my arm around a skinny ten-year-old kinchin, trying to keep her bones from shaking out of her freckled skin. People might tell me things, but that doesn't make me practiced at piecing those people back together. And maybe I was as big a milksop as I ever am, and no damned good after all. But God, what a try I gave it.

Bird shivered tearfully. 'I've felt wrong before, but that was different. The blood was new. Like I'd never get it off. Like nothing would help.'

'I wish I could do something to make it better.'

'Nothing can make it better. I'm sorry I didn't tell you sooner. I just— I liked you. You brought me inside.'

'It's all right, Bird.' If she gets to lie as she pleases, then by God, so can I from time to time. 'You're no different than I am, and it wasn't your fault. Not any of it. We're exactly the same.'

'*That* isn't true,' she gasped.

'It'll get better,' I vowed, only hoping it was a fact. 'Better and better, the farther away you are from it.'

'What do you mean, farther away?'

'People like you and me don't have time to dwell over such things, things that hurt or dirtied us,' I told her, tightening my grip. 'We just keep walking. Nothing is ever clean in New York.'

In late afternoon, I saw Bird and Mrs Boehm off on the New York and Harlem Railroad at the Broome Street stop. Thinking over what was best to do as I walked back, air hanging thick and dirty as cigar smoke in the dimming light, I decided on stopping by the theater and lighting a little inspirational fire under my newsboys. Enlisting those lads had been just about the best idea I'd had, and I'd bribed them fair and square. I deserved some consideration. When I got to Elm Street, though, I discovered that I was already wanted. There was my small ally, looking left, right, and sideways as he trotted in the direction of the Tombs, stopping at the first glimpse of my hat.

'There you are,' said Ninepin, pulling his gold-rimmed ladies' spectacles off and rubbing at them in weightless relief. 'You're something past shady, Mr Wilde.'

'Well, now you've found me.' My pulse sped up a little, for his looks were steady but greyish. The sort of expression you might find on a lad who'd spotted a certain black carriage. 'What's the news?'

'Look leery,' he hissed, warning me quiet as he jerked his neck down Elm toward their theatrical haunt a few blocks away. 'It wasn't me who saw— Anyway, there's been bit of a mitten-mill. I was half spoiling, threw a facer myself. Hurry.'

'What were you boys fighting over?'

'You'll see,' he sighed as we hastened away.

We were at the edge of the Five Points when it happened. The shadows steadily gaining solidity all around us, long angles slanting longer as the sun fell. Poor buildings leaning up against one another, poorer residents propped up against the buildings. The usual scene. Then my gait hitched. And suddenly, too. There's a particular feeling to having a knife poked into your ribs.

A sort of *stopping*, when the point hits flesh, like a magician might have turned you to marble.

'Mouth it, and I'll make a hole in your back right here and now,' growled Moses Dainty's voice over my right shoulder. A Scales-shaped shadow told me he wasn't alone, and that Valentine's twin familiars now outnumbered me. 'Hand over your copper star.'

I did, clenching my jaw as the knife bit inward.

'That's the spirit. Now, turn left.'

I thought as I pivoted, grimacing, to tell Ninepin to run. But he'd vanished into the lazy drifts of smoke, saving me the trouble. So I marched east along bustling Anthony Street with a little trickle of blood already running down my spine. When we'd near reached the heart of Five Points and the Old Brewery, about the most degraded and yet public spot on Manhattan, I thought them out of their heads. But then we turned north again, into an alley, and I knew I was in for a sorry time.

I'd never actually walked into Cow Bay previous. It was pretty clear the instant we set foot down the darkened crevice why I'd avoided it. The corridor that had once been a cow path narrowed as it went along, and the filth rose higher, a cramped stretch of hell. Before the Panic, it had been merry African concert saloons rife with laughter, bawdy houses where coloreds and whites alike could find soft-voiced black stargazers. But that was before the Panic. At first, dim as it was with the buildings looming crazily inward, I saw unmarked stairwells leading down to the sort of saloons most men would call sewers. Here and there a body crouched on the steps in the shade. Too poor to keep drinking, too drunk to walk, and too wearied of life to brush off the flies. But farther down, as the crack squeezed thinner and thinner, the stairs disappeared and there were only disintegrating wooden shacks growing from the piles of mud and shit. Walls with sagging doors. Hardly a window. And not a single breath of fresh air to be found.

Dwelling places, they were meant to be. But not even the free-roaming pigs were wretched enough to venture into the dead-end pit of Cow Bay.

'All right, Tim,' said Moses when we were well out of sight of the main road. 'Back up against that wall.'

I went, my hands at my sides.

'Pretty far from Ward Eight, aren't you, boys?' I hissed.

'Not so far as to make us uncomfortable.' Scales shrugged, his broad, smashed, sneering privateer's face well satisfied.

'Fine police work the pair of you manage. You'd have done better to kill me by now, you know.'

'Hear, hear,' put in Moses.

'Well, we would have, too,' admitted Scales. 'But we need to ask a question first, before you're too quiet to answer.'

'What makes you think I'll answer now?'

'We'll find that little girl again.' Moses Dainty flashed me a smile from under his pale moustache. 'And then we can kill her just as slow as we like. Maybe after we've gotten to know her a bit better. We can kill you slow too, if you'd rather.'

'What we want to know is,' Scales announced, 'did you tell George Matsell about Bird Daly padding in your ken? Does the chief know anything of her at all?'

'He knows everything,' I lied. 'Knows where she is right now, and has a guard set. He'll have you bastards locked in a cellar before you even have time to report back to Val.'

Scales looked a bit downcast.

'Guess in that case, the little Wilde dies fast, then,' he muttered to Moses.

At least, I think that's what he said.

I was distracted, launching myself off the wall with my open hands clutching for Moses while he played with his knife like a kinchin in short pants, throwing him with all my weight into his partner.

However else I felt about Valentine, I'd one huge advantage simply by virtue of being his brother: I am a small man who knows how to fight large men.

You have to be quicker.

Uppercut, pivot, rush, kick, everything faster than them though your heart is racing. Everything cleaner than them though you're not near as tall. And that's how I fought that day.

Swifter. Sharper.

Better.

Because the instant two bigger men push one smaller man to the ground, it's over.

And then Scales caught my jaw with a crack like a pistol shot. I fell as if it was one in fact, flat on my spine in whatever muck fouls the back end of Cow Bay, my ears ringing. I remember wondering, when Scales's boot came down on my throat and Moses wielded his knife again, if I could have picked any more pitiable way to die than this: sprawling in dung, gutted by a pair of fellow copper stars.

I thrashed once, helplessly, the boot crushing down against my larynx.

Everything drifted away.

And then someone screamed, and it jerked me back from the edge like a towline.

'Don't touch me, you smoked Irish *bastards*—' another voice snapped.

I still couldn't move, but that lasted only a second.

Air rushed into my lungs. And thank God that's a mindless task, or I'd have missed the opportunity, dancing at the edge of something wide and black as I was.

Another scream, this one softer. A *thud*.

When I could see again, I'd already rolled to my knees, gasping like a drowning man. Otherwise hale, though. There was no sign of Moses Dainty and Scales any longer. Or there didn't seem to be. All had gone inexplicably quiet.

Soon as I could, I dragged myself up to my feet toward the smear of sunlight so very far above that miserable stretch of alley.

I was completely, entirely surrounded by ghosts.

They had carved-out gouges for eye sockets – brown eyes

intact, but within genuinely starving faces. The decaying rags hanging from them might have been clothing, or maybe just the shreds worn by spirits in picture books. But spirits didn't smell this way, and I hoped spirits didn't look as much in pain. I couldn't tell their exact ages, though there were women as well as men. About twelve of them, all told. All as silent and motionless as if they were already dead and not just well on their way to it. All staring at me as if I were the apparition, as if I cut the figure of the magical specter and not them.

They'd come from the surrounding houses, I realized. Every last one of them black. And then I remembered who lived at the end of Cow Bay. Cow Bay, where even the Irish wouldn't go. Or not thus far. Not yet.

'You're Timothy Wilde,' a woman said.

I tried to answer but fell back against the wall awkwardly, nodding instead.

They waited.

'Where,' I rasped when I could, 'where are the other two copper stars?'

One man stepped forward, shaking his head.

'Don't be wasting your time asking after that pair, Mr Wilde. You're all right?'

I nodded, though my throat still pulsed like a smashed insect under my fingers. The colored man I'd never seen before in my life placed my copper star in my free hand.

'I won't waste another thought on them,' I vowed.

My voice was about as good as a stick drawing words in a patch of sand. But it did the job.

'Well, you seem all right, Mr Wilde,' the man said as one by one the ghosts peeled away. 'Anything else we can do?'

'Thank you. Shake hands with Julius Carpenter for me.'

The remaining men and women turned slowly and deliberately back to their homes. Looking, under thick layers of hunger and want, grimly satisfied.

'Oh, any of us see him as knows him, that we will, Mr Wilde,' he agreed, as he too faded back into the shadowland from which they'd come.

The stab wound, I thought, was only a tiny hole. Beneath my notice. Staggering back toward the mouth of Cow Bay, I met with my second gang of thugs that early evening.

Ninepin had disappeared to a specific purpose, that much was obvious. Fang stood at their head with a weighted club hung slack in his fingers and the scar on his lip tugging up like a Punch-and-Judy puppet. Behind him slouched six others including Matchbox, Dead-Eye, and the bigger soldiers from *The Thrilling, Gruesome,* and *Bloody Spectacle of the Battle of Agincourt*. I was more than half touched to see them. Herding the vigilante crew back streetside, I burst into dying sunlight once more.

'They hemped you bad,' said Matchbox worriedly. 'Can't you breathe?'

'I'm fine.'

'Then why look so ketched?'

'This is what a fellow looks like when his own brother sends a pair of footpads to hush him.'

Not as if he didn't warn me, I added in my head.

We tramped the remaining few blocks to the theater in darkening silence, went inside and down the steps toward the lamp-lit stage. Shadows hung unnaturally that evening already, or so I thought. The streaks of gloom looked like a scene painted by a kinchin who'd lost perspective halfway through, and I remembered with a dull ache that the public had seen

Marcas's corpse, that everything was surely ruined already no matter what I did.

The remainder of the news hawkers idled on the stage, shuffling their feet or lying on their backs playing cat's cradle. I could see a new worktable, busy with paper and fuses and packages of gunpowder. Hopstill had paid the newsboys a series of calls, then. And none of them seemed to have blown their own faces off. Three of them, however, were christened with black eyes and split lips.

'What is going on?' I demanded.

'We had a scrap.' Matchbox's eerily adult eyes seemed more tired than usual. He brushed his fingers through his black hair, slumping Indian-style in front of the melted heaps of wax footlights.

'You found the black carriage,' I supposed.

Silence. One of the bashed-up youths snorted softly in disgust, turning the page of his newspaper. But I felt a thick rush of pride. Something I'd tried had actually worked. 'Listen, this entire city has doubtless turned for the worst, you'd best go on and leak it to me.'

'Was there really,' began Dead-Eye, rubbing anxiously at the marble stuffed in his face, 'a croaked kinchin-mab hitched up like Je—'

'Yes,' I owned tightly, 'and you know how word travels. If it wasn't in your afternoon papers, it's for no reason other than the chief of police.'

'It *was* in the afternoon papers,' Fang corrected me.

That one took me a moment to breathe through.

'I *need* that carriage, lads,' I pleaded.

'You heard him,' drawled Fang to the little knot of fight-marked boys in a tone I couldn't well fathom. 'Leak it.'

'I leaked it to *them* right enough,' the lanky youth snapped, pointing a grubby finger at Ninepin and Matchbox. 'And I got a punch in the daylight for my trouble, too.'

'You'll get one again if you don't change your story, Tom Cox,' growled Ninepin.

'You won't, so long as I'm here,' I said firmly. 'Spill it. Where is the carriage?'

'Dunno. We lost it,' Tom Cox muttered.

'You *what*? Well, where *was* it, then?'

'Outside a chophouse near to St John's Park, where we was hawking afternoon papers, already pulling away when we eyed it. We stopped work, shadowed it for a mile and a half through slow traffic, thereabouts, and it pulled up in front of a brick autum. Then *somebody* got out of it,' he added, glaring spit-bright and defiant at Ninepin. '*Somebody* went into the autum. Shut the door behind as the rotan drove off again. I keeked it *clear as day*. So did these lot. After that, we shoved off, came back here. Didn't know what to think.'

'For the last time, who got out of the carriage in front of the church and went inside?'

'Say Mercy Underhill again,' snarled Ninepin, pulling his spectacles off his face and handing them to Fang, 'and I'll go as many rounds as it takes to keep your great gaping potato-trap shut.'

'Sod off,' snapped Tom Cox, leaping to his feet. 'She'd that green dress on, the one that's off her shoulders with the fern pattern, we've all seen it a score of—'

I caught Ninepin by the collar as he pitched headlong into the fray. He wasn't on my mind, though. Just in my hand.

The green dress, off the shoulders as most of hers are, with the fern pattern. The one I last saw her in when she was standing across the street from Niblo's Gardens in March.

Like a history book. Such a very long time ago.

She'd the basket slung over her arm at the same angle her eyes drifted sideways, and it had been stuffed full of half-finished short stories. Mercy had been trapped indoors for days with a bad case of ague, but well recovered by the looks of her color, and I hadn't known she was well again, I'd the day before handed the reverend a bottle of cordial and a used book from a stall. He'd thanked me as if the mere tokens were great talismans, because Thomas Underhill loathes Mercy's falling ill like he loathes nothing else on earth. But there she was, off balance like the best of statues, and she'd finished the ode she'd been working on while laid up recovering, and I read it in the middle of the street, rays of sunlight flashing white off her black hair.

If Mercy had been descending from the carriage owned by the man in the black hood, then she was in danger. That was all there was to it.

'The autum was Pine Street Chuch, yes?' I questioned.

'It was,' agreed Tom Cox, face flushed with the readiness to send Ninepin starry eyed and bleeding into the ground.

'Stop scrapping, then. Miss Underhill's in trouble.'

Everyone stopped.

'Thank you. You're all dead flash rabbits. Stay here tonight, and off the streets,' I ordered, letting Ninepin go as I turned toward the exit.

That she hadn't known whose carriage she was in, I was certain. There are things a man is right about, things he knows. Things like *Mercy needs my help.* I whistled for a hack on the first street corner good enough to encounter one, and told the driver to deliver me to the Pine Street Church.

Chapter Twenty-One

How many people of the United States are probably aware of the fact that the Pope considers the Crusades as still in existence, and issues a bull every two years, inviting soldiers to engage in them?

American Protestant in Defence of Civil and Religious Liberty Against Inroads of Papacy, 1843

Darkness was gathering her thick skirts around New York as I pulled up at the corner of William and Pine. My breath came easier as the minutes rolled past, which was a blessing, though now that I could breathe I couldn't see a damn thing. Streetlamps in these parts are left for dead when the glass cracks. I stepped down, paid the hack. My world seemed muffled. The carriage ought to have made more sound as it drew away.

Nothing would have happened the way it did if Mercy Underhill hadn't stepped out her own front door seconds later, out of the little brick house under the trees by the Pine Street Church. And nothing would have happened the way it

322

did if she'd seen me standing there under a broken streetlamp. A man without any light.

But I did see her, and she didn't see me, and something in my mind slotted into place like typesetting. It wasn't a conclusion, though, which only goes to show how paper skulled I truly am. No, it was a question.

Where is she going?

So I followed her.

She walked rapidly for the first few blocks west along Pine, wearing a light summer hood in pale grey over her hair. I can stay quiet when I want to, so she didn't hear me. I walked close enough to defend her if she met an enemy. Far enough to linger behind if she met a friend.

Mercy hailed a hack when she reached Broadway. So did I, urging the driver quietly to follow as the moon broke through the cloud cover. By that time, I didn't need the newsboys to have told me that the latest atrocity was in the afternoon editions – I could read it clear in the pedestrian traffic patterns. For every local walking clean and brushed and satin buttoned in front of shop windows, there were two speaking together with trim lips and faces stretched like canvas drying. Dandies and swells and stockbrokers of the type I'd used to listen to, distracted for a moment from their clothes and their money. I knew which words they were saying without even bothering to read their lips.

Irish.

Catholic.

Outrage.

Savage.

Nuisance.

Danger.

When Mercy alighted from the hack at Greene Street,

within sight of Silkie Marsh's bawdy house, I was already convinced she was headed straight inside it as I paid my own driver from half a block back. They were known to each other, there were a hundred reasons for her to visit. But then she stopped under a striped awning before a tea shop and waited. Hood pulled low, eyes glancing back and forth to either street corner.

About two minutes later, a man walked up to her. Not known to me. Handsome, his waistcoat sporting more embroidered flowers than Valentine's and his swallowtails tight across the chest, brushed a clean blue-black. I disliked him immediately. The moon shimmered along the curve of his beaver hat. I couldn't hear Mercy speak as she approached him, but I saw her face in the spider's-silk glow, and so I didn't have to.

I've been so frightened, she said. *It hurts to be this frightened. Quick, quick, or I'm lost for good.*

His reply was unknowable, as his face was turned from me. They set off down the moonwashed road about ten inches apart.

I followed. They went into Silkie Marsh's house after ringing her bell. Lights blazed from every windowpane. I could see the bits of mirror and candle and carpeting that tempted men inside, all the tugging shine of the hardwood and the crystal. For maybe as long as ten minutes, I only waited. If I followed Mercy into Silkie Marsh's brothel, then that was exactly what I was doing: I was *following Mercy*, no two ways about it. In the end, I simply forced my feet to move. Mercy going abroad at night was unusual but could be explained with a bit of effort. A kinchin with scarlet fever, a poor man thrown from a horse, a midwife who needed another pair of hands. Mercy meeting a strange fellow hours after being seen in the carriage of the man in the black hood, though – I couldn't possibly have conscienced not learning what it meant.

I told myself that, anyhow.

When I dove across the street at last, I didn't bother with knocking. The front door was unlocked, and I burst through. My eyes took in the empty foyer, gleaming with rich color. I brushed past it all, past the oils and the ferns, and invaded the parlor.

There were about nine of me in the floor-length Venetian mirrors, all looking as if I'd barely survived an encounter with Cow Bay. And about nine of Silkie Marsh, too, who sat perched in her amethyst velvet chair mending a stocking, of all things. She looked up at me, momentarily startled. Seeming very young and petal like for an instant, the sweetness of her face fairly glowing above the severity of fashionable black satin. Silkie Marsh is right to wear such things, for they don't suit her and make her seem a girl trying out an elder sister's ball gown. Black satin, unlikely as it sounds, makes you suppose she isn't dangerous.

'Mr Timothy Wilde,' she said. 'You look very near to collapse. Might I offer you a drink?'

I said no, but she ignored me. She set her stocking and her needle on the chair and went to the sideboard by the piano, pouring a pair of neat whiskeys, sipping hers as she handed mine over.

Finding I needed it after all, I bolted the drink and passed the glass back to her. 'Thank you. Where is Mercy Underhill?'

'I don't know whether that is any of your business, Mr Wilde,' she said sweetly. 'In fact, I am sure it isn't.'

'I know she's here, and I need to speak with her. Tell me where she's gone.'

'I don't like to tell you. It's an ugly matter. Please don't make me, Mr Wilde, you're not a forceful man in that way. You'll think still worse of me than you already do.'

'You needn't worry much over that.'

'I don't like betraying secrets, as I'm a woman of my word, Mr Wilde. But if you must insist, she's just down the hall there, through the door next to the Chinese vase. I know you'll never find it possible to like my company, but don't try to speak with her at the moment. Please don't, for mercy's sake.'

I'd crossed the hallway in under five seconds, I think. The Chinese vase rested on a pedestal with a pretty shaded lamp hanging on the papered wall above it, the pale amber shine making a circle.

Shoving the door open, I entered.

The small chamber's lights were dim, more shade than shape. But there was a startled sound, and a quick, frantic little thrashing. I saw figures on the bed, one of them bare from the waist up, face twisting to look at me with eyes wide and unfocused. And the man was there too, above her but half under the coverlet, glancing backward, wearing nothing at all. His hand covered Mercy's pale curve of breast and his smallest finger traced the line of her rib.

'This room is *occupied*,' he drawled. 'Kindly—'

I hauled him off of her, which shut him up.

'However you've hurt her, I'll pay you back triple,' I vowed, with one hand bruising his forearm and the other nearly tearing out his hair.

'He isn't hurting me, you fool,' Mercy gasped. She'd sat up in the bed, pulled the coverlet more fully over herself. 'Does it *look* like he's hurting me?'

I let him go, and the dandy staggered back.

'Mr Wilde,' Mercy began. Her eyes closed now, breathing fast through her nose. 'You need to—'

'Oh, bugger this, it's all off now,' gasped the stranger flailing helplessly about the room for his fine clothing. 'What do you think me? I'm a sensitive man, I could not possibly – not after – and you *know him*?'

Mercy's mouth opened, but nothing came out. She clutched her fist into the coverlet, kneading it ruthlessly. My back encountered the wall, and I slid down it to sit on the bare boards. Watching the stockbroker – no, exporter-importer more likely, his accent was all New York but his shoes and watch and the silk of his waistcoat foreign – regain what was left of his dignity.

'Well, whether you know him or not, I am sorry to be of such poor service to you and the proposed transaction, as – I don't – oh, confound it, best of luck, Mercy. You'll come by the money somehow or other. As for me, well . . . another time, perhaps.'

With that, he was out the door, shutting it behind him. I shuddered. Standing up, I turned to face the window, away from Mercy.

'I don't know if you realize what you've done,' came her voice from behind me, 'but will you tell me please why for heaven's sake you've done it?'

'He was going to pay you,' I whispered. 'And he paid Silkie Marsh for the furnished room.'

A rustling of fabric as she rose from the sheets.

'How long?' I attempted. 'Tell me. Please. How long has this been happening?'

A dark chuckle emerged from the bed. It ended in a gasp, as if she were drowning, and it sent a frigid chill through my gut.

'How long, you ask? How long have I known the company of men, or how long have I been paid for it?'

I couldn't answer her. So she continued regardless.

'About five years, in the first case, since I was seventeen. And about five minutes, in the second. Since I was ruined.'

'Ruined,' I repeated numbly.

'I don't suppose when you were reading *Light and Shade in the Streets of New York* that you ever suspected you knew the author.'

I didn't mean to turn, but in my shock, I couldn't help it. Of course, she was breathtaking. Skin like fresh-fallen snow on a frozen river, eyes shining pale blue as she gathered up her dress. Every curve subtly beautiful, hair impossibly black and caressing the swell of her breast before falling past her hips, center of gravity wonderfully askew. I looked away, actively hating myself, forcing myself to hear what she had just told me.

'*Light and Shade*,' I repeated, picturing Mrs Boehm's magazine and her embarrassed blush. It was tales of wicked social scandals, acid Wall Street tragedies, the plight of emigrants, and the stifled rage of the poor. One had told the story of an Indian wrongly suspected of stealing chickens who had been stoned through the streets, another the saga of a morphine addict who sold his winter coat for a dose. They were wildly sexual, sharply heart breaking, the finest sort of melodrama, and I'd read every one. 'By *Anonymous*.'

'Such a boring pseudonym, really,' Mercy answered, in the dullest of cottony murmurs.

Passing a hand over my eyes, I pulled air into my lungs and then forced it out again. That she'd written those stories didn't surprise me. She'd probably seen most of them lived in the flesh, at one time or another.

What surprised me was that I hadn't been able to tell.

'But – wait, *ruined?*' I stammered, getting a fraction of my brain back.

'I'm lost now,' she affirmed. 'It's hopeless. But God, it was a near thing. I'd almost six hundred dollars saved up yesterday morning, before Papa found it and caused something of a . . .' The memory stopped her cold for an instant. 'There was a scene. Now I'll never find another place to hide any store of coin, never, nor be able to write another phrase in that house without supervision, and my . . . actually, my father's opinion doesn't bear speaking about.'

'And so your answer was to – to *sell* yourself?' I cried, entirely repulsed.

'There wasn't any alternative,' Mercy answered dully as the new friction of her cotton dress rubbing against itself trembled in my ears. 'I have to *leave here*, I can't possibly stay in New York, I have to get away, you don't know what it's like at home, I— Why did you *do* it, Timothy?'

I turned around once more. Mercy had more or less donned the green dress, though it was askew as ever. Her eyes, when I met them, were despairing. Blue pools a man could drown in.

'I wanted so to get to London,' she said. 'To live there. To make my own way. The entire state of New York could have been lined up to stop me and I would still have— Everything is different in London, can't you understand that? None of this disgraceful Puritan *hatred*. There are reformers in London, and Bohemians, and philosophers, people like my *mother*, and— Here I try to save children, and they tell me that poor children don't *matter*. Here I try to live my life, including romantic attachments, as I please, but God forbid I ever openly walk from one street corner to another with any man other than *you*, Timothy Wilde. Here I have a desk and paper and ink, and Papa from the time I was small kisses me and tells me he's proud I want to write, compliments my nature poetry and my hymns and passion plays. And then I finish scores of short stories and twenty-three chapters of a novel, and yesterday he finds the novel sitting on my desk. I was stupid, distracted, my mind on the children, on your investigation, *so stupid*, I never never leave it out, and there it was in plain sight when he came up to tell me he'd fried us both some rashers and a pair of eggs. And now I may as well try swimming to London. It would be better than dying *here*.'

Physically biting my tongue, I told myself, *Wait. Don't talk. Wait.*

Listen.

I could well believe that she had kept *Light and Shade* secret – no lady of my acquaintance could manage to admit *reading* it without blushing. Less excusable but also comprehensible was that her father might be dismayed at Mercy's producing highly secular material. But it was a shock to learn that London crooned her name from across the ocean so, beckoned her more urgently than I'd ever perceived.

Not the biggest shock I'd had that night, though, not by half.

'Your father made a scene and it ruined you?' I demanded at last. 'He made a scene, and you—'

'My savings are now *gone*,' she snapped. 'Gone. He took them. Gone. As for my novel, he called it *trash*, and it ended its days in his fireplace.'

My mouth fell open idiotically as I tried out a number of things to do with my hands – hanging them still, cocked on a hip, drawn over my lips. Nothing worked particularly well.

'No,' I said softly, for it was wrong to picture such a thing happening. Thomas Underhill causing his daughter any pain.

The reverend can't bear to see Mercy with so much as a scraped knee. She'd cut herself on the left thumb peeling potatoes once, after her mother died – just once – and he'd permanently taken over the mindless task himself. 'No, he couldn't have. That's horrible. He loves you.'

'Of course he loves me,' she choked out. 'And yes, he *could*. He *burned* it, every page of it, all my words, my—'

Mercy stopped, pressing her fingers against her throat, forcing herself to calm as her voice came to a strangled halt. 'I know that none of that is your fault,' she continued when she was able, 'but I lost all my money, and Robert was going to pay—'

Sad as it is to confess, I lost the trail of the conversation about then.

I'd listened to every heartbroken word she'd said up to that point; however, it's difficult to claim I'd absorbed it very well. My eyes fell shut. *I've been going the wrong way about it*, I thought as the sickness curled luxuriously in the pit of my stomach. *Thinking her a prize and not a person.* I'd have cut off my hand for her if that was what she cost, and she'd never bothered to tell me that in fact she cost—

'Who is he?' Why I wanted to know, I can't imagine.

'A merchant trader who gives a great deal of support to reform societies. We've been friends for ages, and he's always had his eye on me. I wasn't interested before, but he's kind enough, and I didn't know what to *do*.'

'This is how Silkie Marsh knows you,' I realized. 'Not because of charity at all. Isn't it? When you started, did someone like her hurt you, did they make you—'

'I don't have to answer any of this.'

'Answer anyhow, damn it.'

'The first time, I did it for pleasure, though I thought it was love. It was beautiful in its way, but it didn't last, so it couldn't have been love, could it? Afterward . . . It was always by choice, I *liked* them, Timothy, I liked feeling desirable, liked being wanted for something other than a source of ipecac and turnips,' she hissed at me. 'So I arranged to be introduced to Silkie, and whenever I need a private space to share with a friend, that friend rents one of her rooms. She's glad of a little extra income. And I hate her, but she's so very practical about these matters that I knew that she'd never give me away to Papa, and there you have it, the entire tale, every so often she allows me use of one of her bedchambers and I come and go precisely as I please. It isn't as if I can be seen entering a hotel with an unmarried gentleman, is it? Or his rooms? But here, anyone would assume I was making a charity call. And this was the first occasion when . . .' Her jaw set suddenly, wrath blazing through the hurt. 'Stop *looking* at me like that, it's horrifying. *I* am the only thing I have. A man can't ever understand that, I have *nothing else to sell*, Timothy.'

'Don't call me that.'

'Why not? It's your name. Could I have sold my book to Harper Brothers after it burned to cinders? Should I have stopped the charity work I love, stopped tending the children, and sewn men's shirts instead? I do as much as I can, on my *life* I do, and it will never be enough. Should I have married an old fool with a bank account and lived as a whore every second until he died? I couldn't stomach that. Doing it once, for a princely sum and with a friend, seemed . . . easier.'

If you look at it right, almost everyone is a whore in these parts, one way or another, I thought madly. It's a question of degree. Women who troll the back alleys of Corlears Hook in search of their next shilling aren't generally doing it out of preference, but they aren't the only ones who sell bits and pieces of themselves. There are friendly lasses who stargaze when they need a new pair of boots, mothers who spit into their palms only when the little ones are sick and the doctor an easy sort of man, lady birds who yearly survive the dark, dark winters by letting men under their skirts. There are thousands of debutantes who marry bankers they don't love and don't intend to. Girls who'd done it once for a lark and thin-skinned bats who'd done it a thousand times. Pretty molls who rented rooms when they felt the urge to, just as Mercy had. Common enough practice. All too common. I'd never thought to blame them for it, for needing money more than they needed dignity. And it wasn't a fair picture of women, I knew that even as I was thinking it, that plenty of girls could never countenance such a choice. That I was being revoltingly cynical. Heartless, possibly. But I couldn't be sure in that moment which nauseated me more – the fact of Mercy's being paid or the fact of her pleasure coming from anyone on earth apart from me.

Meanwhile, what I ought to have noticed just then was how upset she was, how her fingers wound tight in her skirts to keep them still. The way her breathing wouldn't even out. The fact that watching your novel burn while you stand there helpless to save it might feel a bit like watching someone slice off your finger. After the humiliation she'd just suffered, I ought to have treated the most charitable woman of my acquaintance in a thousand charitable ways that hellish night.

The fact that I didn't can still sicken me, when I let it.

'How could you?' I asked numbly. 'And *here* of all places, here where kinchin disappear into black carriages—'

'No, that's wrong,' Mercy choked, her voice breaking. 'I'd not been here since . . . since all that began. Your investigation. Don't think that of me, I'm begging you. I'd never glimpsed a hint of trouble here beforehand, not an inkling, I swear on my life, I only used a room now and again, and anyhow I've precious little contact with her children save when they fall ill, months go by without my ever seeing them. Over a year in Liam's case. But when Papa found my savings yesterday, I panicked, and I had to make one last effort to get away. I was so desperate. I didn't want to come here, see her again, wonder what she knows. It was ghastly, Tim. Please believe me. I hadn't any choice.'

'There's always a choice. How could you do this to me?'

'But it has nothing to do with you, I tell you, it—'

'It has *everything* to do with me!' I cried, taking her hard by the arm, harder than I'd meant to. 'You aren't stupid, the last fucking thing you are is stupid, you've watched me for years trailing after you, the way I look at you, it's obvious to the entire goddamned world, you can't stand there in front of me and claim not to have known it. How dare you say it has nothing to do with me? It's the cruelest thing I've ever heard. Everything about you has to do with me, and you've known it for years. *Are* you stupid, or are you simply a liar? How can you pretend not to know I once had four hundred dollars in silver and marrying you was all I ever thought about? I'd have gone to London. I'd have done anything.'

I let her go and Mercy's perfectly imperfect face softened. Relented a bit, like she'd remembered now who I was and not simply what I'd just done.

'I did think you might have matrimony on your mind.' She turned toward the dressing table, beginning to put up her hair. 'And I could have done worse than marrying my closest friend. But did you ever ask me?'

'Not after— *Look* at me. How could I? I hadn't any case to make.'

'How can you say that about yourself?'

'I hadn't anything. I still don't have anything. Just a mad brother and twenty little corpses.'

And then my heart nearly stopped.

It came of stating the two facts next to each other, I think. As if I'd taken a picture and torn it in bits and rearranged it.

Val. Valentine.

My mind spun right off its tracks.

That the two spiteful letters from the Hand of the God of Gotham had been the work of a rabid Nativist copper star had always been likely. More than likely. That third letter, though. The one both disturbed and disturbing.

The one under the influence of . . . of something.

Of morphine, maybe? Mixed with whatever else was ready to hand? Lye fumes, hashish, laudanum?

I felt sick.

But it can't be, I insisted desperately, my blood crawling backward through its vessels and my brain reeling. *Just because he's trying to kill you doesn't mean . . . He's trying to kill you for the sake of the sodding Party, and dead little ones are the last thing they need. He took you to see Liam in the first place, damn it. And Bird. Bird trusts him, Bird . . .*

Knew him from the days when he'd frequented Silkie Marsh's house and had been dragged off to the House of Refuge hours after seeing him again.

Was he capable of questioning Madam Marsh, with me in the room, and the pair of them weaving a tale to utterly blind me? Had I understood nothing that day, and my own brother the blankest void of all?

My hands were shaking so badly that I laid them flat against each other, palm to palm. I tried out the list again, Val's list of dubious pastimes, in my head.

Narcotics, alcohol, bribery, violence, whoring, gambling, theft, cheating, extortion, sodomy.

Ritualized child murder.

'It can't be,' I said out loud. 'No. It can't.'

'What can't be?' Mercy questioned, still doing up her hair.

'My brother. He's been on my back to quit this investigation, but it can't be because he's afraid it'll lead me to . . .'

'To *what?*'

'To him.'

Mercy caught her lip in her teeth, shooting me a scrap of pity from under her eyelashes.

'Val would never hurt kinchin. You do know that about your own brother, don't you?'

I stared back at her.

Mother of God.

I don't know whether I couldn't breathe for the next five seconds, or if breathing no longer seemed like a very practical hobby.

People tell me things they don't mean to. I'm a walking confessional in the form of a square-jawed, wiry-limbed, short-statured star policeman with green eyes, a dirty blond widow's peak, and a partial face, and I might as well be a walking coffin box for all the good it's ever done me.

'You just called him Val. The first time was him, wasn't it?'

The silence I'd expected to hear fell between us.

The one that meant yes.

'We were always there, at your house,' I added idiotically, simply to shatter the screaming quiet. 'When you thought it was love, you meant Val.'

Mercy didn't answer me. Her hair was finished, save the tendril on the back left side that never agrees to go anywhere.

'Why are you so against Valentine?' she murmured. 'Enough to suppose him capable of child murder?'

'He did just try to kill me.'

Scowling, Mercy pulled on the grey cloak. It was a kindly scowl, if that's possible.

'Your brother did no such thing. Someone is playing you for a fool. Who was it that came after you?'

'Scales and Moses Dainty, Val's twin lapdogs.'

Mercy laughed. 'You mean Silkie Marsh's lapdogs, though she pays them well enough to keep quiet about it.'

Of course, I'd been dead wrong. Silkie Marsh had seen the nightdress and wanted Bird back. Silkie Marsh had wanted me to stop wondering why her kinchin-mabs turned up in trash bins, and Val had warned me that she'd try to quiet me. That she'd once out of spite tried to quiet *him*.

'Do you think it matters now?' I questioned, voice thin as a honed blade. 'Knowing you wanted him and not me?'

This time when she didn't answer me, her lips parted. She tried, bless that tender spirit of hers, no matter how her life had just exploded. She tried. Mercy just couldn't think of a damn thing in the world to say.

'I wonder if you think it's better this way,' I added. 'Is it better that I'm going to try to kill him and not the other way round?'

Her breath caught.

'Tim,' she attempted. 'You mustn't—'

'When you were in a carriage this afternoon, the one that let you out before your door in Pine Street . . . That coach belonged to the man in the black hood. You were with him.'

Color flamed into her face and then faded fast as a scrap of cheap paper burning. What was queerest about the expression was that I'd seen it before. Like an inner bomb, everything shifting and everything fiery and everything flying, and then watching the dust settle back. I'd seen it on Bird's face last, when I'd rescued her from the carriage careening toward the House of Refuge.

'I wasn't,' Mercy gasped. 'No, I wasn't.'

'The newsboys saw you. Tell me who he is.'

'No,' she cried, shaking her head wildly. 'No, no, no. You're wrong. They were wrong, there must be two carriages. That's it! There are two, of the same manufacture.'

'You truly want to shield him from me? A lunatic kinchin murderer? *Why*, Miss Underhill?'

Mercy put two white, trembling hands on my waistcoat. 'Don't call me that, it's so ugly coming from you. It's impossible, you must believe me, the lads were wrong, I know it. The man who owns that carriage doesn't believe in God at all, and he doesn't give a damn about politics. I tell you it's *impossible*.'

'Are you going to tell me his name next? I am going to make him pay, you know, one way or the other. If I have to kill him myself.'

'No, telling you just now will only make it worse, you'll make a horrible mistake,' she whispered as I gently pulled her fingers away from my plain black vest.

'Let me hurt him – you know he's earned it. *I've* earned it, for God's sake.'

'You're frightening me, Tim. Don't look like that. I can't tell you when you look like that.'

I thought over one or two ways of *making* her tell me, but nothing was workable. Mercy is the sort of woman who walks past mad Irish bruisers to free a colored fellow she scarcely knows, so I'd have needed to break her in a number of pieces, and even if that was remotely possible for me, I was pretty sorely distracted. There was someone else who needed killing.

'Maybe you're right,' I muttered. 'Yes, you're right, I think. At least I know about Valentine, and you certainly shouldn't have told me that.

'I'd have warned you sooner, if I'd known,' I added as I walked out the door. 'No one ever ought to tell me anything. I'm sorry about your book, on my word I am.'

'Don't leave like this, please . . . Timothy!'

I left her there, wearing a slate-colored hood with her hair up, reaching a hand out toward me. I had a brother to grind into the pavement, and I wasn't going to lose any time in finding him. As I swept back past the front saloon, Silkie Marsh interrupted me, her face all guilty concern.

'Are you all right, Mr Wilde? I feared, you see, that the exact . . . situation between myself and Miss Underhill was not entirely clear to you.'

'You said just what was needed to send me straight through that door,' I reminded her through my teeth.

'But that isn't *true*. Please don't, I said.'

Please don't, for Mercy's sake.

It had been her name, not a plea. This sad, disgraceful thing I'd just uncovered – the knowing it was entirely my own fault.

'But perhaps you misunderstood me?'

By now, Silkie Marsh was smiling. The identical smile I once saw a much uglier woman wearing as she informed a friend of hers in a coffeehouse that her cousin had developed an incurable cancer.

'That whorish little hypocrite,' she lilted prettily. 'You love her, I think? Yes, it's obvious, though I can't see why. You *cannot* imagine the way she has looked at me, time and again, when tending to children *I feed and clothe*, and in my very own *home*. I'd not wish misfortune on anyone, Mr Wilde, but perhaps it will lend that slut a fraction more human sympathy, now that she knows what the rest of us feel like when our legs are open.'

I'd seen a similar expression once, but not in a human. It was in the eyes of a yellow dog turned evil with hydrophobia seconds before a civic-minded hydrant inspector bashed in its head.

'I'll tell you something about *mercy*,' I said as I strode to the door. 'I'm not arresting you for sending that pair of idiots to hush me. That would be ridiculous. But this is the last shred of *mercy* you'll ever get from me. And you'll need it, mark my words.'

A sick, inside-out feeling struck me when I reached the street again. Leaning over, I propped my palms on my knees, breathing as if I'd just been pulled from a torrent half drowned. I've never been good at feeling lost. When I've been brought that low, I don't know what to do with myself, whether to erase my sorry life with a quart of whiskey or to let fly at a wall until I've broken my own hand. Both are vivid distractions, I've tried them, but neither is permanent.

I'm very skilled, however, at feeling angry. At rage, I'm a bloody professional.

And since I couldn't hurt Mercy, and she wouldn't give me the man in the black hood, and I'd made a promise to Bird that precluded me from walking into the forgetful Hudson just yet, killing my brother seemed just about the only good idea left to be had.

Chapter Twenty-Two

*Last day of the election; dreadful riots between the
Irish and the Americans have again disturbed the
public peace. The Mayor arrived with a strong body
of watchmen, but they were attacked and overcome,
and many of the watchmen are severely wounded.*

From the diary of Philip Hone, April 10, 1834

Silkie Marsh's brothel was a five-minute walk from
Valentine's station house, and it was nine o'clock at night.
My brother would be in his office. And if not there, then at
the Liberty's Blood. I got halfway to the police station before
I knew something far worse was wrong with the city than my
evil temper: our pathetic attempts at secrecy had come to
nothing at last. The afternoon edition of the *Herald* had ruined
us.

People along Greene and Prince streets had pulled their
front curtains across their windows, and some had even
shuttered them despite the noxious heat. A foul aguey sweat
glimmered on the closed panes. Every few brownstone and

red brick rowhouses, I could see nervous fingers twitching draperies back, so as to stare out into the road. One man, well dressed enough to be a clerk but muscled enough that I knew him for a Party rabbit, sat on his front steps smoking a cigar with a cudgel propped between his knees. Waiting for the thunderclap. And from the looks of things, the wait wouldn't be a long one.

I knew what it all meant before I'd been told, so I changed my direction, veering right into the jungle. When I saw a group of star police approaching from a side street, most of them familiar enough members of Valentine's engine company, I stopped short. They carried torches and elegantly tapered leaded clubs. A few of them walked with pistols slung from their belts. But none of them proved quite mountainous enough in silhouette to be my brother.

'Is that Timothy Wilde?' one called.

'Something like him.'

'Fall in with us, we're wanted. Every copper star. We're the last of Ward Eight, your brother's already on the muscle.'

'Where's the riot?' I asked as I made an about-face, taking a heavy club from a stout Irish fellow who'd seen fit to bring two of them.

'Where it's least necessary, as ever,' spat the policeman. 'Five Points. The only sinkhole on this island that couldn't get any worse.'

'That's my ward you're riding,' I pointed out.

'Sure, and Captain Val told me. God help you.'

Not so far today, I thought.

The shouting reached us first, before the stench of burning trash winnowing through the air, before the sparks. Glancing into the sky, I saw that at least the patchwork summery sheet of low-flying storm cover was yet grey, no darker stain marking a building afire. The moon appeared and disappeared like a restless spirit. A pair of respectable Yidisher secondhand shopkeepers hastened past us nodding, glancing behind them, doing their best to keep out of the way. At almost the same moment, a pack of tiny kinchin, howling like pups, raced down Anthony Street toward the sinister glow, doing their best not to miss anything. I thought of Bird in Harlem, where the stars are clearer even when the sky turns stormy, and tightened my grip on the club.

'Looks like a hell of a spree,' I remarked. 'Do we know who started it?'

Whatever the newspapers and journals say about riots springing up like wild mushrooms, they're mistaken. I know two facts about riots: they are always about the same thing, and they are planted. Always. Riots are farmed, and then when they bloom, the farmers get to smash their bitter fists into the face of an entire city.

'Seems to have been Bill Poole.'

'I've met Bill Poole,' I said, picturing the drunken thug whose eye I'd blackened outside of St Patrick's. 'We didn't get on. He's to blame for this?'

'He bein' a piece of it anyhow, and scores of Nativist rabbits at his back, ready to break what they can, heads or windows. We're meant to keep order, if possible. Matsell might try palaverin' them peaceful, but you know Bill Poole.'

'I'm beginning to.'

'Crazy little sod, Bill Poole,' an American copper star muttered. 'What does he want to do with the Irish if not get votes out of them, I'd like to know. They're here now. They're staying. You'll as soon deport the cockroaches.'

'Fuck off,' the Irish fellow said.

'No offense meant,' the other returned readily. 'I'm

marching next to you, aren't I?'

After crossing Ward Six's border and continuing east for two and a half blocks, you'll reach the Five Points. It's called Paradise Square, of course, as we never did lack for humor – the eye of the pit where the five streets crash together. Neither paradise nor a square, but an infected triangle. There are parts of this city where, during the drier stretches of summer, the boot-deep mud will harden fully, and its smell lessen. Not in Five Points. There are parts where the gin-sotted mabs will go indoors at four or five in the morning, when more than half naked and no longer keen to stand up. Not in Five Points. And in most parts of the island, the people who live there have just barely coin enough to be cruelly snobbish about their neighbors' race. But in Five Points, where we stood beside Crown's Grocery with the giant five-story monstrosity of the Old Brewery looming pale and cracked as an old skull across from us, all races live together. Because once a man is poor enough to seek shelter there, no other hell exists for him to sink to.

Bonfires blazed on the damp sewer-ground throughout the plaza. I wanted to think that we stood in recently used coffee grounds, but I knew better. People gathered in clotted packs of three, or of seven, or of twelve, lighting torches at the nearest blaze and seeking out folk of their kind. Knots of Irish mainly, who'd probably been called out. A few blacks, but they stood before their own tenements, looking wary. Clumps of other police too, scores of them.

Right before the Old Brewery stood most of the Bowery Boys. You can see the difference between aggressors and defenders by the way they hold brickbats, and these particular Nativists were lightly draping them along the ground as if using them was going to be an awful flash summer lark.

Dressed like simon-cheap versions of Val down to a man. Every shirt collar turned over, every vest screaming with flowers, every dinted hat high brushed silk. And the highest hat of all, atop the cruelest head, belonged to Bill Poole. He'd a cigar between his lips and stood in the exact middle of Cross Street at the triangle's southern tip, looking lit up like the Fourth of July.

'. . . and now this festering plague of a religion is allowed to *flourish*!' he was booming. 'No longer hid in low hovels and rotgut cellar groceries. They build a *cathedral*! And then what do these white savages do, you might ask? They take one of their own kinchin, and they sacrifice him to the Antichrist of Rome!'

Grotesque applause at this from Bowery types, disgusted snarls from the Irish. Blacks waiting to see which of their homes would be burned down to pig-level this time.

'Right. This can't go on,' said the man to my left, glancing nervously down at his copper star. 'Stopping a riot before it happens is one thing, but—'

'If I were you, Bill Poole,' came a voice that cut through bonfire haze like an alarm bell, 'I'd go home and sleep it off. And I'm in a pretty fair humor tonight, as it happens. So I'm going to *let* you go home and sleep it off.'

George Washington Matsell stood before every single one of his eighteen captains and thirty-six assistant captains. Never have I seen a deadlier-looking collection of firemen, street brawlers, Party thugs, and fighting entrepreneurs in my life, and they made Chief Matsell's hiring practices pretty clear. If you were loyal to the Party or maybe even a good watchman, you could wear a copper star. If you looked like you've killed a man with your bare hands and aren't shy about doing it again, you could be a captain. Valentine was just behind

Matsell himself, glancing around him with a cudgel elegantly tilted over one shoulder.

'You all see whose side this standing army, these so-called police, choose to fight on?' screamed Bill Poole. 'They're an affront to Democracy! Patriots bow to no gang of street thugs.'

'Funny you should say that,' drawled Matsell. The quivering points of torchlight surrounding him all seemed to be listening hungrily, holding their breath. 'I'll tell you once again: citizens, disperse! If you don't know what that means, it means go on the hell home while we find the son of a bitch who hurt that kinchin.'

'And I say don't disperse,' sneered Bill Poole. 'So what of that?'

'People will get hurt. I don't want that, Poole, though you might. So I'll put it like this: *you'll* get hurt.'

'If you can't collar a sick Irish lunatic, you think you can bully an *American*?'

'I think I can arrest a tongue-pad,' Chief Matsell growled resignedly. 'Why don't you do the honors, Captain Wilde?'

'It's damned queer,' said Valentine, walking easy as you like toward Bill Poole with a pair of iron cuffs and a wicked smile. 'And I always thought disperse meant *sod off*. How are you, Bill?'

'Men!' shouted the chief. 'Keep them at bay!'

For several simultaneous eruptions had taken place. I blinked as I was shoved hard to one side, right into the sagging porch of Crown's Grocery. The square looked suddenly like one of Hopstill's calculated lightning displays, leashed fury bursting into the swinging of brickbats from every direction. From behind me, the Ward Eight copper stars surged forward, and I careened toward the Old Brewery and the thick of the trouble thinking, *At last.*

A fight. And one worth winning too, by God.

Not being used to battling with a cudgel, the first one that came at me might have staved my head in. It meant to. But I ducked, and it hit the mud, spraying filth in all directions. Whirling as best I could in ankle-deep grime, I brought my own leaded stick down on the drunk rabbit's hand, snapping something or other. He cried out, backing away, toothless without a weapon.

So I found another fight, as good as the first had been.

Brass knuckles flashed from several directions, a single pistol fired just before the fool's neck met with a brickbat, and I thought, *More of this. More.* I saw so clearly that night, felt the merest breath of rogues behind me and spun to drive a heavy club into their guts. Some of them ran when once hurt. I didn't mind. That was flash. I'd no desire to punish anyone, just to win at *something*, any *something*, in the lawless den of dogs I'd somehow landed myself in, or so I thought as I caught a nasty-looking thug in the torso, sending him crashing into a public water pump.

We were at open war – windows breaking, men prone in the mire, screams woven into a howling maelstrom of sound. It was a seething, snarling dust-up between American dead rabbits, Irish scoundrels, and the copper stars, who were composed of maybe half and half. That's important to me. Because we weren't splitting apart, I saw with a feeling a little bit like watching my brother box, and we weren't turning on each other. None of us. One saw another endangered and blocked a brickbat with his own club. One saw another fall, and he helped him up. No matter the color of their hair or the cast of their features.

It was a bit of a miracle, truth be told. Or it was to my mind, and the sort I'd stopped expecting from New York.

Then the air turned rottener.

I found myself in the doorway of the Old Brewery, sweating like a draft horse. I'm not sure how I came to be there. It must have been at least thirty minutes later, for the cloud cover was blowing over, and the stars were painfully sharp. Many were still fighting. But some had fallen, or had been arrested and were being forced into wagons.

Whoosh.

It was one of Bill Poole's henchmen. I recognized his gin-sour teeth and his absolutely apelike hands. It couldn't have been called his fault, maybe, that the man was built for destroying.

I stumbled back.

That had been a knife, not a cudgel. And it had sliced a good way down my forearm. The cut felt shallow enough, but at least ten inches long.

My brother appeared on the Brewery threshold, licking his lips like a French tourist. Completely untamable and entirely familiar. He took in the scene.

'Well, if it isn't Snatch Smith,' he said cordially. Val's linen was mussed, but otherwise no one seemed yet to have touched him. 'Is my brother giving you a beating, then?'

'Not by half,' the villain sneered.

'Then he was planning on it. Eh, Tim?'

Slashed down my arm though I was, I couldn't find the blood much impeded me. That sad sot was enough distracted by Valentine that when I came after him again, he was off his guard, taking a solid blow under his arm. The knife he'd been gripping flew into the darkness of the Old Brewery.

But I'd missed incapacitating him. Guessing the bigger threat, he'd his huge meaty hands around Val's throat before either of us knew what was happening. Lucky thing for the pair of us that he'd guessed wrong.

I knocked him cold with the cudgel. And I dropped to the floor myself immediately after, staring up at black rafters, exhausted. Wrecked and bloody and too long sleepless and my head throbbing. An ancient wooden staircase rose above me. I heard a dog snarl, half-hearted yells from outside.

Val stood, half garroted but well and truly alive.

'Snatch isn't too keen on the hospital,' I heard my brother rasp out as he launched the unconscious man through the door. 'A nap in Paradise Square will give him time to think over his choices.'

'I was wrong,' I told Valentine from the ground. 'About Bird. It was Silkie Marsh wanted her bundled off to the House of Refuge. Probably would have had her hushed once she arrived. I was wrong to blame you.'

'You get the most goosecap ideas,' Val gasped. 'If you want to live a long, plump life, keep your mazzard shut and do what I tell you. Let's go.'

'Where?'

'The riot's near enough to quashed, and Piest has found something. Some blowsy country hen who'd a secret lover north of town where the kinchin were buried. You and I are for the Tombs, chief's orders—'

I sat up.

'You bedded Mercy Underhill, didn't you.'

It wasn't a question. My brother, who'd checked over his throat and decided it wasn't any more crushed than it should have been, reached his right hand out to pull me to my feet. I accepted.

Valentine's lips twitched. 'Aye, I've tilled her garden. A long while back, though. Why do you ask?'

That wasn't a question I could get my head around.

'Pretty wench, isn't she, and she doesn't know a thing about it either,' he coughed. 'There's the charm, in my book.'

It was the fact that he was right that made me want to scream. 'You bedded Mercy,' I said again.

'Well, and haven't you? You've been paper skulled over her for years, yes? Where's the fuss? Every free-born American son has occupied Mercy Underhill if she fancies his measure, and you a barman with plentiful chink all that time, enough to show her some sport. Jesus Christ, Timothy, what the devil has gotten into you? A red-blooded woman's entitled to a little fun. You really mean to say you *haven't* bedded her?'

It was too much. I flew at him.

I wanted to see his blood pooling, to hear a good honest yell of pain out of the wretch. First there were feints, a nimble twist on his part. My fist hit his eye nevertheless, with a snap like a firecracker, and I wanted more of that feeling. That he could be *taught* something. Be dragged dówn to my level of defenselessness or else hauled up to my sort of sympathy.

Then he'd pinned my right arm behind my back and my face smashed against the crumbling whitewashed wall with his hand holding me by the neck like a new-littered kitten. At least his temple was bleeding. That was satisfying.

'Buggering *hell*, Timothy! Are you wholesale insane? Why should *I* matter more than any of the others? You know as well as I do—'

Val stopped because at those words, I'd winced visibly and knocked my own head against the peeling paint, saving him the trouble. I felt his paw on my neck shifting, thoughtful.

'You didn't know. You found out just now that she's . . . available. And you weren't after a tumble with her,' he added softly. 'You were thinking along . . . churchish lines.'

'For once in your life, please shut your mouth.'

A silence like a yawning chasm.

'Tim, I'm sorry,' he said. It was a strange thing to hear from a man pinning you down by the neck. 'I can't say as I know the feeling exactly, but I'd be caved too.'

If my brother had ever apologized to me before, I couldn't recollect it. The fingers holding my arm in an oaken grip loosened.

'If I let you go, will you stave my face in?'

'Probably.'

He released me, and I turned to peer at him. A good amount of blood oozed from the cut I'd made by his eye. I still wanted to add to it, but somehow couldn't when I saw his expression. Valentine looked almost sheepish.

'Well, God knows you've cause to stave my face in,' he said with the saddest smile I've ever seen. 'You'll have another swing at me, gratis, and we'll go to the Tombs. I've done considerable worse to you before ever meeting an Underhill, after all.'

'Becoming a fireman is not worse than bedding the woman whose name I want to change.'

He paused. 'You're one too many for me tonight, Tim, and that's a fact. What's wrong with my working as a fire rabbit?'

I couldn't believe my ears. 'Don't play stupid.'

'God damn it, Tim, this is me *being* stupid. What's wrong about it?'

'Our parents died *in a fire*,' I snarled at my brother as he loomed over me, my eager fists balling uselessly at my sides. 'You remember, don't you? And practically the next day you were charging headlong into them.'

Valentine's green eyes narrowed into fast-turning carriage spokes, thoughts flickering sharply through them. 'Maybe that was hard at first. But that's not why you've been angry with me all this spell. Me fighting fires. I'm meant to fight fires.'

'You're going to make me watch you burn to death,' I spat at him. 'What could possibly bother me more, precisely?'

Val started laughing.

It wasn't his usual regretful chuckle. And neither was it the apologetic full-throated variety. This was a laugh that sent a gash through your belly. Val could laugh at a hanging, I grant, but this made gallows humor seem like smiling at a kite in midair. I felt I was watching someone being gutted, and grew so frightened for a moment that I went and gripped his arms with both my hands. He was wincing as usual, but this time he said the thought aloud.

'It isn't funny. It isn't the smallest bit funny, not a wooden jack's worth.'

'Val,' I said. Then, 'Stop, Val.' But he wasn't listening.

'You're telling me,' he gasped, 'that all this time you've been angry—'

'Because the instant our entire family burned to death, you started up charging into every fire you could find. Yes. Val. *Valentine.*'

It was the only moment I could recall being taller than him, for he'd doubled over with his hands on his knees, tawny hair hanging in his eyes as he laughed like a man who'd long been sentenced to hell.

'Oh, that's rich. *That* kittles me. You want to hear something, Timothy, a real gapeseed of a story? Eh? You might as well know what I *thought* you were angry over. Christ, my lungs.'

'Val,' I said. My own weak voice echoed grossly in my ears, and I thought insanely, *You confounded idiot, be more like him.*

Val turned his head to look up at me, blood still running

freely down his cheek, and he straightened his shoulders. 'About that fire. The first one. The one made you learn to tend bar and me to cook supper.'

'Yes,' I said.

'I lit that fire,' Valentine said.

He wasn't in front of me any longer. He was a thousand and a thousand and a thousand miles away. It was a ransomed look. One he'd never before showed me. And since he'd never shown me, I'd never known it was there.

'I was smoking a cigar in the horse barn, instead of mucking out the stalls like I was meant to. I smoked the fucking cigar, Tim, and it lit in the straw, and when I rushed to free the horses, they . . . I opened the stalls because we needed them, Dad couldn't farm without the horses, and what sort of . . . and I was running out of the . . . I was sixteen years old, Tim, and I thought you saw me. You *did* see me, tearing open all the stall gates, trying to coax the horses out of them. Running about like hell was at my heels. And it was. All right? You stood in that open doorway and you *saw me* light that fire. Didn't you? All this time, I . . . you were frozen stiff when I turned. And then I didn't see that it had gotten as far as the kerosene, all that kerosene. By the time I'd dragged you out. We couldn't. You remember. Not with the buildings attached, and the blaze in the doorway. It was ended. I never did it on purpose.'

When Val stopped talking, he drew his fingers over the back of his neck, looking away. A cry sounded in a near room, followed by a cackle and the merry smashing of glass. I longed to say something. But whatever link there was between my brain and my mouth had been severed, just as sure as the link between my mouth and the distant thump in my chest.

I watched Valentine flick my copper star. 'You're what a

star police is meant to look like. I knew it. I was never glad of your being scarred up, but I was glad of the fire downtown if for no other reason. I'll take myself off, and that way you'll rest easier. You won't have to see me anymore. Go meet Matsell and make sure that New York is still standing tomorrow. Goodbye, Tim.'

He walked away with his hands in his pockets. Straight out the wide front door. Every individual piece of me wanted to stop him. Even the parts that were still furious, and even the bits he'd just exploded like a kerosene keg.

But I couldn't get myself to move quick enough. By the time I'd run into the street with his name on my lips, it was as if Valentine Wilde had been a figment of my imagination.

CHAPTER TWENTY-THREE

This is the way: make Americans only acquainted
with the simple truth respecting Romanism, and they
will scout it out of countenance, and even its adherents
will deny its claims or practices, out of pure shame.

American Protestant in Defence of Civil and
Religious Liberty Against Inroads of Papacy, 1843

I didn't go meet Matsell, as it happened.

No, I dragged myself home to Elizabeth Street. More than half delirious, and only luck to thank for keeping possession of my wallet for the whole journey. The house was very empty when I got there. No one kneading, no one sketching.

I pumped as much Croton water as I could bear to carry and started a fire in the grate. Heated the water in kettles, in soup pots. Whatever I could find. Filling the hip bath I'd pulled out from behind the stacked flour bags was one of the more irksome jobs I'd done all night, and it wasn't even properly night now, not any longer, but nearer to chalky late-summer dawn. I didn't have a choice, though. The little stab point in my back throbbed horribly, the gash down my arm not much better, and it's a bad job to die of infected blood.

It's a bad job to die when you've unfinished business, anyway. And I'd a full cargo's worth. Three very important priorities.

Keep Mercy Underhill safe. Get your brother back. Stop the bastard who's done all this.

I wasn't too sure about the order of importance, so I let that go and determined to accomplish all three as best I could at the same time.

Settling back into the hot water hurt like all hell. Not as much, though, as when I spooned a heaping pile of pearl-ash alkaline salt onto one of Mrs Boehm's clean rags and started scrubbing out every part of me still bleeding. The pale powder spat and hissed when it touched the water, and I wasn't being gentle about anything. That was purposeful. It isn't easy to slip into unconsciousness when you're in that much pain.

After I'd rubbed pearl-ash into every cut I could find, paying harshest attention to the tiny gouge pulsing in my back, the water was a rosy hue and I was as fresh awake as I'd ever been in my life. Drying quickly with another slop sheet, dousing the fire with pink water from the hip-bath, I fetched more clean cloth for bandaging and wrapped up my burning cuts. They would keep, now. And I'd been hurt worse. It was when I looked over my face in the pane of window glass, finding it bright shiny and watery textured – hideous, but on the whole healthy – that I suddenly knew what I had to *do*.

What was *next*. And it wasn't Piest or Matsell.

With the sheet gathered around my waist, I ran upstairs for butcher paper, a hunk of charcoal, and my only clean shirt and trousers. I suffered a dizzy spell on the way, but I fought it off, more annoyed and impatient than anything. Returning just as quickly, I spread the brown sheet out on the tabletop. I poured myself a splash of brandy. Cautiously, knowing a measure of pain would keep me alert. Next, I turned back to the chair I'd hung my filthy togs over and reached into my inner frock coat pocket. Then at last I sat down at the table holding Palsgrave's letter, the only letter that sounded as if it had been written by a lunatic and not a stage villain, and I spread it out on the grainy wood.

I can see only it.

I can see it and nothing else see it ever and ever amen only the body so small and so broken.

I stopped reading that part. It was madness without any markers, any facts to speak of. But that letter, in combination with the way Marcas had met his end . . .

It gnawed at me. *Something is wrong.* And of course it was, I'd learned that much from poor little Aidan Rafferty long since. But if I thought of all this as a *story*, as the way people *do things*, as the way someone sitting in my bar with his tongue unhinged would *tell it to me* . . .

Something was wrong.

I picked up my charcoal and I stood up from the table and I drained the brandy. Still a bit dizzy. Near to two full days awake, slit up pretty nastily, wearing only trousers and a half-buttoned shirt, on that huge piece of blank butcher paper I wrote in one corner:

THINGS A PERSON WOULD KILL FOR:
God.

Politics.
Defense.
Money.
Madness.
Love.

I looked them over. Maybe an argument could be made that money and self-love are the same, or that politics and God are similar, but I liked it well enough. So I continued, this time taking up more canvas. Drawing the following words in separate areas all throughout the middle, circling each with a thick black line like a fence:

19 buried (nameless – Jack Be Nimble of the Newsboys
*   among them?)*
1 trash bin (Liam)
1 escaped (Bird)
9 rescued (Neill, Sophia, Peter, Ryan, Eamann, Magpie,
* Jem, Tabby, John)*
1 publicly desecrated (Marcas)
1 mistaken for a rat (Aidan)

I'm not sure why I added the last name. He was so very long past, and not a bit connected. But I wanted him there. He was important to me.

So.

Twenty-two dead, and Bird sleeping warm and peaceful in the middle of a rambling berry patch farmstead in Harlem. Or so I hoped.

But then I began to notice something. I poured myself another small brandy, just for something to do with my hands when I stopped to think. Oddly enough, my hands as they were writing and circling and busy felt alive. I thought, *Yes, this is working, don't stop, everything you can think of belongs on this piece of butcher paper. Everyone depends on it.*

. Leaning over, I started drawing. I drew a quick sketch of Silkie Marsh. I drew Mercy as she'd been at St Patrick's, with her eyes wide and her hair down. I drew one of the buried corpses, cracked open and bones bare. I drew Marcas, in cruelly broad lines, because that's what his murder had looked like. I drew Bird's new dress. Just little pictures between the spaces, spooling the cobwebs from out of my head.

It worked, too. When the pictures were out of me, I started remembering words.

And the right ones this time.

People tell me things they shouldn't. Things they ought to be powdering over, shoveling underground, facts they ought to be stuffing into a carpetbag before dropping into the river and quietly drowning. I wrote the series of statements in another section, deciding 'Statements' was a fair enough name for them. Bits of sentences from Mercy, from Palsgrave, remarks that hadn't seemed to have any connection to each other.

By the time I was through scribbling them out, they didn't look like spoken phrases at all. They looked like a map. A map of hell, maybe, but a map nevertheless, and my breath caught in my throat.

I pulled the letter – the only letter left to me – out from where it lay half covered under the butcher paper. I read it over.

Nothing made sense, but everything fit.

I felt a bit like laughing, but that would have been horrible. And anyway there had to be *some* difference between me and Val. So I finished my sheet of butcher paper instead.

First I circled *Love*. From under 'Things a Person Would Kill For'. And then *God* too, for that was a part of it. And then *Money*.

Next I wrote the following questions:

What did Piest find in the woods and tell the chief?
Who attended Father Sheehy's Catholic school proposal meeting?

A knock occurred just beyond the bread display.

I approached Mrs Boehm's door, having stopped on the way for a kitchen knife. Rankly exhausted, sick at heart, buzzing with savage and unnerving butcher-paper knowledge. Grasping the knob, I lifted the blade she used to quarter chickens.

And there stood Gentle Jim, of all the people in the world, with my brother's treelike biceps draped senselessly over his shoulders. When I'd first spied Jim with his head lolling off the crook of Val's arm at the Liberty's Blood, I'd have called you a liar if you claimed he could support his own scant weight, let alone Val's. But I'd have been dead wrong, and Valentine didn't presently appear to be much up to walking by himself. I guessed nine reasons for that, and then settled on one overarching one, which was his brother Tim is a purblind milksop.

'Good Lord,' I managed. 'Thank you. Come in, for God's sake. I'll take his legs.'

'It would greatly endear you to me,' Jim replied exhaustedly.

That didn't end up happening. What did seem to work was me slinging both of Val's arms over my shoulders and walking up the stairs with him hanging on my back, Jim following with my brother's ankles so the man wasn't dragged up each and every step. Though in that state, he'd never have noticed. I've seen it a hundred times.

Reaching my room, I dropped him pretty hard on my straw tick mattress. Not out of spite, for once, but because he's damnably heavy.

'What the *devil*,' I prompted.

'Yes, well.' Gentle Jim tugged at the paper collar of his laundered shirt wearily. 'I never did set any stock in his perfection. Only his tremendous appeal.'

'He says he's not a sodomite,' I remarked stupidly.

'And just *what* do you mean to insinuate about *me*, if you please?'

I liked him fine after that. As perfect replies go, that one was all aces. And if sodomy had just saved Val's hide, it was now my hands-down favorite of his indulgences.

'What was he doing, just now?'

'The unfortunate rogue met a sea captain at the Liberty's Blood and signed on for a voyage to Turkey,' he sniffed. 'However, every mother's son drinking there owes Valentine far too much money and far too many favors to allow him such a . . . career misstep. We objected. Strenuously. Not molleys,' he added, rolling his eyes before I could say a word. 'I venture to surmise I am his only intimate acquaintance in the City Hall Park set, actually, or . . . my goodness. I *hope* I am. What a dreadful line of thought, Timothy. Anyhow, the dockworkers didn't like to see him shipped off either, what with his role in their Party, and all. Thus I was charged with escorting him home. Val grew rather uncultured with me en route, dreaming of the open sea as it were and finding himself thwarted in his aims, and threw his house key into a sewage sink. I am above retrieving it from such a place. And here we are.'

I was trying to work out if my brother was still breathing. The odds seemed fair that he was. I'd given him one hell of a black eye, but someone had carefully cleaned the place where the skin had split.

Yes, I like this Jim fellow considerably, I decided.

'Have I gotten him home, then?' Gentle Jim inquired, genuinely worried.

'You're a fine friend to the pair of us,' I answered. By way of an apology.

'Don't you dream of thinking that,' Jim laughed as he walked toward my staircase. 'When once he wakes up – I don't know what troubles have recently beset the two of you, he always claimed you were quite close – you shall doubtless suppose me an utter bastard. Val coming off that much morphine is a grand and a glorious thing. I wish you all the fair luck in the world, because that is how much you will need.'

I was too much anxious over Val to leave for the Tombs. Not because I thought he might finally have used himself too hard, but because there was no guarantee that if I left and he awoke, the bloody-minded scoundrel might not set sail for Brazil. And so I found some stomach-calming dried mint and brewed a pot of tea instead. My brother endures the sweats and the chills with remarkable calm, and the bit where his heart rate starts resembling a hummingbird's doesn't much vex him. But this one looked like it had been a real out-and-out. That meant I needed mint tea, and – supposing the tea didn't work – a bucket. I fetched them.

Thankfully, I waited only about twenty minutes. I was sitting with my back to the wall by the straw tick in my relatively unfurnished room when Valentine sat up, looking like a savage who'd just crawled out of a cave and stolen a dapper Party man's togs.

'What,' he said in a voice the texture of tree bark, 'am I doing here?'

'Sleeping off the morphine,' I said amiably. 'Gentle Jim delivered you.'

'That prancing little hobbyhorse.'

'I like him fine.'

Val rubbed his hand up and down his face a few times. 'You never want to see me again.'

'I changed my mind.'

'Why?' he wanted to know, shoving his index finger and thumb hard into his eyeballs.

'Because I'm not a very good brother, but I'd like some practice at it.'

Val coughed up something that belonged on the ground in Five Points and tugged his red silk kerchief out of his pocket.

'And just how do you calculate to learn that lay, Tim?'

'I'll watch you, I guess. That's my plan.'

'Then you,' Val rasped into the cloth, 'are thick as cream.'

'I know.'

I had spent more than half a lifetime believing that my brother's foulest crimes against me consisted of firefighting, morphine use, and moral depravity, in that order. And I'd never had the smallest intention of forgiving him for any of them. Not that Val had asked. But knowing that his greatest crime was actually a bloodstain so dark it could blot a man out entirely . . . Miraculously, that was easier. An instant had passed the night before, as I staggered home, when I realized I could be rid of the person who'd robbed me of my parents. That I could simply let Valentine go. And then I'd thought about my twisted maelstrom of a sibling's exactitude in

stuffing pigeons with butter and suet and marjoram before
stewing them, and how whenever we'd had a window it had
always been scrupulously clean, and the occasion we'd run
out of handkerchiefs and he'd actually cut an old waistcoat
into squares and hemmed them. I'd thought about the quality
of spine required to walk into a fire in which people are
burning. I'd thought about reasons for doing so. It had been
all I could manage not to start shouting his name down
Elizabeth Street.

'Is that mint tea?' Val croaked dubiously, opening one eye.

'Yes.'

'Is it really that bad?'

'Yes.'

And it was. But that only ever takes about half an hour –
the bucket period, I mean to say, and when the nausea had
been conquered, Val stuck his head in my basin and washed
up, and we went back downstairs. I soon found day-old bread
Mrs Boehm had wrapped and put in the cupboard, a piece of
farmer's cheese, and some house beer. The dawn was now far
from grey, and the air had cooled from the passing storm
overhead. A mutely watchful morning. When I'd finished
making coffee, I sat down across from my brother. Val was
staring at my butcher paper, eyebrows raised.

'Your coffee,' Valentine said, 'smells like the underside of
an Irish boot.'

'I ought to tell you right off that you won't be seeing Scales
or Moses Dainty again. It's not by my hand, but they're . . . in
no position to be found. They were hedging with Silkie Marsh
and met some who objected to them trying to kill me.'

My brother was too drug-sick to grieve properly. But he
did slump a little further. 'There's a question solved. Do you
know, I thought that pair of cross-coves were beginning to

smell like rats. But they'd run with me so long, I couldn't swallow it.'

'I need to know what you learned from Matsell and Piest. I could go find them myself, but—'

'But they leaked to me already. You've turned murder artist,' he added with his eyes on the brown paper.

'It helped. What did Piest find in the woods and tell the chief?'

'That piece of old Dutch toast is really as sharp as they make them.' Val sighed, putting his elbows on the table and staring at the bread darkly. 'I suppose you know he unearthed a rank lot of sheepskins by the grave. Well, he found the wench they'd been occupying too, and she was all the go to spill for him. Name of Maddy Sample.'

Maddy Sample was a lovely and apple-cheeked farm girl of seventeen who lived in the midst of a cherry orchard bordering the woods where the shields had been found. Mr Piest, bless the mad rogue, had discovered her by visiting the nearest pub to the gravesite – a saloon called The Fairhaven, on the assumption that the girl lived very near – and then pretending to lech after every moll who'd bother speaking with him. He enjoyed zero success, as might be expected. But this behavior gave the menfolk the impression he was hot after their property. And soon enough a fellow by the name of Ben Withers, who was more chivalrous than clearheaded, warned him not to gawk after Maddy if he didn't want Ben's fist in his eye.

'Which would have been bully,' Val explained, 'but Maddy Sample isn't married to Ben Withers. He lives at a brewery a quarter mile away. *Also* bordering the forest. Which made our Mr Piest wonder what the devil dear little Ben was so worried about.'

Mr Piest hadn't yet encountered Maddy Sample. But he found her soon enough at the cherry orchard when he told her parents that his wife was ailing, and needed a part-time companion of sunny disposition. For a large sum of coin, a few of which he handed over to them as a gesture of good faith. The Samples wished his wife a swift recovery and in the meanwhile sent him straight to their vegetable garden to speak with Maddy. When he'd gently told her what he'd found, what he wanted, and what he'd pay her for pretending to call on his wife, Maddy washed her hands and rode with him to the Tombs.

'Matsell and Piest questioned her, and the pair of them know what they're about, making a moll comfortable.' Val dunked a piece of bread in his small beer and hazarded a bite of it. 'The doxie was spinning yarn after yarn as soon as a glass of French cream was in her hands. Ben Withers is a real out-and-outer, but he's not yet through his brewers' apprenticeship. Ben Withers is a bit peppery about who she talks with. Ben Withers has a fine ankle for a jig. When they'd got her off the topic of her young man, she admitted they go to the woods to play plug-tail, and when they asked if she'd ever spied anything dusty, she said there's a carriage comes there at times. Saw it twice.'

'My God,' I said softly. 'Did she see what they were about?'

'Didn't want to get caught, did she? So she kept her distance. Whenever they appeared, she and Ben turned tail.'

'What else?'

'Just one thing. The carriage had a picture on the side. She said it was an angel.'

'An angel?'

'Sure as taxes, an angel. That's why Matsell wanted us. It truly *is* a religious nutter, Tim. Which means last night was only a taste. We're buggered if we can trace him, and buggered if we can't.'

'No,' I said on a tiny, hushed little breath. 'It doesn't mean that at all. I know what's happened. Right down to brass tacks.'

It's a good job Val hates my coffee and is downright snobbish about it, or I think he'd have spit it out. Meanwhile, I felt like I was flying and free-falling at the same time. It's not a bit pleasant.

'*How?*' my brother demanded.

I pointed dumbly at the sheet of butcher paper.

'Mother of God. Then what are we doing here, young copper star? And are you going to leak?'

'Will you get uppish if I don't tell you yet?' I asked, rising.

'Yes. No. Christ, Tim.'

'I have to see someone.' I was buttoning my vest, casting about for my boots, tying the thin strip over my scar. 'Can you do one thing for me? Please?'

'When I can stand,' Val said judiciously, 'and when you've poured me a whiskey. You rankly inhospitable cow's teat.'

I went for the liquor. 'Can you ride at once up to Harlem and find a farm called Boehm? Marthe Boehm. My landlady is there, and Bird Daly. They plan to come back to the city today, but they need an escort. If you're on the muscle, I'll know nothing can go wrong.'

'Is anything likely to go gammy where *you're* headed?' he asked pointedly.

'It's all bob, Val, trust me,' I said, assuring him of my safety. 'Just one or two people I need to speak with.'

'I've taken orders from bigger flats than you, I suppose.'

Cocking his head in a measuring sort of way, my brother poured himself a second glass of whiskey. Bigger than the first.

I'd my frock coat on and was nearly out the door when I turned back.

'Why didn't you just tell me you had nothing to do with Bird's being dragged off to the House of Refuge?'

'Because you go deaf when I talk, Tim.'

He said it in the same tone as he'd say, 'Why not, if the weather's fine?' or 'Because you can't add lemon to milk that way, tit-brains, it'll curdle the sauce.' Didn't meet my eyes either, just pulled out his tiny appointment book and began jotting down *Boehm* with a pencil stub from his frock coat. I hadn't much liked having my heart broken by cruel chance the night before. This new crack through it seemed fair, though, because I have apparently been an instrument of merciless punishment for seventeen years and because Valentine Wilde does not ever – despite his habits, never needs to – write anything down in order to recall it. Which meant that risking a glance in my direction seemed long odds to him just then.

'I thought so,' I said when I could manage to talk at all. 'Val, I'm sorry for it. Please don't go to Turkey. Promise me.'

He did look at me then, and his eyebrow twitched with dark amusement. 'The life of a sea-crab has lost its sheen.' Val paused, tucking his appointment book away again. 'You won't go charging up against the Party half cocked? They're dangerous. I've been trying to tell you so.'

'It's not them I'm fighting, turns out,' I called back as I left him, settling my wide hat over my brow. 'I'm thick as cream, just like you said. It's absolutely everyone else.'

CHAPTER TWENTY-FOUR

They gather the sons and daughters of Protestants,
and even of some professors of religion, into the
schools, and gradually accustom them to the worship
of Catholics . . . I could give some facts corroborative
of these remarks, which have occurred here, had I
room.

a correspondent of the 'Home Missionary', 1843

I quit the hack at the intersection of Chambers and Church streets. The combined house and practice shone, a beacon of good health in the form of housing. About as far a cry from Five Points as you could imagine. Its steps newly scrubbed by his servants, and the knob on his door flashing merry arcs of light in the sun. Glancing over the brass plaque announcing DR PETER PALSGRAVE, PHYSICIAN TO YOUTH, I rang the bell.

A butler appeared, looking parched and skeletal.

'Dr Palsgrave cannot be disturbed.'

Polishing the copper star with my coat sleeve did the trick.

He sighed, looking grieved at the sad pass New York had finally come to.

'Very well, then. Dr Palsgrave is lecturing at New York University. You will find him there,' he droned while the door was shutting.

By the time I'd arrived at Washington Square, it was nearly midmorning. The sun was perched high over the trees, and students streamed from place to place like ants in their brightly colored hose and squashed hats. Fresh cheeked and worried ill over nothing whatsoever. The third one I hailed pointed me to the medical lecture hall and public dissection forum. I set off, feeling about thirty years older than him and not the more probable five or six.

The door to the hall creaked when I pulled it. Light gushed through the opening, glancing wildly off the dust in the air. Down in the central lecture pit it was pretty dim, though the twelve-foot windows hadn't any curtains over them and a number of lamps glowed. A few wigged heads turned to glance at me, but soon shifted away again. Dr Palsgrave stood behind a corpse with a hole drilled in its head and a metal hook screwed into it, the hook tied to a rope with a pulley. He tugged, raising the body's torso upright from the head. The ribs were already spread wide, skin peeled off like an orange rind, mouth grinning in unlikely good will.

'And so you see,' he continued as I descended, 'that the thoracic cavity does not end abruptly at the height of the uppermost rib. It allows the thymus, trachea, esophagus, and the longus colli muscles to extend higher, for one, but we shall continue to focus upon the left common carotid artery's progression upward into the skull for the moment.'

'I need to speak with you, Doctor,' I said at the bottom of the stairs.

The little man looked up. Golden eyes molten, corseted spine crackling with annoyance. Then he returned his full attention to science and science alone.

'I am *busy at present*. Can you not see that? As if enough trouble has not come of this so-called police force—'

'It would be very, very much *better*,' I insisted, 'if you took me someplace private.'

'Out of the question! I would be *wasting* a very valuable speci—'

'Get one of your fellow doctors to take over the lecture. I'll wait.'

Seething, Dr Palsgrave did as I asked. With an angry flick of his wrist, he led me out of the lecture hall and into another interior corridor. His posture balletic, his white whiskers mad as a cat's, his formal coat very brushed and very blue, muttering infamies at me all the while. When we'd reached the end of the passage, he threw open a door – which also, I noted, had his name engraved above it.

Dr Palsgrave had a second alchemy lab at the school, I realized when we entered the office. And he was in the midst of an experiment, an assistant wearing a robe hovering over the delicate equipment. Retorts were burning away, little fires dancing with the liquid metal above them. There were bits of tissue pinned to boards, vials filled with mysterious poisons. I hadn't the slightest notion what Dr Palsgrave was about, but it all looked to be so wonderfully full of *promise*. As if he could see a future where some as-yet-undiscovered substance made a fraction of a child whole again. I dreamed – just for a moment – that I was the very person to watch him do it.

It wasn't true. But I wanted it to be.

'Please leave us, Arthur,' the doctor sighed.

When his assistant had quit us, I turned to face Dr Palsgrave.

Feeling pretty awkward about procedure under the circumstances, but not able to waste any time either.

'I know,' I said quietly. 'About the kinchin. The burial ground outside the city is yours. I need to talk to you about it.'

A puppet with cut strings would have been a kinder sight. His eyes flew back to me and I could see whole civilizations, cities that he'd built and cherished and planned for, like the model of an entire world, all crumbling. Dr Palsgrave turned white. And then he started panting, his hand over his heart shaped into a claw.

'Stop,' I gasped, lurching toward him. 'I never meant to say it like that. If I could have done the same, with your education— I just need to know I'm right, Dr Palsgrave. Tell me I'm right and stop shaking so.'

It took several more seconds, but he did. I'm not in any particular sense good at lying. But I'm extremely good at telling the truth, so he believed me. He shuddered a few more times, and then out came a toxic-green kerchief worth ten dollars as he wiped the sweat off his neck. Quickly, I set myself to extinguishing all the open flames, and then returned to stand before him.

Lifting both his hands, Dr Palsgrave dragged them down his white side whiskers. 'How did you find me out?'

'Mercy Underhill gave a piece of it away, though she never meant to. You told me the rest yourself. And you were seen.'

'*Seen?* By whom?'

'By a girl who lives in a nearby cherry orchard. She never spied your face, but she saw your carriage. I'm afraid she's already told the chief of police that it carries the insignia of an angel. But it doesn't, of course. It's the staff, the snakes with the wings. A caduceus. What else would you paint on your coach?'

I hold Dr Palsgrave in the highest regard. And so I don't wish to dwell over the moments just after he was found out. He really isn't a dignified man, apart from the corset. And I wish that his version of the world would come true quicker. So I'll just report the first sensible thing he asked me after I'd fetched us both chairs and he'd collapsed into one.

'When did you begin to suspect me?'

'Honestly, I never suspected you until about three hours ago. But I'd started asking myself why any man would do such things, and I'd several other . . . pointers. When did you start performing autopsies on recently dead kinchin?'

'Perhaps five years ago,' he murmured. 'I never lied to you when I did the autopsy on the children from the common grave. They ranged from five years dead to recent, and somehow you fathomed—'

'That you knew each and every one of those kids, having first cut them open and taken which organs you pleased,' I supplied for him. 'Your reaction to the very first corpse ought to have posted me. Liam. You were terrified that we'd called you in to examine him on purpose, you thought it a ruse meant to force a confession. The reasons you suggested why someone would saw a body open were ridiculous, Doctor. Swallowed a valuable? You an anatomist and giving every reason save for an autopsy. I'll grant your autopsies don't look a bit like most I've seen – they're *wider*, yes, along the rib cage? The cut below the breastbone? They let you see better?'

He nodded exhaustedly.

'They were never meant to be the symbol of the cross at all. But for all they look so foul, you couldn't expect me to believe they were *cannibalism*, or—'

'I didn't know what to tell you. It was all so sudden, so horrible, and putting the body of that child in a . . . in that

373

trash bin . . . was the worst thing I've ever done in my life,' he whispered. 'I'll never forgive myself for it.'

'Tell me from the beginning,' I asked him calmly. 'I'll start it off for you. Bodies are extremely scarce. Bodies of kinchin specifically, and the fresh deceased sort you needed for your studies still more rare. What sane parent would ever hand their dead kinchin over to you to be hacked open? But in the bawdy houses . . .' I paused. 'They fall sick pretty often.'

Dr Palsgrave passed a hand over his mouth, wincing. 'The bodies of kinchin are anatomically very different from those of adults, and when I could not obtain the materials for study I needed, I grew . . . morose. I had lost so *very* many already, Mr Wilde, and so very *long* before their time. I could not erase brothels from New York, but I thought I saw my way to a solution five years ago when a little girl under my care passed away due to a severe heart defect. Her madam in life, Silkie Marsh, asked me whether I had any use for the remains, as she was in poor straits and could not afford to bury the girl herself.'

Dr Palsgrave had protested that he'd no right to the body, and that the university would surely demand answers if he tried to dissect an unidentified corpse there. But Silkie Marsh was quick on the trigger with a solution. He could return that night, masked or hooded. She would clear out a space and a tarp and put a table in her cellar. All for just fifty dollars. Dr Palsgrave could bring whatever other equipment he required, and spend as long as he liked at his work.

'I suppose when you cautioned Madam Marsh that you would need a way to dispose of the dissected remains without anyone getting peery, she offered another compromise,' I ventured. 'You'd supply the carriage, for who would question a doctor, and she'd summon the manpower.'

'Their names were Scales and Moses,' Dr Palsgrave answered. 'They were most efficient about the burials outside of town. It was good work, Mr Wilde, I vow that it was *good* work. Finally I could perform dissections that meant something to me, to the *children.*'

It went on for five years, all told. When a kinchin-mab died, Dr Palsgrave was summoned back. He paid his fifty dollars. He performed his life's work. He saw that the child was given a burial, each and every time, no half measures. He thanked them aloud as they were being put into the shallow ground. It was no shallower than any other pauper's grave, after all. And they were doing good meanwhile, all in the meanwhile, every sin atoned for during that meanwhile. Dr Palsgrave never doubted it.

There had been nineteen dead, all told, the results of pneumonia and of fevers and of pox and contagion. Then one day Dr Palsgrave had arrived in his black hood, the kinchin had all been bid to stay in their rooms, and he and Silkie Marsh had gone to carry Liam's body down to the cellar chamber. When they entered the room, it looked like a slaughterhouse.

'Liam suffered from pulmonary trouble,' Dr Palsgrave explained, 'and I was performing alchemical experiments using blood. I still am, the results have been . . .' He trailed off, abstracted and achingly hopeful momentarily, and then snapped back to earth. 'But no matter. I bid Madam Marsh that – should the unfortunate child fail to recover – she should inform me as soon as possible, for I wanted to drain the blood. There are French researches suggesting that blood contains elements of metal, and I wanted to see if I could distill it into the rarefied essence of itself. The notion of purifying blood is very promising. I was duly informed, raced to the brothel when the boy met his end, and siphoned the unfortunate child's blood into a bowl. So hurried was I, I extracted it in his sickroom rather than using the basement. But then I found that I had stupidly forgotten the vessel I meant to carry it away in, and so I rushed back to the carriage.'

'The room was left dark when you did,' I said. 'Why?'

Amazement and fear vied for control of his features. 'How can you know that? I took my lantern with me. I tried to be as discreet as possible upstairs, whenever I was forced to do any research in proximity to the other children. I came back within three minutes, but—'

'But you walked into a butchery. Someone had found you out, someone who'd spilled the blood everywhere.'

'Madam Marsh stifled a scream, and I fear that I myself experienced a *severe* palpitation.' Dr Palsgrave pinched his fingers over his nose regretfully. 'It may have played a part in my actions. I cannot say. We tracked footmarks into another bedroom and found the window open, a makeshift ladder tied to the catch. Madam Marsh ordered me to dispose of the body, without making any other employment from it, just as she demanded that I help her scrub the blood from the floor. Moses and Scales were in the house within twenty minutes.'

'But then you rebelled.'

'I *could not do it*,' he gasped, clenching his fist upon his knee. 'To *waste* a child's shell that way, the blood being lost, and I needed a spleen. I am sorry I told you it was rats. I demanded use of the cellar. Silkie Marsh refused at first. But then I told her I would never darken her door again if she failed to give me ten minutes, that our entire arrangement would be off for good and all, and so she allowed it.'

'Go on.'

Dr Palsgrave's mouth turned down, hiding something sour

and pained and weary seeming. 'I took the organ. We bundled the poor kinchin into my carriage. We were headed north to the burial site, but I freely confess that we had gotten only as far as Mercer Street when the most awful *panic* overtook me. I had spent ten additional minutes that Madam Marsh had claimed could be disastrous. The evidence was at my very feet, and a witness – God only knew who, I never was told precisely how many children she employed at any given moment – was at large, and probably frightened to death, the poor creature. I stopped by a trash receptacle outside a chophouse.'

He stopped dead.

'I . . . it will *never* leave off haunting me, Mr Wilde.'

I believed him, too. It's no easy lay to look that stricken over a point of honor when you're not honorable. 'Silkie Marsh learned what you did from Moses and Scales. Did she object to how close the body was to her ken?'

'No, or if she did, she never mentioned it. Next morning, she informed me that the missing child had been found. She told the kinchin that Liam had gone through a bloodletting before he peacefully passed, and the child believed her, thank heaven. She'd handled the situation, and all could go back to normal, Madam Marsh said.'

'Knowing all about the deaths, the letters must have confounded you even though they did deflect attention from you,' I hazarded. 'The only one printed publicly, the Hand of the God of Gotham message in the *Herald*, you managed to keep quiet through. But then you were sent something very sinister in tone. Addressed to you personally, and you the man behind it all in fact. It gave you a scare. You couldn't imagine what to make of it, so you sought me out, knowing you couldn't destroy the thing and keep a clear conscience. Then you saw Bird Daly.'

'Yes,' he said readily, very near to smiling. 'I'd never before viewed her in the sunshine, which was a treat.'

'Did you mention seeing her in my company to Madam Marsh?' I asked. Slow and careful.

'Oh, yes, I believe so. I recall saying that she looked very well, very healthy, since she had left Madam Marsh's employment. Not a great deal more.'

I smiled without thinking. It was likely a godawful cold one, because Dr Palsgrave looked perplexed. So I wiped it off. For his part, the doctor was fading to grey a bit around the cheekbones, rubbing two fingers nervously over the shawl-collared waistcoat, just about in the region of his heart. And I knew his mind at once. There had been a single death unaccounted for, an abomination that he could never have authored, ripped open and nailed to a door with mad crosses painted all around him like a sickly white swarm. Marcas, who had not died for science. Marcas, who had not come from the Marsh establishment.

'I know,' I interrupted him. 'I can't tell you what happened, but I will see to it personally that the culprit pays.'

'Has it to do with the letter I gave you? I can hardly bear even to think of—'

'And you needn't any longer. I've got it well in hand. Doctor, there's one single thing more.'

'Yes?'

'A small boy who went by the name of Jack Be Nimble once took a keek inside your carriage as you were disposing of a corpse. He was about to open the sack when you interrupted him. In front of Silkie Marsh's ken. What did you say to the boy?'

'*Incredible.* You're really quite incredible, Mr Wilde, I – yes, I do recall it. Not his name, I never knew that. And you're right, he'd not yet opened the bag, only the passenger door, though he gave me such a start as took ten years off my life. He was quite underfed, I believe. Used to wild living, the barbarous ways these boys have. I gave him a coin and told him to ask the mistress within for some good chicken stew. Madam Marsh's profession is entirely repellent, but she keeps a very fine table, that I'll never deny.'

I stood up, holding my hand out. 'Thank you for your honesty, Dr Palsgrave. Sorry for mentioning it so harsh, but you need to stop. No more corpses from Silkie Marsh's brothel. Not ever again.'

He shook my hand, likewise rising. 'I couldn't, anyhow. My heart would fail me. Mr Wilde, wait – you truly mean to do nothing against me?'

'Truly.'

'No, please, I must know – you said that *Mercy Underhill* gave me away? How is that possible? She knows nothing about this, I swear it.'

A smile crept onto my lips, a warmer one. 'She was seen quitting your carriage yesterday, by kinchin who'd reason to believe you a smoky character. You must have been tending to some sick little ones together. But she told me that the man who owned that carriage didn't believe in God, or politics. It reminded me of you ready enough.'

'I see. Yes, I see.' Dr Palsgrave wavered, shoving down his natural pride. 'Mr Wilde, stay for a drink at least, as I cannot ever repay you in kind.'

'I've urgent business,' I answered, putting my hat back on.

'Of course. I'll be grateful to you another time. But how will you ever begin to solve what happened at St Patrick's? Only a savage would do such a thing.'

'By returning to the scene,' I told him.

'And then?'

'I'll ask one question.'

'One question? But what do you suppose will happen after that?'

'Then I'll have an honest-to-God murderer to call on,' I said, gravely tipping my hat to him as I shut his office door.

By the looks of St Patrick's as I reached its corner, nothing unholy had happened during the riot. All was clean. A needful, thorough, frenzied sort of clean, from the granite steps to the red stones to the three wooden doors. I'd not have been half surprised if Father Sheehy had scrubbed down the oak in the side yard, and I'd not have blamed him either. A changeable, pleasant breeze blew over the strangely quiet street.

Inside the cathedral, an altar boy dusting the pews sent me straight to the priest's sacristy. I knocked at the door and heard a gentle cue to come in. Father Sheehy wasn't working, though, or didn't look it. He stood with his hairless head cocked thoughtful and still at a religious painting. The artwork was old and pictured a man of about sixty, with white hair and a kind face, holding a staff leafed in gold.

'Mr Wilde,' Father Sheehy greeted me. 'Have you been enjoyin' much in the way of progress, then?'

'Not enjoy, no. Who's that you're mulling over?'

'Saint Nicholas has always been a man after my own heart, and lately it often seems to me best to have a word with him, on account o' his being the patron saint of all children.'

'Is he?'

'Indeed he is.'

'That seems a mighty heavy job,' I couldn't help muttering.

Father Sheehy only nodded, understanding my meaning. 'He's the proper choice, though the work must be endless. You see, there's a story, Mr Wilde, in which Saint Nicholas visits a famine town. Nary a crop flourishin' there, all dead as dust. Terrible sufferin' falls on the village, then worse sufferin' still, day after day, such as I'm fearin' might be faced in my homeland in the year to come. Until one mornin' a man driven mad wi' hunger and poverty slaughters three kinchin and butchers them. All along plannin' to sell the meat, you understand. But our Saint Nicholas, having been blessed of God and a holy man, sees through the ruse. And exposes him.'

'That's a terrible story.'

The priest smiled sadly. 'And yer thinkin' it's too familiar a one. But Saint Nicholas did go one further – he raised all three from the dead. And so I've been sayin' to him that we'd be much appreciative of his prayers on our behalf. Delivering the message that, as he isn't here to work his miracles, we are doin' the best we can.'

'What happened to the butcher?' I asked as Father Sheehy went to his desk, waving me into the chair across from him.

He looked surprised, passed an active hand around the top of his pate. ' 'Tis the best question I've heard in some time, Mr Wilde, and thus a pity that I can't go far after answerin' it. When Bishop Hughes returns, I shall inquire. I was forced to send him word of the recent tragedy, and I believe him to be makin' the journey back from Baltimore. But can I do better by you some other way?'

'I've just one question,' I replied slowly. 'The night before Marcas was found, you'd a meeting. About educating New York's Catholic kinchin in Catholic schools. Irish kinchin, that is to say, in Irish schools.'

'Aye.' His tone was dry as nails and just as pointed.

'It didn't go well?'

'I wonder, Mr Wilde, if ye've ever read a tract called *Is*

Popery Compatible with Civil Liberty?' he questioned with an entirely humorless smile. 'If not, have y' ever explored a rippin' tale from Harper Brothers called *The Awful Disclosures of the Hotel Dieu Nunnery?* Nay? Well, then, perhaps y' weren't yet aware that priests make a holy practice o' rapin' nuns and then buryin' the tiny products of those unions in holes in the basements of monasteries. Naturally there are *concerns.*' The last word was spat so hard, a grown man might have flinched from it.

'I know you're angry at being slandered. You've a right.' I paused. 'But do such things ever actually happen, Father?'

His teeth set. 'They do. All over the world, and every day, among Hindoos and Turks and Anglicans and Protestants and Catholics. I'll stop such revoltin' acts nae faster by denouncin' my God, Mr Wilde, for without my God on my side, how will I ever succeed at anythin'?'

I sat up, leaning my forearm on the edge of his desk.

'After that meeting, as the men were all dispersing. Did any one of them make a donation? To the orphanage or to the church?'

The priest's eyebrows lifted. 'That one o' them did, and the result of many, many friendly overtures on my part, as well as the bishop's.'

'It was clothing or food, a large sack of some kind? And it was late, and you were talking to important people. You thanked him. You were happy he'd come around. You were pulled in all directions and left it to be sorted later.'

'Aye,' he said. A helpless, confused flutter crossing his kindly face.

'Is the sack still here?'

The priest went as white as if he'd been erased, a hand rising to cover his mouth. As if the answer was poisonous, and he'd absorb it through his tongue once he spoke it. I felt for him, but hadn't the luxury of waiting.

'Father, please write down the name of the donor. Put it on a piece of paper and hand it over to me. Otherwise it's just my word.'

His hand twitched once before he was able to move it. But move it he did, reaching for paper and a quill, his face just as frozen as St Nicholas hanging on the wall.

Weirdly, as he sealed a man's fate, and as I watched him, I didn't think about what came next. About what I'd do, what that paper *meant*. I thought about what Mercy had said in Washington Square Park. That writing things down was a map after a fashion. And that she'd never learn her own inner borders without penning them – like a surveyor with a rope and an astrolabe, staring thoughtfully at a river. I realized, not being any dab hand with words, I do the same with butcher paper. Then I thought of her burned book and felt a shame at having left her the night before such as I'd never experienced.

The priest passed me the name. But it wasn't a surprise, so I just folded it and thrust it in my waistcoat pocket.

'I'm new at this,' I said. 'But trust me to set it right.'

I shook his hand. I turned to walk away.

'Saint Nicholas was barely five feet tall, Mr Wilde, so they say. He was a very small man.'

Glancing back at the painting, I said, 'I don't follow.'

'God makes use o' the right vessels.' He spoke quietly, staring down at his hands. 'No offense meant, and beggin' your pardon.'

'Might I borrow that pistol of yours?' was the only sensible reply.

I wondered as I quit the cathedral with his gun in my coat which God he'd meant, seeing as how I didn't have a specific one. Every second of that whole wretched investigation had been built on my blood and my sweat and my brains and my need to know. But if there was an invisible force on my side, I'd have been a fool to cross it just then. So I let all that pass, let it go by with a silent *thank you*. To anything and everyone who might have helped me without my knowing it, right down to Maddy Sample and her healthy appetites.

Half an hour later, I knocked at the Underhills' door.

CHAPTER TWENTY-FIVE

*I sincerely rejoice to hear that you are still engaged for
the good of the Roman Catholics. For a long time, the
church considered that the conversion of the Jews was
hopeless, and even now we seldom hear a prayer
offered up for them. With regard however to both the
Roman Catholics and the Jews, we may inquire, 'Is
anything too hard for the Lord?'*

Letter written to the *American Protestant in
Defence of Civil and Religious Liberty Against
Inroads of Papacy*, 1843

No one answered. But the front door was unlocked. So I
went inside, taking time and care to be quiet about it.

Right off, I knew that something was wrong.

First of all, a sound met my ears. A brittle stillness,
something just beyond my hearing – as if, when I entered,
something else had *stopped*.

I listened harder, but nothing came of it. So I went on.

When I walked into the parlor, there were the bookshelves,

there the green carpet and the lampshades and all the trappings of a happy home. There the tomatoes hanging brilliantly red beyond the window. Not long for this world. Not with the cold coming, as everyone knew it would.

It was all wrong, though. It was identical to how I'd left it.

And by identical, I mean *exactly* the same. The papers the reverend had been working on when we'd had our last conversation were still on the table. Nigh deliriously tired, I pondered when that might have been. Five days back? I couldn't recall exactly. The pair of sherry glasses rested next to them. One of them mine, one of them his. The sherry glasses and the silence meant their serving girl, Anna, was long gone. The papers meant I was right. It hurt to see a thing like that in person, when it was someone you cared for. Someone who'd once done you an irreplaceable kindness.

I pulled the pistol out of my coat. There was already a bullet lodged in the gun, well packed with powder. I hoped beyond my ability to state the feeling that I wouldn't have to fire the thing. But I was already more than glad I carried it, because of the smell.

A whiff of kerosene had been my first greeting, I realized. Bone-deep unsettling wheresoever you encounter it. To me in particular.

I went into the Reverend Underhill's private study, and there I had my answer.

He'd strung a rope up and through the slender iron arms of the chandelier, done in a noose knot. Well tied, too. The light fixture hung above and just in front of his desk, and below that on the simple braided rug was a pile of clothing. Done in pale dyes, dipped only for an instant, subtle blues and yellows that reminded you of birds' eggs, fragile colors you can only truly identify outdoors in the sun. Dresses and

THE GODS OF GOTHAM

chemises and stockings and shawls, all in a heap stewing in kerosene.

Of course they were all Mercy's and of course I knew every piece.

It jarred me terribly. The first question I'd planned on asking hadn't been *What have you done with your daughter?*

A candle glowed on the desktop, and the reverend sat behind it. Staring at the scene he'd created.

'I thought you'd come, Timothy,' he whispered.

I'd like to say I'd never seen a face like that before. So hurt and so raw and so helpless. He was sitting there in only his shirtsleeves, staring with tired blue eyes at the candle, but he was repulsively *open*. His mind, the expression on his face. It was wrong to look at him, the way it had been wrong to look into the glistening innards of his single murder victim hanging there in St Patrick's. He'd looked half this bad the last time I'd seen him, narrow face pinched too small and his hands lost at the end of his wrists, and I cursed myself for not previously knowing what the beginning looked like. Because I *had* seen a face just like this one, finalized. On Eliza Rafferty.

'Where's Mercy?' I left the pistol at my side for the time being. 'Why do you mean to burn all her clothes?'

'Mercy is quite gone,' he said, voice rattling out from a hollow shell. 'This is all that's left of Mercy, I fear.'

I went completely still about then. The gun very heavy in my hand.

'Tell me what you mean by *gone*, Reverend. Did you hurt her?'

'What's this?' he muttered, looking up for a moment. 'Why should I hurt my little girl? She was very feverish, burning in her skin. I did what I could, but it's too late now.'

If you've ever been on the deck of a ferry in stormy

November, I don't have to describe the seasick feeling that washed over me.

You left her there. You cruel, cruel coward. You left her standing in the middle of the room wearing a green dress, calling after you.

'She was well enough last night,' I said desperately.

'These things happen so quickly. Everything always happens so quickly, Timothy. I meant to burn the way she did, you see, but perhaps now you'd be willing to bury her? To bury us? Would you? I'll tell you where she is, but first we have to talk. I don't imagine you understand quite yet.'

I finally noticed what was sitting on the desk beneath the candle. A small diary. The pages I could see were scrawled with at least six different hands, most of them far from educated, and a single nicely worked sketch of a little flop-eared dog. Marcas's journal. If I could have felt any more sick to my stomach, I might have done.

'What do we have to talk about before you tell me where Mercy is?'

'I didn't like doing it, but no one would listen,' he went on dully. 'Not even you, Timothy, even after I warned you in detail. And no one would print my letters after the first, and then what with the police discrediting them— I didn't like doing it, you must understand that much.'

All the letters, of course, had been written by the same man. The Hand of the God of Gotham, who'd first adopted a poor imitation of a cloddish emigrant. But all I had left to me physically was the final note, the brutally honest picture of a broken mind. I pulled the crazed rant the reverend had written to his friend Peter Palsgrave out of my inner coat pocket. We needed to be finished talking. When I put the obscene note on the table, phrases of it winked at me dementedly.

'I knew it was from you when I'd looked at it hard enough,' I told him. 'Just tell me where to find Mercy.'

Silence.

'You said, *So small it's an abomination.* That was Aidan Rafferty. And it was, and far worse, but to think that it shattered you so – and then the rest of it. Dr Palsgrave is your closest friend. *Mend the broken things.* That's what he does, bringing kinchin back from near-death, though you aren't aware of— Christ, it's unspeakable. You wanted him to stop you before you committed murder. The same sort of murder you supposed all the others to have been, but this time in the public street. For all the world to see at last. And pinned on Father Sheehy, of all people.'

The reverend dropped his face prayerfully into his palms.

'It could only have been you. That was Scripture, wasn't it? "I am a broken jawbone"?'

'The jawbone of an ass. A cruel, dark, base weapon. A fitting one, so I became it under the circumstances.'

'Fitting?' I cried, forgetting myself and gesturing with the pistol. '*Fitting? And how?* How did that child ever deserve—'

'We're *infested*,' he ground out. Standing, the reverend shut the diary and lifted the candle. 'You simply haven't lived long enough to learn the consequences of a vermin infestation, Timothy – or perhaps you've learned it today, since Mercy's fever can only have come from such dens. When the same sort of contagion finished Olivia, I thought perhaps it might be a part of God's plan for me. To make me suffer, that I might learn to sacrifice more willingly. To hurt me, that I might understand pain. I supposed that perhaps I was being tested, and I would be found worthy only if I remained ever dedicated, remained pure. How can one remain *pure* within a *dung heap*, Timothy Wilde?'

The dead kinchin's journal landed with a pathetic flutter in the cold fireplace as I stared at him. It made sense. It fit in a line. The self-obsession, the devotion, the righteousness, the atmosphere that made Mercy think only *London, London, London*, the fire lighting her eyes when she'd talked of her planned escape in that wretched rented bedroom the night before. It was only a downward slope, watching a man march to the bottom of a hill. This was merely the man who wouldn't give Aidan Rafferty cream unless his mother had first denounced the pope.

I recalled him shouting at Mercy that day I'd caught sight of them, framed in their parlor window, her face flooding red with mortification, and nearly bit off the end of my tongue when I realized too late what sort of conversation they'd really been having.

'Oh, come, my opinion cannot possibly surprise you,' he scoffed. 'First they pour into the city, our city, like locusts, blaspheming God wheresoever they go. Then God sends His plagues to follow after them despite their migration, and what do Olivia and Mercy do? They *help* the sufferers. They die alongside them, these rats that look like humans. And you see how we are repaid – look at Eliza Rafferty. *Look at her*. She saw through the charade at last, knew her infant for damned. And so then, like a true heathen, she slaughtered him with no more ceremony than might be afforded a stray dog.'

'You supposed that the sudden news of twenty cut-apart corpses might be a way of purging the Irish from the city,' I supplied, wrenching us back to the purpose. 'Mercy was the one who told you. Mercy informed you of the bodies we copper stars found, and so you wrote those letters to defame the Irish. You sent them to the papers. You sent me one, for God's sake, to warn me what was coming. I'd thought it for Val, but it was always meant for me.'

'I thought you would take better precautions if I warned you, perhaps even keep one eye on my daughter. I hoped so. There was clearly a monster at loose, carving crosses in child whores, and how could I help but be frightened for her safety, given the filth she daily associated with? It was obvious what was happening. I only publicized the problem, told New York what it needed to know. What did the details matter? Did you ever get a hint at the culprit, Timothy? I can't claim to have held any hope that you would, for this vile breed is devious. But I knew that some good could come of it, a purging, once the secret had been exposed for public view.'

'And so you tried to tell everyone. You supposed that there would be a riot. That the Nativists would drive the Irish out. Mercy knew what I knew, and so you did as well. *Where* is Mercy now?'

A martial drumbeat couldn't have been more steady, the sunrise more predictable. *Where is Mercy?* I had dreamed about exposing the kinchin killer all that while, supposed that it would feel righteously grand when I caught the bastard. Instead it felt irrelevant. I'd have objected to such a cold reward if I hadn't deserved every second of it for the night before.

'It was such a disappointment when you impeded their circulation,' he said distractedly. 'I knew then that I had to do something much more drastic. But I never wanted to,' he added, looking thin as parchment and haunted all of a sudden. 'As I told Peter, I—'

'You never signed your message to him. He has no notion it's from you.'

'Hasn't he? I couldn't focus just then, knowing what was coming, I couldn't begin to think clearly. I knew the act itself would be repulsive. But I had direction from God. There was a clear sign, and I obeyed it, and for that I cannot apologize.'

I thought pretty hard for a few seconds. Over what his clear sign might have been. But then my own stomach twisted away from me like a frightened cat. I knew just what he meant.

Mercy, alive if only in my memory, was talking in my ear . . . *Now I'll never find another place to hide any store of coin, never . . . and my father's opinion doesn't bear speaking about.* I'd supposed ever since the butcher paper that she'd suspected her father. The reason she'd rushed with her hair down to St Patrick's was that she'd feared her own father was a killer when he returned home in the middle of the night. Thomas Underhill's mind had snapped so clean that he'd likely arrived half soaked in gore.

The part I hadn't yet grasped was that she'd accidentally triggered the murder in the first place.

'First they kill my wife,' the reverend murmured. 'She was so beautiful. You don't recall her rightly, that would be impossible, but I remember. And then they contaminate my only daughter's mind and spirit to the point that she turns into some sort of *pornographer.*' He breathed that last word in a gentle caress, as if trying to keep it from choking him. 'She's no better than a whore now – how could Mercy have written such filth otherwise, if she hadn't known the touch of many men? Everything they encounter they turn to muck, can't you see that? Even my daughter. I took the wages of her many sins, and I threw them into the street. It was gone in seconds, of course. Picked up by vagrants, other bawds, every sort of human street trash. And then I knew what I had to do. A man cannot shirk a task given him by God, and what charity can be offered to a race whose very *children* are so disposed to be whores?'

I closed my eyes, my pupils blank and burning. Picturing Mercy's coins scattering in the street – the ones she'd worked for, counted upon. Seeing my own money as it had melted in July. I'm not greedy. I didn't suppose Mercy ever was either. We were never stockbrokers, or landlords, or Party officials. But there isn't any pity in New York. And so, lacking pity, we all need a lifeline.

I don't know if you realize what you've done, but will you tell me please why for heaven's sake you've done it?

'I can scarce picture it,' I said. 'Finding Mercy out, and then taking what was hers. Going to the dockside bawdy house. You took a drunk little boy and you gave him enough laudanum not to care where he went.'

'Yes,' he exclaimed. 'And even at that darkest hour, I was alert to signs and signifiers, Timothy. Had anyone stopped me . . . it would have been an omen. Can't you see? No one else cared where he went either. Not even his keepers cared, no one cared, they are past help. I had to warn the city, had to publicize their wrongs before a single other person was infected. They took my beautiful child and they taught her to—'

'You stuffed him in a sack under . . . togs, I assume,' I kept on relentlessly, 'cloth being lighter, and packed yourself some paint and some nails. After you'd endured Father Sheehy's meeting, you simply slipped into an alcove, and there are plenty of them. I can't stomach it, Reverend. Back luck for you Marcas wasn't quite dead.'

'Yes, there was a great deal of blood for a dead boy,' he breathed, passing a hand over his eyes. 'A very great deal of blood.'

'Did he wake up?' I demanded.

'I don't know.'

'You *do* know,' I snarled. 'Answer me.'

'I can't think, he was very slight, and then the task itself went quick enough. I can hardly remember what passed just before I let myself out the front entrance, but perhaps—'

I lost my temper.

'You remember.' I'd closed the gap between us, and my pistol was at his brow. 'Tell me.'

Even men who want to die shudder at cold metal pressed into their skin, and so did Reverend Underhill.

'He said nothing,' the madman answered in a liquid, rippling voice. 'So he felt nothing, then. There was merely . . . there was just a very great deal of blood.'

'How could you have burned Mercy's book?' I asked next.

Holding Father Sheehy's gun to his skull I felt like a thug, no better than the men who'd shoved a turnip between Julius's lips. But I was learning what Val had likely discovered a long while ago. When enough terrible things have happened, doing them stops being quite so uncomfortable.

'I burned Mercy's book for Mercy,' he answered, surprised. 'How could you know about that? She refused to speak of it with me afterward. It was wild – erotic in a shameless fashion, so lyrical and ripe as to be completely untamed. The sort of thing that could have done her reputation tremendous harm. She would have been a mother one day, she was meant to be, and how could she face her children as the author of luxurious trash?'

If I knew one thing for a certainty, despite all my blindly adoring illusions about Mercy, it's that she's incapable of producing trash. I've read *Light and Shade in the Streets of New York*, after all. Many upon many a time. Just picturing that lost book, the one she could have sold the way Frances Burney or Harriet Lee or a score of others had done, shut my throat like a bear trap.

'Mercy,' the reverend murmured. 'I'd have given anything

to have saved Mercy. She was a piece of Olivia. And now the only way to see her again is to die by my own hand. A fitting penance, for a part of the blame is mine – I ought never to have allowed her such freedoms. This is my fault. I begged her to repent of her folly before the end, I begged Olivia the same over fostering blasphemy, but they both refused, and I cannot face eternity without either one of them. Mercy has cost me my soul.'

Thomas Underhill looked like a child by that time. Just as lost as was possible, not seeing his own study, feet uncertain on his own carpet.

'Where is she?' I insisted.

'You're here to bury us after all, aren't you?'

I tried another tack.

'What did my brother say to you,' I questioned, 'the day after we met, long ago? When he'd recovered from the drugs and came to speak with you alone, before you asked us to tea, what did he say?'

'I couldn't possibly—'

'I very much need to know,' I pleaded.

The reverend's anchorless eyes drifted to the wall. 'He asked me if I thought that God could forgive any act, no matter how vile. You know why, naturally. And of course I said yes.'

My eyes fell shut as I blessed the world entire for that one tiny grace.

'And then,' Thomas Underhill continued, 'he asked if human beings were capable of the same.'

'What did you tell him?' I whispered.

'I said to keep trying and find out.'

'Thank you,' I told him, as feelingly as I've ever said anything. 'God, thank you. Where is Mercy?'

'She's dead.'

I forced him back into the armchair with the pistol. Scaling the desk, I used my pocketknife to cut two lengths of hemp rope from the trailing end of the noose. I left the grim circle intact for meditation and quickly tied his wrists to the arms of the chair.

'I'm here to arrest you,' I said. 'Did you take her to a doctor? To a church, a hospital? Tell me where she is now, and I'll bury her. Wait any longer, and I'll drag you to the Tombs first, then think your request over in a month or two.'

I'd never been any dab hand at lying, but this time my heart was in it.

'She's upstairs in an ice bath,' he cried at once. 'I tried, I tried. She was already slipping away from me when—'

Losing the rest of his sentence wasn't deliberate, but I was halfway up the staircase by that time.

My eyes took in a blinding scope of familiar details as I raced up that flight. Dozens of useless facts about the Underhill staircase. And pure facts are pretty well respected, in my new profession. But they leave out the *story*. They're just markers, blank tombstones. That's what I've come to learn by way of being a copper star, and it wasn't Bird Daly taught it to me either. It was Mercy sitting in Washington Square Park after she'd fought tooth and nail for a member of a long-despised race, just the way her mother used to do. Mercy said that words can be cartography, and this is what she meant:

There exists a 2.5 inch scratch in the pale brownish wallpaper in the Underhills' staircase, just above the eighth step. Nothing about that is important. What's important is that I was sitting there at the age of sixteen, silent and miserable even after a hearty dinner, because my brother hadn't been home for two days. I supposed, as usual, he was

dead. I supposed, as usual, he'd burned somehow. I
supposed myself alone. So I pulled my pocketknife out, and I
drove it right into the wall. And the next thing I can recall,
Mercy had decided to place herself at the bottom of the
stairs, stating that she must now read the poems of William
Cullen Bryant aloud to her father. To her father, who was
in his study with the door open twenty yards off. And not
sitting on the eighth step.

Facts aren't important on their own.

People are important. Their stories and their kindnesses. Stories happen to be, according to Mercy – and I understood her better by then – the only thing that's important.

The facts went like this.

At the top of the stairs directly to the right is Mercy's bedroom. I went inside. It's done all in a cheerful, clean blue. But it might as well never have been painted for all the bookshelves, the hundreds of titles bound with string and rabbit glue tumbling onto the floor. Books with their spines broken from savage love, books with their jackets regularly dusted, books twice bought because the first volume shattered into ink flakes. The wardrobe stood open. Emptied, the dresses downstairs and not in a fit state to be spoken of.

Mercy had been in an ice bath only recently. That was a fact I'll never erase. But she'd thrashed her way out of the rudely cut chunks of frigid water. She was on the planked wood floor now, despite the fact that her ankles were tied with the identical hemp rope I'd encountered downstairs. Also despite the fact that she'd been wrapped into a dressing gown with her arms stuffed inside the long sleeves and the empty wrists tied behind her like a strait-waistcoat.

Her lips were blue, and the upper one still fractionally

shadowed the lower. Her face looked carved in bone by that time. I'd have been tempted to say that even her eye color was fading. But that wasn't the case. It's just that blue rings look one way against white, and another against dull red. And the whites of Mercy's eyes were so very empurpled from exertion and exhaustion that they'd have been unrecognizable, maybe. To someone else.

Those were the facts.

The story, though, went like this.

Mercy Underhill was still breathing. I could see those breaths come one after another as I whirled around that chamber. Wherever I turned I could still see them, as I cast about for ways to get her dry. Ways to get her warm. It was a bit like watching a child who'd fallen. In the bad sort of fall where the kinchin flutters within itself, testing hurts. They were little breaths. About the depth of my thumb if I'd measured it against her breastbone.

I got all the rope off her, and the icy fabric. She went first into my frock coat and second into every single piece of Thomas Underhill's clothing I could rob from his wardrobe. Getting her warm was paramount, beyond even fetching a doctor, and so I carried her downstairs to the kitchen and made a soft nest out of quilting before the iron stove.

If a fire was lit faster in the history of North America, I don't know where or when.

Oddly, by the time I'd used enough of my breath to turn Mercy's fingers the color of her piano keys and not her blue wallpaper, I'd gone a ways toward forgiving the Reverend Underhill. Only for that part of it, mind. Not for the dead kinchin, and not for the letters. But I knew he loved Mercy. He loved Mercy like a man who had no other family left.

And I thought then that it would be the grimmest pit of hell to hurt the person you loved most simply because your mind was wrong. I'd hated putting Eliza Rafferty in a wet cage filled with the rats that had already haunted her. She'd no excuse, and I'd no alternative. And yet.

I've done mad things myself. Stupid things. Never quite that mad or quite that stupid, but after all it wasn't for lack of trying.

When Mercy started to come back to herself, she looked around her as if I was the only shape she could recognize. I had her cradled against me with my back to the wall, waiting. As she awakened, eyes drifting to and fro again, lips growing just that shade less chalky, I pulled her slightly closer. It was mesmerizing.

'You were never sick, were you?' I questioned softly.

Mercy's lips formed *no*.

'Are you cold now?'

She closed her eyes, shaking her dark head. Her hair and her temple hit my upper arm lightly. Seconds later she bit out, 'He's gone mad. He thought me diseased. I wasn't. Timothy, I wasn't. I'm not feverish just because – I'm *not*.'

'I know,' I whispered into her hair. 'And I'm sorry, love. I'm so very, very sorry.'

It might have been wrong to let Mercy start sobbing without any attempt to settle her delicate state back into quiet. But I don't suppose women very delicate in general, and I don't suppose humans all that quiet. So apart from providing a warm structure to cry against, I let her alone. It was warming her. It was maybe the best thing she could have done. Medically speaking. But Mercy's very clever, so that didn't surprise me.

'Is my father all right?' she asked at length.

'I don't think he is, actually.'

'Tim, I was the one who told him about the hidden bodies.

It was my idea, I thought he may have heard something useful, this is—'

'Don't say it,' I told her fiercely. 'Don't you dare apologize to me. It's a number of people's faults, but never yours.'

After an hour more of silence and occasional shivering, she fell asleep. Heated through at last, with her head on my shoulder and her three pairs of breeches falling over my knees. Very, very beautiful. No less so for the frozen cracks on her lips or the blisters all over her hands.

When I went back into the study to check on the reverend, none of the new facts came as any surprise to me.

I never told Mercy how loose I'd tied those bonds. How easy I'd made it for Thomas Underhill to free himself.

I'd done it for Mercy, after all. So that isn't the sort of thing I can mention to her. That I sent the reverend to hell a bit quicker, if there is one, rather than subject her to visiting him at the Tombs.

Thomas Underhill had hanged himself weird and savage, his spine badly broken, face both purple and swollen, neck stretched an inch at least though I've never studied anatomy.

People who slit kinchin open out of mad hate and bitter memories ought to get worse than their own nooses around their necks. They ought to be served with jail time. Communion with the rats they're so fond of comparing actual people to. I think that when those sort get a chance to visit with real rats, they begin to forget the comparison to words like *Irish* and *black* and *thief*, maybe even *whore*. And they deserve every minute of it, to my mind. But it wasn't about me.

I left Mercy well blanketed by her stove as the heat dwindled. I left the reverend locked in his own chapel's gardening shed. Twisted up with the shovels and rakes, for the moment. Not wanting Mercy to find him, I took the keys.

Breathing deep, steadying myself, I looked out across the churchyard at the peaceful gravestones. An amber hue hung over everything. The sun wasn't quite setting by then, but I could feel its tug. It would be an autumn light almost, I imagined, swiftly falling. August suns linger for the worst news generally, but that sun showed better charity. I needed charity. I was tired enough to feel dead.

When I'd closed the garden shed door, I went looking for someone whose time could be purchased. That took forty seconds, and ended by being a hot-corn girl with a very slight harelip. Paying for her entire stock with Party money, I sent her to bring Dr Peter Palsgrave, whom Mercy clearly trusted, to the Underhill residence.

Then I set off to confront the coldest killer I could ever have imagined. The reverend was mad, after all, and my new quarry owned no such convenient excuse.

CHAPTER TWENTY-SIX

*Now let it be remembered, that Popery is the same
thing at the present time, that it was in the Middle
Ages. The world has altered, but the popish creed,
feelings, avarice, and ambition, are all the same.*

American Protestant in Defence of Civil and
Religious Liberty Against Inroads of Papacy, 1843

Silkie Marsh wasn't at her establishment, more's the pity,
so I was sent on to the theater within Niblo's Garden on
Prince and Broadway – the establishment Hopstill spent all his
time building fireworks for, though I doubt he'd ever seen an
actual show.

By the time I'd arrived there, the yellow had left the air. A
clear fall blue bloomed in the sky above the lush plant life and
the lusher crowds packing the brass-fitted saloon. Brushing by
candied apple vendors and the great green blades of the
landscaping, I walked into the theater. It was to be a vocalist
that night, a break in the endless parade of acrobats. I gave a
coin to a boy in a cocked paper hat who was selling peanuts,

and I asked where Silkie Marsh was sitting that night. He told me readily enough. Flashing my star in place of a ticket, I walked up the stairs.

Silkie Marsh was perched within a gem-stand of a box. Herself the crown jewel, of course. Brittle as cut stone, and about as likely as diamonds to crack. Clear and cold and perfect looking. And the only thing I could count on, the one weapon at my disposal, was the fact that I could see clean through her.

'Gentlemen,' I said to the pair of swells seated in the box. They were all oiled moustaches and artfully tailored sleeves, pretty as pictures and just as flat. 'You're taking your leave.'

'Mr Wilde,' Silkie Marsh said sweetly, eyes blazing hot with annoyance, 'you are of course welcome to join our little party, but I can think of no earthly reason why my friends should depart.'

'No? I can conjure two, actually. First off, I've a burning need to interrogate them on the subject of New York's brothels down at the Tombs. That might take hours, I'm thinking. If they don't scurry off before I even notice they're gone, that is. And second, they might enjoy occupying children at your establishment, but I'll bet even if they've a taste for kinchin-mabs, they don't want to palaver about dead ones.'

They were a memory after another five seconds. My tone had all the while been friendly, measured. A pretty tune with dark words set over it. I needed her off balance, angry enough to make a single mistake.

Silkie Marsh didn't flex a muscle when I sat down in one of the newly emptied velvet chairs. Didn't even spare a blink. And that's not what unnerved me. No, what unnerved me, with a prickling tingle of disgust along my lower back, was that she didn't spare a glance after her companions either. Once gone from her immediate view, it was as though they were really *gone*: small and lifeless as chess pieces, and just as disposable.

'I'd grown to think of you as somewhat brutish, Mr Wilde, but now you seem to have entirely forgotten how to behave around people.'

Leaning forward toward a bottle of champagne in an ice bucket, she poured us a pair of drinks. She wore a red satin gown of watered silk that made the blue ring in her eyes look much bluer, and her flaxen hair was pinned up with a black velvet band. Everything as rich as it was tasteful.

'Tell me,' she said softly, leaning back as light sparked off her champagne flute like shattered prisms, 'are you here to inform me finally of what happened to poor Liam? Have you caught the culprit? I would be most grateful to know that when you speak of dead kinchin so graphically, it tends to some purpose.'

'It does. Why don't you tell me how many of your kinchin you purposely hushed before selling their bodies for autopsy to Peter Palsgrave?'

Shock on most people looks like fear. On Silkie Marsh, it looks like pleasure. Her mouth dropped open and her head tilted back as her pale eyelashes fluttered. I wondered if she'd cultivated that. It can't have been easily mastered.

'That's a lie,' she gasped.

'No, it's a question. I just want to know how many it was. I haven't a scrap of evidence, so here's all my cards on the table. I can't prove a thing. I'm bust. Tell me.'

Tell me.

You told me you grew up a kinchin-mab, and you didn't mean to, hated the confession afterward. So tell me this. I'm honest, and you're a remarkable liar, so we'll each play to our strengths until one of us wins.

'I think you ought to tell me what you accuse Dr Palsgrave of doing,' she said with another scared fluttering motion, switching topics. 'This is all too vile to countenance. He's a very good man, a philanthropist at heart, the sort who isn't satisfied unless he's giving back to the human race.'

'And he also admitted to me that he paid you fifty dollars a corpse. I've evidence enough against *him* to put him under the ground, but I want to know how many of the chits you sold him died natural. You put them to sleep, didn't you, poisoned them maybe? Scores of poisons wouldn't have been traceable, even by Dr Palsgrave, and anyway the bodies have long since decayed. The proof has rotted away by now. It can't hurt you to answer.'

Arcing her torso forward as if it were a knife blade to my throat, Silkie Marsh brought her glass up to her lips. Just touching it to the lower one, subtly and flirtatiously.

'If you know nothing,' she said, 'I can't imagine why you think I'll tell you.'

'I'll know just how clever you are. Won't that be satisfying?'

'Why ever would I want to kill my own employees, Mr Wilde?'

'I never said you wanted to. I said you *did*.'

'This is so very tiring,' she sighed. 'Even supposing I did allow the good doctor to dispose of the bodies incurred by illness – and I don't deny it, he wanted them very badly, Mr Wilde,' she added in a caressing tone, like a viper's tongue flicking at my skin. 'He wanted all the corpses he could lay his hands on, and what position was I in to tell him no? I a bawdy-house madam and he a renowned physician on whom I relied for medical help? He insisted upon my cooperation, and how could I refuse him when he had such power over my household? It was tantamount to blackmail.'

LYNDSAY FAYE

I eyed her critically. It didn't wash.

So after a pause, she concluded, 'I like you knowing nothing, Mr Wilde. I think I prefer to keep it that way.'

'You've murdered two for a fact. That's not quite the same as knowing nothing.'

She smiled amiably. 'Which two of my beloved brothers and sisters did I murder, then, Mr Wilde?'

'Liam, for one. He'd had pneumonia. But he'd also recovered. I don't know if you needed the money or if it was your usual practice, but you made him sick again.'

Silkie Marsh was starting to look, of all the wrong expressions, bored. She was watching the admirably small bubbles in her champagne flute. I suddenly knew why Val had been fascinated by her. She was probably the only person Valentine had ever met whom he couldn't figure out.

'The musical program is just about to begin. I wish you good night, Mr Wilde, though—'

'The one I know you killed a bit more viciously went by the name of Jack Be Nimble.'

Her eyes flashed to mine instantly.

And that was all I needed to continue. That look was as good as a confession.

Why should she know the name Jack Be Nimble if she hadn't rid herself of him the same night they met, when Jack had poked his head into Dr Palsgrave's carriage and then gone indoors for a plate of hot chicken stew? Whether she'd tried to employ Jack first was anyone's guess. But dead he was, and by her hand. She couldn't possibly have allowed him to live, once she'd learned he associated her with Dr Palsgrave's carriage and a dark, silent bundle on its floor.

So I stopped playing by my own rules.

'You'd have to have buried that one without Palsgrave,' I mused. 'He'd have been too suspicious, a healthy newsboy like that suddenly falling ill in your establishment. I'm sure you only hushed the chronically sickly so as never to arouse the doctor's suspicions, and I'm sure you were unspeakably careful. Jack, though, he needed fast solving, having keeked in Palsgrave's carriage, seen a man in a black hood outside your door. Where did you bury him? I'm not surprised you got away with hiding the body – you're cunning enough, and anyhow there weren't any copper stars.'

'You've no proof,' she whispered. 'And I've not said a thing either.'

'I told you already that I'm through being merciful, Madam Marsh. That means I don't need one single piece of what you call *proof*. I could shut you up on any charges I like tomorrow. Just so long as you're a whore and I'm a copper star.'

'And that is meant to convince me confession is the best policy?' she cried. 'The fact you're keen to bury me alive in that dungeon you call the Tombs?'

'I'd like nothing better. But if you tell me how many,' I answered, leaning forward, 'I won't.'

Bribes generally set my teeth on edge. I wanted so badly to *understand*, though. Like I'd never wanted anything. I wanted Mercy, but that was written on the underside of my skeleton. Everyone wants money and comfort, but those were too vague to feel by comparison. I wanted Valentine to live better than he did, and that want lived in a part of me that couldn't be touched.

But this – I suddenly wanted *facts* as if they were clean water. Pure, cold, storyless *facts*.

Silkie Marsh set her champagne glass down. The animated doll was gone, replaced by a creature a bit resembling . . . well, a stockbroker. Measuring odds and looking for patterns and taking a long shot. It was artful.

'I killed seven of them, and yes – they had been chronically sick. They'd each cost me a fortune in medical procedures. Bleedings, sweatings, poultices, cordials, and yet the little parasites couldn't quite manage to *die*. It was a kindness, stopping their pain. The rest passed without any help, unexpectedly. Part of the money always paid for decent food for the others, you ought to know. And anyway, why should I have cared about their deaths when I made their *lives* so much easier than mine was? I'd have liked my fish to be fresh when I was their age and in the same line of work.'

Not knowing whether any particle of her own history was true or meant to play me, I kept my peace. I suspected it was honest, though. How else could she ever have learned to exist so?

'Thank you,' I said. 'My curiosity was getting out of hand.'

'I should say so. Though why you want the number so badly, I'll never know.'

'You'll know right this minute, actually. Seven of them. That's three hundred and fifty dollars, isn't it?'

'Why?'

'Because I want every cent of your blood money. In cash.'

Let me be perfectly clear: everything I'd said to her initially – that I hadn't two solid face cards to keep each other company – was the God's honest truth. I had no evidence against her, proof of literally nothing. I couldn't even prove those corpses had ever set foot in her establishment while alive. As for Scales and Moses, the ideal witnesses, they were stone dead. Could I have jailed her for whoring? Yes, for a week or two, however long it took her to bribe her way out again. Judges, not unlike copper stars, have a difficult time caring much about stargazing.

I would have been forced to track down the men who'd bought her and compel them to testify in court for a conviction to stick, which was about as likely as her making a full confession. Val might have testified, but Val probably hadn't paid in the first place. My options, therefore, were limited. The way I saw it, in fact, I had two of them, since the notion of doing nothing was nauseating:

1. *Wring her neck myself.*

I couldn't stomach that one either.

2. *Make her pay in a way that matters to her. Tell the chief. And bide my time.*

At the moment, Silkie Marsh was beyond the law's reach. The person I could punish, the one whose carriage had been seen, was Peter Palsgrave. But jailing him would have been a cruel and fruitless spectacle without any meaning behind it. He'd fought so hard for them. He'd done his best. He'd keep saving more of them, over and over again, until the day he died. How many fatalities would be on my hands if I locked him away, how many more kinchin dead, and this time on my account?

As for Madam Marsh, I thought, I will watch her relentlessly from this day onward. Watching her will be my religion. And one day, the murderess of seven children is going to dangle from the end of a rope.

Silkie Marsh was on the verge of stuttering, but she spoke clear. 'The day I agree to such an outrageous—'

'I have the ear of Chief Matsell and keys to the Tombs lockup. Who do you think you're playing with? I don't care about *evidence*,' I lied. 'For God's sake, I could plant mountains of the stuff and save myself any further trouble. I want money. Three hundred and fifty dollars.'

She must never have learned how to spit in a man's eye.

That was the only answer to why she didn't. Madam Marsh only drew herself up a little straighter and smoothed the wrinkles from her long, lavish crimson skirts.

'Since you've given more than that to the Party, I don't see the problem,' I added pleasantly.

'Of course not. You don't seem to see much of anything,' she snapped. 'Drink your champagne, Mr Wilde, I've already paid for it and you've driven off my friends.'

I upended the shimmering glass and then set it back on the table.

'Why should you hate me so very, very much over things that don't affect you?' she questioned in a final miserable-sounding bid for pity.

'They deeply affect me. You tried to kidnap Bird Daly and drag her back to the House of Refuge to be silenced. Neat trick of yours, signing *Wilde* to the papers you tried to inter her with. And you paid Scales and Moses Dainty to kill me. You'll not see them again, by the way. I made them both easy.'

Let her think I killed them myself, spread rumor of my violently unpredictable new status of dead rabbit, I thought. I'd a convincingly deadly brother to flesh out the picture.

She drained her own glass, looking downcast. 'Even supposing you are right, I don't know why you think you'll live to make anything of it. A man can only ride so far on his brother's coattails. Even with Scales and Moses to your account.'

'You're threatening to kill me again,' I said, grinning. 'But you're not going to.'

'You suppose not? For what reason?'

'For the same reason you only tried to hush my brother the one time. It was once, yes? I'll have to hear that story from him, it'll kittle me. You only tried to hush Val once, Madam

Marsh, because when he'd lived through the first time, you were glad of it. You'd like to have Val back, I think. Someday. And I plan to inform him that if anything ever happens to me, if I die anywise other than ninety years old and of pure placid boredom, it's your fault. And I'm not very fair to him most of the time, but here's a fair statement: if that happens, you'll never have him. Not if hell froze in July.'

'You're a monster,' she snarled at me.

'Well, then I'm a monster whose good health you ought to worry about. And I want three hundred fifty dollars in cash. Delivered by someone harmless, before dawn.'

Madam Marsh drew her fingertips down her neck and flung me a smile that reminded me of a fresh-honed razor blade.

'You're right,' she said. 'I'm not going to hush you, though how you could suppose I'd ever dream of such a cruel thing is quite beyond my ken. I am going to do something else, though, because you are a thief, and thieves are the lowest form of filth.'

'What's that?'

'I intend to *ruin* you.'

It would be a lie to say that I enjoyed hearing it. Or that I didn't think it worth worrying over. But I couldn't call myself the smallest bit surprised.

'And I wonder if you know, Mr Wilde, just how very far a man can be ruined without being killed. You'll understand what I mean one day.'

'I will,' I said. 'And I'll get better and better at this. The policing. I'll take to it like a bird to air. You'll see that I will, as I'm not going anyplace.'

I made my exit.

The gardens below were strung with glowing orbs of all sizes – hectic fireflies in the bushes and the paper lanterns in the trees and above all the rest, just beginning to flicker, a dusting of powdery stars in the infinite distance. People moving through the shadows laughing, waving fans before faces, spilling drops of champagne on the grass. For some reason, I liked the thought that the three sorts of light touched everyone alike, from the stars to the candles to the lightning bugs. Everyone fading as the daylight gave up the ghost, marked only by silvery edges and the flare of lucifers meeting thin cigars.

My dream of being a ferryman on the waters of the Hudson, I realized just then, had always been a dream about being somewhere *else*. Having a little spread on Staten Island or in Brooklyn, doing work that lets a man be out of doors, possess and keep up his own rusting and saltwater-pocked means of livelihood, that's the sort of thing a barkeep is required to dream about. Property, daylight, countryside. I'd dreamed of that summer when I'd been twelve years old and suddenly happy on the water with the salt in my hair because I'd so often been terribly unhappy since. No other reason. It's like a pretty picture tacked on the wall of a windowless tenement room. Just a reminder that other lives are different, that maybe you felt peaceable once and could do so again. A tune you write to whistle the daily aches away.

And I'd been lazy about mine. Picked a vision I supposed might fit my shape and never bothered to try it on properly. Because I hadn't *chosen* New York. People come here, keep coming, thousands upon thousands, miserable crowds thick enough that some feel frightened they'll bury us, but no one realizes that they're the fortunate ones. The emigrants decide where they belong. Not what they'll become or if they'll succeed, of course, but simply *where* they are. Geography and will twined into one forward motion.

Telling Silkie Marsh that I wasn't going anyplace felt good. As if, for the first time, I'd deliberately chosen something that wasn't simply drifting with the fairest tide. I'd planted my flag in the ground. And that choice might get me killed sooner or later, if she had anything to say about it, but the stake and the land were *mine*.

So I tugged the mask off. It didn't fit quite right anymore, had been fraying at one edge ever since the riot, and I've never been good with a needle. I dropped it at the exit of Niblo's as I left the manicured lawns and the silhouettes of city dwellers and the countless spheres of light.

I found George Washington Matsell at his office at the Tombs. Hunched over his stack of parchment, scribbling flash words and their meanings as the blueish sky through the window behind him dulled to black.

He didn't look hangdog over the riot, or even very tired. That almost annoyed me. I could feel collapse vibrating hard and relentless behind my eyelids, having run myself so ragged. But then I grasped that he was writing the lexicon to understand better. Remembered that the chief had already passed through a score of riots, and watched half of lower Manhattan burn down to a sad set of statistics not two months back, when he'd been a justice and the police hadn't existed.

'What in hell do you think you're doing here,' he said without bothering to look at me, 'when I wanted you here in August?'

'Today's September. The first, I think,' I said absently, marveling. 'You're right, I never noticed.'

'Then maybe you noticed that my mood isn't very good. Did you notice that I've over thirty men in lockdown, and eight copper stars at the New York Hospital? Or that the Five

Points is one giant sea of broken window glass? I wonder if you'll notice when I sack you in a moment, no matter who your brother happens to be.'

'It's over, Chief. We're through with this business. I've fixed it.'

Chief Matsell glanced up in considerable surprise. He traced his jowls with his fingertips, arms snug over his enormous blue waistcoat, taking my measure. Searching my face like the front page of a newspaper. Then he read me, and he smiled.

'You worked it all out, back to front?'

'Everything.'

'And you found the culprit?'

'Two and a half. There were two and a half culprits.'

He blinked, grizzled brows twisting like caterpillars. 'Twenty-one victims in all, yes? No recent bad news?'

'Right.'

'How many arrests?'

'None.'

'Mr Wilde,' he said, leaning forward and lacing his fat fingers together over his lexicon, 'you're generally better at talking. I suggest you regain your eloquence. Now.'

So I told him everything.

Well, most things. Parts I couldn't look in the eye myself just yet, and those ones I left out. Mercy having saved her own life, wet and still and blue on the floor of her bedchamber. Dr Palsgrave feeling so ashamed he'd put a corpse in a trash bin that he could scarce speak without his heart faltering.

How loose I'd tied those knots. How very, very poorly I'd fastened the reverend to a chair.

When I came to the end, the chief sat back. Put the gentle feathered end of his quill against his lower lip. Thought it over for a while.

'You are certain that Dr Peter Palsgrave knew nothing of Madam Marsh's hastening deaths?'

'I'd stake my life on it. It would have violated everything he stands for.'

'Then frankly, I don't feel any necessity of subjecting him to charges of what is in essence grave robbery when there were never any graves in the first place,' he said slowly.

'Hear, hear,' I agreed.

'Thomas Underhill made a full confession before he hanged himself, you say?'

'Yes.'

'That's all you have for me? A story?'

I removed the little journal from my frock coat and set it on the desk. 'The diary of the St Patrick's victim, Marcas. The reverend kept possession of it, God knows why. It was in his study.' Next I pulled the piece of paper with *Reverend Thomas Underhill* written shakily on it out of my waistcoat pocket. 'What's better, Father Sheehy identified him as the only man to bring a large bundle into the cathedral that night, and the only man he failed to observe leaving. The sack, which held the drugged child, was no longer inside St Patrick's when Sheehy discovered the body. It explains the lack of break-in. It all fits.'

'That's what put you onto the reverend? His carrying a bundle with him to the school meeting?'

'No, the other way around. I didn't know he had a sack, but I knew there was a meeting and I knew there was no break-in.'

A near-smile floated around Chief Matsell's lips. 'That all just . . . occurred to you at random.'

'No,' I sighed wearily. 'I used butcher paper.'

'Butcher paper.'

LYNDSAY FAYE

Nodding, I let my head drop onto one closed fist. I didn't know when last I'd eaten, and the edges of my eyelids burned with fatigue.

'So, as far as we are concerned, the doctor is not worth touching and the reverend is beyond our justice. You say we can't convict Silkie Marsh of any crime.'

'Not honestly. She needs very careful watching. We'll catch her out sooner or later, and she'll find herself at the end of a rope.'

'I agree with you. I do imagine, however, that you've confronted her?'

'Three hundred and fifty dollars' worth.'

I'd not have thought it possible, but George Washington Matsell's lungs hitched a bit. It was a nice thing to see. It was good to think that my taking an enormous bribe actually startled a man who generally couldn't be alarmed by a charging bull.

'Are you handing it over?' he asked dryly, next.

'I can spare fifty for the Party if you must, but the rest is for one of the victims.'

'Ah. I will accept fifty, for an unnamed police charity, and you will donate the remainder to . . . what victim? Bird Daly, I take it?'

'A victim,' I said steadily.

The chief chewed on that for a minute. Made up his mind.

'I'd like to offer you something, Mr Wilde,' he said, standing up. 'Copper stars, supposedly so that they do not grow arrogant or corrupt, must be rehired every year. I don't like this policy and I never did. It negates the very idea of expertise, and as for stopping corruption— But here is what I propose. So long as I am chief of police, you are a copper star. We'll set you up solving crimes, you see, rather than preventing

them. If you want a title, I'll come up with one. I'm very apt
with words. And you've done a fine job at surprising me.'

I know the sudden small glow wasn't sensible. It should
never have satisfied me so deep that I could keep that job.
Maybe it was just a novel sensation, being good at something
entirely new.

'Thank you,' I said.

'That's settled, then.'

'I've a single condition.'

The chief turned away from the window he'd been
contemplating, silvery brows quirked in annoyance. Clearly, I
was pushing.

'I only meant to say that you ought to keep Val too,' I
offered more humbly.

'Mr Wilde, I will get your measure one of these days,'
sniffed Chief Matsell, sitting back down and lifting his quill.
Still looking downright bustled. 'You are a genius with butcher
paper, apparently, and then of a sudden you are thick as
lumber. Your brother – provided he doesn't get himself
croaked, or elected to public office – will doubtless be a copper
star captain until the day he dies.'

'I'm grateful you think so, then.'

'Mr Wilde,' the chief said, 'get out of my office. You look
ready to faint in it, and I don't want the trouble of stepping
over you.'

On my way out of that great fortress of stone, I encountered
a strange fellow, walking furtive and fluid like a crab, with
thick Dutch boots, without a chin, with wild tinsel hair, and
rushing up to me the minute we'd spied each other.

'I must inform you of the evidence delivered by a Miss
Maddy Sample, Mr Wilde. We see the light of dawn at last!'
Mr Piest whispered, clutching my arm in his dry claw.

'It's morning already,' I answered gratefully, as the moon outside began to rise. 'Supply me with some bread and coffee and I'll tell you all about it.'

And yes, it was morning in my head. All was going better than I could ever have expected. I owed so much of my success to Mr Piest that I'd have been a turncoat not to stop and deliver the story. Just two problems plagued my mind as I finished filling in the blanks for my colleague over steaming tin cups and a heaping plate of beef and stewed cabbage.

What will happen? I thought. Not to me. That much seemed settled. But there was a pair of girls I didn't like to let down, one very much younger than the other. Both fates undetermined. Both lives marred and mended and marred again.

And the worst betrayal of all just then was, I didn't strictly know whether either one of them was alive or dead.

CHAPTER TWENTY-SEVEN

The tide of emigration which now sets so strongly
towards our shores, cannot be turned back. We must
receive the poor, the ignorant, and the oppressed from
other lands, and it would be better to consider them as
coming filled with the energy of hope for happier
days, and more useful labors, than they found at
home. No one, I presume, seriously believes they come
with bad intentions.

The Sanitary Condition of the Laboring Population
of New York, January 1845

A very uncomfortable mix of pricklish sensations haunted
me as I arrived back home. First, the fact that I didn't
have two bodies, and couldn't check whether Mercy was nursed
fully back to health at the same time; and second, the thought
that maybe no one would be there. That maybe Silkie Marsh
could whisper instructions to blackbirds and send them flying
up to nameless assassins in Harlem. Ravens croaking out 'Kill
Bird Daly' and then lazily winging back to the city.

When I opened my front door, though, the coiled-up feeling melted. There was Valentine, sitting at the bread-kneading table with Mrs Boehm. He'd gotten a pitcher of gin, and two tumblers were out, alongside my landlady's supply of precious chocolate, a plate of pastries much finer than she usually bakes, and a deck of playing cards. The entire room smelled of butter. Mrs Boehm herself was flushed to her sparse hairline, grinning so wide that she might have knocked the gin pitcher off the table. She'd clearly just laid down a hand, and I could see it upside down. A full house.

'No argument is possible,' she was saying, clapping her hands once. 'You are a . . . tell me again, please. What word is it, for a man who so badly loses at all cards?'

'A flat,' Val answered. 'And proud to lose to so square a republican as yourself, though not as proud as I am to teach you the lingo. Timothy Wilde, copper star! You look like death passed you over, thinking he'd already done his job. You've lost your mask as well, but that looks pretty flash.'

'It's wonderful to see you both,' I said. 'I need to ask Bird a question.'

'She is probably not yet sleeping.' Mrs Boehm poured an ounce more gin into Valentine's glass and then sipped at her own with German delicacy. 'If you are quick.'

Bird wasn't yet sleeping, though she'd curled up on the trundle pulled out from Mrs Boehm's bed. The simply stitched curtains were pulled back from the window. As I walked quietly in, Bird's square little chin jutted eagerly up in my direction.

'You're all right,' she said. 'I knew you would be. Mr V said that you were nowhere you couldn't gammon your way back again.'

'I wasn't. Bird, can I ask you something?'

Bird sat up readily, tucking her knees cross-legged beneath the counterpane.

'When you said all that time ago that I'd kissed the girl in that picture I'd drawn,' I questioned softly, 'what did you mean? You seemed troubled over it, and you know Mercy Underhill. You must have met her, where you used to live.'

'Oh,' Bird whispered. 'Yes.'

She thought about the question for a bit too long. Long enough for me to notice that she supposed I'd not like her answer. But I waited her out, for it was plaguing me.

'Well, I didn't think her quite right, you see. She was doing . . . the same thing, exactly the same as me, but she could come and go as she pleased and I couldn't, so when you'd her picture, I supposed . . .' Bird trailed off, puzzling worriedly. 'I thought she must have been your mistress, if you'd her picture. But I don't understand her. Who'd ever want to just for, if . . . and if they could get out again, why—'

'No, hush,' I said as she grew panicky. 'Thank you for telling me. It's not easy to understand, but I do want you to know . . . she wished your lives better. You savvy, I think?'

'I see that,' Bird murmured, nodding. 'Everyone else loved her. Just not me. But if you ask me to really like Miss Underhill, and not pretend, I'll do it.'

'No, I'd never ask that.' I squeezed her shoulder once. 'She has enough people who love her. No one is ever going to decide that sort of thing for you again.'

I arrived back downstairs in time to see Valentine slipping out my front door. So I went after him. Having already criminally missed going after my brother once, I didn't mean to do it again anytime soon. When Val heard the door shut, he glanced back, his boot on the lowest of our three steps to the street. Not wary, exactly. But cautious. Tugging my hat off tiredly, I raised an eyebrow at my brother – the one on the more expressive side of my face.

'It's all over,' I said. 'I solved it.'

'Bully.' Val fished a cigar end out of his pocket and tucked it in the corner of his mouth.

'That's all you have to say?'

'Aces,' Valentine answered, winking.

'You don't want to know what happened?'

'I'll get it from Matsell tomorrow. He tells a better story.'

'You're a prick,' I marveled.

'If you're keen to have me recollect any more of this in the morning, I'd not waste words now,' my brother suggested, checking his pocket watch. 'Anyway, I'm off to a clandestine Party meeting. I have to ogle over a score of Irishmen and decide who's fit to guard future ballot boxes. Waste no more of my time, Tim.'

'Regarding this afternoon,' I persisted, leaning back against the side of the house. 'Your escorting Bird and Mrs Boehm back here. That was bene enough. You did me a good turn. But staying with them the whole time, until I returned, not knowing what I was about?'

'Mmm?' he said, already looking back and forth and over and under for a hack. Walking backward into Elizabeth Street, not paying me any attention. Just exactly the way he always acts.

It's infuriating.

'Thank you,' I called out.

Valentine shrugged, standing in the middle of the road. The bags beneath his eyes lightened an ounce or two as he glanced back at me. 'It wasn't much.'

'I'll see you tomorrow at the Liberty's Blood. Try not to

take so much morphine you're half croaked by the time I arrive, all right?'

Valentine caught the sort of grimace he gets when he's laughing. It passed, though, and the gleaming-bone wolf's smile appeared in its place.

'Sounds dead flash. Try not to be such a comprehensive cow's teat in the meantime, will you, my Tim?'

'That seems pretty fair,' I answered sincerely.

I never went back to the Pine Street Church, or to the Underhill residence.

Mr Piest, whom I'd confided in very closely over our shared meal, 'discovered' the body in the garden shed half an hour after I'd told him of it. Since I'd given him the key and all. The Reverend Underhill had obviously been strangled to death, but there were no witnesses. Nor clues. Nor suspects. It was a sad crime, obviously a murder.

But what could the copper stars do under the circumstances?

My colleague saw to it that within five more hours he was buried, in a quiet place under the familiar apple trees, in the Pine Street churchyard. We learned later that the reverend's earthly properties were fast tied up with his pastorate. And anyhow, he'd been a charitable man long before the end, serving the needs of poor Protestant families. After the burial, there was only the house owned by the parish, and its furnishings. None of it valuable as anything but aids to memory. His will left his extensive library to a nearby free school. *And that was just exactly like him after all*, I thought. It hadn't seemed to have ever once occurred to Thomas Underhill that his daughter might need more than she had, when so very many had so much less.

I didn't plan on forgiving him for that either.

After sleeping for a few scant hours, I waited at home all through the night for a knock on the door.

When the hesitant rap came, I went outside and took a small woven bag from a beggar woman who'd lost the main balance of her teeth. I gave her a second coin for her trouble, though she told me she'd already been well paid not to look in that bag. And that if she did open the bag, the sender would know, and the pigs would eat her when she was left for dead in the streets. I asked where she'd come from, and she pointed to a grocer half a block away. A man on its porch watched us from under a straw hat brim, silent and cheerless.

I didn't acknowledge him, though. Thanking the tattered moll, I pocketed my delivery and set out on foot for Pine Street.

But I never reached it. Passing rows of modest brick houses with their white-painted lintels brightening, the third time in a row I'd watched morning spread out buttery and thick over the city, I glimpsed Mercy walking in the opposite direction. That is, toward me.

Mercy wore a dove-grey dress that didn't quite fit her. From the saleable charity pile at the church, I assumed, for it was very clean and neatly sewn. Its bell-shaped skirt hung a little loose around her waist, though, and its wide neck draped even more off one shoulder than her frocks normally do. She'd taken half the time with her hair as usual, and I could see from a distance her lips were lightly blistered and her hands bandaged in a few places.

I thought, *This is what Mercy looks like in a grey secondhand dress on the last day you will ever see her,* as our steps met in the dead center of the western Pearl Street sidewalk.

'Mr Wilde,' she said.

'Hello,' I said.

It was a start.

'My father is dead,' she murmured. 'You were there, you – you know, I think.'

'Yes.'

'The policeman was kind, but he wouldn't let me see. And he said *murdered*. But that wasn't the way of it. I don't believe him.'

'I'm so sorry.'

'You shouldn't be sorry. You helped. You didn't want me to have to – for what really happened to be known.'

She'd been crying, but not for long. The edges of her eyes were merely pink, still glistening a bit, and the angry red color from being forced into an ice bath was fading. The rest was very blue, her hair very thick and very dark. Mercy hadn't asked me a single question yet, and suddenly I realized why. What had just happened to her, the dark, ugly realizations, the exposed secrets that burned when you touched them . . . They couldn't be bettered by learning *more*. I wondered if Mercy would ever ask another question again in my hearing.

'The buried kinchin were autopsies,' I told her quietly. 'They weren't desecrated at all, they were used by Dr Palsgrave for science after they'd passed. It's complicated, but a better outcome than we could have hoped for. I haven't arrested him and I'm not going to. But I wanted you to know that everything's . . . over with, now.'

I said nothing of Marcas and the church door. That image was already tattooed on her corneas as she stared at me, saying nothing, as dazed and hurt as any creature I'd ever witnessed.

'I've a gift for you.' I held out the little purse.

Mercy touched her teeth to her lower lip. No questions, though.

Who'd have thought that the very worst thing ever to happen to you would be Mercy losing question marks, I thought, then forced myself to stop thinking.

'It's three hundred dollars in cash. It comes from a . . . very appropriate donor, and one you never need feel *debt* toward. It isn't mine or Val's or anyone's you might think, but it's . . . it's *yours,* and you're going to London. Three hundred is enough to be getting on with, although . . . I'm sorry your togs were ruined, or can you wash kerosene out of clothes?'

I stopped.

When she tugged open the drawstring and saw the actual coin, Mercy's mouth fell open entirely, like a ribbon bow being pulled.

'I don't see how this could be mine.'

'Trust me,' I insisted. 'I know I'm not entirely to be trusted in your eyes just now, but please trust me. I'm sorry about all of that. You're getting away from this place. And if you find you need do nothing more in London and grow tired of it, or if you go elsewhere, to Paris or Lisbon or Boston or Rome, and then later want to see New York again . . . I'll be here.'

There were too many blisters on Mercy's fingers. I wanted to wipe them smooth again. It was a relief, in a way, to know she wasn't in love with me. I could carry on as before.

Whatever is best for Mercy. Nothing much else need be considered.

'Are—' Mercy stopped, struggling. 'Are you staying in New York forever, then?'

I breathed considerably easier after that. And *what* a question for her to want the answer to. It was enough.

'I've a career now,' I confessed. 'And a brother who belongs locked in a cranky-hutch. I think I might hate them both, but I think I'm the right man for both jobs.'

Mercy's eyelashes flicked. 'I can't. I can't take this from you.'

'Go to London,' I said, pushing it into her hands.

'Timothy, why are you doing this?'

'Because you'll write a map.' I was already walking away from her.

'But why do you want that of me?' she called softly.

Giving me one more invaluable question.

'I want that for a very good reason,' I answered, keeping my pace. 'If you ever want me to understand something, any piece of you . . . well. If you've written a map, then I'll know where to look.'

By two weeks later, September had made itself better felt. The charcoal-sketched notions of trees in City Hall Park burst violently red and then faded back into line drawings. The air was fresher, for now. Down by the docks it smelled of tar and fish and sweat and smoke instead of constantly rotting animal remains. Everything was brighter for being so much more muted. And everyone alike indifferently happy for the three or four days September lasts before winter sets in.

I wanted to kill my brother again by then, but I didn't hate him yet, and I hoped I wouldn't any longer.

I found out where a light-fingered apprentice had cached his master's best cutlery, which was the second crime I'd solved in as many weeks.

It felt good.

On a beautifully fresh Sunday morning, I opened my copy of the *Herald* at the kitchen table and read this passage:

The office of the Irish Emigrant Society is at present located at No 6 Ann Street, in a plain and unpretending building.

427

Occasional scenes of an amusing kind occur in the office.
Crowds of anxious expectants are seated there, looking out
every minute for a chance, in comes an employer in search of
a steady man, or decent girl, when buzz! fifty candidates for
the piece of good fortune are on the alert, and on their legs
in an instant.

Failing to see the humor in the anecdote, I tossed that
particular copy into the bread oven when I was through with
it. Not that the press had failed to serve police interests, by
any means. George Washington Matsell, in a stroke of genius
I could never have anticipated, gave out to the newspapers
that the kinchin called Marcas found so gruesomely slain at St
Patrick's was hushed by a pair of insane Nativist political
radicals, with wicked English ties and a history of outrageous
violence in the name of vile European anarchy. They went by
the names of Scales and Moses Dainty, and had both been
killed in the Five Points riot the same day they enacted their
heinous, utterly anti-American assassination. One reporter
had the nerve to ask whether they'd been copper stars. Matsell
said no. When I checked the records myself, Matsell turned
out to be right, too, which only goes to prove the chief is
thorough as well as clever, and knows when it's beneficial for
the reputation of the police force to erase particular names
from Ward Eight's roster. Plenty of people knew different, of
course, and a few knew still better than that. But regular New
Yorkers can't be bothered to dwell on the same crime for
more than a fortnight. Things returned to normal: brutal,
greedy, frenzied, and secretive, but with less talk of mad Irish
kinchin killers.

Mrs Boehm and I reached a decision. And so, to tell her
about it, I invited Bird Daly on a trip to Battery Park.

After a few hours and several small meals, the sun was sinking low and we'd grown tired of wandering. The grass there is much better kept than anywhere else on the island, though, and being close to the sea was still pleasant rather than unspeakably cold. So when we felt like stopping, we sat under a spreading oak near to where I'd been buried in a stack of Bibles when Valentine found me. I didn't mind so much thinking of it any longer.

The time seemed ripe, so I set to. I told Bird that she was going to live at a home founded by Father Sheehy and go to school. An Irish Catholic school. Mrs Boehm and I not being very learned, and learning being absolutely necessary.

It didn't go quite so well as I'd expected.

That is, I'd expected it to go badly in the first place. But I'll skip the next few minutes of Bird's ranting at me, and proposing herself for various jobs if we couldn't afford her, and her using language she shouldn't have picked up yet. It doesn't show her in her best light, and I don't like to think it ever really crossed her mind that we might be tired of her company. Bird Daly is plenty warm company, and I convinced her of it eventually. So she sat there, all angry eyebrows and outraged freckles, staring at the throngs of people.

'I think I can't manage it,' she said finally. 'I think I'll miss you, and Mrs Boehm, and not . . . not manage it.'

'Here's what I think about it. Shall I tell you?'

Bird nodded, grey eyes shimmering like silver coins at the bottom of a deep fountain.

'I think that you won't have to miss me, because I'll see you when you like. Maybe sometimes when you wouldn't like, because I'll drop in unannounced and you'll have to leave off learning sums, or playing at hopscotch. And soon enough you'll never want to leave the place, to go off and be a grown young lady, because there will be so many other kinchin who you'll miss when the time comes.'

Bird's throat seemed to be working at something pebbleish. 'Will there be other . . . will there be kids like me there?'

Working out exactly what she meant took me two seconds. When I did, I looked very hard at a passing carriage, shamming as if I knew the society lady being dragged about by horses with improbable feathers on their heads. So that Bird wouldn't see what my face was really going on about.

'Kinchin-mabs?' I said clearly. 'A great many. You mean, apart from the ones I sent there myself? Neill and Sophia and all the rest?'

My little friend nodded. Resigned, if not content.

And so we watched the people passing us by, knowing things about them. The both of us. Knowing things by the dirt on their sleeves and the hard look in their pistol-sight eyes. Knowing things because we were safer, and richer, for knowing them before they did. And happy in the notion that we were reading the same letter of the same sentence on each and every human page.

We never said a word.

After leaving Bird with a score of her former friends and her future friends the next day, I went back home. Bird wasn't there any longer, and that went hard. But Mrs Boehm smiled at me with her wide lips as I passed her on the staircase. And I smiled at her, and it was something.

I still hadn't any furniture to speak of. But I hadn't needed it until then, and maybe I would think about it now. Matsell had secretly raised my salary to fourteen dollars a week. Picking up the magazine that had long been resting on the boards just inside my door, waiting until I was ready to touch it, I sat under my window and read the last installment of *Light and Shade in the Streets of New York*.

The scullery maid who had been seduced by the aristocrat died in childbirth. But the baby was delivered to the earl, who wept with remorse for his coldness, and he took the infant girl in his arms. The tale was lush with imagery, keenly insightful despite the popular cliché of its premise. Like the rest of the series, it was about passionate people creating tragedies because they didn't know how to do otherwise.

I lay back on the straw tick and fell asleep at midday. As deeply as I ever have.

I dreamed that Mercy went to London and met a rich earl and married him. But soon enough, the vision shifted. She had idle hours and paper aplenty.

Suddenly, I was reading her book:

I careen through chapters at a furious rate. The writing itself is now sidelong, much more like Mercy's manner of speaking than her tales. Hinting at great loves and losses, but never any direct story. By the end she's Patience on a monument, watching the people of New York pound like the breaking Atlantic surf all around her.

I look for myself in words that sound like me. In the spaces between period and capitalized letter.

Naturally I do. The dream is mine.

And so I search for a man, strongly built but short in stature. A twist to his lips at once bitter and thoughtful, blond hair that sweeps in a deep peak down his brow. I pore over her society parties – tables covered in oyster shells, the smell of fried beets in the heavy air, a black fiddler playing outside her window. Searching for a pair of green eyes that have seen too much, and that love her.

But she hides me away, of course. She imprisons me in
metaphors, fragments me into secondary characters. Saloon
keepers and servants. I follow the ink trail she's left, yes, but
I recall at the same time how she used to look at me, the
corners of her lashes forever snatching at glimpses of
something else.

I can never quite fathom what she wanted of me. Not even in
the dream. Only what she turned me into.

Having woken up sweating, I threw open the window. The
air was cool enough, with autumn marching toward us so
steadily. But the dust still blanketed Manhattan's fields and
churches in a sheet of sunny brilliance. Too keen to view
directly. I shut my eyes.

And because I love her past all reason, as I found myself
losing the words she'd written in the vision, I struggled to
memorize them.

He had all manner of pet names for me. To the degree that
when the gentleman at long last uttered my right name
aloud, it seemed the only true expression of myself, as if all
men heretofore had mispronounced or forgotten it.

An empty exercise. A mad one. She was never talking
about me.

THE GODS OF GOTHAM: HISTORICAL AFTERWORD

The history of New York's Five Points is rife with legend, speculation, and controversy, but I have done my best to present its conditions accurately. In 1849, the *Herald* ran a sensational story about an infant who had been discovered 'in the sink of the dwelling house No 6 Doyer Street. From the appearance of the child when found, it was evident that foul means had been used, as, around the neck of the little innocent, a cord had been tied tight, causing strangulation'. Despite the severe poverty of Ward Six, murder was far from common, and the residents who found the body were shocked, calling at once for the police. When the copper stars arrived, they were directed to the mother's chamber by neighbors. Eliza Rafferty was 'sitting very composedly in a chair in her room, making a dress, that being her profession'. The coroner determined that the infant had been murdered, despite Rafferty's insistence that the baby was already dead before being placed in the sink. What exact circumstances drove her to infanticide remain unknown, but many Five Pointers lived hand-to-mouth in such desperate and miserable circumstances that survival was a daily exercise in will.

New York's formation of a police force lagged behind that of other large metropolitan centers like Paris, London, Philadelphia, Boston, and even Richmond, Virginia. There were many reasons for this delay, but not least the fact that New Yorkers have never much liked being regulated, and the revolutionary spirit of autonomy and independence was still running strong in the antebellum period. It is much in evidence today, as a matter of fact. But in 1845, following a period of increasing crime and civic unrest, it was finally decided that the streets could not go unattended any longer, and the now legendary NYPD was formed despite vocal opposition and political controversy. In the same year, a recently arrived blight called *Phytophthora infestans* spread widely across Ireland and the Great Famine began, leading to the death or relocation of millions of Irish and prompting a social upheaval that still shapes New York City today.

New Yorkers have always been avid theatergoers, but none more so than the news hawkers and the bootblacks of the Five Points. The playhouse founded by the newsboys was in fact on Baxter Street, and they were responsible for everything from the stage properties to the musical underscoring, mounting full productions of such scripts as *The Thrilling Spectacle of the March of the Mulligan Guards*. The house seated fifty, and once played host to the Russian grand duke Alexis when he toured the notorious slum, after which the boys proudly renamed their theater company The Grand Duke's Opera House.

New York City in the middle of the nineteenth century, already the undisputed center of the publishing world in America, gave birth to a new genre: nonfiction urban sensationalism told in alternately harrowing and uplifting accounts of life in the squalid streets of the Western world's newest mega-metropolis. Unlike long-established capitals such as London or Paris, New York boasted only 60,515 residents, according to the United States census for the year 1800, a figure that would explode to half a million by 1850. Consequently, the city struggled wildly to keep up with its population, its poor, its infrastructure, its culture, and its social strictures, and urban sensationalist literature dramatized the sort of shocking occurrences that resulted from this upheaval. Often titling their works with variations on themes of gaslight and shadow, shade and sunshine, authors like city reporter George G. Foster thrilled readers who hailed from more pastoral landscapes, while at the same time attempting to illuminate the plight of the destitute Manhattanite. Mercy's articles are based on these works.

George Washington Matsell published his flash dictionary, *The Secret Language of Crime: Vocabulum, or, the Rogue's Lexicon*, in 1859. The necessity of writing such a book surprised even Matsell, who remarked dryly in his preface, 'To become a lexicographer certainly never entered into my calculation, or even found a place in the castle-building of my younger days; and if a kind friend had suggested to me that I was destined to fill such a position in life, I would simply have regarded him as a fit subject for the care of the authorities.'

Matsell was a widely read, highly intelligent, and bluntly forceful character, much despised in working-class neighborhoods and yet an avid scholar of such social trends as gang warfare and child vagrancy. He suggested that, while to the police an understanding of the underworld's slang was critical, the average citizen would also find his dictionary useful, as the ancient British criminal jargon known as thieves' cant was quickly infiltrating Fifth Avenue society. The spread of flash talk to the general population would prove to be a permanent shift in the English language. When you say 'so long' to your 'pal' in parting, you are participating in a subversive cultural phenomenon dating back to 1530 and the Derbyshire scoundrels who first developed a secret language all their own.

ACKNOWLEDGMENTS

In one sense, it requires many people to produce a book, and in another sense it requires only one, and I'm by no means referring to myself. If my husband Gabriel weren't the sort of fellow who constantly told me I was in the right line of work when I was sure I should take up longshoring, and who told me to go to the library rather than telling me to get a real job, I would never have written *The Gods of Gotham*. Thank you, Gabriel, for making this book happen, and for being the person you are. And thank you to my family, who tenaciously repeated the absolutely mad encouraging phrases he kept spouting.

To Amy Einhorn and to her entire phenomenal staff at Amy Einhorn/Putnam, thank you for taking a manuscript and turning it into a far better book than I dreamed it could be. Amy, you're a tireless advocate for powerful storytelling, and as passionate a reader as you are an editor, and I couldn't be more grateful for your insights. Thank you for the enormous gift of helping me to bring these people into the world.

Erin Malone met Timothy Wilde when he existed in only six terribly overwritten chapters, and somehow still wanted to see him in print. And when there were twenty-seven terribly overwritten chapters, she fixed them. Erin is my Mickey Goldmill. Thank you for believing in this book. Thank you also to the rest of the brilliant minds at William Morris Endeavor, including but by no means limited to Cathryn Summerhayes, Tracy Fisher, and Amy Hasselbeck for shocking me constantly with the level of your Awesome. To all my foreign publishers, thank you for caring about these characters, and for sharing them with other parts of the globe.

I owe a huge debt to the historians and scholars I relied upon so heavily to make this world as authentic as I could. Thank you to the New York Public Library and the New-York Historical Society for existing, and thank you to Tyler Anbinder, Edwin G. Burrows, Timothy Gilfoyle, Mike Wallace, and many others for immersing me in the history of the most fascinating city in the world. All remaining screw-ups are entirely on my head. Many of my major sources were original, so thank you to all the nineteenth-century diarists and journalists and pamphlet writers and speechmakers who left bread crumbs behind in the forest.

Thank you to Sir Arthur Conan Doyle for teaching me what a hero story looks like, and to Jim LeMonds for teaching me how to write and self-edit them.

I have an invaluable network of friends whose love and support define generosity, and whom I'm terrified of naming individually lest I leave one out. But to all those who take care of me, to my early readers, Feaster guests, fellow artists and actors and sketch comics and photographers and musicians and barflys, to my Shakespeare in the Park groundlings, to all the Sherlockians and Markt Restaurant employees and BLT Steak veterans, to the people I share micro-brews with and who are kind enough to eat my cooking, you helped make this happen. Thank you. I couldn't be luckier.

THE
GODS OF
GOTHAM

Bonus Material

Q & A with Lyndsay Faye

'*The Gods of Gotham* is the story of the first cop on the first organized beat in New York City, set during the strife-torn summer of 1845 when the Great Irish Famine began. I started with just that simple a concept: Day One, Cop One.

'I hope this book is at heart about the choices good people are forced to make when confronted with the ugliest sorts of poverty, bigotry, and tragedy. It's the story of a man who, having lost everything, finds an avocation and a cause. I'm fascinated by the intersections between luck (good or bad) and bravery (wise or foolish), and the way lives can be rebuilt following utter destruction. So to my mind, those are the important points.' Lyndsay Faye

How did you get started?

One day I picked up a novel in a Barnes and Noble pitting Sherlock Holmes against Jack the Ripper and, skimming it, thought *that's not how I'd have done it.* That notion became my first novel, *Dust and Shadow.* And it taught me two important lessons: first, I could sit down for long enough to write a novel. That was shocking. And second, writing about where you've been is excruciatingly boring. Writing about where you've *never* been, where no one alive has ever been – that's the ticket. Thrilling.

What compelled you to write this book?

I am one of those walking clichés who is deeply and entirely in love with New York. The people, the pace, the resilience, the history, the architecture, the clashing and melding and morphing and adapting of cultures. And for a very long time, since I was ten and introduced to Conan Doyle's works, in fact, I've been fascinated by the methods used in crime-solving when *there was no exact method to crime-solving*. Previous to established systems of forensics and psychology and science, how were crimes avenged? *The Gods of Gotham* is a marriage of those two fascinations. But it bears mentioning that those factors are the details, not the blood and guts of the piece. This book (I dearly hope), and every crime book I love is about passionate people doing passionate things in the face of terrible situations, and sometimes getting it right and sometimes getting it wrong.

I wanted to write the story of the first NYC cop, and walk in his shoes, and see what he saw. But there's a bit more to it, of course. When the Muslim community center planned for downtown Manhattan was widely vilified by the right-wing press, I got riled up to the point of outright anger. But more disturbing to me than the nasty feeling I get when listening to otherwise nice people make bigoted remarks on FOX television, I felt a profound sense of déjà vu. *Haven't we done this before? Isn't it time we got over it?* First the Irish came, and were roundly trashed. Then the Italians, the Jews, the Chinese, and more recently Hispanics. None of them deemed fit to be here by the already established people who – for reasons that are myriad and complicated – tried as best they could to keep immigrants out of their neighborhoods. Of course not everyone has been anti-immigrant, I don't mean to imply such a thing. But people fresh off the boat are almost perpetually deemed too poor, too strange, too lawless to be given a leg up in NYC.

So here we are, and immigrants have proven time and again to be the lifeblood of the city. Here we are, with good American Muslims who died tragically in 9/11, fighting a war of wills against genuinely evil extremists, and meanwhile screaming at each other about a community center. Every time I encountered a racist anti-Irish sentiment during my research, it sounded familiar, and it riled me. Thus my protagonist got riled against intolerance too.

Did anything surprise you during the course of writing the book?

It shocked me that the Potato Famine began at almost the exact moment the NYPD was founded. As if I wasn't already fired up enough about finding such disheartening parallels between modern anti-Muslim rhetoric and nineteenth-century anti-Catholic rhetoric.

What else should a reader know about this book?

Well, the NYC details are as accurate as I could make them. If I say a roundsman worked 16-hour shifts, it's because I found that item somewhere after scrupulous digging, and the same goes for as many details as I could possibly incorporate. The language of 'flash', in particular, tries at being as exact as I could make it and still be understood by a modern audience.

When Charles Dickens visited America in 1842, New York left a strong impression on him. Here are his frank and vivid descriptions of the city, including a visit to the Tombs and an excursion into the infamous Five Points.

EXCERPT FROM *AMERICAN NOTES* BY CHARLES DICKENS: NEW YORK

The beautiful metropolis of America is by no means so clean a city as Boston, but many of its streets have the same characteristics; except that the houses are not quite so fresh-coloured, the sign boards are not quite so gaudy, the gilded letters not quite so golden, the bricks not quite so red, the stone not quite so white, the blinds and area railings not quite so green, the knobs and plates upon the street doors not quite so bright and twinkling. There are many by-streets, almost as neutral in clean colours, and positive in dirty ones, as by-streets in London; and there is one quarter, commonly called the Five Points, which, in respect of filth and wretchedness, may be safely backed against Seven Dials, or any other part of famed St. Giles's.

The great promenade and thoroughfare, as most people know, is Broadway; a wide and bustling street, which, from the Battery Gardens to its opposite termination in a country road, may be four miles long. Shall we sit down in an upper floor of the Carlton House Hotel (situated in the best part of this main artery of New York), and when we are tired of looking down upon the life below, sally forth arm-in-arm, and mingle with the stream?

Warm weather! The sun strikes upon our heads at this open window, as though its rays were concentrated through a burning-glass; but the day is in its zenith, and the season an unusual one. Was there ever such a sunny street as this

Broadway! The pavement stones are polished with the tread of feet until they shine again; the red bricks of the houses might be yet in the dry, hot kilns; and the roofs of those omnibuses look as though, if water were poured on them, they would hiss and smoke, and smell like half-quenched fires. No stint of omnibuses here! Half-a-dozen have gone by within as many minutes. Plenty of hackney cabs and coaches too; gigs, phaetons, large-wheeled tilburies, and private carriages – rather of a clumsy make, and not very different from the public vehicles, but built for the heavy roads beyond the city pavement. Negro coachmen and white; in straw hats, black hats, white hats, glazed caps, fur caps; in coats of drab, black, brown, green, blue, nankeen, striped jean and linen; and there, in that one instance (look while it passes, or it will be too late), in suits of livery. Some southern republican that, who puts his blacks in uniform, and swells with Sultan pomp and power. Yonder, where that phaeton with the well-clipped pair of grays has stopped – standing at their heads now – is a Yorkshire groom, who has not been very long in these parts, and looks sorrowfully round for a companion pair of top-boots, which he may traverse the city half a year without meeting. Heaven save the ladies, how they dress! We have seen more colours in these ten minutes, than we should have seen elsewhere, in as many days. What various parasols! What rainbow silks and satins! What pinking of thin stockings, and pinching of thin shoes, and fluttering of ribbons and silk tassels, and display of rich cloaks with gaudy hoods and linings! The young gentlemen are fond, you see, of turning down their shirt-collars and cultivating their whiskers, especially under the chin; but they cannot approach the ladies in their dress or bearing, being, to say the truth, humanity of quite another sort. Byrons of the desk and counter, pass on, and let us see what kind of men those are behind ye: those two labourers in holiday clothes, of whom one carries in his hand a crumpled scrap of paper from which he tries to spell out a hard name, while the other looks about for it on all the doors and windows.

Irishmen both! You might know them, if they were masked, by their long-tailed blue coats and bright buttons, and their drab trousers, which they wear like men well used to working dresses, who are easy in no others. It would be hard to keep your model republics going, without the countrymen and countrywomen of those two labourers. For who else would dig, and delve, and drudge, and do domestic work, and make canals and roads, and execute great lines of Internal Improvement! Irishmen both, and sorely puzzled too, to find out what they seek. Let us go down, and help them, for the love of home, and that spirit of liberty which admits of honest service to honest men, and honest work for honest bread, no matter what it be.

That's well! We have got at the right address at last, though it is written in strange characters truly, and might have been scrawled with the blunt handle of the spade the writer better knows the use of, than a pen. Their way lies yonder, but what business takes them there? They carry savings: to hoard up? No. They are brothers, those men. One crossed the sea alone, and working very hard for one half year, and living harder, saved funds enough to bring the other out. That done, they worked together side by side, contentedly sharing hard labour and hard living for another term, and then their sisters came, and then another brother, and lastly, their old mother. And what now? Why, the poor old crone is restless in a strange land, and yearns to lay her bones, she says, among her people in the old graveyard at home: and so they go to pay her passage back: and God help her and them, and every simple heart, and all who turn to the Jerusalem of their younger days, and have an altar-fire upon the cold hearth of their fathers.

This narrow thoroughfare, baking and blistering in the sun, is Wall Street: the Stock Exchange and Lombard Street of New York. Many a rapid fortune has been made in this street, and many a no less rapid ruin. Some of these very merchants whom you see hanging about here now, have locked up money in their strong-boxes, like the man in the Arabian Nights, and opening them again, have found but withered leaves. Below, here by the water-side, where the bowsprits of ships stretch across the footway, and almost thrust themselves into the windows, lie the noble American vessels which have made their Packet Service the finest in the world. They have brought hither the foreigners who abound in all the streets: not, perhaps, that there are more here, than in other commercial cities; but elsewhere, they have particular haunts, and you must find them out; here, they pervade the town.

We must cross Broadway again; gaining some refreshment from the heat, in the sight of the great blocks of clean ice which are being carried into shops and bar-rooms; and the pineapples and watermelons profusely displayed for sale. Fine streets of spacious houses here, you see! – Wall Street has furnished and dismantled many of them very often – and here a deep green leafy square. Be sure that is a hospitable house with inmates to be affectionately remembered always, where they have the open door and pretty show of plants within, and where the child with laughing eyes is peeping out of window at the little dog below. You wonder what may be the use of this tall flagstaff in the by-street, with something like Liberty's head-dress on its top: so do I. But there is a passion for tall flagstaffs hereabout, and you may see its twin brother in five minutes, if you have a mind.

Again across Broadway, and so – passing from the many-coloured crowd and glittering shops – into another long main street, the Bowery. A railroad yonder, see, where two stout horses trot along, drawing a score or two of people and a great wooden ark, with ease. The stores are poorer here; the passengers less gay. Clothes ready-made, and meat ready-cooked, are to be bought in these parts; and the lively whirl of carriages is exchanged for the deep rumble of carts and waggons. These signs which are so plentiful, in shape like river buoys, or small balloons, hoisted by cords to poles, and dangling there, announce, as you may see by looking up, 'OYSTERS IN EVERY STYLE.' They tempt the hungry most at night, for then dull candles glimmering inside illuminate these dainty words, and make the mouths of idlers water, as they read and linger.

What is this dismal-fronted pile of bastard Egyptian, like an enchanter's palace in a melodrama! – a famous prison, called The Tombs. Shall we go in?

So. A long, narrow, lofty building, stove-heated as usual, with four galleries, one above the other, going round it, and communicating by stairs. Between the two sides of each gallery, and in its centre, a bridge, for the greater convenience of crossing. On each of these bridges sits a man: dozing or reading, or talking to an idle companion. On each tier are two opposite rows of small iron doors. They look like furnace-doors, but are cold and black, as though the fires within had all gone out. Some two or three are open, and women, with drooping heads bent down, are talking to the inmates. The whole is lighted by a skylight, but it is fast closed; and from the roof there dangle, limp and drooping, two useless windsails.

A man with keys appears, to show us round. A good-looking fellow, and, in his way, civil and obliging.

'Are those black doors the cells?'

'Yes.'

'Are they all full?'

'Well, they're pretty nigh full, and that's a fact, and no two ways about it.'

'Those at the bottom are unwholesome, surely?'

'Why, we DO only put coloured people in 'em. That's the truth.'

'When do the prisoners take exercise?'

'Well, they do without it pretty much.'

'Do they never walk in the yard?'

'Considerable seldom.'

'Sometimes, I suppose?'

'Well, it's rare they do. They keep pretty bright without it.'

'But suppose a man were here for a twelvemonth. I know this is only a prison for criminals who are charged with grave offences, while they are awaiting their trial, or under remand, but the law here affords criminals many means of delay. What with motions for new trials, and in arrest of judgment, and what not, a prisoner might be here for twelve months, I take it, might he not?'

'Well, I guess he might.'

'Do you mean to say that in all that time he would never come out at that little iron door, for exercise?'

'He might walk some, perhaps – not much.'

'Will you open one of the doors?'

'All, if you like.'

The fastenings jar and rattle, and one of the doors turns slowly on its hinges. Let us look in. A small bare cell, into which the light enters through a high chink in the wall. There is a rude means of washing, a table, and a bedstead. Upon the latter, sits a man of sixty; reading. He looks up for a moment; gives an impatient dogged shake; and fixes his eyes upon his book again. As we withdraw our heads, the door closes on him, and is fastened as before. This man has murdered his wife, and will probably be hanged.

'How long has he been here?'

'A month.'

'When will he be tried?'

'Next term.'

'When is that?'

'Next month.'

'In England, if a man be under sentence of death, even he has air and exercise at certain periods of the day.'

'Possible?'

With what stupendous and untranslatable coolness he says this, and how loungingly he leads on to the women's side: making, as he goes, a kind of iron castanet of the key and the stair-rail!

Each cell door on this side has a square aperture in it. Some of the women peep anxiously through it at the sound of footsteps; others shrink away in shame. For what offence can that lonely child, of ten or twelve years old, be shut up here? Oh! That boy? He is the son of the prisoner we saw just now; is a witness against his father; and is detained here for safe keeping, until the trial; that's all.

But it is a dreadful place for the child to pass the long days and nights in. This is rather hard treatment for a young witness, is it not? What says our conductor?

'Well, it an't a very rowdy life, and THAT'S a fact!'

Again he clinks his metal castanet, and leads us leisurely away. I have a question to ask him as we go.

'Pray, why do they call this place The Tombs?'

'Well, it's the cant name.'

'I know it is. Why?'

'Some suicides happened here, when it was first built. I expect it come about from that.'

'I saw just now, that that man's clothes were scattered

about the floor of his cell. Don't you oblige the prisoners to be orderly, and put such things away?'

'Where should they put 'em?'

'Not on the ground surely. What do you say to hanging them up?'

He stops and looks round to emphasise his answer:

'Why, I say that's just it. When they had hooks they WOULD hang themselves, so they're taken out of every cell, and there's only the marks left where they used to be!'

The prison-yard in which he pauses now, has been the scene of terrible performances. Into this narrow, grave-like place, men are brought out to die. The wretched creature stands beneath the gibbet on the ground; the rope about his neck; and when the sign is given, a weight at its other end comes running down, and swings him up into the air – a corpse.

The law requires that there be present at this dismal spectacle the judge, the jury, and citizens to the amount of twenty-five. From the community it is hidden. To the dissolute and bad, the thing remains a frightful mystery. Between the criminal and them, the prison-wall is interposed as a thick gloomy veil. It is the curtain to his bed of death, his winding-sheet, and grave. From him it shuts out life, and all the motives to unrepenting hardihood in that last hour, which its mere sight and presence is often all-sufficient to sustain. There are no bold eyes to make him bold; no ruffians to uphold a ruffian's name before. All beyond the pitiless stone wall, is unknown space.

Let us go forth again into the cheerful streets.

Once more in Broadway! Here are the same ladies in bright colours, walking to and fro, in pairs and singly; yonder the very same light blue parasol which passed and repassed the hotel-window twenty times while we were sitting there. We are going to cross here. Take care of the pigs. Two portly sows are trotting up behind this carriage, and a select party of half-a-dozen gentlemen hogs have just now turned the corner.

Here is a solitary swine lounging homeward by himself. He has only one ear; having parted with the other to vagrant dogs in the course of his city rambles. But he gets on very well without it; and leads a roving, gentlemanly, vagabond kind of life, somewhat answering to that of our club-men at home. He leaves his lodgings every morning at a certain hour, throws himself upon the town, gets through his day in some manner quite satisfactory to himself, and regularly appears at the door of his own house again at night, like the mysterious master of Gil Blas. He is a free-and-easy, careless, indifferent kind of pig, having a very large acquaintance among other pigs of the same character, whom he rather knows by sight than conversation, as he seldom troubles himself to stop and exchange civilities, but goes grunting down the kennel, turning up the news and small-talk of the city in the shape of cabbage-stalks and offal, and bearing no tails but his own: which is a very short one, for his old enemies, the dogs, have been at that too, and have left him hardly enough to swear by. He is in every respect a republican pig, going wherever he pleases, and mingling with the best society, on an equal, if not superior footing, for every one makes way when he appears, and the haughtiest give him the wall, if he prefer it. He is a great philosopher, and seldom moved, unless by the dogs before mentioned. Sometimes, indeed, you may see his small eye twinkling on a slaughtered friend, whose carcase garnishes a butcher's door-post, but he grunts out 'Such is life: all flesh is pork!', buries his nose in the mire again, and waddles down the gutter: comforting himself with the reflection that there is one snout the less to anticipate stray cabbage-stalks, at any rate.

They are the city scavengers, these pigs. Ugly brutes they

are; having, for the most part, scanty brown backs, like the lids of old horsehair trunks: spotted with unwholesome black blotches. They have long, gaunt legs, too, and such peaked snouts, that if one of them could be persuaded to sit for his profile, nobody would recognise it for a pig's likeness. They are never attended upon, or fed, or driven, or caught, but are thrown upon their own resources in early life, and become preternaturally knowing in consequence. Every pig knows where he lives, much better than anybody could tell him. At this hour, just as evening is closing in, you will see them roaming towards bed by scores, eating their way to the last. Occasionally, some youth among them who has over-eaten himself, or has been worried by dogs, trots shrinkingly homeward, like a prodigal son: but this is a rare case: perfect self-possession and self-reliance, and immovable composure, being their foremost attributes.

The streets and shops are lighted now; and as the eye travels down the long thoroughfare, dotted with bright jets of gas, it is reminded of Oxford Street, or Piccadilly. Here and there a flight of broad stone cellar-steps appears, and a painted lamp directs you to the Bowling Saloon, or Ten-Pin alley; Ten-Pins being a game of mingled chance and skill, invented when the legislature passed an act forbidding Nine-Pins. At other downward flights of steps are other lamps, marking the whereabouts of oyster-cellars – pleasant retreats, say I: not only by reason of their wonderful cookery of oysters, pretty nigh as large as cheese-plates (or for thy dear sake, heartiest of Greek Professors!), but because of all kinds of caters of fish, or flesh, or fowl, in these latitudes, the swallowers of oysters alone are not gregarious; but subduing themselves, as it were, to the nature of what they work in, and copying the coyness of the thing they eat, do sit apart in curtained boxes, and consort by twos, not by two hundreds.

But how quiet the streets are! Are there no itinerant bands; no wind or stringed instruments? No, not one. By day, are there no Punches, Fantoccini, Dancing dogs, Jugglers, Conjurers, Orchestrinas, or even Barrel-organs? No, not one. Yes, I remember one. One barrel-organ and a dancing monkey – sportive by nature, but fast fading into a dull, lumpish monkey, of the Utilitarian school. Beyond that, nothing lively; no, not so much as a white mouse in a twirling cage.

Are there no amusements? Yes. There is a lecture-room across the way, from which that glare of light proceeds, and there may be evening service for the ladies thrice a week, or oftener. For the young gentlemen, there is the counting-house, the store, the bar-room: the latter, as you may see through these windows, pretty full. Hark! To the clinking sound of hammers breaking lumps of ice, and to the cool gurgling of the pounded bits, as, in the process of mixing, they are poured from glass to glass! No amusements? What are these suckers of cigars and swallowers of strong drinks, whose hats and legs we see in every possible variety of twist, doing, but amusing themselves? What are the fifty newspapers, which those precocious urchins are bawling down the street, and which are kept filed within, what are they but amusements? Not vapid, waterish amusements, but good strong stuff; dealing in round abuse and blackguard names; pulling off the roofs of private houses, as the Halting Devil did in Spain; pimping and pandering for all degrees of vicious taste, and gorging with coined lies the most voracious maw; imputing to every man in public life the coarsest and the vilest motives; scaring away from the stabbed and prostrate body-politic, every Samaritan of clear conscience and good deeds; and setting on, with yell and whistle and the clapping of foul hands, the vilest vermin and worst birds of prey. No amusements!

Let us go on again; and passing this wilderness of an hotel

with stores about its base, like some Continental theatre, or the London Opera House shorn of its colonnade, plunge into the Five Points. But it is needful, first, that we take as our escort these two heads of the police, whom you would know for sharp and well-trained officers if you met them in the Great Desert. So true it is, that certain pursuits, wherever carried on, will stamp men with the same character. These two might have been begotten, born, and bred, in Bow Street.

We have seen no beggars in the streets by night or day; but of other kinds of strollers, plenty. Poverty, wretchedness, and vice, are rife enough where we are going now.

This is the place: these narrow ways, diverging to the right and left, and reeking everywhere with dirt and filth. Such lives as are led here, bear the same fruits here as elsewhere. The coarse and bloated faces at the doors, have counterparts at home, and all the wide world over. Debauchery has made the very houses prematurely old. See how the rotten beams are tumbling down, and how the patched and broken windows seem to scowl dimly, like eyes that have been hurt in drunken frays. Many of those pigs live here. Do they ever wonder why their masters walk upright in lieu of going on all fours? And why they talk instead of grunting?

So far, nearly every house is a low tavern; and on the bar-room walls, are coloured prints of Washington, and Queen Victoria of England, and the American Eagle. Among the pigeon-holes that hold the bottles, are pieces of plate-glass and coloured paper, for there is, in some sort, a taste for decoration, even here. And as seamen frequent these haunts, there are maritime pictures by the dozen: of partings between sailors and their lady-loves, portraits of William, of the ballad, and his Black-Eyed Susan; of Will Watch, the Bold Smuggler; of Paul Jones the Pirate, and the like: on which the painted eyes of Queen Victoria, and of Washington to boot, rest in as strange companionship, as on most of the scenes that are enacted in their wondering presence.

What place is this, to which the squalid street conducts us? A kind of square of leprous houses, some of which are attainable only by crazy wooden stairs without. What lies beyond this tottering flight of steps that creak beneath our tread? A miserable room, lighted by one dim candle, and destitute of all comfort, save that which may be hidden in a wretched bed. Beside it, sits a man: his elbows on his knees: his forehead hidden in his hands. 'What ails that man?' asks the foremost officer. 'Fever,' he sullenly replies, without looking up. Conceive the fancies of a feverish brain, in such a place as this!

Ascend these pitch-dark stairs, heedful of a false footing on the trembling boards, and grope your way with me into this wolfish den, where neither ray of light nor breath of air, appears to come. A negro lad, startled from his sleep by the officer's voice – he knows it well – but comforted by his assurance that he has not come on business, officiously bestirs himself to light a candle. The match flickers for a moment, and shows great mounds of dusty rags upon the ground; then dies away and leaves a denser darkness than before, if there can be degrees in such extremes. He stumbles down the stairs and presently comes back, shading a flaring taper with his hand. Then the mounds of rags are seen to be astir, and rise slowly up, and the floor is covered with heaps of negro women, waking from their sleep: their white teeth chattering, and their bright eyes glistening and winking on all sides with surprise and fear, like the countless repetition of one astonished African face in some strange mirror.

Mount up these other stairs with no less caution (there are traps and pitfalls here, for those who are not so well escorted as ourselves) into the housetop; where the bare beams and rafters meet overhead, and calm night looks down through the crevices in the roof. Open the door of one of these cramped hutches full of sleeping negroes. Pah! They have a charcoal fire within; there is a smell of singeing clothes, or flesh, so close they gather round the brazier; and vapours issue forth that blind and suffocate. From every corner, as you glance about you in these dark retreats, some figure crawls half-awakened, as if the judgment-hour were near at hand, and every obscene grave were giving up its dead. Where dogs would howl to lie, women, and men, and boys slink off to sleep, forcing the dislodged rats to move away in quest of better lodgings.

Here too are lanes and alleys, paved with mud knee-deep, underground chambers, where they dance and game; the walls bedecked with rough designs of ships, and forts, and flags, and American eagles out of number: ruined houses, open to the street, whence, through wide gaps in the walls, other ruins loom upon the eye, as though the world of vice and misery had nothing else to show: hideous tenements which take their name from robbery and murder: all that is loathsome, drooping, and decayed is here.

Our leader has his hand upon the latch of 'Almack's,' and calls to us from the bottom of the steps; for the assembly-room of the Five Point fashionables is approached by a descent. Shall we go in? It is but a moment.

Heyday! The landlady of Almack's thrives! A buxom fat mulatto woman, with sparkling eyes, whose head is daintily ornamented with a handkerchief of many colours. Nor is the landlord much behind her in his finery, being attired in a smart blue jacket, like a ship's steward, with a thick gold ring upon his little finger, and round his neck a gleaming golden watch-guard. How glad he is to see us! What will we please to call for? A dance? It shall be done directly, sir: 'a regular break-down.'

The corpulent black fiddler, and his friend who plays the tambourine, stamp upon the boarding of the small raised orchestra in which they sit, and play a lively measure. Five or six couples come upon the floor, marshalled by a lively young negro, who is the wit of the assembly, and the greatest dancer known. He never leaves off making queer faces, and is the delight of all the rest, who grin from ear to ear incessantly. Among the dancers are two young mulatto girls, with large, black, drooping eyes, and head-gear after the fashion of the hostess, who are as shy, or feign to be, as though they never danced before, and so look down before the visitors, that their partners can see nothing but the long-fringed lashes.

But the dance commences. Every gentleman sets as long as he likes to the opposite lady, and the opposite lady to him, and all are so long about it that the sport begins to languish, when suddenly the lively hero dashes in to the rescue. Instantly the fiddler grins, and goes at it tooth and nail; there is new energy in the tambourine; new laughter in the dancers; new smiles in the landlady; new confidence in the landlord; new brightness in the very candles.

Single shuffle, double shuffle, cut and cross-cut; snapping his fingers, rolling his eyes, turning in his knees, presenting the backs of his legs in front, spinning about on his toes and heels like nothing but the man's fingers on the tambourine; dancing with two left legs, two right legs, two wooden legs, two wire legs, two spring legs – all sorts of legs and no legs – what is this to him? And in what walk of life, or dance of life, does man ever get such stimulating applause as thunders about him, when, having danced his partner off her feet, and himself too, he finishes by leaping gloriously on the bar-counter, and calling for something to drink, with the chuckle of a million of counterfeit Jim Crows, in one inimitable sound!

The air, even in these distempered parts, is fresh after the stifling atmosphere of the houses; and now, as we emerge into a broader street, it blows upon us with a purer breath, and the stars look bright again. Here are The Tombs once more. The city watch-house is a part of the building. It follows naturally on the sights we have just left. Let us see that, and then to bed.

What! Do you thrust your common offenders against the police discipline of the town, into such holes as these? Do men and women, against whom no crime is proved, lie here all night in perfect darkness, surrounded by the noisome vapours which encircle that flagging lamp you light us with, and breathing this filthy and offensive stench! Why, such indecent and disgusting dungeons as these cells, would bring disgrace upon the most despotic empire in the world! Look at them, man – you, who see them every night, and keep the keys. Do you see what they are? Do you know how drains are made below the streets, and wherein these human sewers differ, except in being always stagnant?

Well, he don't know. He has had five-and-twenty young women locked up in this very cell at one time, and you'd hardly realise what handsome faces there were among 'em.

In God's name! Shut the door upon the wretched creature who is in it now, and put its screen before a place, quite unsurpassed in all the vice, neglect, and devilry, of the worst old town in Europe.

Are people really left all night, untried, in those black sties? Every night. The watch is set at seven in the evening. The magistrate opens his court at five in the morning. That is the earliest hour at which the first prisoner can be released; and if an officer appear against him, he is not taken out till nine o'clock or ten. But if any one among them die in the interval, as one man did, not long ago? Then he is half-eaten by the rats in an hour's time; as that man was; and there an end.

What is this intolerable tolling of great bells, and crashing

459

of wheels, and shouting in the distance? A fire. And what that deep-red light in the opposite direction? Another fire. And what these charred and blackened walls we stand before? A dwelling where a fire has been. It was more than hinted, in an official report, not long ago, that some of these conflagrations were not wholly accidental, and that speculation and enterprise found a field of exertion, even in flames: but be this as it may, there was a fire last night, there are two to-night, and you may lay an even wager there will be at least one, to-morrow. So, carrying that with us for our comfort, let us say, Good night, and climb up-stairs to bed.

George W. Matsell

George W. Matsell, Special Justice, Chief of Police, etc., etc.

THE FIVE POINTS THROUGH THE NINETEENTH CENTURY

The Tombs, or City Prison.

The Dead Rabbits Riot in 1857, on Bayard Street in the Five Points. What started as a small-scale street fight between gangs became a two day riot. Taking advantage of the disorganized state of the city's police force, the fighting spiraled into widespread looting and damage of property by gangsters and other criminals from all parts of the city.

The 'Petition to Have the Five Points Opened' of 1831 described the Five Points as 'this hot-bed of infamy, this modern Sodom'. But even towards the end of the nineteenth century it was still a place of poverty and danger. Pictured here in 1888 is Bandit's Roost, located in the notorious Mulberry Bend – a street scene similar to those that Timothy would have encountered in 1845.

DISCUSSION POINTS

- Timothy Wilde's understanding is deeply hampered by his own misconceptions about his loved ones – in particular, Mercy Underhill and his brother Valentine. How unreliable a narrator is Tim? In what ways is he careful to present the whole story, and in what ways does he fail to do so?

- The city of New York itself is a significant character in *The Gods of Gotham*. How would you characterize Timothy's uneasy relationship with New York? How is it affected by the fact that he was born there?

- In reference to an Irish laborer being taunted by an American in Chapter Seven, Timothy says, 'It's always *someone* in these parts, being made small, being made to wear that look.' In what ways were the hardships endured by the Irish immigrants comparable to or different from later groups like Hispanics, Asians, and Middle Easterners? Have we overcome xenophobia, or does it still plague attitudes to new communities in our cities today?

- Timothy watches the unfolding battle between the Catholic and the Protestant Gods with a certain detachment, but he is constantly making moral judgment calls. How spiritual a man is Timothy? What role do you think religion plays in his life? How has it affected him to grow up in two worlds, one Protestant and one highly secular?

- Mercy Underhill and Silkie Marsh are very different women, but each is immensely affected by the narrow role relegated to females in the nineteenth century. How does each make her own bid for independence? How closely are economics tied to autonomy for Mercy and for Silkie, and in what ways?

- Valentine Wilde's list of 'dubious pastimes', according to Timothy, includes *narcotics*, *alcohol*, *bribery*, *violence*, *whoring*, *gambling*, *theft*, *cheating*, *extortion*, and *sodomy*. Despite this, Timothy often defines himself in direct comparison to Valentine's attributes. Do you find Val a sympathetic character? What is the true north of Valentine's moral compass, and how does he adhere to it?

- In what ways is flash language a dialect? How about a code, a lifestyle, or a community? Are people defined by their language in *The Gods of Gotham*, and are they still defined by language today?

- In the nineteenth century, children were often required to earn their own livelihoods, both on the streets and in other settings. In what ways do characters like Bird, Neill, Ninepin, and the other newsboys and child prostitutes act like adults? Would their behavior seem strange to the modern observer? Many types of class warfare are delineated in *The Gods of Gotham*; is the struggle of children vs adult predators another example?

- The Reverend Underhill is a mentor of sorts to Timothy, and yet he proves also to be his adversary. To what extent are Timothy's feelings about Mercy mixed up with his final treatment of the Reverend? Is the Reverend ever a positive force? To what extent are Thomas Underhill's actions motivated by love? To what extent are Timothy's, and how do his actions differ from the Reverend's?

- George Washington Matsell was a very divisive figure during his era. Were you surprised to find that so many were against the formation of a police force? Matsell was also a student of popular civics and family planning, which were both scandalous reading material at the time. How do you feel about the first NYC Chief of Police endorsing birth control? Do you think Matsell was socially or politically ahead of his time?

...... wrote and presented the
_......_ ...... adult sex education videos which
are n...... ...... languages around the world.

Andre...... been agony uncle for various women's magazines
over twenty years; has broadcast widely in the UK and abroad;
and has lectured and taught in many countries.

Penny

Penny [illegible] [illegible] [illegible] married [illegible] [illegible] [illegible] in helping [illegible] [illegible] [illegible] [illegible] dren, Susannah, A[illegible] [illegible] [illegible] [illegible] [illegible]

Penny Stanway qualified in medicine in 1968 at King's College Hospital Medical School, London. She spent some time in general practice and at the Institute of Child Health, where she studied developmental paediatrics and child neurology and did some research into the causes of spina bifida. Later she became a senior medical officer in community child health in Croydon.

Her interest in breastfeeding began while working in the community and intensified after her first child was born, when she realized that most of the information easily available to mothers and health professionals was inaccurate and unhelpful. An enormous and varied amount of research around the world, plus her own experiences and her husband's valuable insights and collaboration, resulted in the first edition of the enormously popular *Breast Is Best* in 1978.

Penny then spent some years as a full-time mother and many more as a medical writer, exploring health in general and women's and children's issues in particular. She has written nine further books, including the *Mothercare New Guide to Pregnancy and Babycare* (Conran Octopus, 1994) and *Healing Foods for Common Ailments* (Gaia, 1995). She is a member of the Professional Advisory Board of La Leche League International, health columnist for *Woman's Weekly*, and enjoys lecturing and broadcasting.

Andrew Stanway qualified in medicine in 1967 at King's College Hospital Medical School. He became a member of the Royal College of Physicians in 1970, since when he has written thirty-eight books about medicine and health for the public and has run a medical film business for ten years.

His main p[illegible] [illegible] and relationships. He has had [illegible] [illegible] exual and marital